CUT
TO THE QUICK

A Novel

DIANNE
EMLEY

BALLANTINE BOOKS • NEW YORK

Cut to the Quick is a work of fiction. Names, characters, places, and incidents are the products of the author's imagination or are used fictitiously. Any resemblance to actual events, locales, or persons, living or dead, is entirely coincidental.

A Ballantine Books Mass Market Original

Copyright © 2008 by Emley and Co., LLC
Excerpt from *The Deepest Cut* copyright © 2009 by Emley and Co., LLC

All rights reserved.

Published in the United States by Ballantine Books, an imprint of The Random House Publishing Group, a division of Random House, Inc., New York.

BALLANTINE and colophon are registered trademarks of Random House, Inc.

This book contains an excerpt from the forthcoming hardcover edition of *The Deepest Cut* by Dianne Emley. This excerpt has been set for this edition only and may not reflect the final content of the forthcoming edition.

ISBN 978-0-345-48620-2

Cover design: Chris Sergio and Julia Kushnirsky
Cover photograph: © Shutterstock

Printed in the United States of America

www.ballantinebooks.com

OPM 9 8 7 6 5 4 3 2 1

Dedicated with love and respect to
my mother
Theda A. Pugh
and my mother-in-law
Marie E. Emley

ACKNOWLEDGMENTS

First and foremost, I'd like to recognize my brilliant editors and pals, Linda Marrow and Dana Isaacson. Your wise guidance and astute editorial sensibilities have enhanced and elevated my work.

Assistant editor Dan Mallory deserves a special nod for his contributions.

Heartfelt thanks to everyone on the fabulous Ballantine team, especially: Gina Centrello, Libby McGuire, Kim Hovey, Rachel Kind, and Cindy Murray.

I'm grateful also to my wonderful agent, Robin Rue, and everyone at Writer's House, especially Beth Miller.

I must also acknowledge the fine work of my tough copy editor, Teresa Agrillo.

The events and people depicted in this book are fictitious, but they would not have the same impact without the kind assistance of several law-and-order professionals. Any errors are the fault of this author.

Officer Donna Cayson of the Pasadena Police Department was again generous with her time.

Thanks also to the many Pasadena police officers and brass I worked with throughout the past year. I continue to be impressed by your dedication and professionalism.

Karla Kerlin, Special Assistant District Attorney, Los Angeles County, again cheerfully let me pick her brain about criminal law.

Retired police captain Steve Davidson was immensely

helpful, both for insights into police life and for his comments on the manuscript.

Gerald Petievich, author, former Secret Service agent, and buddy, made substantial contributions to the manuscript and aided my understanding of law enforcement personalities and tactics.

Ann Escue kept me from going astray regarding psychiatric facilities and methods, so critical in this book.

Ron Escue and Jon Redyk provided valuable insight on firearms.

Warren Bentley was helpful with information about small-claims court.

Thanks to my posse of friends, perceptive readers all, who beat up the manuscript: Jayne Anderson, Mary Goss, Toni Johnston, Leslie Pape, and Debra Shatford.

A grateful huzzah to friends who endured my whining: Rosemary Durant, Katherine Johnson, and Dottie Lopez.

Last, but never least, kudos to my family, who always contribute in ways both great and small. Special thanks to my nephew, Mark Pasqua, for observations about "lake life." Hats off to the rest of the clan. The Emleys: Charles III, Robert, and Sally. The Kawaokas: Jeanine, Craig, and Cameron. The Pasquas: Sheila and Carl. The Pasquas II: Mark, Jennifer, and Carter. The Prices: Carole, Ed, Jeffrey, and Eric. The Pughs: Bill, June, Eric, and David. And the Pughs II: Chana, Jonathan, Aaron, Justin, Katherine, and Marie.

And of course, to my wonderful husband, Charlie, my safety net, my love.

ONE

Nothing bad ever happened to Oliver Mercer. He hadn't followed Mercer long before he'd figured that out. Nothing really bad. Having your teeth kicked out bad. Watching someone slit your girlfriend's throat in front of you bad. Watching someone slit your girlfriend's throat while you're gurgling through your own slit throat bad. Or losing all your money. A guy like Mercer probably thought that was the worst thing that could ever happen to him. Or handing over his Rolex to a robber. Or finding his girlfriend in bed with his best friend. The fool.

Mercer had all the advantages. Born into money. While following Mercer around Pasadena, he'd heard people call it "old money," like that made it even more important and special. Dough was dough as far as he was concerned. No better cushion from life's problems than a mountain of cash. If at all, real trouble had just skimmed the surface of Mercer's life, its misery lasting as long as a tiny baby's frown. And when his troubles were over, those little tears and that wrinkled brow melted away, leaving nothing behind. It took decades of worry for those frown lines to dig in. That's what Mercer was, as far as he was concerned: a big, fat baby acting like he's something special because he has money he didn't earn. Having airs and looking down on people. He'd seen Mercer do it. He'd gotten that close. He'd worn his favorite disguise, but Mercer would have looked right through him anyway. He was one of the little people.

He smiled. Sometimes little people had big plans that could whip around and bite a guy like Mercer right in the ass.

He'd heard Mercer go on about a billboard company he'd bought into. "Outside advertising," he'd called it, like that dressed it up or something. Guess it made Mercer feel like he had a real job. A well-placed billboard, Mercer had said, like the ones along the Sunset Strip, could earn fifty grand a month in rent. Billboards, for crying out loud. Who knew? Mercer's partner had been having problems with the law for allegedly poisoning some expensive trees, city property, that were blocking his signs. Personally, he thought that was funnier than hell and had to hand it to the guy, if the story was true. Mercer had used unkind words when speaking of his business partner. Well, you gotta know who you're getting in bed with, so to speak.

One thing's for double damn sure, Mercer wouldn't have gotten his girlfriend if he was a working stiff. Babe like her wouldn't have given him the time of day. That's all anyone needs to know about life right there.

Bad things did happen to good and to so-so people too, for no apparent reason. Mercer hadn't learned that life lesson yet. He was about to show Mercer a different view of the world.

Looking through binoculars from his vantage point across the Arroyo Seco, he caught himself holding his breath. He let out a small sigh when all the lights in Mercer's glass-walled home turned on at once, as they did the same time each evening. The house, designed by the much-discussed Spanish architect Santiago Torres, was striking on the hillside. The lights spectacularly set it off. He was sure that's why Mercer turned them all on. That was okay. Then everyone could enjoy it a little bit. The worker bees commuting on the 210 freeway could look up at the big house shining on the hill and have their spirits raised. It was like looking at a faraway castle. Sometimes just the suggestion that life can be different is enough to get you through another mean day. That was another astute observation, if he said so himself. Astute meaning "smart." And if life is being difficult, sometimes you take things into your own hands.

He was grateful for Mercer's attention to appearances for another reason. The lights made watching Mercer easier. The lights could pose a problem later, but he'd deal with it. He tapped ash from his cigarette into the car's ashtray.

The globes on the antique lampposts along the Colorado Street Bridge near where he was parked also turned on. That was a pretty view from the freeway too. It was the first Saturday of September, the middle of the Labor Day holiday weekend. The evening was just how he liked it—clear, warm, and not too smoggy for the city. Not much traffic or people. It would be a fine weekend to go fishing, but the payoff of the sport he was engaged in now would ultimately be more satisfying.

Mercer walked out onto one of the terraces, holding a martini. The man was a creature of habit.

"Look at him up there, acting like he's master of his domain," he nearly shouted to no one. "King of the hill. What's that old Beatles song? The fool of the hill. No, *on* the hill. That's it. 'The Fool on the Hill,'"

He hummed a few bars of the tune. Grinding out his cigarette, he said, "Showtime."

He craned his neck to look at himself in the rearview mirror, then turned the key in the ignition. He circled the cul-de-sac and headed for the bridge to cross the arroyo.

At Mercer's driveway, he punched in the code to open the gate. He'd gotten it by watching the housekeeper when she came to work. Even the stupidest criminal wouldn't have trouble getting into this place. And he was not a stupid criminal.

He rang the doorbell, impressed with the pleasing musical notes it emitted. He turned his back to the peephole, knowing that Mercer would open the door for a blonde. He could almost count the steps it took Mercer to get to the door from the terrace. He'd look through the peephole and wonder what the intrusion was about. Then he'd open the door, still holding his martini.

The door opened and there was Mercer, holding the martini.

"Hello, Oliver. I love it when people fulfill my expectations."

Mercer blinked at his visitor, as if having trouble taking it all in.

"Such an ugly scowl, Oliver. Not very hospitable."

"Who the hell are you? Maybe I should ask *what* are you? A man dressed like a woman?"

"I hate when people criticize things they don't understand."

Before Mercer could close the door on him, he kicked it open, knocking Mercer to the floor, the high heels doing a good job. The hunting knife was out, and he started stabbing and stabbing.

Later, after whacking off another piece with the chain saw, he cut the motor and stepped back to admire his work, taking a drag on his cigarette. If he had it to do over again, he would have rethought the chain saw. It made such a mess, splattering bits of meat all over him and everything else. He took a bottle of Miss Dior from the pocket of his plastic apron and dabbed more beneath his nostrils.

The doorbell rang, followed by rapid knocking. Still holding the chain saw, he wiped a gloved hand against the apron in a wasted gesture. He was covered in blood and gore. His dress was ruined. He had figured it might be, so he hadn't worn one of his favorites. He looked through the peephole and *tsked tsked*.

Standing behind the door, he opened it a crack.

Lauren Richards tentatively pushed it and leaned inside. "Oliver? Are you playing games with me?"

She gasped at the trail of blood in the marble entryway and took a step toward it in spite of herself. Her mouth twisted in horror, her eyes fell upon the corpse of Oliver Mercer on the living room floor. At least, she thought it was Oliver. His arms and legs were in pieces, disassembled at the joints, the hands and feet cut off. The severed body parts were rearranged.

She made strangled squeaking noises through her palms pressed against her mouth.

A hand snatched her arm and flung her inside, where she slipped on the blood-slick marble. The door slammed closed. She looked up from the floor to see him and the bloody butcher's apron, women's clothes, and blond wig. She didn't know if his mouth was covered in blood or smeared lipstick.

He still held the chain saw. A burning cigarette dangled from his lips.

He shook his head.

"Oh, honey. Talk about wrong place, wrong time."

TWO

Detective Nan Vining felt the murders before she saw them. The spilled blood. The screams of unbridled fear spewed from that place deep inside where words have no value. She could feel it beneath her skin, a flush of her own hot blood prickling beneath her scalp. It was residue from her journey. She'd been to hell and back. Or maybe it had been Heaven. She wasn't sure. All she knew was, she had the scars to prove it.

She stood in the driveway of Oliver Mercer's home. She was tall and lean, taut and muscular. She'd pinned her long, nearly black hair into a bun, showing off her ears, which were adorned with simple gold studs, and her graceful neck. She'd stopped caring about hiding the long scar that marred her neck, trailing from her left ear down beneath the collar of her blouse. She had another, smaller scar on the back of her right hand. She'd come to view the scars as quirky characteristics, like her slight overbite and the gap between her front teeth. She'd prefer that they weren't there, but she wasn't about to spend time and money on vanity.

She wore little makeup, just eye shadow and mascara that set off her deep-set, green-gray eyes. She'd been told that she was pretty, but didn't believe it, choosing to believe that the men who said it were attempting to get her to relax her guard. The only appearance she cared about was maintaining a command presence. Pretty didn't help her on the Job.

Standing where two people had been recently slaughtered, Vining could sense the karma. It was easy to name: evil. This was something she knew first-hand. She'd been up close and personal with evil. Too close. Too personal.

Houses and other places have karma. They carry an imprint of the small and large dramas that take place within their walls and seep into the soil. An empty house, waiting for a new family, gives off a wistful yet hopeful aura. An abandoned house seems wickedly stubborn, still standing, like a ruined beauty hints at former glory in her clouded eyes. Why else do people fall silent when standing upon great battlefields of the past? Why are people drawn to hotel rooms and homes where the notorious or merely famous have laid their heads? Why do homes where murders and suicides have occurred linger on the market and sell for less than they should?

Vining had come to embrace the concept, but was skeptical of taking it further.

When Vining's fourteen-year-old daughter Emily was ghost hunting, an activity that, happily for Vining, the girl had since relegated to the dustbin of once-adored adolescent hobbies, she had shown her mother a photograph of an old prison electric chair. The photograph captured shadowy yet distinct images of faces in agony. Em had presented it to Vining as one piece in the mosaic she was crafting that proved the existence of the netherworld. Vining agreed that it was strange, but said that it could be trick photography. Emily accused her mom of being in denial.

Practical Vining enjoyed this indulgence. She didn't indulge in too many luxuries.

Death changes everything. Vining had been dead for

just over two minutes. She'd been living-challenged— the gallows-humor term she'd adopted when the more insensitive jerks around the station had asked questions that were none of their business.

While she didn't completely accept the person she was now, she'd stopped fighting her. Like a stray dog who decided she'd found a home, that person would not leave anyway. Vining reluctantly invited her inside. The dog circled around and plopped in front of the fire, like she'd always been there. After all, Vining decided, everyone's life is crowded with ghosts. The ghost of the person one used to be. The ghosts of children now grown. The ghost of love once hot, now cold. Ghosts were everywhere. All one had to do was close one's eyes. Or open them.

Vining and her partner, Jim Kissick, were among the first to arrive at the murder house. Only Pasadena police officers were there. A PPD helicopter circled above. The grisly deaths were still the PPD's secret, but not for long. News of the double homicide in the Linda Vista neighborhood was dispersing like a toxic spill at sea. Oliver Mercer's and Lauren Richards's corpses, at least the idea of them, would not only enter the lore of this street, this neighborhood, this police department, and this city, but would belong to the world.

They strode through a mass of blue uniforms in the street near the house.

"What up, T?" Kissick greeted Sergeant Terrence Folke, an African American whose size and muscle mass made him stand out among the patrol officers.

Crime scene tape extended across the street end of the driveway. The gate was open.

Folke was terse, in contrast with his usual easygoing demeanor. "Kissick. Vining." He led the detectives beneath the yellow tape onto the property. His style tended to be crisp, but his rundown today was a model of brevity.

"I'm setting up foot patrols for knock-and-talks. I've got the CHP en route to shut down the San Rafael exit off the freeway. No one's been on the property except Pincher and Orozco, who were the first on-scene, and me. And no one's going to get inside who doesn't have a reason to be there."

He pointed to a sobbing woman sitting on a stone bench being comforted by Officer Susie Pincher, a petite and athletic former high school cheerleader with an unfortunate surname.

Folke explained, "That's the housekeeper, Rosie Cordova. She doesn't usually work on Sunday, but came in because she's going to a Labor Day picnic tomorrow."

The big man was getting the job done, but his efficiency and control couldn't hide that he was unsettled.

Kissick patted Folke on the shoulder. "Thanks, Terrence. Good job." He called over Ray Orozco, the other uniformed officer, with a jerk of his head.

"Ray, how ya' doin'?"

Orozco had twenty-two years on the force and a waistline that expanded with each anniversary. He'd never been promoted, nor tried to be, and he'd been around the block more than a few times. There was little he hadn't seen. By his grave expression and the pallid tone of his normally bronze complexion, Vining guessed that today was the day he'd finally seen too much.

He shook the detectives' hands, then pulled out a handkerchief and blotted his brow. It was mid-morning and already in the nineties.

"Hey, Nan. Jim. Bad scene in there. Nightmare stuff."

Kissick squinted at a rustling noise. Two squirrels ran across the branches of a giant magnolia tree in the center of the vast drive. "What's the housekeeper's story?"

"She's worked for Mercer for three years. Said she didn't touch anything. She's confident the male victim is Mercer. She recognized a scabbed-up spot below his left shoulder where he recently had a tattoo removed."

"She can't give a positive I.D.?" Vining asked.

Orozco huffed out a laugh but the source wasn't humor. "You'll see."

"What else?" Kissick planted his hands on his waist and leaned his lanky frame forward, a pose he subconsciously adopted when speaking with people shorter than he.

"She said Mercer was having problems with his partner in some billboard company. Heard Mercer shouting at this guy on the phone, calling him an asshole and an idiot. Scoville, I think she said his name is. Regarding the female victim, name of Lauren Richards, Mercer had been dating her for two months or so. Rosie doesn't know much about her except she's divorced with a couple of young kids. As for Mercer, he was a lifelong bachelor. Born into money. Playboy."

Orozco accompanied the sobriquet with an arched eyebrow toward the grand house and the new Lamborghini in the driveway. Parked behind the expensive car was a several-years-old Nissan Pathfinder.

Vining got his drift. Even with all of Mercer's advantages, he wasn't immune to a determined psychopath with cutting tools. Now it was the job of a group of civil servants to look after his interests and seek justice, the same as if he'd been a homeless man kicked to death on a sidewalk.

Vining took latex gloves from her slacks pocket and put them on. "Any idea about the number of perpetrators?"

Orozco sucked in his full cheeks. His eyes grew veiled as he mentally revisited the interior of that house. He came back to them and shook his head. That would be the last time he'd force himself to go to that place. However, he'd unwillingly revisit it at unguarded moments for the rest of his life.

"Want us to take Rosie to the second floor?"

Orozco was referring to the second floor of the Pasadena Police Department, where the detectives worked.

Kissick also put on gloves. "Thanks, Ray. Make her comfortable. Let her call her family. We'll be there as soon as we can."

Vining and Kissick walked up the long driveway, which was composed of paving stones in variegated hues of gray.

She looked back toward the driveway gate. "If I were him, I would have driven my car up to the house."

They knew nothing concrete about the killer, yet they could begin building a profile based upon experience. The killer was likely male and between eighteen and forty-five years old.

"It would be more secluded than parking on the street and hopping the fence. He either came in on someone else's tail or had the gate code."

Kissick tried the door to the Pathfinder. It was locked. Women's clothes wrapped in dry cleaners' plastic were hanging from a hook above the passenger's window.

The Lamborghini's door was unlocked. The registration and proof of insurance Vining found in the glove compartment showed Mercer Investments as the owner.

They continued toward the house, stopping at a patch of paving stones a few yards from the front door that were smeared with blood.

"Transferred from something else," Kissick observed.

"Maybe he stripped off his bloody clothes here," Vining said. "Wonder if he brought something to change into. Was this planned or random?"

Kissick leaned over, put his hands on his knees, and pointed at the ground. "A long blond hair right there. Looks synthetic. Was Lauren wearing a wig?"

Bent over, Vining examined a mark on the ground. "Bloody footprint, made by a woman's high heel."

"Lauren's?"

Vining placed her foot, clad in cushioned flats, beside it. "My feet are big. The shoe that made this was huge."

They looked at each other.

"Either Lauren is a big lady or our bad guy likes women's clothing," Vining speculated.

"Maybe Mercer had an appointment with Helga?"

"Helga?"

"Big strong Russian masseuse," he said with a fake Slavic accent.

"Something you know about?"

"Mmm . . . strong hands."

She gave him a peeved look and continued to the front door.

It was ajar. Blood was smeared on the polished brass handle.

In a flowerbed was a placard from a security company. On the porch, a sign by the front door instructed guests that this was a shoe-free house, implying there were acres of pristine white inside. A teak shoe rack and a collection of slippers were helpfully provided. In a grotesque twist, Oliver Mercer and his girlfriend had created the worst, ineradicable stain.

They took paper booties from their pockets and slipped them over their shoes. Kissick produced a small bottle of Vicks VapoRub. They dabbed some beneath their nostrils.

With a shove of his index finger, Kissick pushed the heavy door.

It silently swung open on well-oiled brass hinges. The

metallic yet sweetly organic odor of blood was carried out on a blast of refrigerated air.

Vining felt screams escaping, rushing past, rustling her hair, seeking release in the open. As she stood on the threshold of that house, she knew the horrors within would leave their mark on her. That was part of the Job. She took in a shuddering breath.

The sight of blood, even buckets of it, no longer bothered her. After she had crawled through her own blood, spilling from the fatal wound in her neck, had felt its intense heat and velvety texture, fresh from her arteries, after she had felt it oozing around the knife that jutted from her flesh, a stranger's blood was academic. What bore down on her now was the terror of those attacked in that house. That was as palpable to her as a thick fog.

The dead did tell tales. Three months ago, when Vining had looked upon the battered face of LAPD Vice Cop Frankie Lynde, the dead woman had conveyed more information than Vining wanted to know. Vining hoped these new corpses held no such surprises. She didn't assume anything anymore. She sometimes felt she was following an agenda penned by an unseen hand. She hated it, but there it was.

"You okay?" Kissick grasped her upper arm and gave her a squeeze.

She was glad for Kissick's tall, solid presence beside her, unable to deny that she found it comforting. Still, she looked at the hand on her arm, then up at his eyes, perhaps too coldly. They'd crossed the fine line between camaraderie and intimacy before. She was giving him, she thought, a subtle reminder of her boundaries. He would have gotten the message with less.

"I'm fine. Thanks."

He released her, his expression and the atmosphere

between them now strained in a way that no outsider would detect.

"Look." He pointed at her shoulder, a winsome smile erasing the pinprick.

A butterfly had lit there. She craned her neck to see. It slowly opened and closed its wings, which were yellow with black spots and rimmed in black. It leaned away when Vining blew at it, but nothing more. She blew again. It canted leeward on delicate legs but still did not budge.

When Kissick flicked at it, it took flight, only to again land on the same spot.

"Guess it wants to see," Vining said.

"Does it have a tiny camera attached to it?"

"Probably. In one of the black dots."

The simplicity and beauty of the butterfly calmed Vining. It made her remember that there was more to the world than the Job and their sworn oath to put right to the extent that it was humanly possible what had gone wrong in that house. Bearing a delicate token of the natural world on her shoulder, Vining followed Kissick inside to witness horror that belonged to the domain of humans.

The first thing they saw was blood but they heard the soothing sound of water burbling.

"Fountain somewhere," Vining said.

They wove a story from the grisly artifacts.

"Arterial blood spray." Kissick drew his hand in an arc, tracing the path of the blood against the white entryway wall. The blood added a splash of unexpected color to a black-and-white painting of a nude female. "One of them got it right here, opening the door."

The entryway bore testimony to a massive struggle. It looked as if gallons of blood had been tossed onto the white marble floor prior to a wrestling match. A woman's strappy, high-heeled sandal lay beneath a narrow table of off-white granite against the wall. Parallel tracks of blood trailed across the foyer and disappeared down steps to the living room. Someone had lost the battle and the war.

"That didn't make the footprint we found outside," Vining said about the lost sandal. "Too small."

Kissick pointed at an indentation on the front door. Holding the door with his gloved hand, he swung it back and forth to catch the light.

"Maybe forced open by a stick or a poker."

Vining looked at the small round mark. "Or kicked open by someone wearing high heels."

He closed the door, revealing a cocktail glass that had shattered against the marble floor and the contents that had spilled from it. Bending, he stuck his finger into clear liquid, and brought it to his nose. "Gin. Looks like a martini with two olives and a twist."

"Last call," Vining cracked.

The house was modern—glass and chrome, white and beige, circles and angles. The décor was as unobtrusive as an art gallery, designed to set off the paintings and sculpture displayed throughout.

While making their way down the entryway, Kissick nudged Vining and tilted his chin toward the living room wall. The words scrawled there fit in oddly, like another piece of art:

ALL WORK

NO PLAY

A large abstract painting was on the floor, leaning against the wall. It had apparently been removed to provide a grand canvas for the killer's message. Recessed lighting, intended for the abstract painting, brilliantly illuminated the graffiti.

Kissick completed the adage: "Makes Jack a dull boy."

The letters were two feet tall. There was plenty of blood to do the job. It had soaked the pale area rugs and pooled into puddles on the marble floor. The puddles, now many hours old, had grown sticky. Yellow plasma separated along the edges, like oil pulling apart from vinegar.

The detectives' silence was almost reverential. Gallows humor was common among those whose work involved the dark side of life. Whistling past the graveyard. But this carnage had the power to mute any therapeutic wise-cracking. Nothing would mitigate this horror.

On the opposite side of the room, a sheet of water, like a transparent wall, flowed from the twenty-foot-tall ceiling and burbled into a shallow bed of smooth white pebbles.

Vining's eyes flashed on the bodies and quickly moved to the fountain, unable to process the mound of body parts at once, as if easing into a cold swimming pool.

Kissick cannonballed in and moved closer.

She steeled herself and took a good look. She was relieved. *Thank God I can't see their faces.*

Once she had looked, it was impossible to tear her eyes away. It was like trying to figure out an optical illusion. Was she looking at a goblet or two women in profile facing each other?

In the background, the fountain sounded like a babbling brook.

Kissick broke his trance and marched across the room, flicking off a switch on the wall, taking a guess. The water stopped. The room fell into a suitable silence.

He returned to the bodies and dabbed on more Vicks. He held the container out to her and she did the same.

"There's just one word for this. *Sick.*"

She was surprised that she felt slightly light-headed. The menthol aroma of the Vicks didn't help. Talking did. "When I rolled out to my first homicide, Bill Gavigan told me, 'Think of them like dolls. They're just dolls.' "

"That work for you?"

"No."

"Me neither."

"But I have to say, I'm having a hard time processing that these *are* people."

The bodies had been arranged with childlike whimsy, the combinations displaying adolescent prurience.

Lauren Richards still wore tight jeans. Her blouse and brassiere had been cut open, exposing her breasts. One foot was bare. A high-heeled sandal matching the shoe lost in the entryway dangled from one foot. Her body was intact, resting on its back against Mercer. Her head and neck were twisted at unnatural angles. Her face was pressed into his crotch.

Mercer was nude. His clothes had been cut off and strewn around the floor and atop the furniture. His limbs had been hacked into pieces. Nothing was where it was supposed to be or logically oriented. His severed head was laid into the V of her crotch. One of his legs, dissected at the knee, was bunkered up to his left shoulder. His right hand was butted against the ankle and rested atop her head, as if holding it against his genitals.

"Female's neck looks broken," Vining said. "The M.O. between the two victims is completely different."

Not using the victims' names was a way for the detectives to keep emotional distance.

"There was rage against the male," Kissick said. "Overkill. The mutilation probably took place postmortem. No surgical precision. The way the skin's chewed up, I'd guess he used a chain saw. But the female's murder looks efficient. More like an execution. I don't know who he did first, but I don't think she was the target."

"Where's the dog?" Vining pointed at a thick braid of multicolored string on one of the white couches. "He's a big one, based on the size of that toy."

She picked up a woman's wallet, lying open on the floor. She read the driver's license. "Lauren Richards. Caribeth Avenue, South Pasadena. Credit cards are here. Cash is gone."

She looked through photographs encased in plastic sleeves, stopping at one of Lauren with a boy of about ten and his younger sister, who looked to be seven or eight. The three of them were wearing red sweaters and were posed in front of a Christmas tree. She slipped it from the sleeve and shook her head.

"She's got two kids. They're wondering where she is." Vining hoped they never found out the details, how the psycho had snapped Lauren's neck like vermin that had invaded his party. At some point, when they were adults, they would seek the truth, wrongly assuming that knowing would bring peace.

There was evil in the world. It left young children motherless and with grief that time would numb but never obliterate. Thinking time healed all was a feel-good delusion. A fantasy of those who'd never endured profound tragedy.

Vining returned the wallet to where she'd found it. Giving a wide berth to the gore on the floor, she unlocked a glass door and slid it open. She walked onto a terrace, leaving the cool house for the mounting heat. Leaning over the edge to look at the garden below, she saw a large doghouse. She didn't see bowls for food or water.

She looked at the 210 freeway where it traversed the Arroyo Seco Wash on what locals called the new bridge.

The old bridge, the Colorado Street Bridge, was south of it. To the east was the area of restaurants and retail establishments called Old Pasadena. It was bisected by Colorado Boulevard, which cut across the city, disappearing into haze and smog. To the north were mountains, their presence hinted at by a slight darkening in the distance through the brownish air.

Something on her shoulder drew her attention. The yellow butterfly was still there. She blew at it again, seeking to release it outside. Again, it weathered the onslaught and stayed put.

She watched Kissick through the open door.

"Where's Mercer's right hand?" Kissick ran his palm across his sandy brown hair. He'd just had it cut and the edges were razor sharp. "Unless it's underneath, it's missing."

He joined her outside, leaning against the railing with both hands as he looked out.

The sounds of large engines drew their attention skyward.

"Old prop planes." He grinned as he pointed at a quartet of planes flying in formation. "That's a Bearcat. There's a Tomahawk. That's a Nieuport 28, like Eddie Rickenbacker flew in World War One. Must be an air show someplace."

His mouth gaped boyishly as he watched them cut across the sky, making a tremendous noise before fading into the smog.

It tickled her to see that side of him. He didn't reveal that facet of his personality at work, so she never saw it anymore. That was her fault. He'd always liked aircraft and flying. When they'd briefly been an item two years ago, he'd talked about taking flying lessons. She hoped he had.

They turned at the sound of vehicles approaching the house.

She followed him inside.

Vans from Pasadena's forensic team and from the county coroner's office were in the driveway. Crime scene technicians and coroner's investigators were unloading equipment. Sergeant Folke was directing uniformed officers, putting feet on the street.

Vining and Kissick reviewed what they'd learned with the forensic professionals, who set about their tasks.

Vining gazed at the bloody message on the wall: ALL WORK NO PLAY.

"Think his name is Jack or he's just messing with us?" Kissick asked her.

"One thing's for sure. He's the bad man."

"But not T. B. Mann," he said.

She looked at Kissick with surprise. It was jarring to hear that name uttered by someone other than herself or her daughter, Emily. She had told it to Kissick just once. T. B. Mann was the nickname she and Em had given the unidentified male who had ambushed and almost murdered her and escaped. T. B. Mann was her personal bad guy.

It had been months since she'd conjured his face or said his nickname. The scars he'd left went deeper than her skin. They had begun to take over her life. After being obsessed with hunting him down, she'd set her rage on the back burner. To salvage her life, she'd had to let him go.

Thus she lived in twilight, neither light nor dark. She felt in her bones that this in-between time was going to end. Something was in the works. He was out there, calling from the shadows for her to step into the light. The fresh blood of the murder victims had awakened something within her. Somewhere out there, she felt him stirring too.

The butterfly rose from her shoulder, spiraled around, and flew away.

THREE

A sign on the shoulder of the 101 freeway said, THIS HIGHWAY MAINTAINED BY BAD BOY BAIL BONDS.

Kissick exited at Melrose and headed west. This was the seedy side of Melrose, with family-owned *carnicerias* and *tiendas* and storefront attorneys specializing in immigration bookended by EZ Lubes and supermarkets surrounded by iron fences. The traffic on the surface streets was not much lighter than that on the freeway.

He said, "I think our guy brought his own chain saw, indicating premeditation. The housekeeper said she'd never seen Mercer with a tool more serious than a screwdriver. The gardeners came once a week and used their own equipment. There were no tools in his garage. Mercer did not like to get his hands dirty."

"He was murdered by someone who certainly didn't mind."

Vining shuddered, recalling seeing Mercer's dead face for the first time when the investigators had disassembled the "still life with body parts." First to be removed was Mercer's head, gently raised between a coroner's gloved hands.

Vining had been focusing with moderate success on

quieting her escalating pulse as the moment of revelation grew near. When Mercer's face was unveiled, a small gasp went up. No one there welcomed another surprise. It took Vining a moment to take in what she was seeing, the grotesqueness overwhelming her apprehension.

Mercer's face had been clownishly made up with his own blood. They found the tool later in the kitchen garbage—Mercer's toothbrush.

Lauren Richards's face had held no surprises, other than shock over what was happening and the briefest struggle to prevent it.

Now riding in the Crown Vic's passenger seat, Vining took out Lauren's family Christmas photograph. Looking at the sweet faces of the boy and girl, she mentally heard their mother's voice loud and clear.

Get him.

Vining turned down the air conditioning and said to Kissick, "Our guy, or maybe he prefers to be called a gal, worked alone, and planned ahead. Mercer's housekeeper said the Great Dane died of suspected poisoning two weeks before the murders. It's possible she ate a poisoned rat or squirrel, but that sounds like coincidence."

"Let's hope Mercer had the vet do an autopsy. Mercer clearly loved the dog and would have shelled out the dough to find out what happened to her."

In the house there had been a portrait of Mercer and Marilyn the Great Dane. Mercer's arm circled the pooch, his right hand, the severed appendage that so far had not been located, against the dog's broad chest. The portrait provided another clue. Mercer's ring finger bore his USC class ring.

Driving down Melrose, Kissick passed Paramount Studios' famous wrought-iron entry gate. He continued to North Rossmore Avenue and turned left, entering the

rarefied boundaries of Hancock Park. The neighborhood had managed to remain an old-money, largely
Caucasian enclave of sprawling mansions in the middle
of L.A. Encompassing the exclusive Wilshire Country
Club, it was bordered by Hollywood on the north and
Koreatown on the south, making it the defiant caviar
middle of an encroaching lower-class sandwich.

The hustle and grit of Melrose fell away as they drove
down quiet, tree-canopied streets where imposing
homes were set back on manicured lawns. Signs warned
that the Neighborhood Watch was in effect. Patrol cars
from private security firms were highly visible, demon-
strating that the citizens did not rely solely on vigilant
neighbors, nor did they have sufficient confidence in the
LAPD to keep the wolves at bay. Even still, the area was
plagued with crime.

The residents were all but invisible, a curiosity Vining
recognized from Pasadena's well-heeled neighborhoods.
Most of the vehicles on the streets were the pickup trucks
of Latino workers engaged in the many rehab projects
under way on the older homes, or economy cars driven
by household help. Pea-green Andy Gump portable toi-
lets were ubiquitous.

Kissick wandered the meandering streets, mistakenly
turning down one cul-de-sac and then another, rolling
over the speed bumps that attempted to keep traffic at
the posted 15 mph. While they were stopped to look at
a map, a Hummer loomed behind them. The driver, an
attractive blonde holding a cell phone to her ear, blasted
the horn with her free hand before zooming around.

Vining wasn't being helpful in trying to locate the
home of Mark Scoville, Mercer's business partner. Still
gazing at the Richardses' family photograph, she said
absently, "We're dealing with a devil."

"In a blue dress?"

"That's *so* not funny."

"In bad taste, but funny." He glanced at her, goading her. "It's funny, Vining."

"Okay, okay . . . Ha ha."

He frowned, looking for the street. "I didn't pass it, did I?"

"So we gently break the bad news, tell Scoville we'd like to ask him some routine questions. Best to do that at the station. If he won't go to Pasadena, we'll find someplace private in the house to interview him. Did you check the microrecorder before we left?"

He hooked his thumb toward the backseat, where their jackets were. "It's in my pocket. I just put in new batteries. You wanna take charge? I'm thinking that's the best strategy because we want him to talk and to talk a lot and not to feel like he needs to lawyer up."

"What are you saying? That I won't strike fear into his heart?"

"Who, Quick Draw? Poison Ivy?" He teased her with her two well-known monikers around the station, nicknames he knew she hated.

She had a reputation for shooting first and asking questions later. It wasn't completely true, but had its roots in an incident five years ago in which she'd fatally shot a man who claimed his girlfriend, dead from a bullet through her eye, had killed herself. The department had deemed it a good shooting. In policy. But the monikers had been born and stuck. Unfortunately, her reputation had caused her to hesitate when she had faced another soulless killer. Because she had hesitated, T. B. Mann was free.

They found Oakwood and Rosewood and then finally Pinewood Lane.

Kissick stopped the car in front of an imposing Tudor Revival mansion set atop a low knoll surrounded by a spike-topped fence. It was a corner house with a tall wall covered by thick vines along the side.

"That's it," Kissick said. "Billboards have been veddy veddy good to Scoville."

Sprinklers sprayed waves of water across a vast lawn and formal garden of sculptured topiary and seasonal flowers even though drought conditions had been declared and water was becoming as dear as gasoline.

Even the brick house was a snub to the will of the land in earthquake country.

The two-and-a-half-story mansion had steep gables. There were dozens of narrow casement windows with diamond-shaped panes of glass in a lattice pattern. Colored glass was scattered among the clear. On the roof were several chimneys with multiple shafts, each with a decorative chimney pot. False half-timbering on the upper stories was filled with patterned brick. Creeping vines laced the walls. Large fir trees, their branches extending over the house, gave it a foreboding aura.

"That house could stand some of the rehabbing that's going on around here," Vining observed. "Look at the roof and the paint."

"Still, a house that size in this neighborhood . . . That's a big corner lot. His wife couldn't earn enough cohosting that local TV morning show to support this spread."

Kissick drove up the driveway to the callbox near the closed gate.

"The wife's on TV?" Vining asked.

"She's on *Hello L.A.* I watch it every morning."

"You mean that show with the older guy and the two women who wear short skirts and low-cut tops to do their so-called news?"

"Yep." He responded to her head-shaking with a bemused, "Except for the older guy, what's not to like?"

"Which bimbo . . . I mean *newscaster* is Scoville's wife?"

"Dena Hale." He said her name as if savoring it.

"The big blonde."

"She's a healthy specimen."

"I thought you spent your time at home reading when you're not with your boys."

"I do. At night. In the morning, I look at the paper and watch *Hello L.A.*"

"Just to see Dena Hale, apparently."

"She's hot."

"She didn't look so hot in her mug shot, drunk and bruised after she crashed her Ferrari on the Pacific Coast Highway a couple of years ago." Vining hated the tinge of jealousy that roiled her blood. Her physiology was showing she cared while her mind insisted she didn't.

"She's been sober since then."

"How do you know?"

"Oprah." He gave her a mischievous smile, daring her to make a comeback.

"You know she's in her forties. I saw her on some TV show about being forty and fabulous."

"They say forty is the new thirty."

"I thought fifty was the new thirty."

"You get the point."

"What does that make me at thirty-four?"

"Younger and hotter than Dena Hale."

She smiled crookedly at him. "There you go again."

"You started it."

"Did not."

"Did too. You gonna finish it?"

With her index finger, she slid her sunglasses down her nose and peered at him.

He cocked an eyebrow.

After a second, she pushed her sunglasses up. "Press the buzzer."

Hot air blasted in when he rolled down the window. He pressed the call button and they heard a phone ringing through the speaker.

After several rings, a woman drowsily answered. "Hello?"

"This is Detective Jim Kissick of the Pasadena Police. I'm here with Detective Nanette Vining. We need to speak to Mr. Mark Scoville about a matter of some importance regarding his business partner, Oliver Mercer."

The sleep disappeared from the woman's voice. "Pasadena . . . *Police?*" Sounding as if she'd turned her head away from the phone, they heard her say, "The police are at the gate. Something about Oliver."

There was a man's voice in the background. "Let them in."

The woman said, "Please, drive up."

The gate rolled open. Kissick cursed when the sprinklers splattered the windshield as they drove up the long cobblestone driveway. They circled a turnabout with a fountain in the middle that was not running. It began shooting water as if someone had just turned it on.

Getting out of the car, they grabbed their jackets from the backseat and put them on. The spray from the sprinklers floated toward them. Vining turned her face toward it, letting out a sigh of pleasure.

A man and woman exited one of the home's tall double doors and stood on the porch. They looked as if they'd been hanging out by a pool.

Vining watched as they shot nervous comments at each other. She judged by their body language that they were genuinely nonplussed by her and Kissick's visit.

Mark Scoville wore a T-shirt over knee-length trunks with a bold floral print. Thick, dark hair curled over the shirt's crew neck. A belly pushed the T-shirt out over his waistband. He was more out of shape than overweight. He stood six feet tall but was stoop-shouldered and soft. His dark, curly hair had receded. He wore wire-framed aviator–style sunglasses with nearly black lenses. They looked expensive and were worth every penny because they made the spreading and balding Scoville look cool. His deep tan and the healthy impression it conveyed covered a multitude of shortcomings.

Vining knew from the information they'd pulled that Scoville was forty-five years old. He had one DUI and had received several speeding tickets over the past few years.

Dena Hale hurriedly pulled off an elastic band, releasing her long blond hair. She combed it with her fingers and again fashioned it into a ponytail. She pulled on a billed Lakers cap and pulled her hair through the opening in the back. Unlike her husband, she was edges and angles. Long tanned and toned legs extended from beneath her short white bathing suit cover-up. Big designer sunglasses with white frames and her cap hid all but her button nose and full lips. Sharp cheekbones and an adorable tilted chin complemented her heart-shaped face. Her winning smile was always turned on full blast during her television show. She was not smiling now.

The detectives flashed their shields.

"Mark Scoville?" Vining asked.

"Yes." Scoville came down the steps to meet them.

"I'm Detective Nanette Vining and this is Detective Jim Kissick. Are you Mrs. Scoville?"

Hale nodded, remaining on the porch, holding herself with crossed arms.

The sun reflected off Scoville's sunglasses.

"Did something happen to Oliver?"

Vining's voice was somber. "Mr. Scoville, I'm sorry to have to tell you this, but Oliver Mercer was murdered."

"*Murdered?*" Scoville drew his heavy eyebrows together and his mouth gaped.

Hale gasped and ran down the steps to join her husband, clutching his arm.

They both began talking at the same time.

"My God. What happened?"

"Where? How?" Scoville tore off his sunglasses and searched Vining's face.

She noticed his eyes were heavily bloodshot and had dark circles. "I can't go into that right now, Mr. Scoville, but we need to get going on this investigation as soon as possible. Would you and Mrs.—"

Scoville reeled, dropping his sunglasses. "I can't believe this. Oliver murdered?" He ran his hands through his hair. He broke away from his wife and started up the front steps. "This isn't happening. I . . . I have to sit down."

Hale scooped the sunglasses from the ground and started after her husband. She turned back to the detectives. "Please come in. It's hot outside anyway."

Vining caught Kissick watching Hale's legs as she jogged ahead of them up the steps.

The interior of the house was polished woods, threadbare Oriental carpets, stiff portraits, sedate landscapes, and ornate furniture upholstered in delicate but tired fabrics. The furnishings looked as if they'd been passed down through generations or selected to appear that way. The sun shone through the tall front windows and cast diamonds of light on the hardwood floor and the long runner that extended the length of the foyer.

The old house was of a type that used to intimidate Vining. She had worked to eliminate that phobia, and it was one thing she'd managed to overcome. To her, this house seemed musty and somehow sad. There had been laughter here, but its echoes had long ago faded.

Scoville hovered in the foyer, arms dangling at his sides. He was bathed in white sunlight from the windows that was shot with bright patches of red, blue, and green from random pieces of colored glass. The effect made him look as if he were trapped beneath a bell jar, lost and detached from the world.

His wife went to him. "Honey, why don't we sit in the library?" Taking off her sunglasses and hooking them on to the neck of her swimsuit cover-up, she turned to the detectives and flashed a tense smile. "Through here, please."

The detectives followed the Scovilles off the main hallway into a comfortable room lined with floor-to-ceiling built-in shelves crammed with books and objets d'art. A wooden ladder on wheels gave access to the higher shelves.

Through French doors, Vining saw a garden with a pool beyond. A female wearing a bikini, perhaps a teenager, was peering toward the house with a hand on her forehead to shield the sun. Vining heard a distant shriek as the girl wheeled around, raising her hands to defend herself against an attack by two young boys who pelted her with water from squirt guns.

Scoville slowly lowered himself onto a large leather chair and massaged his chin with his hand. "I apologize, but I've never had anything like this happen before. It's like it's happening to somebody else."

Hale nervously flitted around the room. Her sunglasses again in her hands, she opened and closed their arms before tossing them onto the coffee table. "We just had dinner with Oliver and his girlfriend, Lauren, when, Mark?" She looked at Scoville and then answered her own question. "Last month."

Kissick glanced at framed photographs of Hale with the notable people she'd interviewed on her television show. Her statement caused him to exchange a glance with Vining.

Hale caught the glance and paled.

Vining announced, "Lauren Richards was also murdered."

Hale dropped onto a couch, one hand pressed against her mouth.

Scoville moaned and buried his head in his hands, his elbows on his knees. "This is a nightmare. Can you tell us what happened?"

"The housekeeper found their bodies in Mercer's home this morning."

Vining pulled a Windsor chair from a secretary desk and sat. She leaned forward, her hands clasped on her lap. "Mr. and Mrs. Scoville, time is of the essence. We need to get all the information we can as quickly as possible. We'd like to ask you both some routine questions to help guide us. We're best equipped to do that at our police station in Pasadena. We'll drive you there and bring you back. We won't take much of your time."

Kissick spotted a box of tissues on an end table and handed it to Hale, who had begun to weep.

She looked up at him, tears spilling from her big blue eyes and mouthed, "Thank you."

"Mr. and Mrs. Scoville, does that sound okay with you?"

Scoville looked at Vining. "Of course. We want to do everything we can, but I don't know how much help we'll be."

"Any information will be helpful."

Vining pointed toward the French doors. "I see you have children. Is there someone who can watch them?"

Hale took off her cap. "Dahlia, my seventeen-year-old. She can stay with our son Luddy and his friend. She had plans to go to the movies with friends, but she can change them, for once."

She opened one of the doors, leaned out, and musically called, "Dahlia . . . Dah*lia*." She huffed when she received no response and resorted to yelling, putting the full force of her broadcasting training into it. *"Dahlia!"*

Kissick, standing near the glass doors, saw the girl stretched out on a chaise reading a magazine. She should have been able to easily hear her mother, but she didn't budge.

"She's ignoring you, as usual," Scoville commented.

Hale picked up a telephone handset and punched in a number. By the pool, the girl answered her cell phone.

"Dahlia, I have no patience for attitude right now. The Pasadena police are here. Mark's business partner, Oliver Mercer, and his girlfriend were murdered. The detectives want us to go to Pasadena, and I need you to stay with Luddy and his friend until we get back. I know you have plans. You'll have to change them. Too bad, darling."

She scowled, one hand on a hip. "For crying out loud, it's not the end of the world. You're staying here. End of discussion. You can drive my Jaguar your first day back at school, okay? Fine." She jabbed the END CALL button.

Scoville looked sullenly at his wife. "Two people were murdered and she's pissed off over not going to the movies."

"She's just being a seventeen-year-old girl. I was the same way."

"That's what I'm worried about."

Hale's jaw tensed but she let the comment go. "Can we change clothes first?"

Vining hesitated, and then said, "Of course." She

didn't want them out of their sight, but she had no cause to stop them and wanted to stay on their good side.

The detectives followed the Scovilles into the foyer and watched as they went up a staircase with ornately carved balusters. On the landing at the top of the stairs, Hale headed in one direction in the vast house and Scoville headed in the other.

The detectives looked at each other.

"Separate bedrooms?" Kissick asked.

Vining heard two doors shut. "Not even on the same side of the house."

FOUR

W*hy aren't* you talking to Dena and me at the same time?"

Mark Scoville sat at a table in an interview room in the Detective's Section on the second floor of the Pasadena Police Department. Vining and Kissick sat across from him. The interview was being videotaped.

Scoville continued, "In the police TV shows, that's what they do when they think people are hiding something. The police try to trip them up."

Vining opened her hands as if she were an open book. "It's procedure, Mr. Scoville. We take your statements independently so that you won't influence her responses and vice versa."

"Statements . . . I thought you just wanted to ask us

general questions about Oliver and Lauren. Who they knew, where they went . . . Stuff like that."

"We call that making a statement."

"Sounds like you think I had something to do with it. Maybe I need to call my attorney."

Vining made a face as if she were surprised by his level of concern. "That's always an option, Mr. Scoville, but nobody's guilty here, right?"

Her rhetorical question rankled Scoville. "Of course not. Like I said, I'm happy to help any way I can. I'm just trying to figure out your methods. I've never been in a situation like this before."

"I understand. We really appreciate you coming down here during the holiday weekend."

"No problem. Oliver and I had our differences, like any business partners, but he was a good guy. And Lauren . . . I've never had anything like this happen to me. Guess I've led a sheltered life."

It wasn't lost on Vining that Scoville had turned the murder victims' tragedy into his own. "The sooner we wrap this up, the sooner you can go home."

"Sounds good."

"Mr. Scoville . . . Or may we call you Mark?"

"Please."

"Mark, what did you do last night?"

"I was home. My wife and I had a dinner party with three other couples. Let's see, we had Joan and Peter Shapiro, Michelle and Fred Lane, and Angela and Ty Kerrigan. The Kerrigans are new friends from the country club. It was the first time they'd been over, but we've known the Shapiros and Lanes for years. We barbecued steaks and halibut in the backyard. Ate outside. I made my grilled radicchio salad." He paused as if waiting for a response.

Vining made a noise conveying that it sounded good.

"It's delicious. One of my specialties."

Kissick jotted down the names on a yellow pad while Vining continued the interview.

"When were your guests there?"

"Six-thirty until nearly eleven. Afterward, Dena and I picked up. Our housekeeper had the weekend off. We didn't get into bed until after midnight."

Vining took in his bloodshot eyes and mottled complexion, which was more pronounced under the station's fluorescent lighting. "Late night for you and your wife?"

"For Dena. With her job, she gets up before dawn. Me, I've always been a night owl. Being my own boss, I can pretty much set my own schedule."

Vining waited to see if he'd confess to being hungover. When he didn't, she went on. "Were your children home?"

"Luddy spent the night with his friend Jeremy, who lives a few blocks away. Dahlia came trailing in after her curfew, as usual. She's Dena's daughter from an early and short marriage to this B-list actor." Scoville snorted laughter. "Chad-David Clayton."

Kissick perked up. "Chad-David Clayton? He played Horatio Raven in *Babylon Tomorrow.* That show was a classic. I thought it was much better than any of the *Star Treks.* Is he still around? He kinda dropped from sight."

"He's still around." Scoville was irked by Kissick's veneration of Dena's ex. "He retired from acting and sells insurance in Idaho. Shows up at these fan conferences and sells his signature. Calls Dahlia once in a while."

Kissick shook his head, amazed by the coincidence. "Horatio Raven. . . ."

Vining moved on. "How long have you and Dena been married?"

"Nine years."

"And Luddy is your son with Dena?"

Scoville beamed. "He's my boy. Named after my father, Ludlow. He was the apple of the old man's eye."

"Your father passed away?"

"A few years ago. He was a larger-than-life character, old Ludlow. Came out from Matawan, New Jersey, in the sixties with hardly two nickels to rub together. Bought land along the freeways that was dirt cheap then and put up billboards. Marquis Outdoor Advertising is the largest privately held outdoor advertising firm in Southern California. We don't have as many billboard faces as the big guys, but our boutique includes some of the most valuable in the world, including most of the signs on the Sunset Strip."

Scoville took his wallet from his pants pocket and handed Vining and Kissick business cards. He grew animated as he settled into familiar territory. "The big signs on the Strip are as much a part of its cachet as those in Times Square or Tokyo's Ginza district. It's all due to my father's foresight in seeing the emerging car culture in Southern California and snapping up key locations."

Kissick listened with interest. "Billboards. Who knew it was such a big business?"

"A high-profile, high-traffic face can lease for a hundred grand a month."

Vining raised her eyebrows at Scoville's number. "Sounds like your dad was a visionary."

"He was."

"Did you always work for him?"

"No. I did during summers in high school and college, but was on my own for many years. I joined the firm full-time when my father was diagnosed with lung cancer. When he died, he left the business to me. A year after my dad passed away, my mom went from a heart attack. I think the stress of my dad's illness killed her."

Vining moaned sympathetically. "Any other family involved in the business?"

"No. I had a brother, but he died when he was in high school."

"That's sad," Vining said.

"Yeah, well . . . I spent a lot of years trying to distance myself from my dad. Make my own way. I'm sure my son will do the same with me. The old man was no walk in the park, for sure. But we came together at the end and had a couple of good years." Scoville grew wistful.

The pieces clicked for Vining. "The beautiful Hancock Park house, was that your parents'?"

"My childhood home. Now I'm bringing up my son there."

"How great. It's a wonderful house." She nearly shuddered, thinking about growing up in that moldering manse. "How many rooms does it have?"

"Thirty-two."

"Whoa."

Kissick sat quietly, letting her take her time getting where she was headed.

"Lots of room to spread out," she said. "I noticed that you and your wife took off in different directions when you went to change clothes."

Scoville laughed uneasily and shifted his gaze. "I'm a night owl, like I said, plus I snore. With Dena's early schedule, she needs her sleep. We have plenty of together time." He gave Kissick a wink.

Kissick commiserated with a raised eyebrow.

Vining guessed that Kissick was imagining Hale with the vaguely slimy Scoville. She savored the thought. "You're a lucky man. Dena's not only accomplished, she's gorgeous."

"I am. I'm very lucky. I have a wonderful life."

"Seems like it's right out of a storybook."

Kissick squelched his smile in response to Vining's sappy comment.

"Well, I wouldn't go *that* far," Scoville conceded. "But it's a great life."

"Except for problems with an adolescent stepdaughter." Vining grinned.

"Right. There's that."

Vining had achieved her goal. Scoville was more relaxed and unguarded than when they had first sat down, and she'd confirmed their separate bedrooms. She tried a new direction. "What do you know about Lauren Richards?"

"Not much. We had them over for dinner a month, six weeks ago, like Dena mentioned. That was the only time Dena and I met her. I know she was divorced. She was an administrator or something for the modern art museum in Pasadena. Oliver was on the board. That's how they met. They'd been dating for a couple of months. She had two small kids. A boy and a girl, I think. Oh, and she was a Rose Parade princess when she was in high school. Oliver made sure we knew that. Oliver always had an attractive woman on his arm. He liked them tall, slender, and brunette." He pointed at Vining. "He would have liked you. You're his type."

Scoville's attempt at flirting with her felt creepy, but Vining remained enigmatic. She smiled closemouthed, hiding her overbite and the gap between her teeth that men inevitably found sexy. She didn't want to encourage him. "Did you socialize much with Oliver Mercer?"

"Not really. Ours was primarily a business relationship."

"How did Mercer contribute to the business?"

"He was a silent partner. That was our agreement

when I sold him a hunk of Marquis. I retained control of the day-to-day operations."

"How long had you known him?"

"About three years. We met through this investor group we both belong to. Belonged, I should say."

Kissick jumped in. "Bringing an outsider into the family business must have been a big deal."

"It was. I couldn't have done it when my father was around. I was ready to grow the firm, and Oliver had money he wanted to invest." Scoville shrugged. "He was rich. His grandfather was the founder of the Wall Street firm Mercer Brothers. Made a fortune. Oliver's father tripled it. Oliver's brother is still with Mercer Brothers. Oliver took his own path. Was with a venture capital group based in Pasadena for some years before he decided to go out on his own. Apart from the money Oliver brought to the table, he also brought years of experience growing and expanding companies. I needed somebody with business acumen."

Kissick asked, "How much of the firm did Mercer own?"

Scoville's eyes darkened and he laughed without amusement. "Too much."

"Half? More than half?"

"It's a privately held company." Scoville leaned back in his chair and crossed his arms over his chest. "We don't have to open our books."

"We've heard that you and Mercer had been arguing a lot lately," Vining said. "What can you tell us about that?"

Scoville raised a shoulder in a gesture that bordered on juvenile. "We were having a disagreement over the direction the company should take."

"Tell me more."

Scoville widened his eyes and spoke slowly, as if it

were necessary for them to understand. "Like I said, Marquis is privately held, and our affairs are nobody's business. Except the IRS."

Nobody laughed at the lame joke.

Vining leaned toward Scoville. "Mark, your business partner and his girlfriend were brutally murdered. We're going to find out what you and Oliver were arguing about. I bet a lot of people know. Your secretary, your chief financial officer, your golf-club buddies . . . Oliver probably talked to his people about it. Since we're going to find out anyway, you can save us a lot of time by telling us now. Frankly, it's making you look like you have something to hide."

Scoville ran his hand over his receding hairline and then gestured toward himself. "Hey, I don't have anything to hide. I already told you that. I want it understood that I had nothing, *nothing* to do with those murders. You want to know what Oliver and I were fighting about? Here it is. He had cooked up this deal with the CEO of an outdoor advertising firm in Vegas that wants to break into Southern California. The firm's name is Drive By Media. They're big in Vegas, which is an outdoor advertising mecca. I can't go into details. Doesn't mean I'm *hiding* anything. Just means there's a deal on the table and it's confidential."

Kissick pressed. "You still haven't told us what you and Mercer were arguing about. Mercer's housekeeper said one day you and he looked like you were about to come to blows."

"His housekeeper." Scoville sneered. "Rosie. . . . By the way, you probably don't know that he was bonking her as well as half the other women in his vast social circle. All those private clubs and boardrooms, the museum, the philharmonic, the Playhouse, the endless fundraisers, riding on the coattails of his family money and name. Oliver was laying pipe all over Pasadena. He'd fuck a snake if you could hold it still."

The detectives let him wallow there, waiting to see if he'd add anything else.

He glared at the table and stewed.

After a minute, Vining ventured, "What about Dena?"

Scoville bristled. "What about Dena?"

"Did Oliver make a pass at her, or more?"

"Everyone makes passes at Dena. That's nothing new. When you're married to a woman like Dena, you learn to live with it."

"Does she flirt back?"

"When she wants to piss me off."

Vining pressed, "Does it go any further than flirting?"

"I'm pretty confident it doesn't."

"Why is that?"

"Because Dena's too ambitious. One of the big networks is courting her for a national morning show. She wouldn't tarnish her all-American image for a roll in the hay with Oliver Mercer, or anyone else." Scoville sniffed. "My point is, you should take what Consuela tells you with a grain of salt."

The derisive way he dismissed the housekeeper got to Vining. "Rosie Cordova."

"Whatever."

Kissick leaned back. "So Mark, I'll ask one more time. What were you and Mercer so heated about?"

Scoville sighed, tiring of the questions. "The deal with Drive By was bad—long story short. Oliver thought he was an astute businessman, but he didn't know his ass from his elbow. He was a spoiled brat who'd gotten his way his entire life and hated to be told no."

"But you said you'd brought him into the firm for his . . . business acumen, I believe were the words you used."

Scoville leveled a gaze at Kissick. "I don't like your tone, and I don't like the direction this conversation is taking. I came down here on the pretense that we were going to talk about Oliver Mercer and his girlfriend and where they went and who they knew and things like that. Now I'm feeling under attack. You think I had something to do with those murders. I'm thinking it was a big mistake to talk to you without my lawyer."

Kissick appeared hurt and surprised by Scoville's outburst. "Mark, I apologize if I came on too strong. Like Detective Vining said, these are routine questions. It's just procedure."

"Procedure my ass. I know how you cops operate. The fact that you're coming after me shows you don't have shit. You're grasping at straws. You'd be happy to hang this thing on me and call it a day."

Scoville wagged his index finger at Kissick and turned it on Vining to show that she was included. "I want you to understand one thing very clearly. I had *nothing* to do with those murders. And any insinuation that I did is simply ridiculous. It's more than ridiculous. It's stupid. You know what? I'll take a lie-detector test right now. You think I'm hiding something? I have nothing to hide." He crooked his fingers. "Bring it on."

"Mark, you're being so cooperative. Thank you." Vining gave him her best gap-toothed smile, which she knew helped her look guileless. "I apologize for my overzealous partner." She shot a you-bad-boy glare at Kissick, who took on a hangdog look. "I mean, we bust in on you while you were having a nice afternoon with your family. Thanks for helping us out."

"I'm sorry I got so heated," Scoville said. "This has been a bad day."

"Yes, it has," Vining agreed. "So let's see about setting up that polygraph." She looked at Kissick.

"I'll do that." Kissick left the room.

Alone with Scoville, Vining sensed that he was traveling to a dark place. She milked it. "These murders . . . my God."

He blinked at her. "It was bad?"

"Worst I've seen, and I've been at this a while."

"What happened to them?"

"Can't talk about details, Mark. Let's just say it was nightmare stuff." She chewed her lip. "Both of them in the prime of their lives. Everything to live for. . . ."

"Oliver and I weren't best friends, but live and let live. I'm sure he'd say the same about me. It's awful. I still can't believe it."

"Your mind can't help but go to their final moments on earth. The horror."

Her suggestion seemed to implant scary images in Scoville's mind. Shaking his head slightly, he fell quiet and frowned at his hands.

She went on. "And their loved ones getting that knock on the door that everyone dreads. Praying that it's all a bad dream. Then the realization that there's no waking up from this nightmare."

Still shaking his head, he murmured a small, agonizing sound.

Kissick returned. "Polygraph is set up for tomorrow at nine."

Slightly dazed, Scoville asked, "Here?"

"Yes. Go to the information desk in the lobby and ask for Detective Vining or myself."

"All right." Scoville started to get up.

Vining put out her hand. "Mark, just one last question. . . . Is there anyone you know who might want to harm Oliver or Lauren?"

Halfway out of his seat, he again sat, following the direction that Vining moved her hand. "No. No one."

"Anyone who might want to harm you or your family?"

Scoville thoughtfully shook his head.

"Any clients, suppliers, competitors. . . ."

Scoville continued shaking his head.

"Husbands of women Mercer was involved with . . . women who Mercer spurned . . . men Lauren was involved with. . . ."

"No."

"Anyone with a grudge, who felt Mercer or you did them wrong. . . ."

Scoville suddenly frowned and pulled himself straight. He stared at the table.

Vining and Kissick exchanged a glance.

Kissick asked, "Mark, did you think of something?"

Still frowning, Scoville wouldn't look at them.

"You look as if you've seen a ghost, Mark," Vining said. "What's going on?"

"Nothing. I . . . I just remembered that I promised to take my son somewhere. I'm late. I've gotta go. To answer your question, I don't know anybody like that." He stood. "Looks like we're through."

"Sure," Kissick said. "We'd like to spend a few minutes chatting with your wife, if that's okay."

He avoided their eyes. "I just told you. We've gotta go."

Vining began, "What if Detective Kissick drives you home and I'll take your wife back to Hancock Park later?"

"What's so important about talking to her? She barely knew Oliver and Lauren."

"Again, it's routine investigative procedure," Vining said. "No one here has anything to hide, right?"

Scoville rubbed his hands together and shoved them into his pockets. "Right."

Kissick came around the table closer to Scoville. "Mark, what's troubling you?"

"I told you. My son's waiting."

"Where are you taking him?" Vining asked.

"You know, I've had enough. I'm outta here. But go ahead. Talk to Dena. Bring her home later. That's great."

"Good deal," Kissick said. " 'Cause it's no problem for us."

Scoville held up his hands as if to smooth everything out. "No problem for me either. No problem at all."

FIVE

*A*fter Kissick left with Scoville, Vining walked Hale to the interview room, passing Detective Tony Ruiz and newly minted Detective Alex Caspers.

Caspers's eyes bulged as he watched Hale pass by in a snug baby-blue velour jogging suit, his focus laser-like as he followed the rear view.

Shortly afterward, Vining came out to get Hale something to drink.

"Caspers, your mouth is hanging open." She playfully pushed up the chin of the oversexed young detective.

"Damn," he said as if in pain. "Let me say it one more time. *Damn.*"

Ruiz was less enthused. "Who's she?" Hostility was Ruiz's typical M.O. when it came to things Vining. They had a long history. His station moniker was Picachu, as he resembled the bald, rotund cartoon character. He had briefly trumped her, having assumed her desk in Homicide while she was absent for nearly a year taking Injured on Duty leave. Their boss, Sergeant Kendra Early, had since moved him to Assaults, where the energetic Caspers ran circles around him. And Vining was back at her old desk.

With the Mercer/Richards murders, Sergeant Early had brought in detectives from other desks under her control to assist Kissick and Vining, who were the only full-time homicide detectives. Vining would again have the pleasure of extended face time with Ruiz and Caspers. Vining found alpha male Caspers, who didn't appreciate how wet behind the ears he was, easier to work with than Ruiz. What you saw was what you got. Ruiz, a nineteen-year veteran, was smoke and mirrors.

Vining said, "That's Dena Hale, wife of Mercer's business partner, Mark Scoville."

"Isn't she on TV?" Caspers looked at the wall of the interview room in which Hale was ensconced as if wishing he could see through it. The two-way glass was on an interior wall.

"Yeah? What show?" Ruiz asked with renewed interest. The fringe of hair around his bald pate still managed to litter his shoulders with dandruff.

"*Hell in L.A.*," Vining joked.

Caspers scrunched his face and then grinned. "It's *Hello L.A.* You're bad."

"Meow," Ruiz said.

Vining *was* being catty. It was invigorating. "She looks good . . . for her age. She's forty-three."

Caspers's eyes widened. "*Forty*-three? No way."

At twenty-eight, he had myopia concerning females past thirty. With several colleges in Pasadena, a major hospital, innumerable shops, restaurants, and museums, and a vibrant night scene that drew young people from all over, there was no shortage of opportunities for Caspers and his buddies on the PPD to meet women. Caspers had not even been above dating crime victims, witnesses, E.R. room nurses, and, on at least one occasion, a woman he'd arrested. He protested that he'd collared her for petty theft, it was her first offense, and *she* had called *him*.

"Old enough to be your mother," Vining taunted. It was a stretch, but let him do the math.

Ruiz snorted. "Caspers, like you would turn that down, if she gave you the time of day."

"Like my father says, I wouldn't kick her out of bed for eating crackers."

"Who's that?" Vining took stock of a man sitting in the conference room.

He appeared to be in his thirties. His head was shaved. He wore glasses with heavy black frames, the color stark against his pallid skin. His fresh white dress shirt was tucked into beige slacks. His long neck protruded ostrich-like above his shirt collar. He was sitting erect in the chair, his hands flat on top of the table. Even though his appearance tended toward nerdish, he was tall and broad-shouldered and could be physically intimidating. He was staring into space, his lips set into a line beneath a dark brown toothbrush mustache.

"You mean Adolph," Caspers joked, referring to Hitler's infamous mustache.

"That's Dillon Somerset," Ruiz said. "The guy who was stalking Lauren Richards. Works as a computer consultant. A few months ago, he did a project for the museum where Lauren worked. Went out for lunch with her and the other office employees a couple of times. The museum's director said he did a good job. Was always polite and on time. No problems.

"Lauren's mother said he asked Lauren out once but

she turned him down, saying she didn't date because of her kids. Her mom said Somerset gave Lauren the willies because he was always staring at her. He'd leave little gifts on her desk. Wildflowers. Rocks. He's big into backpacking in the wilderness. Once he brought her a chrome part from a car engine because he liked the shape of it. After he finished the job with the museum, he started hanging around Lauren's house. He'd stand across the street, just watching. Leave things on her doorstep. When Lauren would head home after work, he'd be standing near her car."

"Would he say anything to her?" Vining asked.

"Just 'Hello, how's your day?' Like that."

Vining understood how the innocuousness of Somerset's actions made them as chilling as if he'd made an overt threat.

"Did she file a stay-away order?"

"Her mom said she was about to. A couple of weeks ago, Lauren and her dad approached Somerset. Her dad told him he was upsetting Lauren and her children. Somerset said he couldn't understand how his being nice to her and watching out for her was a problem. Her dad got heated. Told him it was a big problem and he'd better knock it off."

Vining shot an angry glance at Somerset in the conference room. "And?"

"Somerset started turning red from his neck all the way up to his scalp. All he said was, 'Okay.' "

"Okay?"

"That's it. Okay. He turned and walked away, holding his arms down by his sides, all rigid. Lauren didn't see him after that and they figured it was over."

"Any priors?" Vining inclined her head to look into the eyes of the shorter Ruiz and not at the top of his bald head.

"No." Ruiz looked at Somerset in a way that was almost hungry, as if daring him to look up. The man had secrets, and Ruiz wanted them. "He's a passive-aggressive fucker. You can smell it on him."

Caspers made a gesture like he was breaking a twig in half. "Snap."

"You said he's a computer consultant," Vining said. "Does he work for a company?"

"He did for a couple of years. The human resources person there said he resigned and won't give me anything else without a warrant. Somerset dropped out of Caltech after studying there for about a year and a half. Never got his degree. Now he works out of his home. Lives in an apartment above the garage of his parents' house in San Marino. His daddy owns a company in town that makes some medical technology something. Figures. The loser has a rich daddy supporting him."

Ruiz, like many cops, had a chip on his shoulder regarding the Pasadena area's many wealthy denizens. Pasadena and its neighbor, San Marino, had been a playground for the wealthy since the turn of the last century.

Vining didn't fault Ruiz for his prejudice. She had her own, but also had the conceit that hers was well-earned.

"Did you hear about Mercer's dog?" Caspers went on when Vining indicated she hadn't. "Autopsy showed he'd ingested something that ate his guts out. Probably mixed with ground meat."

"A Prestone patty," Ruiz commented.

"Who would be that cruel to a dog?" Vining asked rhetorically. The human carnage was unbelievable, but the added offense to the animal pushed it over the top.

They fell silent, thinking of the poor dog eroding from the inside out.

"Planned it all out." Ruiz narrowed his eyes at Somerset. "Every step of the way. Just like he was writing a computer program."

"We haven't eliminated Mercer's business partner, Mark Scoville, as a suspect in a murder-for-hire plot," Vining reminded him. "Scoville and his wife had three couples to their home last night for a dinner party that didn't end until after eleven. With the TOD estimated between six and nine p.m. that puts him out of any of the wet work. But he got funny when we asked if he knew anyone who might want to do Mercer harm. He volunteered to take a polygraph."

Ruiz raised bushy eyebrows. "Somerset refuses."

"You should have heard him go on," Caspers said. "It's a matter of principle. The test is ridiculous. Inaccurate and unscientific. He won't lower himself to participate in a carnival game. Says the fact that the results can't be used in a trial proves his point."

"Maybe not, but not participating makes you look guilty." Ruiz had a gleam in his eye. He felt a rush from being within inches of snatching not just a bad guy, but a snarling, drooling monster.

"It's one thing to know something. It's another to prove it." Vining stated the obvious to get Ruiz's goat. It worked.

"Gee, Vining . . . ya think?" Ruiz took off, saying, "I'm getting coffee."

Vining looked at Caspers. "Guess it's up to you, Caspers. You want to help me interview Dena Hale?"

"Ch-yeah," Caspers enthused.

"Remember, eyes on her face. Hands on the table."

"Detective Vining." Caspers feigned insult. "I am a professional."

"A professional what?"

The young detective took a lot of grief from the more-seasoned detectives, but he was an easy target.

Caspers seemed genuinely put off by her ribbing.

Vining grabbed his arm and started toward the room where Hale waited. "Come on, friendly ghost. Let's put the screws to Mrs. Hell in L.A."

SIX

"*Dena's story* jibed with her husband's." Vining used a lime wedge speared with a plastic toothpick to stir the foam of her blended margarita. "Except for one issue."

"The separate bedrooms." Kissick caught the bartender's eye and pointed at his empty wineglass. He said, "Thanks, Paul," when the bartender pulled the cork from an open bottle of cabernet and filled the glass until it was brimming.

It was well past the dinner hour at Monty's. The venerable chophouse had been in the same location for sixty-five years. Off the beaten track from the relatively new phenomenon of Old Pasadena and its mostly chain restaurants and shops in restored historic buildings, Monty's was a beloved locals' joint. Sadly, developers had finally made the owners an offer they couldn't refuse. The restaurant was due to be demolished to make way for an office building.

Vining's cell phone, which she'd set on the bar, jangled musically. She picked it up. "Text message from Em. She's with her dad and Kaitlyn and the boys in Santa

Barbara." She read it aloud. "All good. Major shopping today. Love you."

She snapped her phone closed. "I miss her more than I want to admit."

"Julie and I have been trading the boys back and forth for years. I still have a hard time when they leave."

"Did I tell you that Em's starting a new school?"

"No. Where?"

"The Coopersmith School of the Arts. It's a magnet school that specializes in music and fine arts. It's hard to get in. Emily is so excited."

"That's great."

"She's going to miss her old friends and I'll have to drive her to and from school for the time being."

"She'll be driving before too long."

"That'll be something new to stress over."

"Seems like only yesterday they were in diapers."

Vining sighed and picked up her drink, which was still nearly full. After a pause, she began, "On another subject, how about Mark Scoville and Dena Hale? I don't think *they* miss each other when they're apart. Dena said the room at the left of the stairs is her *salon.* Keeps her clothes there so she doesn't disturb her husband when she gets up before dawn to go to work. Mark said she sleeps there because of his snoring and because he likes to stay up late."

"Maybe she was trying to preserve his dignity. Still, I sense trouble in the Tudor. I bet nothing's happening between the sheets in either bedroom."

"I bet Scoville sleeps in his parents' old bedroom. He still has all their furnishings. Their clothes are probably still in the closets." Vining looked disgusted. "That would send me down the hall to a separate bedroom."

Kissick sipped his wine and glanced at a basketball game on one of the TVs suspended from the ceiling on either side of the bar. "What did she say about Mark's business affairs?"

"Claimed to be the uninvolved wife. Doesn't know anything about it." Vining took a bite out of the remaining half of her cheeseburger. It wasn't on the dinner menu, but the cook would always make one for her. The restaurant's steaks were great, but didn't fit Vining's budget.

"Was she telling the truth?" Kissick snatched a French fry off Vining's plate and dunked it into the cocktail sauce that went with his shrimp.

"Maybe, but she's an actress."

"Newscaster."

Vining flicked her hand, dismissing the title that bestowed additional gravitas. "Anyway, she was pulled together in the way she answered questions."

"Self-possessed."

"Whatever." He had a habit of suggesting more-precise words, just thinking out loud. Normally, she didn't mind. He was a college graduate and read a lot. She'd barely gotten her high school diploma and was damn glad she'd made it that far. Right on the heels of Grad Night at Disneyland, she and Wes, her high-school sweetheart, had married. Emily came along soon after. Then, scant years later, divorce, and the ongoing struggle to support herself and her daughter. She wouldn't dream of undoing any of it if it meant she wouldn't have Em. Street smarts were more important than book smarts in their line of work anyway, unless one had plans to move up the ladder. Still, she'd like to be better educated. Maybe one day.

She knew Kissick wasn't showing off, but she felt peevish. The day was getting to her.

He shook his head at something going on in the basketball game. "Did she know anyone who might do the victims harm?"

"She didn't know anyone who would hurt Mercer or Richards. As for herself, she's had nutty fans. One guy used to hang around this restaurant that Scoville owned when they were first married. When the restaurant went belly-up, the guy disappeared. She talked about how tough the restaurant business is, how hard it was for Scoville to lose his business, and so on."

"Scoville's had lots of failed business ventures. After I drove him home, I stopped by the house of one of his golf buddies." Kissick dredged a jumbo shrimp in cocktail sauce and consumed it up to the tail. "This guy was full of stories. He's also in this investor group that Mercer and Scoville belong to. Said that Mercer and Scoville were having big issues over the billboard company. He laughed when I suggested that Scoville invited Mercer to buy into Marquis because of Mercer's business smarts. He said Mercer was a dilettante. A great guy, but never worked a day in his life and was more interested in acting like he was a businessman than being one."

Kissick ate the last of his shrimp. "This guy said that Mercer owned fifty-one percent of Scoville's company. Sounds like Scoville sold a controlling interest not as a savvy move to bring in expansion money but out of desperation to bail the thing out."

"I bet he's run it into the ground since taking it over from his father." Vining watched a waitress deliver heaping platters of steak to two older men seated at a red vinyl booth along the wall. The waitress, who looked as if she'd worked there since the Nixon administration, used two spoons to mix globs of butter, sour cream, and chives into baked potatoes that were nearly the size of footballs.

"Scoville's chief financial officer said he couldn't talk to me. The next thing we'll hear is 'talk to my lawyer.'"

Vining set the last quarter of her cheeseburger on the plate, wiped her hands, and tossed the napkin beside it. "Even if it was the creepiest murder-for-hire ever, Scoville would have been expecting news of it. There was no denying his and Dena's shock when they heard about the murders. I didn't pick up deception from either of them. Scoville doesn't impress me as a good liar. The only time I felt he was hiding something was when we asked about people who might want to do him or Mercer harm. Maybe they were into a dirty business deal."

"Scoville has a big ol' chip on his shoulder. Sounds like Mercer did too. I can see the two of them making enemies." He pointed at the remaining cheeseburger on her plate. "You going to eat that?"

She slid her plate toward him.

He picked up the burger and bit into it, closing his eyes as he chewed. "Mmm . . . They do a great burger here." He popped the rest into his mouth. "I'm really going to miss this place."

"Me too. Order more food. You didn't eat very much." She realized they were doing it again—acting like a couple. They had been for a few months two years ago. Great months, until she'd ended it. She'd had sound reasons. She had a young daughter at home, and wanted to set a better example than her own much-married mother had for herself. Their relationship could affect their work, even though it wasn't against policy for officers to date or even marry. To be honest, she was scared silly.

He snagged a final, now-soggy fry before shoving the plate away. "I'm trying to take off the weight I gained when I was on IOD leave."

Kissick had been on leave from the injury he had sustained while working their last case.

Vining looked at his lean frame. "What? Six ounces?"

"Seven pounds. I couldn't work out for over a month. Who knows? Someone might want it again." He winked at her.

"There's that." She changed the subject. "I caught up with a couple of Scoville's dinner party guests after I dropped Dena off. They said it was a *normal* evening with the Scovilles. Mark was there the whole time. No unexplained absences."

"And normal means . . . ?"

"Mark drank too much. Got loud. Dena was pissed off. Got quiet."

"She has hard-fought sobriety, and she's living with a drunk," he said. "I'd say that's a problem."

"Hard-fought sobriety?" She didn't hide her amusement.

"You've gotta give the woman her due. She's been open about her struggle. How she crashed her Ferrari. Went to A.A."

"You've gotta change the channel."

He sipped his wine, looking a little irked. "So do the Scovilles' friends have any idea what's going on in that marriage?"

"No one would admit anything. Maybe Dena and Mark keep their private life private. Dena's shown she can be proud. Guess she doesn't have it all after all. I still can't get over the way her daughter treated her. I can't imagine Emily ever being that disrespectful to me."

"My boys toward me either. There are two sides to every story, but still, it's sad. I think Dena's lonely."

"You would."

"What does that mean?"

"Poor little rich girl."

"She seemed down-to-earth."

"I wonder if you'd be so sympathetic if she wasn't so good-looking."

"That's a callous thing to say. I care about all human beings." He opened his palms if cradling the world between them.

"Especially women with good legs in short skirts."

"Why Corporal Vining, I didn't know you cared."

"I don't." She felt her cheeks color with the lie. She tried not to smile, but he was looking at her in that crazy way that he knew always made her crack up. Her lips parted, revealing her overbite. She pressed her tongue against the gap between her front teeth, which she did when she was nervous. That was precisely where he was looking. Men. Simpleminded bastards.

"I never get to see your legs anymore."

She raised her index finger, warning him, her nails on her utilitarian hand short and unvarnished.

He grabbed her finger. When she tried to pull away, he held tight, that silly grin still on his long face. She jerked again and he let go.

"Two glasses of red wine. Went straight to your head. You're a cheap date."

He nudged her melted margarita toward her. "You've hardly touched your drink."

"Can't let my guard down with you. You're trouble."

"Some people live for that kind of trouble." He sidled closer on the barstool until his knees were touching hers. "I remember you getting loose, Nan. Sometimes those memories warm my cold nights."

"Why do we have to go there? Seems like lately we can't have a drink together without going to that place."

"What place is that, Nan?"

"Now you're annoying me."

He sat straight, her comment having had the effect of

a slap. "I don't want to *annoy* you. I thought we were having fun. Guess I forgot who I was with."

Ouch. "Sorry. I didn't mean to come off so strong. It's just—"

"We have to work together. I know. What we had was in the past. You want to ignore this thing, even though it's like an elephant in the room.

"Nan, we've both been given second chances in life. Before I was injured, I thought I understood what you had gone through. But until you see your own blood spilling out of you at the hand of some asshole . . . you can't really comprehend. And what I went through was small compared to what happened to you. I don't want to sound melodramatic, but life is short."

"So what are you saying? We should hop into bed because tomorrow we might die?"

He laughed joylessly. "Gotta hand it to ya, Vining. You can be one tough broad."

He slid off the stool and set enough money on the bar to pay for both of them. "I'm happy to buy your dinner. Don't worry. No obligation. See you tomorrow."

She didn't go after him. She didn't run after men. That included when her ex-husband had walked out on her and two-year-old Emily.

She waited until he had had time to retrieve his car before she left.

SEVEN

Traffic on the curvy old Pasadena Freeway was light. Vining exited at Avenue 43, five miles northeast of downtown L.A. and eight from the Pasadena police station. She turned north at the Taco Fiesta stand, closed for the night, and headed into Mt. Washington, the hilly Los Angeles neighborhood known as the poor man's Bel Air.

The dwellings changed as she went up and up, traveling winding, aging streets. Social class was displayed as clearly as strata in a wind- and water-eroded canyon. The homes in the flatlands, closest to the freeway, were modest bungalows, many with iron bars over the windows. Fences protected tiny yards strewn with toys and bicycles. Icicle Christmas lights were draped from roof eaves year-round. Many homes were painted turquoise and salmon, colors inspired by the residents' Mexican and Central American palette.

Climbing higher, woodsy, funky cottages attested to the area's history as an artist's haven. Farther still, homes grew larger as the view became more expansive. On the flatlands at the top of the mountain were grand old mansions. Mt. Washington was the first home of Los Angeles's nascent movie industry. Charlie Chaplin was a frequent guest of the Mt. Washington Hotel, built upon a sprawling property at the crest. The mission-style buildings are now home to the international headquarters of the Self-Realization Fellowship.

When Vining was recovering from her injuries, she'd take long walks around Mt. Washington, mostly because her grandmother said she should. She resumed her tough workouts at the gym as soon as she was able, but Granny advocated open, if not necessarily fresh, air to elevate her spirits. Her grandmother saw something she didn't—her rage had gotten the better of her. Vining kept her appointments with the department-appointed shrink and she walked.

She did enjoy hiking to a lookout point that had a sweeping view of the hindquarters of L.A., above the noise, the hustle and bustle, the bad guys, the victims. It gave her clarity to step away for a few moments and let the quiet seep beneath her skin, beneath her scars. But rather than mitigate her rage, it sucked out the moisture and weakness, crystallizing it into something pure and powerful. It lodged beneath her skin, like a bullet too close to a vital artery to risk removal. There it resided, waiting until her system pushed it closer to the surface or dangerously closer to the artery.

Vining turned right onto Stella Place, her street near the middle of the mountain. It was one of the few remaining intact specimens of a 1960's development of multilevel homes clinging to the hillside on cantilevers. She and Wes had stretched to buy the house when they were first married. He had since moved onward and upward with a younger wife, newer kids, and a happening McMansion in unapologetically white-bread Calabasas, thirty miles away in the hills east of Malibu.

Vining watched the garage door open. After driving inside, she watched it close, making sure no one slipped in behind her. Unlocking and opening the door into the house set off the prealarm. She punched the codes to reset it.

The house seemed unusually quiet without Emily. She was a quiet child anyway, her hobbies tending toward the bookish, her domain the former rumpus room downstairs, but still Vining felt the absence of her energy. She let her mind wander to a time in the not-so-distant future when Emily would leave for college and Vining would then have nothing in her life but her job. And that bullet of rage.

The house was stifling. Tossing her jacket over the back of a dinette chair, she walked through the kitchen and family room. In the living room, she clicked on the central air. It hummed to life, sending out refreshing coolness. She yanked the drapes back, removed the steel pin that secured the sliding glass doors, slid the doors open, and walked onto the balcony. The daytime heat had ceded to the cool of night. That morning, Vining had French-braided her long, dark hair and pinned it into a coil at the back of her head. She unfastened the top two buttons of her shirt, spread the collar open to the cool air, and ran her fingers over her damp neck, brushing the indentation of her scar.

The crickets loved the late-summer heat. Their songs rose in a great chorus from her sloping, ragged backyard and the dried brush and chaparral beyond the chain-link fence. The heat made the city lights shimmer in spite of the smog. Vining had a bird's-eye view of the unglamorous side of downtown L.A. and points southwest: functional government facilities, working-class and poor neighborhoods, and the Pasadena Freeway. It wasn't a multimillion-dollar view, as from Mulholland Drive, with a blanket of lights stretching to the ocean, but it was pretty at night nonetheless. She liked being above it all and able to see.

As she turned to go inside, she ran her hand across wind chimes that were hanging from a steel arm attached to the wall beside the glass door. The arm had once supported a hanging plant, one of many potted plants around the house that she and Wes had nurtured. Vining had had lots of time then to fuss with things like houseplants. Now anything green that survived did so through blind life force.

The wind chimes had been a Christmas gift from Wes and his wife Kaitlyn a few years back. A description on the box said they were hand-tuned and had a diagram of the musical notes they played. They looked expensive and were totally useless, much like Vining's view of Kaitlyn, who had likely selected the gift. Keeping on top of gifts and celebrations seemed part of stay-at-home mom Kaitlyn's job. The chimes did make nice music when the wind blew, Vining had to admit. However, over the past three months, they'd taken on a life of their own, sounding when there was no wind at all.

Emily had a theory. "It's Frankie, Mom." She was referring to the female LAPD vice officer whose battered body had been dumped by the Colorado Street Bridge last June. While working the case, Vining had developed an uncanny relationship with the dead officer, one that suggested a paranormal connection. It was unsettling for Vining and unwelcome. She didn't want to believe in ghosts.

As the last musical notes faded into the air, and the background noise of crickets' songs again became prominent, Vining thought of Frankie. She again headed inside. Before she stepped over the threshold, she heard a clear, high "ding" produced by two of the smaller steel tubes. She looked back to see the two tubes swaying, ringing once more before slowing to a stop.

Vining stared at the chimes.

Do it again.

They never did, of course. Never on demand. Their silence seemed almost willful.

Inside the house, the answering machine on the kitchen counter showed two messages. Vining began going through her nightly routine of putting her weapons to bed.

She took the Glock .40 from the holster attached to her belt and ejected the magazine, which she stashed in a kitchen drawer behind tea towels. The gun went inside an empty box of Count Chocula cereal in a cabinet. The .32-caliber Walther PPK that she wore in an ankle holster would go beneath her bed pillow, loaded. The rest of her arsenal—Winchester Model 70 Featherweight, Mossberg 500, and Smith and Wesson .38—was locked inside a gun safe. Every month, she and Em took all the weapons for a workout at the PPD gun range in Eaton Canyon. Afterward, they'd grab a bite and spend the rest of the day in the garage, cleaning and oiling the guns and talking until late. It was their tradition.

She grabbed a new box of Count Chocula, pulled apart the inner liner, and ate a handful as she leaned against the sink listening to her phone messages. She doubted that either was from Emily, who had already checked in.

The first message was from her grandmother, wondering how she was doing without Emily and in light of the big double homicide that was all over the news. Vining was Nanette Brown's namesake and proud to carry the flag. She smiled, appreciating the call, wistful as she listened to the tremor of age in Granny's voice, which sounded more pronounced in the recording than in person.

The first syllables of the second message, "Hi, Cutie, haven't heard from you in a while," made Vining shove her hand angrily into the box. Chocolate morsels spilled from her fingers as she crammed cereal into her mouth.

Her mother, Patsy Brightly, never called unless she wanted something, even if that something was to assuage her own anxiety. This time, Patsy, a serial bride with four marriages under her belt, wanted something more tangible: Vining on a double date with her latest flame, Harvey, and his newly single son. Vining's younger sister ducked such requests from their mother. Stephanie's husband and children gave her a built-in excuse.

"Wouldn't that be adorable?" Patsy gushed. "Mother and daughter marry father and son? I told you about Harvey Torma. He's a regional manager for a company that makes polystyrene foam packaging."

Vining made a face at the chemically imbued description. "Like you have a clue, Mom."

Patsy was fifty-one but could pass for thirty-nine in the right light. She invested hard work in keeping her figure. Her voice on the answering machine had that life-of-the-party lilt she poured on in the presence of men or others she wanted to impress. She had never learned that she didn't have to work so hard for the men. They'd come around anyway, at least until they got what they wanted.

Vining immediately felt guilty for having such mean thoughts about her mother.

"Patsy's just being Patsy," she said aloud. "She doesn't really think you're a slave that she bought and paid for by giving birth to you."

Patsy went on. "Things are getting serious between Harvey and me. I'm even taking golf lessons. Me, a golfer. Can you imagine?"

Vining deleted the message before she'd heard it all. She put the cereal away and dusted her palms. She gave Granny a quick call to let her know she was okay. She'd call her mother tomorrow. She could delay no more than twenty-four hours before Patsy would call again and then keep calling.

In her bathroom, she hooked the hanger with her suit jacket on a towel rack, where the steam from her morning shower would freshen it. She threw her blouse in the hamper and examined her slacks to see if she could wear them once more before a trip to the dry cleaners. Using her fingernail to scratch something off the fabric, she decided she could and hung them beside the jacket.

Sitting on the bed, she unclasped her ankle holster and put the Walther PPK to bed, literally, beneath her pillow. She had once resisted being one of those paranoid cops who kept arsenals in their homes, loaded weapons at the ready. T. B. Mann had changed that. She'd grown accustomed to the slight, reassuring hardness of the Walther beneath her pillow. The princess and the pea. Only this princess would blow T. B. Mann's head off if she had the chance.

She'd said as much, promised herself as much, dangled sweet vengeance in front of herself like chocolate cake in front of a diabetic—the very thing that would fulfill her would likely kill her. Yet over the past few months, she'd put her rage on ice. She'd let her incipient private investigation into other possible victims of T. B. Mann go dormant. She hadn't even sufficiently followed the one promising lead she'd turned up: Johnna Alwin, a Tucson police detective murdered a few years ago under circumstances that were jarringly like Vining's ambush.

Peeling off her panty hose, finally free of that cloying second skin, soaked with perspiration after the hot day, she carried them into the bathroom and shoved them into a net bag that already held several other pairs. She seriously had to do her laundry. She took off her bra and grabbed her light summer bathrobe from a hook on the back of the door.

Instead of hauling the laundry hamper into the garage to get a load started, another matter lured her attention. From the back of the dresser drawer where she kept her few pieces of good jewelry in satinette bags or boxes inlaid with squares of padding, she took out a box. From it, she withdrew a necklace, a string of pearls with a pendant. The pendant had a large pearl in the middle circled by glittering imitation diamonds. The pearls were imitation too, but good quality, and the necklace was well crafted. Only a trained eye could discern that the gems were not genuine.

Five years earlier, after Vining had fatally shot a famous man in a high-profile event that had taken on a life of its own, the pearl necklace had shown up in her home mailbox. A panel card was attached to it with a ribbon. She retrieved the card. The satin ribbon was still attached through a hole made with a paper punch. The ribbon was bloodred. The message had been handwritten with a fountain pen:

Congratulations,

Officer Vining

Through a bizarre chain of events distinguished by seemingly otherworldly influences, Vining had come to believe that the necklace was a gift from T. B. Mann. If so, she had attracted his lethal attention a full five years before he had attacked her in the house at 835 El Alisal Road. Pearl was the birthstone for June. It was not her birthstone, however. She was born in April, with the diamond as her birthstone. She and Emily had deciphered a different significance for the pearls. Both of the most deadly events in Vining's life—the day she killed the celebrity and the day she was ambushed—had happened in June. Pearl was her death stone.

Leaving the necklace on the dresser, she proceeded with her nightly routine of making sure the house was secure. She closed and double locked the sliding glass doors and turned off the central air even though the house was barely cool. The electric companies had jacked up the rates during the power shortages a few years before. After the crisis, the rates had not gone down, but had only shot up further. Vining pinched pennies where she could. Wes contributed toward Emily's support, but keeping up the other expenses was tough on Vining's salary alone. She made sure Emily never went without, but she often did herself. She hardly noticed it anymore.

In her bedroom, she opened the windows a few inches each, only as far as they would go before hitting the wood dowels she'd set inside the window frames. She plugged her cell phone into the charger atop her nightstand. In case something happened to her landline, she'd still have her cell.

Such were the more obvious ways that T. B. Mann had changed her life. She'd resisted at first, and then decided she was being as stubborn as if she'd resisted treatment for cancer.

She quickly took a cool shower and put on a light cotton nightgown. She pulled back all the bedcovers except the top sheet.

The pearl necklace was still atop the dresser.

Without questioning why, she put it on, only the second time she'd ever worn it. The pearls gave a cool jolt to her feverish skin. T. B. Mann was, after all, the most important man in her life. He had jealously edged out anyone else. She'd tried many ways to manage him in her life, from blind obsession and overt challenges to attempts to put him behind her to living with the slow-burning rage in her belly, that crystalline bullet lodged within her, leaching its poison. Nothing worked.

She had no explanation for what she was doing now. She was working on instinct. Something was happening. Something had changed. She'd become aware of it at the murder house that morning. She and T. B. Mann were inexorably tied. He'd tugged on the invisible skein of spider's silk and she'd felt it, as if he were a fly caught in her web. Or perhaps she was caught in his.

She wore the necklace to bed, risking it penetrating her dreams, in a gesture to say, "I hear you."

She closed her eyes and quickly dropped off to sleep, faster than she would have thought possible given the day's events. Right before she did, she swore she heard the wind chimes tinkling as if an invisible hand had brushed across them.

EIGHT

Happy Labor Day from *Hello L.A.* We're glad you're spending this lovely Monday morning with us. Hopefully later, you'll be headed to the beach, the park, a movie, shopping, or someplace else fun and cool. By cool, I'm not just talking about making a fashion statement. It's gonna be a hot one today. Remember to drink plenty of fluids. Right now, we're gonna work on keeping you happy right here on *Hello L.A.* To help do that, I'm delighted to introduce a very special guest."

Dena Hale was bright and polished, decked out in a peach skirt suit with a scoop-neck white top that showed off her tan, gams, and famous cleavage. She had pulled herself together in spite of the grueling events of the previous day and night. The media had descended on the murders like white on rice. News vans had lined up outside the gates of their home by the time she'd returned from the Pasadena police station.

The detectives had downplayed the tense interview as simply seeking information, but she knew they considered her husband and possibly even her suspects in a murder-for-hire scenario. She didn't give their questions a second thought, knowing they were grasping at straws, but Mark had been in a state last night, convinced he was going to be arrested for the murders.

Dena had called Leland Declues, the attorney they used for business and personal affairs, and he had been kind enough to stop by. He tried to calm Mark, reminding him that the police needed evidence in order to arrest him, evidence stronger than him having bitter arguments with his business partner. Big deal. Still, when Declues suggested the name of a good criminal defense attorney, Mark's anxiety skyrocketed.

Dena understood her husband's concern—she was concerned too—but found his distress disproportionate to the circumstances. But then, he'd been on a downward spiral before the murders. The negotiations with Drive By Media had really rattled him, making Dena wonder what was actually going on. She feared where this new development would lead.

Declues and Mark had polished off a bottle of pinot noir, with Mark drinking most of it. After the attorney had left, Mark started in on the vodka while Dena handled the phone calls that came in from concerned friends and family—and the voracious media.

She hated it when Mark drank like that and especially hated her kids seeing it. Her sobriety and his drinking had been a big problem between them ever since the old man, Mark's father, had died. She and Mark had both taken the pledge after she'd crashed her car that night and emerged from a blackout in the Malibu–Lost Hills sheriff's station lockup. That was a turning point in their lives. They'd both awakened to a new dawn and were delighted to become acquainted with their new selves. Mark had even stayed the course when he shut down his restaurant and joined his father's business. But the old man's illness and death had unhinged Mark, cut him loose from his moorings, and he had drifted back to the bottle.

Dena didn't know whether Mark was more upset over Oliver's and Lauren's murders or the police interview. She knew that Mark had had nothing to do with those murders. For better or worse, she knew this man, and he didn't have it in him. Behind his boisterous demeanor, he was reclusive and shy. He'd struggled with depression. He was not a man who lashed out. He sucked it in. It was his sweet, sensitive side that she loved the most. Unfortunately, lately, she'd seen that side less and less.

She knew full well it was pointless to ask what was bothering him again until he'd sobered up.

Last night, she'd gone to bed after leaving him in the media room with a cup of chamomile tea, watching a program about crocodiles on Animal Planet.

After one in the morning, she'd been awakened out of a sound sleep by her husband raging incoherently by the pool. She'd pulled on a bathrobe and run outside to find him with a bottle of Hennessey in one hand, a lit cigar in the other, tottering unsteadily by the edge of the water. She'd coaxed him inside and deposited him in his bed, then gone to her rooms in the opposite wing of the house, wondering how much longer she could keep up the ruse of her sham marriage.

Always a professional, Hale had arrived at work on time, prepared, and had left her personal troubles at the door. Only those closest to her would have noticed the slight deepening of the fine lines at the corners of her eyes and the subtle dullness of her normally sparkling blue eyes. They might have attributed it to fatigue, and that observation would have been partially correct. There was also a heavy dose of sadness and frustration. Trying to keep a marriage together while the other party's time and interest were elsewhere was like one hand clapping.

Hale picked up a book and showed the cover to her audience. "You have undoubtedly heard about this wonderful novel, *Razored Soul*. I'm telling you, I couldn't put it down. *I could not put it down.* Critics are calling it *The Catcher in the Rye* meets *The Belly of the Beast*. What's especially remarkable about this book, the author's first, is that he wrote it entirely while he was serving a seven-year prison term in San Quentin for voluntary manslaughter. The book immediately shot to the top of the bestseller lists. The author left prison only last month after completing his sentence. Unless you've been under a rock, you've probably seen the sexy photos of him in the current issue of *Vanity Fair*."

Hale fanned herself. "Whoo! Oh, and there's a wonderful interview in that issue too."

The largely female audience laughed.

"We are so thrilled to have this man on our show to tell us about his astonishing and inspirational journey. Please welcome Bowie Crowley."

Hale stood and clapped. The audience members got to their feet as well, enthusiastically whooping and whistling as Crowley walked across the stage. He cut a commanding figure as his long legs, clad in snug, button-front Levi's, made short work of the distance. His body displayed the results of years of pumping iron in the prison yard. His trademark tight black T-shirt, tucked into jeans, hugged well-developed musculature underneath. Around his broad neck was a large crucifix on a heavy gold chain.

Uncomfortable with the attention, he tossed a nervous nod and a crooked smile to the out-of-control audience. Reaching Hale, he gave her a two-handed handshake and went to the chair as if finding a life raft. He pulled one ankle atop a knee and waggled his foot, clad in a well-worn, rough-hewn boot.

When the crowd quieted, Hale began. "Those photos, Bowie . . ."

"Yeah, those photos . . ." He retracted a corner of his mouth and diffidently shook his head.

"I hear they're making one of them into a poster."

He hiked his shoulders. "It's been talked about, but the only posters I've approved are to promote the book."

Crowley drew his hand through wavy light brown hair that reached his shoulders. His handlers had begged him to cut it. He had conceded to having it professionally styled after years of trimming it himself in prison. They also wanted him to wax his eyebrows, straighten and whiten his teeth, and wear something more contemporary than Levi's 401 boot-cut shrink-to-fits and ragged motorcycle boots. He could have his choice of the hottest designer clothes for nothing. He said no thanks.

He insisted, "That photographer can make anybody look good."

"And he's modest too," Hale pronounced.

He blushed.

Realizing she'd embarrassed him, that he really *was* modest, Hale felt bad.

"Let's talk about your book. *Razored Soul* is a coming-of-age novel about a young man with a troubled childhood. A high-school dropout who hangs with a bad crowd. Drugs, booze, and the rest of it. He's a classic ne'er-do-well, and his life is going nowhere. One day, in a drug-and-liquor-induced haze, he murders a man, a buddy of his. But that horrible event is the catalyst by which he turns his life around. This is a thinly disguised fictionalization of your life, Bowie."

He nodded, pulling at his lower lip with his fingers.

"Why write a novel instead of an autobiography?"

"Because I like telling stories. Fiction gave me the freedom to tell this particular story in the best way possible. I felt the book would be more compelling and inspirational as a work of fiction."

"Writing this must have been therapeutic for you."

"It was. Worked out a lot of demons writing that book."

"I know what it means to do something stupid and bad, something that you think is the worst thing that could happen to you, and it ends up being a blessing in disguise. When I had my drunken car crash, I thought my career in television was over. I thought my husband would leave. There was talk of my kids being taken from me."

While Crowley listened, his restless hand moved from his face to his lap, and he slid his foot to the floor, the better to lean toward her. He took in every word as if they were the only two people in the room, not moving his deep-set, hazel eyes from hers.

Hale was impressed by the vulnerability in his face, which belied his powerful physique. She knew part of the reason the public found him compelling was the dissonance of trying to make the image of the sensitive artiste jibe with that of a cold-blooded killer.

"The worst night of my life ended up turning my life around," she said.

Hale grimaced. The tears had begun their ascent and would shortly spill from her eyes. There was no turning back. She was known for crying on camera. Her detractors claimed the tears were calculated. If crying pretty worked for Oprah . . . But for Hale, not only were the tears never planned, she couldn't always predict what would set them off. When thinking about the interview with Crowley, she'd decided to talk about how alcohol had nearly destroyed her life as a way to get him to open up about his experiences. The saga of her car crash was no secret, and she was usually able to speak of it with detachment. Yet here she was—blubbering.

She was tired and stressed, and fatigue and stress were triggers, but they weren't the only things that had tipped her over. It had been a long time since anyone had listened to her with such sincerity, had really cared about what she was saying.

Crowley reached across the short space that separated them and laid his hand upon hers.

One could have heard a pin drop in the crowded studio, but what one heard instead was audience members snuffling.

"I'm sorry, folks. You know me. . . ." She wiped her eyes with her fingers. Someone sped from backstage with a box of tissues.

Crowley began telling his story, directing the cameras, which loved him, onto himself, giving Hale breathing space.

"Dena, you're right. The hero in my book is a very bad boy. That was me. I was the kind of guy my West Texas grandmother would call a 'no-account.' I grew up in Central California near Lake Nacimiento. People have weekend homes there or come up for the day to use the lake for boating and fishing. But me and my buddies, we were lake locals. You mentioned I dropped out of high school. Dropped out . . . kicked out, more like.

"My uncle got me a job as a journeyman welder in the San Ardo oil fields. Every day after work, me and my buddies met under a grove of live oak trees by the lake. We'd sit on picnic benches there or on the beds of our trucks and we'd get drunk on the cheapest beer we could buy and smoke store-brand cigarettes, the cheapest ones we could find. The women would come for a while, but they'd take off early, having to deal with the kids, or they just got sick of us."

Crowley started sniggering at a recollection.

The camera again went to a quickly touched-up Hale, who was smiling with anticipation.

"We used to watch people back their boats onto the landing. Sometimes one of those guys would show up. You know the kind. Brand-new boat. Brand-new truck. Brand-new trailer. Old wife."

The audience giggled.

"The wife would be driving the truck, trying to back the boat into the lake. The husband would be out giving directions, and they'd be cussin' and screamin' at each other. My buddies and I would sit there, drunk off our behinds. We'd hold up cardboard signs that we'd written numbers on and yell out the scores we'd given them for how well they did backing in the boat." He laughed and shook his head. "We'd yell out, 'Six and a half! Seven!' "

The audience laughed along, vicariously participating in that slacker lifestyle, imagining sidling up to Crowley and his unsubtle sexual energy.

"Stupid stuff. Every day, we'd do this. *Every* day. My best buddy, Dallas, was a lake local. Dallas Star Baker. His father was a die-hard Dallas Cowboys fan. One July evening, about eight years ago, shortly after my twenty-third birthday, we were under the oaks, raising hell. Dallas wasn't there. He was a psych tech over at Atascadero, the state hospital for the criminally insane. A couple of the lake locals were psych techs. Good job, but crazy hours. I had the next day off, so I was more loaded than usual, and it was late. We'd been at it for hours.

"I took off walking home to get some pot I had. My wife, Traci, and I rented this little house a few blocks from the lake. I went inside. The house was dark. Figured my baby boy, Luke, six months old at the time, and Traci were in bed asleep. Traci was in bed all right, but she wasn't asleep and she wasn't alone. When I got to the bedroom door, I heard all this scampering around and whispering. I flipped on the lights and—"

Crowley grimaced and made a noise through his teeth. "There was Traci in bed, naked. There was Dallas, naked with one leg in his jeans. I always carried a bowie knife on my belt. It was my trademark. Spent hours throwing it at targets, wasting time. One day on a dare, I split an apple on Dallas's head with it. When I saw Traci and Dallas that night, I didn't think about the knife. But then Dallas got this look on his face. Sort of, 'I got you good, didn't I?' Like this was just another of our practical jokes. Something in me snapped. The knife was out. I threw it. Hit him in the heart. He stayed on his feet a couple of seconds and then, boom, he went down. My baby, Luke, was in his room next door. Slept through the whole thing, even with Traci screaming.

"I got six years for voluntary manslaughter plus one for carrying the knife. Sent to San Quentin. The Q. I spent a long time being angry and unremorseful. Then I opened my heart to a different way."

Hale had been listening with rapt attention, as had the audience. "Are you truly a changed man, Bowie?"

"I've been clean and sober for eight years."

There was robust applause.

"But I'm the same man inside. I'll always be the same man. That's the human condition, the struggle between good and evil. All of us have light and dark. Right inside us. Right here." He tapped his chest.

"Most people fight that evil side some of the time. Most people, their evil side is so quiet and weak, it's nearly not there. Then there are people like me. Every day, every minute I'm awake, I struggle with that demon. But I don't walk alone anymore. That's the difference." He pressed his hand against the crucifix.

"That's powerful, Bowie."

"That's the way it is."

They gazed into each other's eyes too long, and Hale knew it. When she finally spoke, her voice was hushed. "How's your son, Luke? He's eight now, right?"

"Yes. He's great. He helps keep me centered."

"I know what you mean. I have an eight-year-old son too."

"What's his name?"

"Ludlow. Named after his grandfather. We call him Luddy. I have a seventeen-year-old daughter too. Dahlia."

"Great names." Crowley nodded. "Cool."

"Thank you, Bowie, for being with us today. I want everyone to know that we got you before Oprah and the national morning shows because you didn't want to be on the road and away from Luke."

"That's part of the reason. I'm a big fan of yours, Dena. You project such a generosity and honesty of spirit. It comes right through the television. I see how people react to you. Warm to you. You can be anything you want to be. Don't let anything stand in your way."

Hale's lips parted. "That's so nice. Thank you." She recovered and made a trademark joke. "I already bought your book, Bowie, but now I'm gonna go out and buy ten more."

Everyone laughed.

"Does anyone in the audience have a question for Bowie Crowley? Yes, you in the red."

A woman stood and took the microphone handed to her. "Hi, I'm Laura from La Crescenta. Are you still married?"

There were titters among the crowd.

"I was divorced while I was in prison."

Hale revealed, "Your ex-wife married one of your close friends."

A gasp went up.

Crowley shrugged. "That was tough, but no hard feelings. He's a good guy, and Traci had to do what was right for her and our son. Hey, I was no prize. I still have my doubts."

"Are you working on another book?" Hale asked.

"I am."

"Something similar to *Razored Soul*?"

"Similar but different."

"Okay. . . ." Hale pointed to another woman. "You in the flowered blouse."

The woman said, "I'm Cynthia from West Hills. What's the significance of that tattoo on your arm?"

Crowley bent his right arm, flexing his biceps, displaying a large, ornate tattoo rendered in blue ink culled from Bic pens, typical of prison tattoos. It said: 23:4. The cameraman zeroed in on the money shot.

"My homeboy, Kiko, did this for me in the Q. He's a real artist. Props to you, my man. Kiko told me I couldn't leave the joint without some ink. This stands for Psalms twenty-three, verse four."

"Remind us, Bowie, please. What is Psalms twenty-three, verse four?"

"That's a homework lesson for you." Crowley play-fully wagged his finger at Hale.

"Even though I walk through the valley of the shadow of death . . ."

They all turned to look at the heavy-set man who had spoken. He pushed himself to his feet. "I will fear no evil, for you are with me; your rod and your staff, they comfort me."

"Hi, Donnie," Crowley said. "I saw you sitting there."

"Who comforts my son, Bowie?" Donnie Baker un-furled a poster that bore a photograph of Dallas Star taken at his sister's wedding shortly before his murder. He wore a tuxedo with a white rose boutonniere. The photo-graph had been widely broadcast after Crowley's recent notoriety.

"This is my son, murdered by that man." Baker held the poster above his head and turned to show everyone. "In all the hoopla over the great Bowie Crowley, every-one forgets the life he took. He murdered my twenty-two-year-old son in cold blood, and a few years later, he's a free man."

The audience grew anxious. Guests near Baker left their seats. Security closed in.

Hale clutched her throat as Crowley stood and tried to calm the situation. "Let him have his say. He's earned it. He's not gonna hurt anybody, are you, Donnie?"

The security guards grabbed Baker but he continued to rage. "You're a free man, Bowie, but my son isn't free. He's rotting in a box six feet under, and me and his mother have to live with you going around like a rock star. You're one of us, Bowie. You're no better than us."

The poster was crumpled on the ground as security dragged Baker away.

Crowley stood at the edge of the stage and raised his

hands. "Could you hold up for a minute, please? Can I say something to the man?"

Hale, not wanting to miss this opportunity, joined in. "Please, security, let Bowie speak."

"We've heard enough from you," Baker protested.

"Donnie, I've said it a hundred times and I'll keep saying it until my last breath: I am truly sorry for what I did to Dallas. If I could take back that moment, I would. Just because I've walked out of prison doesn't mean I've paid that debt. I'll be paying my debt to you and your family the rest of my life. The only way I know to do that is to live in the light, to love and care for my neighbor, and to serve as an example to some other guy out there who's acting like the idiot I was."

"Bullshit," Baker spat. "It's all bullshit to sell books. Amazing what a person can accomplish sitting in a cage. Next they'll be giving you the Nobel fucking Peace Prize."

Hale hoped the censors had bleeped the bad words in time.

"Donnie, you'll never find peace until you can find it in your heart to forgive me."

"Don't preach to me, you good-for-nothing, murdering drunk—"

Baker kept cussing as security dragged him out.

Hale quickly wrapped up, well past the time for the scheduled commercial break. She moved to stand beside Crowley. "My goodness. . . . Thank you, Bowie, so much for joining us today. To our audience, you'll find a copy of Bowie's book underneath each of your seats. We'll be back after a break."

The camera scanned the unnerved but enthusiastically applauding audience. The cameraman quickly moved past an unattractive individual with a prominent Adam's apple who was wearing a yellow dress.

Laura from La Crescenta, sitting in the next seat clapping away, hissed into her friend's ear. "I told you that's a man. Look how big his hands are."

The friend leaned forward to sneak a look at the careful clothing, wig, and elaborately made-up yet homely face. Her attention was then drawn to the extra-large hands with pink nail polish and a large school ring. It was too small for the friend to see, but the ring was inscribed with the initials O. M.

"You see what he's wearing?" the friend whispered. "That's a USC class ring."

Laura, a UCLA alumna, took delight in this. "Yea-ah! Go Trojans."

NINE

It was almost noon on Labor Day in Old Pasadena. The disheveled young man with the backpack didn't look out of place. He was unthreatening. He was rumpled, but people had seen worse. No one paid him any mind. He wasn't the type of person to draw attention.

His short, fine hair, blond to the point of near-whiteness, but with brown roots, jutted from his head at odd angles. He wore dark slacks with a white dress shirt tucked into them. A tightly cinched leather belt gathered excess fabric around his thin waist. His clothes were soiled, and his cordovan penny loafers were scuffed and worn. The ruthless late-summer sun had burned his pale skin, making his cheeks and nose rosy and scouring his bone-white scalp. Other than his purple backpack, the sunburn was the only color he had. He looked like a missionary gone astray from his brethren, his pamphlets lost.

Old Pasadena was crowded. People had come from all over to visit the shops, restaurants, movie theaters, and clubs in the restored historic buildings in the neighborhood surrounding Colorado Boulevard between Marengo and Pasadena Avenues. There was always a scattering of panhandlers, many familiar with the locals and the cops. However, the pale man, crisping in the sun, was known to no one. He didn't have the street-hardened look of the homeless about him, yet he shared their disenfranchised mien.

He went into a mini-mart on Fair Oaks. The shopkeeper gave the man a suspicious look when he took a plastic bottle of water from a refrigerated case, twisted off the cap, and drank it down. The shopkeeper was prepared to confront him as he headed for the door, but relaxed when, without a word, the pale man reached into his pocket and set a five-dollar bill on the counter. When he scooped up the change, the shopkeeper noticed his delicate, tapered fingers, soft hands, and shaped, if dirty, fingernails.

Back on the street, he crossed Colorado Boulevard. He cringed from the crowds that jostled him, bumping into the backpack looped over his shoulders. He turned onto Miller Alley, where the tables and chairs on the pavement in front of Jake's were filled with people lunching on diner food served in red plastic baskets. Farther down, the tables in front of the Equator Coffeehouse drew a different crowd.

The pale man looked and watched, scuttling away whenever anyone came too close. He watched as children played old-time arcade games in front of a shop.

An awning over cluttered windows gave respite from the sun. A sign of painted carved wood suspended by two chains said: YE OLDE CURIOSITY SHOPPE.

The children were especially enthralled with a Test-Your-Strength device. A nickel bought a chance to arm-wrestle a metal hand, sending a needle around a gauge. Cartoon drawings described one's achievements. Yellow, the first category, said: Wimp. You'll get sand kicked in your face. The pale man examined the accompanying drawing of a sunken-chested man that could have been a caricature of him. Red, the highest category, said: He-Man. Nobody better fool around with your girl.

The pale man blinked rapidly as he watched the children, the corners of his thin lips twitching. The sound of children at play was spontaneous music.

After the last child had played to his satisfaction, an older sibling holding him up so he could reach the metal hand, their mother, mindful of the pale man, turned down their pleas for more tries. Gathering her children, she hustled them from the broad alley toward the boulevard.

The man approached a glass and wooden case. Painted on the wooden frame in old-style writing in black and gold leaf was: SWAMI WILL TELL YOUR FORTUNE. Inside the case were the head and shoulders of a mannequin. The painted wooden figure was dark skinned, kohl eyed, clothed in robes of satin and velvet with a tall turban on his head. He held a crystal ball in one outstretched hand. His other hand was suspended, palm down, above it.

The pale man inserted a dime in the slot and shoved it in and out. It made a mechanical chi-chink sound. The swami's hand rotated in a half circle over the crystal ball, which flashed with colored lights. His heavy-lidded eyes blinked and his hinged lower jaw trembled up and down. A small card was spit out of a slot in the front of the case.

The man took it out and silently read it, cornflower eyes traveling over the text: A journey of a thousand miles begins with a single step.

He sucked in his cheeks, creating deeper hollows. He put the card in his pants pocket. Withdrawing a handkerchief, he mopped his forehead and scrubbed perspiration from his scruffy hair.

An outside table in front of Jake's became free when a family got up, leaving partially eaten meals in the red baskets. Slipping the backpack from his shoulders, he sat, resting the pack on the seat of a chair. The top of a spiral-bound pad poked from the pack's outside pocket. A couple at the next table paused in their eating to look at the man and the leftover food.

While he was unzipping the pack, a college-aged waitress in shorts, tennis shoes, and a Jake's T-shirt arrived, a pencil stuck through her topknot of hair. While clearing the table she announced, "You have to order if you're gonna sit here."

He nodded. After she left, he hoisted his foot atop his knee and pulled off his shoe. He did the same to the other foot, to the consternation of people at the surrounding tables, even though his black socks were sound. He set the shoes on the ground.

He stood to unbuckle his belt. Down dropped his slacks, revealing white BVD briefs. Laughter and protests went up, and a crowd began to gather. A few people shouted encouragement. The man seemed oblivious to the commotion he was causing and pursued his task with a single-minded focus.

Still standing, he folded the slacks, coiled the belt, and put them in the pack. The briefs came next, to the hooting delight of some in the crowd and the dismay of others. Next to come off was his shirt, button by button, exposing porcelain skin and his nearly hairless, gangly body to the brutal sun. An odd touch enhanced the already-peculiar scene, in the way that only a well-chosen accessory can. In this case, the accessory was a pearl necklace around the man's neck, revealed when he removed his shirt. On the string was a pendant—a dark blue gem surrounded by sparkling diamond-like stones. The necklace remained on.

One zealous man stepped from the crowd, taking it upon himself to seize control of the situation. He reached for the stripper's backpack, perhaps to withdraw clothing, but didn't get the chance. The pale man, nude save the necklace and black socks, wordlessly snatched up his pack. His blue eyes fired off an icy gaze as he shoved his feet back into the loafers. The action riled the misdirected Good Samaritan, who grabbed the man's arm. With wiry strength and an angry grimace, the pale man wrenched free and hoisted the straps of his pack over his shoulders.

He ran.

He ran down the alley, onto Colorado Boulevard. He darted through dense holiday traffic and edgy drivers. Brakes screeched. People pointed. Some parents tried to shield the eyes of young children.

Two Pasadena Police uniformed officers on foot patrol gave pursuit, after shouting a command to halt.

A car bumped the man, sending him careening into the path of another car that barely stopped in time. He nearly lost his balance, long arms windmilling, long legs flailing herky-jerky, but he kept going.

One of the officers became entangled with a bicyclist and both went down.

The second officer, John Chase, who had a recognized

competitive streak and a hunger when it came to catching bad guys, especially ones who ran from him, kept going.

Patrol cars and a mounted unit now joined in. The patrol cars were hampered by the traffic, and the officers pulled over to engage in the foot pursuit. The officer on horseback made good progress until the man headed down Mercantile Place, an alley parallel to Colorado Boulevard. White tents were set up there, and an annual chili cook-off to benefit a local children's home was under way.

Long tables were covered with chili makings and cooking utensils. Cook stations were manned by groups of chili chefs of all stripes wearing aprons with their team names. The team of soccer moms showed off their tanned and toned physiques, to the delight of gray-haired executives. The wives of a certain age tried to pay no mind with mixed success. Beer and wine flowed. A local jazz band played. Everything came to an abrupt stop when the commotion started at one end of the alley and barreled through. Everything except the burbling vats of red.

The officer on horseback could go no farther, stymied by the tents, but officers on foot entered the alley from both ends.

The pale man was fast and agile. Heading beneath the tents, he zigzagged in and out, jostling tables and people, causing mayhem and spilled drinks. Officer Chase remained maddeningly a few steps behind, growing angrier by the second. He stepped it up, scattering the team from a local gym, not even noticing the scantily clad female members.

Chase pulled closer. Finally, he was close enough. He flung himself headlong, latching onto the man's legs, sending them both flying into the work area of the Golden

Oldies team from the local Kiwanis club. They'd just dumped crushed tomatoes from twenty-four-ounce cans into their lucky cast-iron pot, completing the first of three timed phases of potent secret ingredients, and were bringing up the heat on the portable range.

Over went the table, range, chili, and nearly the Kiwanians, most of whom hadn't moved that fast in years. The officer and the streaker slid facedown into the chili, skidding, drenching them both in lukewarm red-hot.

Chase and the streaker grappled on the ground, each struggling for purchase on the chili-smeared asphalt. Chase got his knee against the streaker's back and wrenched one of his slippery arms behind him.

"Why were you running, man?"

Another officer pulled off the backpack, which had stayed in place throughout it all. "Anything in here gonna stick or hurt me?" He shoved aside heads of garlic and assorted produce and meat on a table before unzipping the pack and dumping the contents onto it.

The streaker, his face half submerged in chili where his cheek was pressed against the ground, stared straight ahead and said nothing.

Officers arrived on scene, some of them just to check it out and laugh.

Chase snapped on handcuffs and hauled the man to his feet with another officer's assistance. "What's your name?"

The streaker just looked at the officers, squinting at chili that ran into his eyes, shrinking from an officer who tried to wipe his face with napkins.

"I asked you a question." Chase ran a towel that one of the Kiwanians handed him over his own face. "What's your name?"

The Golden Oldies team from the Kiwanis kept its

distance except for one angry man. "That's our Nitro in a Pot," he cried. "It's ruined."

Officers razzed Chase.

"The Chaser. My man!"

"Looks like a dangerous criminal you got there, Chase."

Chase ignored them, not letting up. "Why were you running? Why did you take your clothes off?"

A citizen came forward with a beach towel that an officer wrapped around the streaker's waist. He passively endured the attention.

"What are you going to do about the Nitro?" The Golden Oldie wouldn't let up. Except for his sour disposition, his long white beard and round belly made him a natural to play Santa Claus at Christmas events.

An officer asked the older man, "Sir, what's the problem here?"

"Our chili. Nitro in a Pot." Santa held one arm out to indicate the spilled mess. "We were a shoo-in to win this year until you cops busted through."

"I'm not finding any I.D. in here," said an officer who was looking through the streaker's backpack. "He's got about forty bucks in cash." Searching his pants pockets, he found the card with the fortune from Swami. "Journey of a thousand miles? You're taking a journey, all right. To the Big G." He used the station jargon for L.A. County-USC Medical Center in East L.A., commonly known as General Hospital.

Sergeant Terrence Folke arrived. "What the hell, Chase? What have you got all over you?"

"Nitro in a Pot," a Golden Oldie offered.

"It's chili, Sarge." Chase drew his finger through a blob of the concoction on his uniform and tasted it. "Good stuff."

"Thanks," the Golden Oldie said. "It's our prize-winner."

Santa pushed his big belly into the discussion. "And we would have won this year too. Sergeant, I want to know what you're going to do about the behavior of your officers here today. They chased this man through here with total disregard for private property."

"My officers did what they needed to do to apprehend this man and to maintain public safety."

"Public safety? Keeping us safe from him?" Santa gestured to indicate the streaker, who had the beach towel wrapped around his skinny frame, the hair on one side of his head matted with chili, and his head hanging. "He looks about as dangerous as a canary."

"Sir, I'm not going to debate this with you. If you feel our actions were out of line, you can file a complaint with the police department."

"I'll do that."

"Lighten up, Frank. They're just doing their jobs." A Golden Oldie handed Santa a beer. "Vera and Marge went to buy more fixin's. We have time to make another pot of Nitro. Have a drink and relax."

"Dangerous." Santa was not appeased. "Doesn't look dangerous to me."

"That's what Jeffrey Dahmer's neighbors said about him," Sergeant Folke couldn't resist adding. He turned his attention to the streaker. "You have a name?"

"He won't talk." Chase was still wiping chili off himself. "Doesn't have any I.D."

Folke got in the streaker's face. "What's your name?"

The pale man cringed, stepping back into Officer Chase, who gave him an angry shove.

"Can he talk?" Folke asked Chase.

"He was making noise when I had him on the ground. Grunting."

Folke tried again. "What's your name?"

The streaker rapidly blinked like a dog that had been rapped on the snout too many times with a rolled-up newspaper.

"What else did he do besides resisting arrest?" Folke asked Chase.

"From what I understand, he stripped off his clothes and ran down Colorado Boulevard."

"Through traffic."

"Yeah."

"That's it?"

"That's what I understand right now, Sarge, without having interviewed witnesses."

"Looks like we've got a fifty-one and a half here," Folke said.

A Golden Oldie said, "Right now, he looks like Nitro in a Pot."

Folke leaned toward the streaker, causing him to rear back again. "Nitro in a pot. Since you won't tell us your name, that's what we'll call you: Nitro." He lifted the chili-smeared necklace that the streaker still wore around his neck. "Where did you get this, Nitro?"

Chase laughed. "Got no clothes but he didn't forget to wear his pearls."

TEN

Kissick's briefing in the detective's section conference room was cutting into lunchtime. Vining's stomach had started to rumble, inaudibly so far, but that wouldn't last. She knew that some in the meeting could go all day without eating. Not her, but she wasn't going to be the first to suggest lunch. They should be breaking soon since Lieutenant George Beltran was scheduled to give a press conference in half an hour on the steps of the PPD.

The location was Beltran's favorite, as it provided a nice view of the Mission Revival–style police station and Beltran a podium suitably above the fray. The blow-dried breeziness of his black-to-silver locks betrayed a visit to the hairstylist that morning in preparation. He carried a year-round tan, but playing golf during the waning days of summer had turned his skin a warm chestnut hue, making his broad white smile stand out all the more. Rumor was, he slept in molds custom-made for his teeth filled with dental bleach. He'd recently shaved his mustache. He liked being in the glare of the media, and everyone else at the PPD was happy to let him stand there.

Vining had been neutral about Beltran until he'd interfered in her last homicide investigation. While he could be a strong ally, she'd learned that his ambitions too often colored his decisions. He also sought notoriety beyond his law-enforcement career. He had been shopping around his screenplay, *Death in a Blue Uniform,* for months and reported interest among Hollywood's power brokers. The gossipmongers sneered that he better not quit his day job.

Kissick outlined what they knew so far. "The knock-and-talks in the neighborhood turned up zilch. None of Mercer's neighbors saw anyone coming or going. The autopsy showed that Mercer died from knife wounds to his chest. The dismemberment was done postmortem. Richards died immediately from a broken neck. Time of death is estimated between eighteen hundred and twenty-one hundred hours.

"Dillon Somerset, Mrs. Richards's stalker, has no alibi. He claims he was at his apartment alone reading a book during the time frame of the murders. Mercer's business partner, Scoville, was having a dinner party. His alibi is solid, but there's a possibility of murder-for-hire, and we're uncovering business dealings that might provide a motive. The style of the murders doesn't suggest the work of a hit man, but maybe they were purposefully done in such a grotesque manner to throw us off. The poisoning of Mercer's dog argues for premeditation. Could be a coincidence, but the little hairs on the back of my neck tell me it isn't.

"What's interesting is how Scoville's gone dicey on us. When Nan and I interviewed him yesterday, he was cooperative through the whole thing. Even volunteered to take a polygraph, which we set up for this morning. At the end of the interview, Nan asked him whether he knew anyone who might want to do the victims harm. Then he suddenly changed. Got real quiet and insisted he had to leave. Later that night, he left a message on my voice mail that he couldn't do the polygraph. Can't say I was surprised. We haven't been able to get ahold of him since."

"Guilty knowledge?" suggested Sergeant Kendra Early. She was the second-highest-ranking officer there.

"That's my guess," Kissick said. "He didn't commit the murders, but he has information about them. I think our interrogation jogged a memory loose."

"You can't jump to conclusions," Ruiz interjected. "He probably just had his fill of questions. Went home and his wife, the reporter, told him not to take a polygraph as a matter of policy. She'd be savvy about things like that."

"That's one theory," Kissick said.

"Do you still suspect a lone killer did the job?" Beltran asked.

"Yes, one guy. He didn't leave fingerprints, so he wore gloves. Also, it looks like he wore women's clothing— size eleven high heels, a wig of long blond synthetic hair, and a garment of blue rayon, based on the fibers we found beneath Mercer's fingernails. Given the strength required to overpower the victims, it's unlikely we're looking for a woman, but probably a man who dressed as a woman either as a disguise or lifestyle. A mark on Mercer's front door matches the bloody high-heeled footprints in and outside the house. Indicates that Mercer or Richards opened the door, only to have it kicked open the rest of the way by their assailant. Mercer's right hand, likely bearing his USC class ring, is missing. Who knows why that was done, but the killer's rage was directed toward Mercer."

Near Vining was a photograph of Lauren Richards and her two children, Sierra, age seven, and Shane, age nine. Richards's parents had released it to the media. The photo had been taken at the garden wedding of Richards's brother that spring. Richards was wearing a not-so-awful bridesmaid's dress, and her two children were adorable as flower girl and ring bearer. Lauren

Richards's smile was fitting for the Rose Parade Princess she'd been as a senior at South Pasadena High School.

Ruiz and Caspers had made the notification visit to Richards's parents, accompanied by a member of PPD's volunteer clergy. Even though Vining and Ruiz had had their differences, she felt for him and Caspers having to do that job. Looking at the photograph of Richards's children, she sensed their grief, that hollow emptiness, as if it were a vapor released into the atmosphere, available to be absorbed into the skin of the vulnerable. Vining was vulnerable. It was not a stretch to transpose her and Emily into the photograph. Richards had been thirty-six. Vining was thirty-four.

While she had leaped on the investigation of female police officer Frankie Lynde three months before, she was happy to let Ruiz and Caspers handle the Lauren Richards component of this new saga.

Lieutenant Beltran asked, "We haven't brought up the issue of cross-dressing with either of the suspects, correct?"

"Correct," Kissick said. "I want to keep that in our back pocket for now. Once we even ask the question, it'll be in the wind, and size eleven heels will disappear from our bad guy's closet. However, word of the writing in blood on the wall has already leaked out." He grimaced.

"People are afraid there's another Manson-style murderer out there." Beltran looked at his watch and stood. "I'm saying little at the press conference other than releasing the tip-line number and trying to put our citizens at ease."

"What about that message, anyway?" Sergeant Early asked. "All work. No play. What's he trying to tell us?" African American and in her mid-forties, Early wore no makeup. Her round face gave her a cherubic look that was undone by dark circles beneath careworn eyes. She had the sage demeanor of a kindly family elder. Standing barely 5 foot 4 inches, with short-cropped curly hair and a waistline giving way to middle age, it was easy for the uninformed to assume she was soft.

"I don't think we should read much into it," Kissick said. "Just like the Manson family's 'Helter Skelter' message, we may not learn the meaning until we apprehend the guy."

"Do whatever you need to get this asshole. Don't worry about O.T. I'll handle it with the people on the third floor." Beltran was referring to the top floor of the building, where the chief and commanders had their offices. "Kendra, we need to get downstairs."

Beltran and Early departed, taking the formality of the meeting with them. During the press conference, Early would stand to the side, ostensibly there to help Beltran field questions. The truth was, Beltran asked her to attend these events for P.R. She was a popular figure whenever she appeared on TV. The public liked her no-nonsense demeanor and droll sense of humor. She made him look good.

Left in the room were Vining, Kissick, Ruiz, Caspers, and Detectives Louis Jones and Doug Sproul, brought in from other desks under Early's command to work the case.

"Helter Skelter?" Caspers shrugged. "What's that?"

Ruiz was incredulous. "You don't know what that is? Don't you know about the Manson family murders?"

Caspers got defensive. "Hey, I wasn't even born then."

"Manson was inspired by the Beatles song 'Helter Skelter.' He had one of his family members write it at the home of the LaBiancas, who they murdered the night after Sharon Tate and her friends." Kissick was a crime encyclopedia, especially concerning notorious murders and murderers.

"They wrote '*Healter* Skelter' in blood on the refrigerator. Misspelled."

"*Healter*"? Louis Jones shook his head. He was African American, not tall, but had a massive upper body from lifting weights every day in the station gym.

They all laughed at the supreme idiocy of criminals.

"So what about our cross-dressing psycho?" Vining mused.

"Does he like to dress as a woman or does he live as a woman?" Sproul asked. With red hair, glasses and a slight build, he looked more like a high school math teacher than a detective.

"To catch him, we'll need to know where he is in the transgender process," Kissick said. "Our guy may be a fetishist and dress as a woman for a sexual charge, but not as a lifestyle. Or he may be a man physiologically but living as a woman. He may be somewhere in between, with his male genitalia intact, but taking hormones to make his breasts grow and his beard shrink. He may have had a sex change operation and may *be* a female. We can't restrict our thinking."

The topic was making Caspers cringe. "That's not something we see in Pasadena. That's a West Hollywood deal."

"Ya think?" Jones goaded him.

"What? *Here?* In Pasa*dena?*"

Ruiz chuckled at Caspers's discomfort. "You have to be careful when you're out on the town, Alex. You not only need to run a criminal background check on your dates, you really should run their DNA, too."

"Please . . ." Caspers, a perpetual-motion machine, rocked his chair back and forth. "It wouldn't get to 'hello.' "

"How can you be so sure?" Vining couldn't resist the logical follow-up.

Caspers retracted his upper lip. "That *Crying Game* thing? Unh-huh. Fuggeddaboutit."

Kissick passed off a guess as knowledge, just to get Caspers going. "Some of them, I hear, you can't distinguish from a natural-born woman even when having sex."

"Come on. . . . No surgery could be that good." Caspers pointed to himself. "I would know."

"That brings up an interesting question," Jones began. "If a man sleeps with a woman who used to be a man, does that make the man gay?"

"Why even go there, Louis?" Caspers looked as if he might punch somebody.

"I think we could use sensitivity training," Vining joked.

Caspers leaped on the opening. "I'll give you sensitivity training."

That started them laughing more.

"Okay." Kissick attempted to get back on track. "We want warrants for Scoville's and Somerset's phone records. We've got good probable cause for Somerset. Lots of witnesses to his stalking behavior. But with Scoville, we'll face our friend catch-22. We can't get warrants without probable cause, but we can't build P.C. without the phone records, which we need to track down a murder-for-hire plot. Unless he was clever enough to never use his own phones."

"Scoville doesn't impress me as that kind of clever," Vining said.

Ruiz pushed his chair back, as if he'd feasted enough at the dinner table. "I wouldn't put too much effort into Scoville. He offered to take a polygraph straight out. Like I said before, his wife probably talked him out of it.

Our time's better spent building a case against Somerset." He pressed his hand against his chest. "In my humble opinion."

Vining nodded as she listened, showing interest in what Ruiz was saying, but not buying it. "I like Somerset as a suspect, but I like Scoville too." Something about Scoville radiated heat for her. There was no evidence that she could use to make her case so far but she knew better than to deny her instincts. "Scoville's hiding something, and I want to find out what it is."

"For the sake of expediency," Kissick began, "I can see if my buddy over at AT&T can get us Scoville's cell phone info off the record. We could never use it as evidence, but it could point us in the right direction."

They came to an agreement over the work to be done and divided it among themselves.

"That's it for now." Kissick held up a photo of the carnage at the crime scene and passed it to Vining. "Have another look so that you don't forget the psycho we're dealing with."

Caspers gave it more than a passing look.

Sproul discerned the object of Caspers's attention. "Enough. Give it here."

Vining got their drift. "Were you looking at Lauren Richards's breasts?"

"That's one hundred percent organic. No implants there." He made a sucking noise with his teeth in regret for the loss, mostly to get Vining going, which it did.

"Can you say 'inappropriate'?" Vining took the photograph and completed the circle by handing it back to Kissick.

He held it up. "This scab on Mercer's arm . . . One of his golf buddies told me how ironic it was that Oliver had just had a tattoo removed because he was unhappy with it and a week later, he's dead. Apparently, the tat-

too was supposed to be Mercer's initials in Chinese."
Kissick started chuckling. "I shouldn't laugh. Poor bas-
tard. Mercer found out that instead of his initials, the
Chinese characters spelled out 'Demon Monkey.' "

Everyone broke up. Everyone except Caspers, who yet
again had a perplexed look on his face.

Ruiz tapped one of Caspers's shoulders. "You got one
of those Chinese tattoos on your back, don't you?
What's yours supposed to say?"

"It's not *supposed* to say anything. It says 'Crouching
Tiger.' "

"Are you *sure*?" Vining prodded. "Was the artist
Chinese?"

"Ernie up on East Colorado. That's where everyone
goes. He knows what he's doing. He used a template."

"Mercer's friend said his tattoo artist used a template
too," Kissick said. "But Chinese characters are so com-
plicated, one swirl in the wrong direction can change the
whole meaning."

"Maybe you better have someone who speaks Chinese
look at it," Sproul suggested. "Is it Mandarin, Cantonese,
or—"

"Haven't you guys had enough of kicking the new
guy?" Caspers was grinning, but his irritation showed
through.

"We're just trying to help you, Alex," Jones said.

"I'll head down to Hunan Palace today," Caspers
said.

"When are you going? Can you pick me up some
kung pao chicken?" Kissick playfully punched Caspers
in the arm.

They were filing from the room when Sergeant Terrence Folke came in, followed by Officer John Chase.

Caspers greeted him. "The Chaser. What's up?"

Chase took Caspers's hand and patted his shoulder.

They were the same age and they partied together. "Craziness."

Vining started toward her cubicle.

Folke carried a manila file folder and looked as if he was in no mood for frivolity. "Sorry to interrupt, but Vining, can we see you for a minute? Jim, if you can spare a moment too. It's important."

ELEVEN

B ehind the closed door of the conference room, officer Chase related the saga of Nitro's curious sprint through Old Pasadena.

"He doesn't have I.D. and he won't communicate. He won't speak, write, use sign language, blink yes or no, point. . . . Nothing. He looks like he's aware of what's going on. He can vocalize because I heard him make sounds when I had him on the ground trying to cuff him. He makes good eye contact, but he won't talk."

Vining didn't know what this had to do with her. She noticed that the usually unflappable Sergeant Folke looked rattled as Chase recounted his tale. Vining had a soft spot for Folke. He had knelt beside her and radioed for an ambulance as she lay bleeding out onto the kitchen floor in the house at 835 El Alisal Road.

She had a sinking feeling in her stomach. Did she hear ghostly wind chimes or was it her imagination?

Kissick was casually leaning against the wall. "Sounds like a fifty-one fifty candidate."

Section 5150 of the California Welfare and Institutions Code provides that if a person is determined to be a danger to himself or others because of a mental disorder, he can be involuntarily placed in a mental-health facility for seventy-two-hour evaluation and treatment.

"That's a possibility," Folke said. "I wanted to discuss it with Nan before we decided what to do with him." He took papers from the manila folder and handed them to her.

Her mouth went dry as she silently examined the pages, passing them to Kissick.

Chase explained. "Nitro had a drawing pad—"

"Nitro?" Kissick repeated.

"It's the moniker we gave him, since he wouldn't tell us his name. He dumped this pot of chili that these old guys were calling Nitro in a Pot. Anyway . . . So he had this drawing pad and charcoal pencils and one of those soft, gummy erasers. The pad was full of sketches, mostly of animals and flowers and such. And then we saw those."

They were photocopies of charcoal drawings, all of women, all violent. They were the work of a skilled artist, rendered with precise details and vivid contrast, like something from a graphic novel–style comic book.

One showed what looked like the interior of a tumbledown garage or barn. Sunlight shone through gaps in the walls where wood planks were missing. A nude woman was tied by her feet and hanging head down from the rafters. Her hands were behind her back, as if they were also tied. Blood had drained from a gash across her neck and formed a large pool on the ground beneath her head. Her physique, with small breasts and slender legs, appeared to be that of a young woman. Thick long dark hair, drawn with care, the curly tendrils flying loose, obscured her face.

Also hanging down from her neck was a necklace. The cloud of her hair kept it from slipping off and dropping onto the blood-soaked ground. It was depicted as a series of tiny white circles in a row, like pearls. In the middle was a larger circle standing out from the smaller ones. To Vining, it looked like a pendant.

Another showed a woman wearing a uniform, with a badge and shoulder patch sketchily depicted. On her head was a round-brimmed ranger Stetson. This woman was not dead. Clutched in one raised hand were two thick straps, the ends extending beyond the edge of the drawing. Her other hand was also raised as she was looking down at a man in the foreground who was holding a gun up at her. He was facing her, so only the back of his head and one of his hands were shown.

The woman had narrow dark eyes and a firm strong jaw. Her broad mouth and thin lips were parted, creating a gash across the bottom of her face. The charcoal strokes conveyed both her plainness and fierceness.

In the background was a large rock that had a distinctive domed shape.

Vining took her time with the drawings, lingering on the details, her apprehension building with each image.

"Are these real crimes or imagined?" Kissick asked.

"Look through the rest and then you tell me," Folke replied.

Vining didn't like the sound of that.

Kissick took the drawing Vining passed him. He tapped it. "This looks like Morro Rock. You know, in Morro Bay in Central California."

"It does," Folke agreed.

Vining looked at the next drawing. It was of a woman lying on the floor of what looked like a storeroom. Her limbs were splayed out. Her back was leaning against shelves stacked with supplies. Her eyes and mouth were both slightly open in a way that suggested death. A dark stain covered her blouse. She was wearing a pearl necklace with a jeweled pendant in the middle.

Johnna Alwin, Vining said to herself. Her palms slick with perspiration yet her fingers ice-cold, she handed the drawing to Kissick, wondering if he noticed the slight tremble in her hand.

He set the drawing he'd been looking at faceup on the table beside the others in the grisly gallery.

The color drained from Vining's face when she saw the fourth and final one, even though she'd expected it. Why else would Folke have brought them to her? Why else would he be standing there, so grave? What had happened in the house on El Alisal Road wasn't her nightmare alone. The oft-told tale of the ambush attack on Vining served as both a cautionary tale and as the nightmare scenario of every officer everywhere. For the PPD, that unsolved crime was a blot on their common psyche.

Kissick, seeing her face, moved to look over her shoulder.

Folke and Chase, knowing what the paper held, shifted uneasily.

The drawing clearly depicted Vining. It showed her from the shoulders up. A man shown from behind was facing her. He had short dark hair. Shadowy reflections of him were drawn in her eyes. The expression on her face could have been mistaken for rapture, had it not been for the knife protruding from her neck and the blood that made a glistening trail down the front of her uniform.

She licked her lips and swallowed. No one spoke. It was her privilege to break the silence. Her mind was elsewhere.

It was a year ago June. She was walking up the flower-lined brick path of the two-story colonial home on El Alisal Road in an upscale Pasadena neighborhood. It was Sunday and she was in uniform, having taken an overtime shift to earn extra money on a weekend when Emily was with her dad. It was nearly the end of her shift and she was about to head into the station when the call came in. Suspicious circumstances. A local realtor, Dale David, was watching a house for the vacationing owners and noticed a window open that he was certain he'd left closed. The man Vining had met at the home resembled the realtor, whose face adorned bus benches all over town. It was all innocent and reasonable. Mundane, even. There was nothing to raise her suspicions until she'd waited a few seconds too long. He had sent her on a journey from which she had yet to fully return.

It happened in the kitchen, where she'd followed him to look at the open window. There things took a strange turn. He began rambling, making much of a set of poetry magnets affixed to the refrigerator. He'd peeled off a single magnet, printed with a tiny word in black on white, and displayed it in his palm.

"Do you see this? Officer Vining, I want you to see this."

The way he'd said her name gave her a chill. He was panting, as if sexually aroused.

She'd already discreetly called for backup, and was waiting, biding her time. She was unnerved but calm. She vowed not to draw her gun too quickly. The last time she'd drawn her gun on a man, she'd shot him to death. This was different, she told herself. That man had drawn on her first. This man's hands were in full view. This was not at all the same.

She couldn't see what he held in his palm and would not move closer to do so. He was already too close, shortening her reaction time if he came after her, which he did, grabbing a knife from a set of cutlery in a wood block on the kitchen island. She'd fired and missed. He hadn't. The knife had sliced the back of her gun hand and then it was in her neck.

He'd held her close, his arm around her waist. She felt his breath on her face. She could almost feel it now, moist and warm and scented of mint. They'd held each other's gaze, like lovers. Had she ever again looked at herself in the mirror and not seen his shadow there?

When the house exploded with pounding feet, he released her, letting her body slump to the floor. He escaped, though just barely, using a carefully planned route.

Sergeant Terrence Folke had been the one to try to keep her calm, to keep her still, to keep her from crawling, trailing a slick of blood, into the kitchen pantry. Among her dense memories of that day, some crystal clear, others cloaked in fog, was the barely controlled panic in Folke's voice.

But she kept crawling, the knife jutting from her neck as she bled to death. Before she lost consciousness, she reached the object of her desire, the poetry magnet that he'd tossed aside, that T. B. Mann had tossed aside when he'd come at her with the knife. It said one word: pearl.

She blinked.

They were all watching her, waiting.

Blood pounded in her ears as if trying to escape, some of it strangers' blood transfused to save her life. It had been a year and three months. Was the blood now hers?

"He could have drawn this based on news reports."

Her ears still drummed but her voice was controlled. She felt disconnected. Everything seemed disconnected, as she had been from her life.

"It was all over the news that I was stabbed in the neck by an intruder in that house."

She didn't believe it, but only she knew that. Whoever had made these drawings knew about Tucson detective Johnna Alwin.

She caught Chase looking at the long scar down her neck, T. B. Mann's incision improved by a surgeon's scalpel. The angry red hue of that scar and the smaller one on the back of her right hand, her weapon hand, where he had first sliced her, had diminished. They were now pink, an innocent color.

Chase looked away.

She set the final sketch on the table beside the other three. "Where's the drawing pad? The originals?"

Folke said, "We've booked it as evidence in a crime investigation. We'll have it fingerprinted."

Kissick pointed toward the four sketches. "It's possible this Nitro didn't draw those. He could have found or stolen the drawing pad."

Vining stood with her legs apart and her hands behind her back. It was a solid stance, in counterpoint to her shaken well-being. "What does Nitro look like?"

Chase responded. "Caucasian. Six feet. One sixty. Blond over blue. Twenty-five to thirty. His hair is dyed nearly white, but the roots are dark brown."

Kissick said to Vining, "Your guy was six feet and Caucasian."

Vining was studying the carpet. She had to clear her throat before she could speak again. "I got a good look at the man who attacked me. I'd recognize him if I saw him again."

Sergeant Early returned and joined them. Folke gave her a summary of what had gone on.

Early asked, "Does he look like he was living on the streets?"

"His clothes were dirty, but he didn't look street-hard," Chase said. "He looks like he just got out of an institution or a dark hole. He's pasty pale. He's thin, but not malnourished. Good teeth. He's had dental work. Wasn't hungry."

Folke added, "His clothes were good quality. Wool gabardine slacks, lined. White dress shirt, button-down collar. Clean new BVDs. Good shoes and socks."

"Labels?" Early asked.

Folke raised his index finger, remembering a detail. "The labels were cut out. Someone went to a lot of trouble to hide anything that might identify him."

"No one saw him get off a bus or out of a car?" Kissick asked.

Both Chase and Folke shook their heads.

"We could post flyers with his picture around Old Pasadena," Kissick said. "Release it to the media. See if anybody recognizes him."

Early raised her hand and let it drop against her thigh. "This guy is either faking or he's crazy. If he's crazy, he needs to be at County. If he's faking . . . What's his motive? How hard did you try to get him to communicate?"

"We got in his face," Folke said. "He acts afraid. Skitters off into a corner. Crouches down on the floor. Tries to hide behind his hands. We pressed him hard. If he's faking, he's good."

Early pursed her lips. "Nan, go down there and see if he's your guy. If he's not, I don't know where we can go with this. We don't have the time or resources to I.D. some mentally ill transient, especially when we've got two people at the morgue and one of them in pieces."

"I'll go with you," Kissick offered.

As they filed from the room, Officer Chase was unable to resist reliving his takedown of Nitro, which was destined to become a favorite among the stories he'd collect during his career. "You should have seen it. We both slid face-first into chili, and we were covered in it head to toe. Here I'm trying to get cuffs on Nitro and this old guy who looks like Santa Claus was complaining that we'd ruined his chance to win the cook-off. The old ladies are covering their eyes because Nitro's buck naked, except for shoes, socks, and get this, a pearl necklace."

Vining turned to look at him. "A pearl necklace?"

"Yeah, a woman's necklace." Chase gestured toward his chest. "Pearls with a stone on it."

Vining gaped at him, stumbling into a chair in her path.

Kissick grabbed her arm to steady her. "Whoa. You all right?"

She quickly moved away from him, nervously smoothing her hair. "I'm fine."

He asked, "Does a pearl necklace have some significance? A couple of the women in those drawings had necklaces."

She responded crisply, "I don't know any significance," but her cheeks colored. She kept her eyes straight ahead as they moved toward the elevator. She hadn't told anyone what she'd learned about murdered Tucson police detective Johnna Alwin and the mysterious gift Alwin had received, a pearl necklace with a pendant. Only Emily knew about Vining's similar necklace, how she'd come to own it, and who she believed had left it. These were tiny leads and she guarded them fiercely. She would reveal all at some point. Her theory about T. B. Mann was still embryonic. It might not survive if exposed to the air. There was too much at stake. Everything in its time.

She hated being deceitful to Kissick, but still, she did

it. Perhaps this test proved that she held her relationship with T. B. Mann above all others.

"It's just strange," was all she said.

TWELVE

*O*nly recently had Vining opened the files on her attempted murder. It had taken her more than a year to gather the courage. She thought that enough time had passed, and that she would be able to look at the evidence with a cool, analytical eye. She was unprepared for her visceral reaction. Seeing for the first time a photograph of the copious blood on that kitchen floor, her blood, had filled her with rage. Now she was facing the possibility of having her fervent fantasy realized: T. B. Mann in a cage within her grasp. She did not feel invigorated and in command. She felt light-headed and queasy.

They took the elevator. Folke inserted a key to gain access to the basement. Chase got off on the first floor, where he had work to do in the report-writing room before his shift ended.

Exiting the elevator into the jail, they approached a set of gun lockers. Kissick and Folke stashed their weapons, removing the key from the lock when closing the small metal door.

Vining removed her Glock .40 from her belt holster, and then took out the backup Walther PPK she wore on her right ankle. Kissick didn't carry a backup weapon.

Vining's had saved her life once. She set it inside the small steel box, locked the door, and put the key in her jacket pocket.

She felt lighter without the guns. There was truth to the slang term describing a person carrying firearms as being "heavy." For Vining, the heaviness had to do with more than the physical weight of the weapons; it had to do with the feeling of substance and power that accompanied it. She liked guns. She liked wearing them. She now felt as if she might blow away. Or get blown away.

The modern jail had pods as cells, with Plexiglas doors instead of bars, built in a circle with a central command station above the jail floor. There a single guard observed every area from a semicircular desk fitted with video monitors that displayed feeds from cameras in each cell and corner of the jail. Men and women were both housed there, in different cells.

They walked past a man reporting to jail who was undergoing a preliminary search by an officer. The man had his mouth open, was pulling his cheeks apart with his fingers, and had raised his tongue while the officer peered into his mouth with a flashlight, without touching him. Some low-security-risk prisoners were allowed to work at their outside jobs during the day and serve their sentences on nights and weekends. Others, depending upon their crimes, were at the Pasadena jail on a pay-to-stay arrangement—a source of revenue for the PPD. People who had the money to pay the per-day fee could choose from a few safer, cleaner suburban jails, and avoid lockups such as the notorious L.A. County Men's Central Jail.

They approached the holding tank, which was crowded with men who had reveled too hard over the weekend. Some milled around, giving a desultory look at Vining. Some were Latino gang members, their hair as short as velvet revealing their gang insignia tattooed on their scalps. Several were sprawled on the floor against the wall, asleep.

Folke stood in front of the clear wall.

Vining did too, her lips pressed together as she searched the prisoners' faces.

"He's not here." Folke got the attention of a female jailer who was passing by.

She was tanned, blond, and fit, and appeared to be in her twenties. Her sun-streaked hair was braided and coiled at the back of her head. A nametag on her uniform said: M. KUROSKY. She was a civilian employee of the police department.

Vining had once held the same job, which she'd landed shortly after Wes had abandoned her and Emily. Her family had thought she was nuts, but it paid well and the benefits were great. Police officers got paid even better. She applied, was accepted, got through the Academy, and never looked back.

Folke asked Kurosky, "Michelle, where's the John Doe we brought in for indecent exposure and resisting arrest?"

"Nitro? I moved him to a pod . . . by himself. Guys were picking on him and . . . I was afraid . . . I thought he was going to get hurt. He's down here." She had that surfer slacker manner of speaking that was unique to a generation of young Southern Californians, nasal, with the vowels drawn out and the ends of words swallowed. The words came fast, then trailed off as if she'd forgotten what she was talking about.

That was one more thing that bugged Vining about Kurosky. She also wore her uniform too tight.

They followed the jailer.

"Has he communicated with anyone?" Folke asked Kurosky.

"No. He's been sitting on the bed, quiet. Acts scared. He lets me come near him but not the men. I'm a psychology major at Cal State L.A., and I studied something called hysterical muteness. I'm thinking maybe Nitro witnessed something so horrible it made him mute."

Vining let out a derogatory snort. "He might be a murderer."

"Murderer?" Kurosky began. "Nitro?"

They passed a pod where a rail-thin man who was high on meth raged at the surveillance camera. He had pulled off his shirt and was trying to fling it over the lens. He'd also pulled the mattress off the platform attached to the wall and onto the floor. His shouts were muffled behind the Plexiglas.

"Joshua, cool it," Kurosky said, slapping her hand against the clear door.

He sent a stream of epithets her way.

Kurosky continued babbling. "We gave Nitro the charcoals we found in his pocket and some paper, hoping he'd write his name or give us some clue to who he is. All he did was draw the pearl necklace he was wearing when he was brought in."

When Vining spoke, her voice was raspy. She cleared her throat. "Where's the necklace?"

"It's secured with his personal belongings," Kurosky said.

"May I see it?" Vining explained for Folke's and Kissick's benefit. "There's been so much talk about it. Don't you want to see it, Jim?"

"Sure," he said without conviction.

A tall African American gang member leaned against the clear door to his pod and peered out, looking bored.

Nitro was in the next pod.

Vining spotted him before he saw her. She would have

recognized him from the descriptions, but it was more than that.

He sat in the middle of the narrow mattress, knees pulled to his chest, wearing the clothes he had stripped off in Old Pasadena. Gangly arms and hands with slender fingers circled his legs. He rested his head against his knees, facedown, and was rocking slightly. The powdery blond of his erratic hair was matted with dried chili. His scalp and the back of his neck were sunburned. He wore only socks on his feet. His shoes were side by side beneath the shelf that supported the mattress.

Kurosky knocked on the Plexiglas. "Hey, Mister. Howya doin'?"

He looked up, first at the jailer, then quickly at Vining.

She inhaled sharply at the sight of his eyes. She was back in that kitchen and T. B. Mann had stabbed her, had plunged the knife into her neck. She'd touched it, feeling flesh, blood, and steel. Warmth and coolness. He had held her, caressed her. She had given in to his caress, allowed him that intimate trust reserved for a beloved. They had gazed into each other's eyes. She knew she was giving herself to him, unwillingly but completely. And he was taking her, stolen yet his nonetheless. His now. Taking her, sucking it all in until her very . . . last . . . breath.

Kurosky asked, "Want me to open the pod?"

Vining said, "No. I can see him fine."

"I'll go get the necklace." The jailer left.

Vining stood outside the pod with her feet planted in a ready position, her arms loose at her sides, prepared for action. Her behavior was instinctive. Her mind floundered. She'd dreamed of this moment. Prayed for it.

Nitro gave her a tentative smile, as if he knew her, perhaps from photos, like one knows a celebrity or a famous painting. Seeing it for real, it's familiar, yet somehow completely different.

She felt that dreaded tightness in her chest. The hobgoblin was back, the eight-armed beast of her imagination. It began its cobra's squeeze, robbing the breath from her.

I am strong. I am fine.

She struggled to remember the psychologist's lessons, the one she hadn't lied to. Or hadn't lied much.

She tried to breathe deeply, still holding his gaze. *I am in control.* She unearthed her feet and moved closer.

He tentatively stood and approached her. Only the clear wall separated them. His nearly white hair and pale eyes stood out against his sunburned skin. With him in socks and her in shoes, they were eye-to-eye.

Kissick might have called her name.

But there were just the two of them there in the world, in their world—her and the thin pale man.

He *was* familiar to Vining. Something about him was T. B. Mann. Yet, *he was not him.*

Kissick and Folke silently watched, as if observing a delicate pas de deux. A cough or rustling among the audience would send the dancers tumbling to the floor.

"Who are you?" she growled.

Beneath Vining's intense scrutiny, Nitro's cornflower-blue eyes shaded from warmth to apprehension. Suddenly, she butted her head against the Plexiglas, startling him. He scrambled back to the bed.

She turned toward the surprised faces of Kissick and Folke.

"It's not him."

"You're positive?" Folke asked, trying not to look at the red mark emerging on her forehead.

Vining thought about it. She would never forget T. B. Mann's eyes when he held her as tightly as a lover during those last moments. She saw the same worshipful glint in Nitro's eyes. But T. B. Mann's eyes held more. Much more. His eyes had the wide stare and hard edges of a carnivore holding the neck of its prey between clamped jaws, achieving a near-hypnotic state as he squeezed the windpipe, feeling the prey squirm until it was still. Only then did he unhinge his jaws and let the corpse drop to the ground. Vining remembered when she was a child how she'd watched her adorable pet cat lunge at a mouse in the yard, grabbing on to its neck. How the cat had wailed when Vining's mother took the dead mouse from it. The ultimate prize.

That look and the possibility of that look were absent from Nitro's eyes.

Vining said, "I'm positive."

"He seems like he knows you," Kissick said.

Vining shrugged.

Kissick took a tiny digital camera from his pocket. "Let's get some pictures anyway."

As Kissick snapped, Nitro cowered on the bed, his back against the corner, his eyes peeking above his knees, which he'd pulled close.

Kurosky returned carrying a Baggie, which she handed to Vining. "You wanted to see this, Detective."

From the bag, Vining slowly withdrew the pearl necklace. She shoved the Baggie into her pants pocket.

Folke pointed at the necklace. "Can you believe that's the only thing he left on other than his shoes and socks? Why wear a necklace?"

Good question. Vining held it draped across her outstretched palms with the same distaste as if she were cradling the limp body of a hated intimate. The imitation pearls were peeling. The tiny fake diamonds surrounding the pendant had turned dark. Some were missing. A fake deep-blue gem was scratched. The design was identical to Vining's necklace, the one she believed had been a gift from T. B. Mann. Her death stone was pearl. The pendant in this necklace held a dark blue stone, imitation sapphire. The necklace was decades old.

The Magic 8-Ball in Vining's head provided the answer: *This is where it started.*

"Hold it up." Kissick aimed the camera in her direction.

She reversed the necklace so the pendant faced the camera. She handled it gingerly, not touching it more than necessary, giving it respect yet at the same time feeling mild revulsion, as if handling the relic of a saint.

The appearance of the necklace had rallied Nitro's courage. He again approached the Plexiglas. He pointed to the necklace, pantomimed putting it on, then pointed at Vining.

Kurosky brightened. "That's amazing. He's communicating. He wants you to put on the necklace, Detective." She did her own pantomime of putting on the necklace, miming Nitro. "What if you try it? This is a breakthrough. Try it."

This encouraged Nitro, and he began agitatedly patting his chest, where he wanted the necklace to lie on her body.

Vining silenced the jailer with a look. She turned her gaze toward Nitro. Raising her hand, she shook the necklace at him and spoke through clenched teeth. "You want me to wear this? You want me to wear this? What will you do? What will you do if I wear this?"

He backed away. He dropped to the floor and tried to cram himself beneath the bed. When he didn't fit, he pulled the bedcovers off the mattress and hid himself under them.

Vining could see only one of his bright eyes. "He's not the guy who attacked me."

"You're sure, Nan?" Folke asked.

"I'm sure."

Folke said, "Nitro, we're going to charge you with indecent exposure and resisting arrest. Let's throw in disturbing the peace too."

Nitro's one visible eye shifted to look at Folke.

"Do you understand these charges?"

Nitro blinked and shifted his gaze to Vining.

"He needs psychological help," Kurosky pleaded. "You're not going to send him to County Jail, are you? They'll eat him alive."

Folke gestured for Vining and Kissick to come with him. They walked a few feet away.

Folke spoke in a low voice. "I've never seen anything like this guy."

"Any prior criminal history?" Kissick asked.

Folke shook his head. "Nothing came back on his fingerprints. We can send him to the Big G on a fifty-one fifty or we can file charges."

"But he can't be arraigned if he won't state his name or whether he understands the charges against him," Kissick said. "The court would have him evaluated to determine his competency to stand trial. Who knows how long before he's determined to be competent, if ever. Why would we go that route over a fifty-one fifty for a couple of Mickey Mouse charges?"

"We'd only do that if we wanted to keep him incarcerated longer than seventy-two hours," Folke said. "It would give us more time to find out about him and what he's up to. Even if we send him to the Big G, there's no guarantee they'd keep him that long. A psychiatrist could determine he's stable and cut him loose before seventy-two hours. Still, it's like he enacted a textbook scenario for a fifty-one fifty. Stripping off his clothes. Running through traffic. Acting as crazy as possible without doing serious damage but showing he's a danger to himself." He looked at Vining. "Your call, Nan."

She paced back and forth, holding the necklace in her fist. Her back to them, she looked at it while she considered her options. After a minute, she turned to face them.

"This guy's got serious mental problems. Sending him to the Big G is the right thing to do."

"You're sure?" Kissick asked.

"Yes."

They walked back to Nitro's pod, where he was still on the floor, covered up.

"Michelle, get that stuff off him," Folke ordered the jailer.

"Nitro, we can't have you on the floor like that." Kurosky entered the pod and pulled off the bed coverings. "Get up." She tugged his arm.

Holding his eyes on Vining and the necklace she held between her fingers, he climbed to his feet.

"Looks like he understands to me," Kissick observed.

Kurosky put the bed coverings back in place while Nitro kept his eyes on Vining's. He didn't cower or act afraid.

Vining stepped inside the pod and moved close to him. Too close. One swift move and he could have embedded his teeth in her face. She was close enough to smell his sweat. The nearness of him sent electricity through her.

It was him, but it was not him.

Kissick and Folke moved near the open door.

"Nan," Kissick warned.

Vining quickly raised her hand that held the necklace. That startled Nitro. He scurried to the wall.

"Why do you want me to wear this?" She came after him, holding the necklace, raising it higher. "This isn't *my* necklace." She punched out with her arm and the necklace hit his face. It then swung, like a hypnotist's charm.

He pressed against the wall but there was nowhere for him to go. His lips trembled. She recognized the fear in his eyes. She knew he wasn't faking it. She relished it. She loved it. She could have killed him or kissed him, they were that close.

"It's *yours*," she said, dropping the necklace inside the plastic bag and drawing her fingers along the seal. She handed it to Kurosky, and said, "Put it back with his personal possessions."

Before Vining left the cell, she gave Nitro a look and mentally sent him a message: *I'll see you again.*

Kissick tensely joked, "I know the necklace didn't match your outfit, Nan, but . . ."

As she passed the others, Vining said, "I'll teach that clown to draw pictures of me."

THIRTEEN

*M*ark Scoville mentally toted up his losses. After the first weekend of college football, he was down fifteen large. While he'd won on Ohio State over Northern Illinois with a ten-point spread, and the UCLA Bruins with twenty-one over Utah, he'd taken a bath on the USC Trojans in their preseason game against Arkansas. He'd called Oliver Mercer after the game on Saturday to ride his ass over the Trojans' poor showing. They'd exchanged playful barbs that were only superficially in jest. Their brief relationship had soured big-time over the proposed merger with Drive By Media. It all came down to money and power. Scoville doubted that even a struggle over a woman could create such animosity between men. Ultimately, the hand would come down on the side of money over the broad any day. All that Iliad and Odyssey fighting over Helen of Troy . . . That was a myth.

Later that same Saturday evening, Mercer would be murdered. His girlfriend too, which was a shame. Just like that, the problems Scoville was having with Mercer were over. The likelihood that Scoville would be tossed from the business his father had built from scruffy patches of dirt along the freeway to LAX was now as unforeseeable as Los Angelenos abandoning their cars for mass transportation. Wasn't gonna happen.

Granted, the police coming around had been unsettling. But that would pass. They had nothing to link him to the murders. They were just fishing. Just doing their job. Just asking routine questions, as they had reminded him a million times.

Scoville snapped open the flip-top on another canned margarita, poured it into a take-out cup of lemon-lime Slurpee, and stirred it with a straw. A frozen margarita was his favorite hangover remedy. The old hair of the dog with shaved ice to cool him down and hydrate. He'd bought the cocktail makings at the liquor store down the street from the Marquis Outdoor Advertising offices on the Sunset Strip.

After his father's death, he'd taken over the big corner office. It was much the same as the old man had left it. The desk had belonged to his father, as had the furniture and the books and the trinkets in the bookcases. The only things his father hadn't touched were the computer equipment, some of the photographs, and the framed sports memorabilia on the walls: photographs, jerseys, bats, baseballs, mitts, footballs, basketballs, and a hockey stick, all signed.

Scoville had a raging hangover after last night. The interview with the detectives had gone just fine until their needling had dislodged a small detail, nothing more than a black joke that he had forgotten as soon as it had happened. He wasn't really sure what had happened, as he'd been sort of blasted then too. Stupid of him to have overreacted like that in front of the police.

He went out the door that led to the rooftop patio. The executive offices were in the penthouse of the three-story building, constructed above the second floor like the top tier of a wedding cake. Doors opened onto the roof, where there were patio tables and chairs beneath an awning. Surrounding the roof was a four-foot wall from which there was a spectacular view up and down the Strip. Straight ahead, there was an unobstructed view across West Hollywood, Beverly Hills, Century City, and West L.A.—all the way to the ocean on a clear day. The old man had always had the touch when it came to real estate. He might not have been much of a father, but he knew property.

Scoville leaned against the wall and sipped the sludgy cocktail through a wide straw. An inversion layer was keeping the heat and smog trapped in the Los Angeles basin. The air was a putrid brownish-gray color. All this weather was good for was perspiring. And coughing.

He liked coming to the office when there was no one else there. It was his last refuge. Even his meandering Hancock Park home had come to feel crowded with Dena and her pain-in-the-ass daughter, Dahlia. Sometimes he even resented the intrusions of Luddy, the love of his life, whom Dena overscheduled with lessons, sports, school, and social events, in his view. The bad vibes were crowding him out more than the people. Eight years of marriage . . . his first. He'd learned something: Nothing was as soul-sucking as a marriage gone sour.

It was early afternoon on Labor Day, and the Strip was busy on this last official weekend of summer. The nightclubs—the Whisky a-Go-Go, the Roxy, the Viper Room—were shuttered until the sun went down. The sidewalk restaurants along Sunset Plaza were full. People were shopping at the high-end boutiques. Scoville could see the big bright yellow building where his favorite record store used to be. He used to spend aimless hours there as a teenager. It seemed incredible that the store had gone out of business. The times were a-changin'.

A posse of young women in low-cut jeans and midriff-baring tops strolling down the boulevard entered Scoville's field of vision, but he paid them little attention. He was ogling one of his most profitable billboard faces, which had just been fitted with an ad for a blockbuster movie. Down the street was another of his faces and another and another. There were even billboards on top of the Marquis building. Each post supported two faces that were angled so drivers coming in either direction would be exposed to an image. Some advertised movies, but most were for designer clothing and accessories, featuring thin, scantily clad models in provocative poses. The message was always the same: "Be like me. Buy Fendi sunglasses."

Scoville heard the cash register "ka-ching" in his head as he calculated the revenue that he sorely needed now. Best of all, the dough was all his again. The owner of Drive By Media had called when he'd heard about the murders. Scoville had had the distinct pleasure of telling him that Mercer's share of Marquis had reverted to him, as per their partnership contract, and the merger was off.

"How convenient for you," the dickwad had told him. "Your partner getting deep-sixed before he can ink a deal that you didn't want."

Scoville had been glib. "Make sure you tell the cops that."

"Detectives Kissick and Vining. I already did."

Whatever. Marquis Outdoor Advertising was his. Well, more or less. And he had to answer to no one except his accountant. He'd worked around that wrinkle before. As for the cops, they had nothing on him, as he had had nothing to do with Mercer's murder. Scoville had heard on the news that an unnamed source at the Pasadena Police had revealed that they had a suspect— some weirdo who'd been stalking Lauren Richards. Guys like that commit crazy-ass murders. Not guys like him. Murder or overt aggressiveness wasn't his style at all. No way.

His father's words still rang in his head. *Stop being a pussy, Mark.*

He had been a tough guy, old Ludlow. A spit-in-your-eye, balls-to-the-wall tough guy. Only when his father got old and sick did he have a change of heart and seek to bring his prodigal son back into the fold, even showing a scintilla of contrition that was so gratifying.

Scoville used to hate being Ludlow's only remaining child. More than three decades ago, after a high school football game, Ludlow Jr. had been thrown from the open bed of the pickup truck in which he'd been riding to a party with some buddies. The driver, the running back on Luddy's team, hadn't been drinking. He'd lost control of the truck when he'd swerved to avoid a skunk, ejecting the five kids riding in the bed. Luddy Jr.

was the only one gravely injured, sailing headfirst into a tree.

Mark was thirteen and already growing into the pet name his father had bestowed early: Fuckup.

Ludlow Jr. was everything the old man had wanted in a son. Everything any man would want in a son: smart, athletic, disciplined, charming, well-mannered, good-looking, and good-hearted. Of course, such a child was too good for this world, Mark's mother had lamented.

After Ludlow Jr.'s accident, there were tense, sad days before the decision to discontinue life support and allow his perfect organs to be harvested—the young man's final heroic act. The lives of a bunch of strangers were thereby saved or strengthened.

Then the Scovilles were three.

Funny how things had turned out.

Funny too about Mercer. A coincidence that Scoville had wished Mercer dead and now he was. Coincidences happened every day. Babies were switched at birth. Accident victims were misidentified and buried in the wrong graves. People switch flights at the last minute, only to learn that the plane later crashed. Look at all the stories about people who escaped being victims in the Twin Towers on 9/11 because they stopped to change mismatched socks or went around the corner for a doughnut. Coincidence. That's all Mercer's murder was. It couldn't possibly have anything to do with that drunken black joke.

Things were good once again. He had Mercer's cash and didn't have to deal with Mercer. He was sorry Mercer was dead. He guessed one could be sorry and happy about such a thing at the same time. He wondered how they were killed. The detectives hadn't offered details. Scoville hoped it had been fast and they hadn't suffered.

He had a fleeting thought about Dena, wondering if

she would leave him. He decided that she wouldn't. She'd made too big a deal about the importance of her family on her TV show, trotting out the kids like trained ponies. Surveys showed her fans liked her homebody aspect. That drunken car crash had nearly destroyed her career. She couldn't count on the phoenix rising from the ashes twice. No, she wouldn't leave him.

Scoville loudly sucked the last of his margarita through the straw. All was well. He decided to do a little Internet gambling before heading home to take a nap.

At a sidewalk table in front of Chin Chin on the sunset strip, a man with a prominent Adam's apple, wearing a sundress that showed his muscular, tattooed upper body, ordered another mango iced tea. From his purse he took a collapsible rice paper fan he'd purchased in one of the few remaining old-style tourist shops in downtown L.A.'s Chinatown, the type of store packed to the rafters with painted parasols, silk slippers, and carved jade. He'd bought his mother a silk robe, knowing she'd complain bitterly about the extravagance, but it wasn't expensive and it was so pretty, decorated with embroidered butterflies. He'd bought one for himself too, crimson, embroidered with a design of a Chinese footbridge. What the hell? It was fun. Everyone had to live a little. He didn't get into L.A. that often.

He snapped open the fan and began fanning himself, running fingertips beneath the neckline of the white dress, frowning at a small patch of hair missed during a home waxing job.

Tracing fingers around the spit curls on the perky brunette wig from the Raquel Welch collection, he caught two women staring from a nearby table. People could be so ignorant. He crossed his legs beneath the full-skirted dress and admired his ankle-wrapped sandals, which set off the French pedicure. He held up his hand, palm out, to see how his manicure was holding up. It was in need of attention. The Saturday night party at Oliver Mercer's house had wrecked havoc with it. He straightened Mercer's class ring. It was masculine, but he liked it. He had Mercer's severed right hand wrapped in plastic in the freezer at home, tucked away to use for incriminating or merely bewildering fingerprints. He liked messing with people for sport, especially cops.

Picking up his field glasses, he saw that Mark Scoville had not returned to lean against the wall on top of the Marquis office building. The drink cup he had set there was now gone.

Catching one of the two rude women again staring, he pulled away the field glasses and said, "There are hawks' nests on top of those buildings. Did you know that?"

"No, I didn't." She gave her friend a tense smile.

"Fascinating, isn't it, that wildlife can thrive in the middle of a big city? Shows how powerful the life force is and how adaptable living creatures are to their environment."

"I guess animals do what they need to to survive."

"Indeed they do. I'm Jill, by the way." He extended his hand.

The woman tittered, offering her hand. "I'm Abby Gilmore. This is my friend Trish."

"Nice to meet you, Abby and Trish." He pegged them as in their late twenties and not from around here. They had sunburns over light tans, trying too hard at the beach. One of them carried a big straw carryall, likely purchased in Tijuana. The other wore a tank top printed with a photo of Arnold Schwarzenegger in sunglasses and leather, carrying a huge automatic weapon, with the slogan "The Governator." Plus no L.A. woman in her right mind would walk around with an open tote bag that almost shouted, "Steal from me." He could see the gal's wallet sitting right on top.

"Are you visiting Los Angeles?"

"Yes, we're here from Ohio. We live in a town outside Dayton," Abby said. "We go home tonight. We've been in L.A. for eight days."

A lot of information to offer to a total stranger, Jill thought.

"It's really been a trip." Trish giggled, resting her elbows on the table, and pressing her fingers against her lips.

She exchanged a look with Abby that Jill found insulting.

"So where have you been and what have you seen?" Jill smiled directly at Trish, killing her with kindness, though in her mind Jill was twisting that scrawny neck and popping off her head with its overbleached hair, like cleaning shrimp for the barbecue. He liked that image and ran with it, mentally shaving back her skin, her limbs with it, and cleaning out her entrails. Then, plop! Onto the grate to sear above hot coals with her screaming like a live lobster thrown into boiling water.

"Oh, all the tourist places." Jill's unyielding gaze had taken Trish's attitude down a few notches. "Disneyland, Universal Studios, the stars on Hollywood Boulevard . . ."

Abby picked up. "The beach, of course. San Diego for two days. Tijuana. The club scene everywhere." She slid a glance at Trish, and that got them both tittering over the memory of shared shenanigans.

Jill set down cash for the iced tea and pot stickers with ginger sauce. Picking up his purse, he pushed back the chair and stood, smoothing his dress. "Ladies, have a safe trip home. It was awfully nice to meet you. Abby, may I give you some unasked-for advice? Be careful about your open purse. At least shove your wallet to the bottom. There are a lot of criminals around here. Predators."

Abby snatched her tote bag closer, sighing with relief when she saw her wallet still on top. "Thank you . . ."

"Jill."

"Jill." The name did not come naturally to Abby, but she got it out with a half-smile.

Before Jill was out of earshot, just passing beneath the restaurant's awning, they began laughing.

Jill thought of telling them a thing or two, or waiting for them around the corner and teaching them a thing or two, but he had more pressing business.

Sashaying down the sidewalk, loving how the rayon-blend fabric brushed against his legs, he paused in front of a prominent display in a bookstore window. Dozens of copies of *Razored Soul* were stacked in a large pyramid. Beside it was a cutout of Bowie Crowley's nude buff upper body. His crossed arms punched out his well-developed biceps and the garish 23:4 tattoo. A gold crucifix settled between his squared-off pectorals. The sensitive lips and eyes, the James Dean angst, were a stark contrast with his bone-crusher physique.

"Have you read that book?" a woman pausing at the window asked a man whose hand she held. "I couldn't put it down."

Big Jackie O sunglasses hid Jill's vengeful eyes. "You think it's great? Well, here's a different review." With a guttural noise, he hacked up a wad of sputum and shot it onto the window over Crowley's face.

The woman gasped and the couple skittered away. She whispered, "Did you see what she did?"

"*She?*" the boyfriend said, taking a final look at the well-made-up, impossibly homely face.

Jill, watching with satisfaction as the glob traced a

slimy trail down the window, issued a challenge to the aghast boyfriend. "My brother, there's a little part of you that would just *love* to find out, isn't there?"

FOURTEEN

*D*ozens of vintage and new motorcycles were lined up in the parking lot of the Rock Store and spilled onto the banks of Mulholland Highway. The old diner, nestled into a hillside of volcanic rock, was more a destination than a pit stop for motorcyclists enjoying the scenic, twisting ride from the San Fernando Valley to the Pacific. The hot holiday had brought motorcycle enthusiasts out in force. It was just mid-morning but the alcohol was freely flowing on the patio, where hearty meals were being cooked on the outdoor grill. Weekend warriors rubbed elbows with guys in chains and bandannas with bugs embedded between their teeth, biker chicks in leather chaps, tourists sweating in their new leather, and Hollywood stars. The crowd was buzzing with talk of Jay Leno, who had just stopped by, riding one of his pricey toys. The cognoscenti also whispered of past visits from Arnold Schwarzenegger and his wife, Maria.

Those who were there ostensibly because the Rock Store was the place for any biker cruising Mulholland to be, but who really half-hoped to spot a star, were not disappointed when Bowie Crowley rode up on his Harley-Davidson Fat Boy with Dena Hale on the back. Crowley was a for-real tough guy. The kind of guy who seemed mellow but who only a fool would mess with. The kind of guy who had come through the fire and out the other side, with a man's blood on his hands, which made him all the scarier—and irresistible.

And Dena . . . well, Dena was just plain cute and hot. She looked thinner in person, which was hard for the women there to process.

Some in the crowd had seen Hale interview Crowley that morning on TV. They'd seen the humble way he'd interacted with the father of the boy he'd murdered and were impressed. They'd also read the unmistakable look in Hale's eyes when she had looked at Crowley. Who could blame her? Most of the audience would have jumped his bones if they had the chance.

No one with a camera missed this photo op, especially the paparazzi, who were always hanging around, waiting for something just like this. Patience has its virtues.

Crowley hung their helmets on the bike's handlebars and cut a path through the crowd, high-fiving and shaking hands while shielding Hale from the throng. They walked past a pair of nonfunctioning antique gas pumps, a favorite backdrop for people to pose for photos with their motorcycles. The prices on the pumps were frozen at .32¼ cents per gallon.

A rotund grizzled biker happened to have a copy of *Razored Soul* and asked Crowley to sign it.

The biker gushed, "I never buy books, you know? But I went out special to buy this one. I said to my wife, I can't believe this dude is for real. You're like a character out of a book or a movie or somethin'."

Crowley penned a special note, using a Sharpie marker he'd taken to carrying. "Thanks, man, but I'm just a guy tryin' to stay out of trouble. Make something of my life so my son will be proud of me."

The man took back his book and gave Crowley a hearty handshake. "That's cool. Real cool."

Hale could barely conceal her admiration.

Inside, they jostled their way through the dining room with its picnic tables, busy but minuscule kitchen, and mural painted across three walls of a Native American in full headdress on a horse looking across Monument Valley. They went up stone steps to a room full of Formica-topped tables and old club-style chairs upholstered in orange vinyl. A guy was tinkling a tune at an upright piano in the corner. A long wooden bar was against one wall.

Crowley found a stool for Hale and sidled next to her. She ordered a Perrier with lime and had to laugh when he ordered nonfat milk.

"What's so funny?" he asked with a wink. "I got in the habit of drinking milk when I was in the joint. Never touched the stuff until then. Builds strong bones."

"Next we'll be seeing you in one of those ads showing celebrities with milk mustaches."

"That one I might do."

She picked up her Perrier. "Have you been approached for product endorsements?"

"A little. This local firm that manufactures biker leathers and gear came calling and a custom chopper shop wanted me to do an ad. I turned them down."

"Does Harley-Davidson know you ride their motorcycles?"

"They might, but no one's come calling. My name isn't as golden as you think. Face it, I'm a convicted felon. A murderer. Big corporations don't want a guy like me pitching their products. A rep like mine, the only thing it's good for is . . . I don't know what it's good for."

"Selling books."

He raised his glass to clink with hers. "Selling books." He took in the scene. "I can't believe you've never been to the Rock Store before, being a Los Angeles native and all."

"I run with a different crowd, I guess. But this is something to see. Thanks for bringing me."

"I'm glad you decided to take a ride with me, Miss Dena. You haven't really lived until you've done Mulholland on a Harley. A little California dreamin'."

"Hope someone's doing some dreaming somewhere."

"Sometimes you have to shake things up. Change your perspective."

"I could use a new perspective." She looked at her watch.

Crowley leaned against the bar. "When do you have to get back?"

"My daughter is out with friends until late. My son is spending the night at Balboa Island with his buddy and his parents. My husband is God knows where." She shrugged. "I guess I'm in no hurry."

"That's my favorite time schedule. And you know what? I'm in no hurry either."

He smiled at her. She felt herself falling into his hazel eyes and felt like a sap for even thinking that. She looked away.

"I'm glad you invited me, Bowie. This is fun."

"I'm glad you had a change of clothes in your locker."

"I'm glad you had an extra helmet. I should be suspicious of a man who carries an extra helmet in case he might have a partner."

He smiled crookedly. "You've gotta be prepared, right?"

"You got condoms in that storage container on your bike? Maybe some sex toys?"

"Dena . . . what do you take me for?"

"Puh-leese. I saw those women in the audience. We had to hose down the place after the show."

"Now you're gonna make me blush."

She gave him a look that said she didn't believe that for a second.

"Hey, I'm very shy."

She turned her head and gave him the same look from the other eye.

"What are you getting at, Dena? What do you want me to say?"

"I've heard the rumors. Your name's in the gossip rags. You're quite a ladies' man."

"I'm not going to B.S. you. When I first got out of the joint, there was a lot of partying. But that's not what I'm about."

She tapped a varnished fingernail on the bar. "I want one thing to be clear. I'm not going to be another notch on your bedpost."

"I'm not going to deny that I'm attracted to you. But you're married. Understood. I never thought—"

"Oh, *really?*"

"Well, come on. Of course I *thought* about it. I wouldn't be a red-blooded American male if I hadn't. Face it, you're hot. And I like you. But I'm telling you honestly, I have no agenda. It's like this. I wasn't busy today and you weren't either."

"So here we are."

"Here we are."

She smirked and shook her head. "I should be the last person to throw stones," she said. "Living in my glass house."

"What's your truth, Dena? The part of you no one knows."

She looked askance and then, for some reason, blurted out the truth. "That my life is not perfect. Or how about this . . . my life isn't even happy. Actually, lately it's been hell."

"I'm sorry to hear that. Anything you'd like to share?"

She blew out a long stream of air, as if she didn't know where to begin. "My husband's business partner and his girlfriend were murdered last Saturday at his home in Pasadena."

Crowley's jaw dropped. "That was your husband's partner? Good Lord. Don't they suspect some guy who was stalking the woman?"

"That's what they're saying on the news. Yesterday morning, two detectives showed up at our house and took us to Pasadena to be interviewed. Mark and his partner Oliver had been having a big fight over the business."

Crowley nodded and said nothing.

Hale was quick to add, "Mark had nothing to do with it. We had a dinner party that night. I know it sounds like he cooked up a perfect alibi and hired somebody to murder Oliver, but Mark doesn't even think that way. He's not the type. Not that there's a *type* per se." Remembering who she was talking to, she winced. "Sorry."

"No offense. Go on."

"Mark internalizes. He drowns his problems, if you know what I mean."

"Oh, yeah." Crowley somberly watched her with those soulful eyes. "That must be tough for you."

Her tears again welled. "Darn! Enough already." She blotted them with the damp cocktail napkin from beneath her drink. "I hate wearing my heart on my sleeve."

"That's part of the reason you're popular. You're honest, and people can see it."

"I feel like I'm coming apart. I hope people can't see that."

He rested his hand on her back.

She sniffed and looked up at him. With a slight movement of her arm, she created an opening into which he stepped. He pulled her close and nuzzled her hair with his nose. Her tears soaked into his black T-shirt.

She abruptly pushed away. "What are we doing? Our picture will be in the tabloids."

He backed off.

She snatched a fresh cocktail napkin from a stack on the other side of the bar and blew her nose. "I'm sorry."

"You've got nothing to be sorry about. If you've done half the things I've done, then you can be sorry."

"You're kind." She folded the napkin in half and in half again. "It's just . . . I don't have anyone to talk to about this. Even my friends don't know how bad it's gotten between Mark and me. My own dumb pride keeps me from opening up. I was down for so long. My life was an endless struggle. Bad decisions. Bad relationships. There was a point where I thought I'd never finish paying dues. All my old friends had gotten their lives together. Good marriages and great kids. The white-picket-fence thing. Normal garden-variety problems. Then there was me. I'd have lunch with my girlfriends and I'd feel like entertainment for them. Diversion from their routines. But guess what? I pulled it together. I not only pulled it together, I soared right over all of them. I have the top-rated local morning show, the rich, successful, handsome husband, the fabulous house . . ."

"And they don't call you anymore."

"Some don't. That still surprises me. A few do. The true-blue friends. Like a marriage, through thick and thin. But even my true friends don't know everything about my life. They don't know that it's a lie."

Their eyes locked.

She repeated, "It's a lie."

After an intense moment, he gave her a broad smile. "I know what you need."

She was sniveling, but managed to fire back the obvious sarcastic response. "I bet you do."

He grinned. "Well, baby, in my humble opinion, I bet your life could use some improvement in that department." He gave her shoulders a shake. "But the next best thing is a fast ride on a Fat Boy."

On their way to the Rock Store, Hale had touched Crowley, just enough to not fall off. On the second stretch that would take them to the ocean, she snuggled close with her legs tightly squeezing his thighs.

She'd called Mark before they'd left the restaurant. He didn't seem to care where she was or what she was doing. She simply said she was out and would be back before the kids got home. She guessed he was happy that she wasn't around to interrupt his excursion into his bleary world, yet would be back in time so he wouldn't have to deal with the kids.

Hale wrapped her arms around Crowley's broad, lean torso, soaking in the scent of hot asphalt, exhaust, and perspiration. They rounded a curve and all of a sudden, the air was cool and moist, and they could see the ocean. It was lost again around a curve. Then the long stretch of coastline from Santa Monica to Point Dume came into view. Land's end. The sight always cheered her.

When they finally stopped at a street light at the Pacific Coast Highway in Malibu, he said over his shoulder to her, "The producer who bought the movie rights to my book is at his ranch in Montana. His Malibu Colony house is empty. Wanna check it out?"

"You have the keys?"

"Yeah."

"Heh, heh, heh. . . ."

"I've never seen it before. Honest." The light changed and he took off, not waiting for her response.

Her knee-jerk reaction was to be miffed by his presumptuousness but another part of her found his decisiveness appealing, even though the caveman style had never been her cup of tea. The only things Mark was decisive about anymore, it seemed, were drinking and gambling. She couldn't keep him away from either vice, no matter what she tried. She of all people should know she didn't have the power to change an addict.

She still beat herself up for not being firmer when Mark had said he wanted to join his father in running the billboard business. All-controlling Ludlow, while not the source of emotionally fragile Mark's addictions, had fueled the flames. Still, the move promised to provide the financial security that relentlessly eluded them. Mark's restaurant had been floundering. As for her, the rug could be pulled out from under her financially the next time her contract was up.

The freedom she felt on this impromptu day with Crowley brought home a truth that had been swirling beneath the surface of her life. It was there, like a drowning victim submerged in a murky pond, but she darted away whenever the angle of the sun changed, revealing it. She didn't love Mark anymore, but she cared about him. At first, it tore her heart out to see Mark spiraling down, suffering. But when he gave up the fight and allowed himself to float away on the high tide of his addictions, her empathy turned to pity and then disgust.

She was prepared to stay in a loveless marriage to avoid disrupting the children—Dahlia, who had already been through too much, and Luddy, who was pure sweetness and light. She didn't want to be the first to dim that light.

Problem was, the edifice of their lives was crumbling, as if the moldering bricks of the old man's smothering mansion were tumbling onto their heads.

Later, she might feel differently and be racked with guilt and regret. Right now, she was prepared to follow Crowley anywhere. She fully expected to never see him again, or, at best, she'd spot him with his latest arm candy at a Hollywood cocktail party. It would be a nonchalant moment for him and awkward for her. So what? She was tired of living in every world except the present. Yet some little part of her, some tiny, long-silenced internal voice whispered: *Could he be my future?*

She didn't notice much about the house beyond the vast windows overlooking the sparkling, calm ocean.

Crowley opened doors that led to a deck and they escaped the stuffy house. They paid brief, appropriate attention to the view before a single glance into each other's eyes led to a passionate kiss from which there was no turning back.

Standing on the deck, they tore at each other's clothing. The deck was in shadows, but still in view of scattered people along the nearly inaccessible beach. She didn't care. It felt good to stand nude in the cool air, free of her sweaty, binding clothing, possessed instead by his strong hands and artful tongue.

He pulled her onto a double chaise longue, its size and location clearly all about seduction. She laughed when he produced a condom from his wallet, then snatched it from him, rolled it on, and climbed on top. Their lovemaking was hard and fast, no more or less than each of them wanted. She dug her nails into his shoulders as she took his best effort and improved on it. She got there first, starting with a whimper and ending by throwing back her head and letting loose a wail that was as primal as dirt. Watching her brought him to the tipping point.

He struggled to keep his eyes open, not wanting to miss a thing.

Sweat-drenched and panting, they looked at each other.

He took in her now-rosy cheeks, the fine lines erased from her face, which was finally at ease. He craned his head to look at his shoulders, rubbing his hand across the welts she'd left there.

Her moment of feeling at one with the world was fleeting, leaving her feeling more fragile than before. "You'll have a hard time explaining that to the next one," she said.

"You have a low opinion of me, don't you?"

She was embarrassed and realized that by diminishing him, she was able to minimize what had happened between them.

He took her face between his hands. "I'm going to work on changing that."

She felt a fluttering inside her chest and inhaled sharply. He had taken her breath away. She hoped he didn't see it.

They raided the refrigerator, snacking on coke, jarred food, condiments, and crackers. Sitting at the kitchen island, eating a stranger's food in a stranger's home, she enjoyed the vacation from her life and tried not to think about what happened next.

He carried her up the open staircase, draped in his arms. She clutched his shoulders like a child. They took a cool shower, after which he went to the bedside drawer and found more condoms. A lucky guess, he'd insisted when she'd teased him.

Later, she'd explored and asked him about the scar on his back—knife fight in high school—and one on his side—grazed by a bullet fired during a barroom brawl—

and one near his shoulder—stabbed by a shank-wielding inmate in Quentin.

She'd dropped off to sleep in the crook of his arm. A short time later, she'd awakened to see him dressed.

"I have a book signing tonight in Pasadena. Why don't you come with me?"

She slowly blinked, considering it for a second. "I would love to, but it's not a good idea."

He took the freeway back to the studio, where her car was still parked in the lot.

"Call me later," he said.

She nodded. Standing in the parking lot, they did not touch, already behaving like illicit lovers.

She watched him roar off on the Harley, looking like a vision from a thousand bad but irresistible movies. Before the exhaust had faded from the air, her mind was already going to all the bad places. She stopped it in its tracks. For now, just for now, she would savor the moment.

FIFTEEN

Vining and Kissick had stopped by the PPD's forensics unit to check on their progress analyzing Nitro's drawing book for fingerprints. The prints the tech found were consistent with Nitro's.

Vining flipped through the drawing book. She had assumed the violent pictures of women were together in the spiral-bound pad, but they were scattered among the images of animals, trees, and flowers. Somehow, that made it creepier.

Back upstairs, she picked up the photocopies of the drawings and put them in her briefcase.

They were at work on the double homicide in the Detectives' Section conference room when Folke called to say that two officers were transporting Nitro to the Big G, where he'd be placed on a seventy-two-hour hold for psychiatric evaluation and treatment.

"He's County's problem now," Kissick commented.

They pushed along on the Mercer/Richards homicide investigation.

Ruiz got his warrants signed for access to Somerset's telephone, financial records, and his computer. When he and Caspers went to Somerset's apartment above his parents' garage in San Marino, Somerset's mother told them he'd left to go backpacking in the Sierras.

Ruiz served the warrants on Somerset's mother, a well-dressed woman with a zaftig figure who was nearly as tall as her son. Ruiz and Caspers both remarked later that her careful blond coiffure looked like a wig.

Ruiz notified the Inyo County Sheriff's Department, which has jurisdiction over the area in the Sierras where Somerset usually backpacked, and asked the park service to keep an eye out for him. They didn't have cause to arrest him yet, but they didn't want him slipping into the wind.

Meanwhile, Kissick called his contact at Mark Scoville's cell phone provider, who would get Scoville's data on the Q.T.

As the afternoon quickly became evening and then night, Vining wondered why she hadn't heard from Emily. She knew the finale of the gala family weekend at the Santa Barbara Four Seasons was dinner with Kaitlyn's parents at the hotel's blue-ribbon restaurant. She and Em had bought a new outfit especially for that dinner. Emily was going to call when they were on the road home. Vining figured the dinner went late. She had not allowed herself to dwell on Em's absence. Now that she was due to be home, though, Vining let herself feel how terribly she missed her. The feeling was scary in its intensity.

Finally, Emily called. In the background, Kaitlyn was babbling, trying to inject herself into the conversation. Vining guessed that Kaitlyn thought it added to the fun to toss out comments off-scene, but it was one of her traits that Vining found particularly aggravating.

"Hi, Sweet Pea. How was your fancy dinner?" she asked her daughter.

"Good." Emily's answer was clipped.

"What did you have?"

"Filet."

"You can't talk."

"Right."

"Are you okay?"

"Yep."

"No, really."

"Really. Dad and Kaitlyn are going to drive me home and then go to Calabasas."

Great, Vining thought. She didn't want to see Kaitlyn. "But your dad has to drive through Calabasas to get to our house. The original plan was to drop Kaitlyn and the boys home because they'd be tired."

"I know."

"What happened?"

"You'll see."

"Em . . . I'm in no mood."

"It's fine."

"All right. I'll be up."

"One last thing." The girl said it like it was one word. "How's the investigation going on the double homicide?"

Emily could have waited for the details after she'd returned home, but Vining suspected the girl had brought it up now to get Kaitlyn's goat. She must have succeeded, because she heard something like a shriek go up from Kaitlyn in the background. Emily's stepmother was not reticent about expressing her opinion that Vining's occupation was a negative influence on the upbringing of a young lady. Kaitlyn's tentacles around Emily had grown stickier since Emily had become a teenager. Maybe it reflected her lust for a daughter. She and Wes had five- and three-year-old boys, Kyle and Kelsey. Vining had heard through Emily that Wes didn't want more children, while Kaitlyn wanted to try for a girl. Thus the push-pull over Emily, though trying to push Emily into something she didn't want to do was like pushing a boulder.

"It was all over the news," Emily enthused. "I saw Lieutenant Beltran's press conference. Do you think it's the boyfriend? Wait . . . Kaitlyn wants to say something."

Vining rolled her eyes as the phone was passed.

"Hi, Nan. How are ya? Hey, I just want to let you know that I bought Emily a new outfit to wear to dinner with my parents."

"Oh?"

"You'll see it because she's still wearing it. It's by Marc Jacobs, and she just looks so cute in it."

"Emily looks cute in anything, but what happened to the outfit she brought?"

"It's adorable, but . . . I thought she should be dressier for the Four Seasons." She lowered her voice when uttering the hotel's name. "I didn't want Em to feel out of place."

"I see. May I speak with Emily, please?" When Em was back on the phone, Vining said, "So that's what's bothering you."

"Yep."

"All right. I'll see you soon."

The prealarm sounded when Vining opened the door. She didn't reset it, not wanting to deactivate it when Wes was at the door, which would make her look paranoid.

"It's by Marc Jacobs," she muttered as she went about her routine of storing her two weapons with extra gusto. She cracked open her bedroom windows as far as the locks would allow. Pausing in the hallway, she clicked on the air conditioning. She hoped it wouldn't take long to cool down the house. She could hear Wes now, walking into her hot house, "That's Nan, won't spend a dollar to turn on the air in a heat wave."

Kaitlyn had been a nineteen-year-old assistant hairdresser at Supercuts when she had begun an affair with Wes, eight years her senior. Vining still didn't know the real reason Wes had left her. She'd thought she knew Wes better than anyone. That assumption was probably correct, as Wes was like an iceberg, only making a small part of his psyche accessible. It had taken her years on the Job as a cop, wading through the worst of human nature, to figure that one out.

As Vining walked through the kitchen and TV room into the living room, she was still fuming over the outfit affair. The dress and jacket ensemble she and Em had bought was adorable.

She turned off the small lamp that automatically turned on at dusk. With the living room now dark, she pulled open the drapes over the sliding glass doors. She'd left the living-room drapes closed to keep out the heat, but that was only one reason. She also didn't want to give someone the opportunity to sit on the opposite ridge and use binoculars to peer inside her hillside home. Like someone who'd lost a limb, she'd made accommodations. It didn't mean she liked it.

Removing the metal pin that bolted the door, she slid the door open and stepped onto the terrace into the cool air. Her bird's-eye view gave her a clear shot of the distinctive towers of General Hospital. Decidedly unglamorous during the day. At night, the massive complex added to the twinkling lights. Today, it gained new significance. Nitro was there. For three days, he'd be there. Then he'd be released and would walk onto the streets and disappear.

Nitro had shown up the same time that a psycho killer was flexing his muscles in Pasadena. The worst possible time for her. The best time to throw her off guard, to rattle her equilibrium. He had shown up in Pasadena and behaved in a manner that was likely to earn him detention at a mental-health facility. Coincidence?

Hardly.

Nitro's pearl necklace and drawings eliminated that possibility.

Those eyes. There was something there that she couldn't name, but it seared her soul. Why when she looked into Nitro's eyes did she sense something of T. B. Mann?

She closed her eyes on the lights of General Hospital. A residue of the outline of the towers remained in her mind. Slowly it was replaced by another memory, one on which she could not close her eyes.

Standing on her balcony a few months ago, after she'd tested her health and vitality and found both strong, she'd issued T. B. Mann a challenge.

Game on, she'd told him. *Game on.*

Then it was summer. The hot days and warm nights had lulled her with their simple pleasures. Lulled that

bullet of rage if not to sleep, then into that twilight state
where the edges got fuzzy. She could almost, *almost* accept that T. B. Mann might always run free.

Did T. B. Mann know that? Did she and he now share
that blood bond, as powerful as parent and child, husband and wife? Was there an equal bond between murderer and victim?

Clearly, he was not through with her, and conse-
quently, she could not be through with him. "Who is
Nitro, you asshole? A messenger?"

In the still air, two steel tubes of the wind chimes
softly and harmoniously rang.

Vining didn't turn to look, knowing nothing she could
see had sounded the chimes. Instead she looked at the
lights of the Big G until the soft high notes had dissipated on the air.

SIXTEEN

Vining went around turning on lamps and fluffing
pillows, irritated that she cared.

She took a shower. She craved vegging out in pajamas,
but dug through her closet looking for something that
looked nice but not like she'd spent a lot of time prepar-
ing. She found a black sundress with a shirred bodice
that she'd bought for a barbecue at the home of her
mother's latest beau and slipped on flip-flops decorated
with sparkling plastic jewels that her grandmother, who
liked that sort of thing, had bought her. She twisted up

her hair and fastened it with a banana clip, leaving tendrils loose. Makeup would shout that she cared. She swiped on a little lip gloss. It wasn't about love, she told herself, it was about pride.

She took the photocopies of Nitro's drawings from her briefcase. In the kitchen, she paused to forage through the refrigerator, grabbing a slice of leftover pepperoni pizza and a bottle of sparkling lemonade. Her diet was miserable when Em was gone. Em had taken to doing much of the cooking, having declared it her new hobby. That was fine with Vining. Em was her anchor in so many ways. More than she wanted to admit. More than she dared share with the teenager. That was too big a burden for a daughter, and Vining knew it.

She went downstairs to the large former rumpus room that Wes had helped her transform into a bedroom and work area for Emily. Wes had bought Emily's computer equipment and paid the bill for a broadband connection.

Vining sat at Emily's desk. She was nearly face-to-face with a framed photo of herself when she was Emily's age. Her daughter had dug it out of some cardboard box in a back closet. The resemblance between mother and daughter was striking, down to the long straight nearly black hair, green-gray eyes, and Mona Lisa smiles. Neither were fans of cameras. Vining had adopted a closed-lipped smile to hide her overbite and the gap between her teeth. Emily's teeth were perfect, yet she didn't flash them. Both were reserved that way. Ironically, Vining had been in the camera's eye, her image published and broadcast, more than she ever thought possible.

Slung over the corner of the frame was the actual necklace that Vining was wearing in the photograph, a confection of crystals on web-like chains, a style popular at the time. It touched Vining that her daughter wanted those mementos. Vining guessed that she was a decent role model, but she didn't see Emily following her path into law enforcement. She thought the Job, although tough for women, made a good career, but Emily was too emotional. Emily was excited about the prospect of college, and was talking about big-name schools in other states. Vining guardedly encouraged her, privately praying she would decide to stay close to home. Emily was still toying with becoming a photographer or maybe a chef. This week, anyway. But lately she had decided that chefs spent too much time on their feet and worked crazy hours. Happily for Vining, Em had already loved and discarded two other occupations, ghost hunter and thanatologist.

Vining turned on the computer, logged on to her e-mail, and downloaded the photos Kissick had sent of Nitro and his necklace.

She looked at the shot of Nitro cowering on the bed, his head barely visible above his bent knees. She enlarged the image, zooming in on his eyes, making them larger and larger, until they disintegrated. She reversed the process, until they again had shape and substance. Smaller, smaller, until . . . *there*. She again caught a glimpse of that nameless something that made her think of T. B. Mann.

She'd watched Emily crop photos, and she fooled around with the software until she figured it out. She clipped out Nitro's eyes and eyebrows and printed the image.

Next she printed the photograph of the necklace being held between her hands.

She looked at Nitro's drawings.

One woman was not dead, but was being held at gunpoint. She was the only one wearing a uniform that suggested she might be a police officer.

One woman was trussed like a deer being bled out before butchering. She was wearing something resembling a pearl-and-pendant necklace. So was the one who had been stabbed to death in the closet, the one who Vining was certain was meant to be Johnna Alwin. The fourth drawing unmistakably depicted T. B. Mann's murder attempt on Vining.

The drawings included telling details. The nude woman hanging by her ankles was inside a ramshackle wooden building. The officer in uniform stood against a distinctive domed mountain that Kissick had thought was Morro Rock. Vining had since found a photo of Morro Rock on the Internet and agreed.

Then there was Detective Johnna Alwin of the Tucson P.D., stabbed seventeen times in a storage closet of a medical office building, as shown in the drawing.

The settings for all the drawings except the one of her were specific. Her drawing showed no background at all. But it did show how close T. B. Mann had stood to her.

Vining had learned about Alwin's murder while she was doing her private investigation into untimely deaths of female police officers. She'd been drawn to Alwin's case when she'd learned that the Tucson police detective had also been involved in a high-profile incident that had put her in the news, like Vining. As part of an undercover operation, Alwin had shot and killed a local drug dealer with mob connections. Vining had learned through a phone conversation with Alwin's husband that his wife had been given a pearl-and-pendant necklace after the shooting. It was accompanied by a small card with a handwritten note: "Congratulations, Officer Alwin."

The circumstances too closely mirrored Vining's to be coincidence.

Vining logged on to the Internet, brought up the Tucson Police Department's Web site, and looked at the memorial page for fallen officers. It included a photo of Alwin. The face in Nitro's drawing was a good rendition, done in the same hard-edged style of the other three drawings. Whoever drew it could have patched the details together from news reports.

Except for the pearl necklace.

During Vining's research on the Alwin case, in which she'd accessed information available to any citizen, she'd turned up no crime-scene photos.

Alwin's husband had told Vining his wife had been wearing the necklace when attacked. She was dressed to meet him for dinner when she was waylaid by an unexpected phone call from an informant.

Months ago, Vining had spoken to the lead detective on Alwin's homicide, Lieutenant Owen Donahue. He told her the case had been long closed, the murder attributed to Jesse Cuba, a drug addict informant whom Alwin had gone to meet. Cuba was later found dead of a heroin overdose in his seedy motel room. Also in his room was Alwin's purse with her blood on it.

The way the case had been tied up seemed too pat to Vining.

And there was the issue of the necklace.

It was presumably still in the Tucson Police Department's evidence room. Alwin's husband had his reasons for never having retrieved it. She didn't know the type of stone in Alwin's necklace. If Emily's death stone theory held, it would be garnet.

She looked at the photo of Nitro's necklace with its imitation sapphire.

She did a search on "birthstone sapphire" and learned that it was the stone for September.

Nitro's necklace was old. Did it belong to a woman murdered years ago? Was it the prototype for the others? Had Nitro himself been a victim of T. B. Mann? Or was Nitro the messenger, delivering the necklace for someone who was to be murdered in September? Vining wondered if she was the intended recipient. Or was it all a ruse, designed to mess with her head?

Nitro wasn't T. B. Mann, but he had to have a connection to him, even if T. B. Mann had paid him to carry out the deranged-silent-man charade.

Vining had never gone to Tucson to follow up on the Alwin lead. She checked flights to Tucson on the computer. There were many available. She couldn't leave town now, during the critical initial hours of a homicide investigation. Plus, she'd come close to losing her cool with Nitro in the jail earlier that day. Kissick hadn't mentioned it afterward, but cops were always watching. Especially each other. She'd worked hard to put the past behind her. The fact that she'd regained her old desk in Homicide showed that she'd succeeded. It could just as quickly be taken away again. There was a lot at stake in their line of work. Like a game of tiddlywinks, when pressure is put on an officer, you want to be confident that you know which way he or she will jump.

She heard a car stop in front of the house and doors open and shut. She quickly gathered her materials and closed down the computer. She jogged upstairs and stashed the drawings and photos in her bedroom. She lingered in the living room until she heard the key in the lock and the front door opening, then walked into the entryway.

"Hi, baby." Vining fiercely hugged her daughter.

"Hi, Mom." Emily unloaded the shopping bags that weighted her arms onto the floor.

"I'm glad you're home. Missed you." She gave Emily's dress a quick once-over and then said hi to Wes. She didn't move to make physical contact. Years ago, she had decided that a handshake was too formal and a hug was too personal, so she'd settled on a wave. He had never indicated that it bothered him.

"Sorry we got Em home so late." He lingered in the doorway, holding the handle of the girl's rolling suitcase.

"It's all right. I've been working late anyway."

"The big case. I heard."

"Sounds like everyone had a nice vacation. You did some shopping. . . ." Vining looked at the bags.

"You know Kaitlyn," he said.

"Mom, we saw an awesome photography exhibit. Dad bought me a print to put in my room."

"You want me to take this downstairs?" Wes indicated the rolling suitcase.

"That's okay. Just leave it there." She hated that she still found him attractive. He was thirty-five, but he had changed little since high school. He'd filled out, taking on a more manly physique, and his hairline had receded slightly. He'd started wearing his sandy blond hair trimmed closer to his scalp. He'd recently acquired an elaborate, colorful tattoo of bamboo trees on one upper arm. Kaitlyn had influenced his wardrobe. The entire presentation was decidedly hipper than when he and Vining had been married.

The way he looked at her made her glad she'd fixed herself up. Part of her still grieved. Part of her wanted him to suffer. She'd become reconciled to the fact that she might never get over being dumped by him. While she and Emily rarely spoke of it anymore—it was a fact of their lives, nothing to do about it, might as well fret over the weather—Vining knew that her father's abandonment was a scar Emily would always carry with her.

Emily did an angry pirouette to display the dress. "Well . . . ?"

It was strapless with a short jacket, white with embroidered black swirls around the hem. It made Emily look sophisticated. Vining had to admit it was cute, and it definitely looked more expensive than the frock they'd bought at J. C. Penney.

Vining shrugged, "It's cute, Em."

Wes hooked his thumbs into his slacks pockets. "Kaitlyn didn't mean to step on anyone's toes. She loves having a daughter to shop for."

It rubbed Vining wrong when Kaitlyn referred to Emily as her daughter. It wasn't inappropriate, but it still ticked her off.

"Mom, Kaitlyn said the dress we bought was tacky."

"Em, she didn't say tacky," Wes protested.

"That's what she meant."

"Emily, you were rude to Kaitlyn when she was only trying to be nice."

"*I* was rude?" Emily's eyes flared. "Kaitlyn said we were going to an *exclusive* restaurant and she wanted me to look *nice* in front of her parents. She picked up the Penney's bag like it had dog poop in it before she even saw the dress Mom and I bought. Then *you* got mad at *me* and said *I* hurt Kaitlyn's feelings. What about *my* feelings?"

"Kaitlyn meant well, Nan." Wes held out his hands, appealing to her. "It wasn't as bad as Emily is making it out."

Emily leaned toward her father, her face red, the tears building. "You don't understand, Dad!" She swatted the dress. "I *hate* this dress. I *hate* you for making me wear it." The tears flew from her eyes as she ran out, and they heard her footsteps pounding on the stairs to her bedroom.

Adolescence, in addition to filling out Emily's figure,

had awakened a previously hidden talent for high drama.

Wes frowned in the direction Emily had fled. "I don't know what's gotten into her lately."

Vining hiked her shoulders as if it should be obvious. "She's a fourteen-year-old girl. And you, Dad, made it worse by picking sides." She wagged her index finger. "Furthermore, it was insensitive and just plain wrong for Kaitlyn to insinuate that the dress Em and I bought was tacky."

"For the last time, she never said tacky."

Vining looked at him with incredulity. "There you go again. . . . And who the hell is Kaitlyn, former Supercuts hairstylist from a lower-middle class neighborhood in West Covina, daughter of a corrugated-cardboard-factory foreman and a part-time home-care worker, to put on airs? We're *all* poor white trash. Kaitlyn can bleach her hair, but those roots will keep coming back, even if she can afford to stay at the Four Seasons."

She brushed him aside and headed out the door.

"Nan, don't start anything," Wes said with alarm. "It's just a dress."

She turned back, her hand on the doorknob, and leveled a gaze at him. *"Just a dress."* She grunted with frustration.

The brand-new Mercedes SUV parked at the curb still had the dealer plates.

Vining distributed warm greetings. "Hello, Kaitlyn. Hi, Kyle and Kelsey. Aren't you two cute?"

She had to admit that the boys were adorable. "Look how big you are. Did you have a good time on your trip? Did you really? How fun. Hey, Kaitlyn, could I speak with you for a minute?"

"Sure, Nan."

"Could you step out of the car, please?" Vining's tone

conveyed that it wasn't a request. She didn't wait for a response, but walked a few yards away and stood with her hands on her hips.

Kaitlyn seemed baffled but climbed out of the car.

She had an attractive face that at first glance looked prettier than it was due to skillful hairstyling and makeup. Vining and she were nearly the same height, but Vining outweighed her by twenty pounds of muscle earned from serious weight-lifting at the gym. Kaitlyn's workouts seemed to focus on keeping her figure reed thin. Her arms looked liked tanned pencils. Vining thought she was even thinner than the last time she'd seen her, which hardly seemed possible. She was seven years younger than Vining, but her face looked gaunt.

Vining could have broken her in half, and had enjoyed many such fantasies in the early years, when Kaitlyn was whispering into Wes's ear while Vining was struggling to make ends meet and put food on the table. Vining's raging flames of resentment had cooled over the years, but she still had no use for Kaitlyn and her ilk. Yeah, she had a chip on her shoulder, but she'd earned it, every gram of it. She'd love to see one of them try to knock it off.

Now, not content to simply spend Wes's money and be happy, Kaitlyn had again dug the heel of her designer shoe–clad foot into Vining's business.

"Cute shoes." Kaitlyn pointed at Granny's jeweled flip-flops on Vining's feet.

"Thanks."

Kaitlyn tugged at her halter dress, which had a plunging neckline. Figure-revealing clothing seemed to be the clan uniform. Then Vining noticed something different. Cleavage. A lot of it. Kaitlyn had had her boobs enlarged. How had Emily missed passing on that gossip?

Kaitlyn noticed what had attracted Vining's rude attention.

"Oh . . . Guess you haven't seen these yet." Kaitlyn cradled her breasts in a manner that Vining thought she would never have considered before the enhancement. The inorganic material somehow put them in the public domain, a commercial product to be prodded and admired, like a nicely marbled rib eye.

"Wes bought them for my thirtieth birthday."

"But you just turned twenty-eight."

"I know, but after two kids . . . I needed it for my self-esteem."

Vining never knew quite how to respond to declarations of plastic surgery. "Ah, very nice." It seemed to work. "Hey, Kaitlyn, look. Regarding Emily and this dress issue—"

"I didn't mean any—"

"I don't care—"

Kaitlyn burst into tears.

Vining took her tears in stride. She'd made bigger and meaner people cry.

Kaitlyn turned her back to the house and car and began sobbing.

Vining wasn't completely callous to the woman's obvious distress. She put her hand on her shoulder. "Kaitlyn, what's going on?"

Kaitlyn choked out a sob while trying to speak, so Vining wasn't sure she'd heard her correctly. She hoped she hadn't.

"Say again . . ."

"Wes is having an af—" Kaitlyn clapped her hand over her mouth but soon tried again. "He's sleeping with this woman he's building a house for."

Vining was stunned. Wes was up to his old tricks again. She had always thought Wes's infidelity was her fault. Now she saw that it was a character flaw in him. Even the implacable sprite inside her couldn't gloat over this news.

She realized that she was probably the only one Kaitlyn had confessed this to. Maybe the only one she could tell. Who else would fully grasp the tragedy in all its colors and not blab the news around her social circle?

"I'm sorry, Kaitlyn. What an asshole . . ." Vining hugged her. She wondered if Wes was stupid or arrogant enough to leave Kaitlyn. She hoped practical concerns would make him think with his head instead of his crotch. He'd have to pay child support for three children and likely alimony to Kaitlyn.

"Come on, woman." Vining held Kaitlyn upright with her hands on her shoulders. "Your children are watching."

"I'm sorry for breaking down."

"It's all right. Does he know you know?"

"I confronted him when we were away."

Vining raised an eyebrow. That accounted for the excessive shopping. Here she'd been having her own pity party about having to deal with human carnage while they were lounging by the pool at a five-star hotel. One never knew what went on behind closed doors.

"Nan, I didn't mean to hurt Emily's feelings."

Vining wasn't sure how anger against Wes got translated into an attack on a teenager's dress, but she responded, "Apology accepted."

Wes came out of the house and walked toward the car. "Ready to go?" He attempted cheerfulness, but the look of trepidation he gave the two women, one of whom had obviously been crying, suggested he felt the wind from the guillotine blade speeding down.

Back inside the house, Vining sought Emily out in her room.

The girl was in her pajamas, the dress thrown over a chair.

Vining didn't rag her about not hanging it up. "It is a pretty dress. It's a sophisticated look for you. Kaitlyn meant well."

"Actually, I like it," Emily confessed. "I just wanted to wear the one we bought, and I didn't appreciate Kaitlyn's attitude."

"Well, hon, Kaitlyn's stressed right now."

"Something's going on between her and Dad, isn't it?" There was no hiding anything from Em.

"She's dealing with some things."

Emily picked at the appliquéd pattern along the dress hem. "Why is he like that?"

"Let's talk about this tomorrow." Vining didn't want to talk about it, and harbored a foolish hope that Emily would forget, knowing full well that she wouldn't.

She kissed her daughter on the forehead and headed for bed.

Vining got ready for bed, but was too wired to sleep. She poured a glass of milk, grabbed a box of vanilla wafers, her favorite one-after-the-other cookie, and curled up in Granny's favorite spot, the La-Z-Boy recliner in the TV room. She clicked on the classic movie channel and covered up with a chenille throw. After a while, she fell asleep watching an old movie about a murder, *A Place in the Sun*.

SEVENTEEN

*M*ark Scoville was in Pasadena earlier than he needed to be. He wasn't sure what he was going to accomplish, but here he was. All too often lately, he felt like a voyeur in his own life, spectator rather than participant, impotently standing on the sidelines, watching what might well turn out to be, he feared, a train wreck. The whole mess had probably started with gambling. But then his drinking fueled his gambling, so maybe it had started with alcohol. It was a chicken-or-egg dilemma, weakness taking nourishment from weakness.

In some ways he was living out his destiny: His father's perennial fuckup son had *really* fucked up. Once and for all. Amen.

He'd spent the morning at his office, following up on mundane tasks already being attended to by his efficient staff. The day-to-day business ran well without him. He had mastered one skill at which his father was inept: delegating. He was the big-picture guy, in charge of overarching decisions. As such, plus the fact that he was finding it impossible to concentrate or sit still, he decided to make the rounds of his local billboard faces, to make sure none had been hit with graffiti or were covered by trees or other obstructions. He'd also scout new locations. The billboard industry was notorious for squatting—illegally putting up billboards without the required permission or permits, collecting advertiser rent until the local city agencies discovered and acted upon the trespass. It had been a fun, father/son activity when old Ludlow was alive, heading out in the middle of the night with a crew.

Scoville had set off in the early afternoon intending to be in Pasadena to attend Bowie Crowley's reading and book signing that night.

After a few hours driving around, he thought about heading to one of the Indian casinos out on the edge of civilization, but didn't want to get stuck in drive-time traffic on the way back. He disliked those casinos, filled with Asians and Latinos, and considered it only out of desperation, like calling a therapist or an old friend whom he'd left on bad terms. Drinking, however, was more flexible. While surveying some of his billboard faces in the San Gabriel Valley, he'd stopped in a couple of bars, winding up in a Pasadena haunt of Oliver Mercer's where they'd raised a glass to the success of their partnership.

Mindful not to overdo, Scoville only drank Grey Goose and tonic, topping off his drink with more tonic water and ice. He wanted only to take the edge off. Keep his thoughts, swirling like toxic free radicals, from creating a deadly chain reaction.

With time yet to kill, he found himself at the last place he wanted to be—Mercer's house. Meandering through Pasadena, he'd come upon the Colorado Street Bridge, from which he picked out the house on the ridge beyond the freeway. While filled with dread at the thought of seeing the murder house, his car almost seemed to take him there against his own volition. The yellow barricade tape across the locked driveway gate and around the surrounding hedges warned: POLICE LINE—DO NOT CROSS. The bright plastic tape jarred him more than the images in the media of the blanket-draped corpses being rolled out.

He wasn't the only one there. A ghoulish driver had been bold enough to park in the driveway in front of the gate. A man posed a woman and two children for a photo with the house in the background. A couple of punks crossed the tape and jumped onto the bottom crossbar of the gate. They debated hoisting themselves over it.

A young man and woman in uniform carrying hand-held radios exited a dark sedan parked across the street. A patch on their sleeves said "Cadet." They looked like college students, the same age as the pranksters on the gate.

The family taking pictures didn't need to be asked twice. Giggling for having been caught, they scurried to their car and left.

The female cadet ordered the pranksters, "Come down off the fence."

"What are you? A girl scout?" one of them joked.

She held up the two-way. "I'll have a patrol car here in two minutes. So unless you want to be arrested for trespassing, I'd advise you to leave."

They did, piling into a high-end SUV, the noise from their squealing tires their final rebellious act.

The cadets returned to their car, parked in the shade of a tree.

Scoville got out of his Porsche 911 Carrera 4S. He crossed the street and got as close as the barrier tape would allow. He knew the cadets were watching, but he wasn't going to do anything. He just wanted to see the house one last time.

He'd always thought the minimalist structure looked like a shoebox with a second shoebox standing on end beside it. A narrow row of windows lined the first story.

A large round window was embedded near the top of the tower. Precisely trimmed vines cascaded over the roof. A flagpole atop the tower was barren. The exterior was gray on gray, and the interior, Scoville knew, was shades of white. The only color was provided by Mercer's copious art collection.

Scoville had been inside three times. Twice to pick Mercer up before heading to a meeting in downtown L.A., once for cocktails before dinner—an effort at team-building by the new business partners. That's when he and Dena had met Lauren Richards. Of course Mercer had warned Scoville prior to the dinner that, while he liked Lauren a lot and she was a great gal, inviting her didn't mean he was *serious* about her. That had caused Dena to dislike Mercer before she'd set eyes on him.

Standing in the street, his hands limp at his sides, the day's heat stored in the asphalt radiating through the soles of his loafers, Scoville's mind willfully skirted around the Grey Goose and tonic fog and went to the last place he wanted to go—inside that house. A kaleidoscope of images about what had happened and what might have happened swirled even with his eyes wide open. He shook his head to stop them, but they kept on, the lights spinning in hues of flesh, blood, and bone.

He vomited in the street.

He staggered to his car, fell against it with his hands on the hood, and retreated when the hot steel burned him. Veering away, he grappled with the car door, got it open, and plopped onto the driver's seat, his feet in the street. He looped his arm over the steering wheel to get his bearings. Again feeling nauseated, he flopped forward with his head between his knees, upchucking until he was dry heaving.

The cadets were watching. The houses on the street

were set far apart behind big yards. He imagined people peeking through their blinds at him.

Who cares? He was innocent. Wasn't he?

He grabbed a tissue from the glove compartment and wiped his mouth. He took a swig from a liter bottle of water he always carried in the car, swished it around his mouth, and spat it out. He poured some on a tissue and wiped his face, seeing the puddle of vomit in the street. Looking at it made him feel nauseated all over again. Time to get out of there.

Scoville cranked the Porsche's ignition. Hearing the engine's throaty rumble as he gunned the engine revived his testosterone and chased away his doubts. He peeled away from the curb and sped down the street. The Porsche's top was off, and the wind was in his hair.

He was fine. Everything was going to be fine.

Just keep your wits about you, Skipper.

The pep talk was comforting. His father had called him Skipper.

A big crowd had turned out to see Bowie Crowley at Vroman's, the landmark Pasadena bookstore, founded in 1894. People filled all the folding chairs and stood against bookshelves lining the walls. Some sat on the carpet while they waited for the ex-con murderer-cum-bestselling author and self-proclaimed reluctant celebrity.

Scoville had arrived in plenty of time to take any seat he wanted, but he selected one at the rear on the end of the aisle, making an unpleasant face each time he had to swing his legs around to let others pass.

He held his already-purchased copy of *Razored Soul* on his lap atop brand-new J. Crew khakis he'd bought in Old Pasadena to replace the ones he'd soiled when he'd gotten ill. He'd bought a shirt while he was at it, a madras plaid in pink and green that reminded him of something his father used to wear that was now, amusingly, cutting-edge hip. He'd had a cappuccino and biscotti at a café on the bookstore's first floor. He was feeling calmer and more clearheaded than earlier, when he'd lost it at Mercer's house.

Dena had called him while he was at the café, wanting to know if he'd be home for dinner.

"I don't know when I'll be home," he'd told her. "I'm doing rounds, like my dad used to do."

"You sound enthused. That's great."

"Now that this nightmare with Drive By Media is over, I can focus on our core business. I've neglected it too long. Everything okay with you?"

"Fine. So you won't be home for dinner."

"No, I think I'll watch the game at the club and grab a bite there. I won't be home until eleven or so."

"I'm just getting caught up on paperwork. See you later, Mark."

He snapped his phone closed. That was done.

The crowd grew. He was glad he'd arrived early. He glanced around, quickly facing forward when he saw something that disturbed him.

Brushing at nothing on his shoulder as an excuse, he looked out the corner of his eye. There was that guy again. He stood against a bookcase with his elbow hooked on one of the shelves. Scoville had first seen him downstairs. He'd been flipping through a book on cigars he was thinking about buying and saw the same guy watching him. The guy had been browsing through a book about having the perfect wedding on a budget. It was an incongruous sight.

Scoville sauntered past and saw the guy had the book turned to a page with photographs of models in white lingerie.

The word that came to Scoville's mind was *thug*. The guy might have been forty, and was beefy with olive skin. His oily hair was combed straight back, brushing his collar. A sheen of perspiration coated his apple cheeks and the rolls around his thick neck. He wasn't as tall as Scoville, but there was something menacing about him. When Scoville took the cigar book to the register along with a copy of *Razored Soul,* the guy was picking up trinkets at a display of Halloween decorations and, Scoville thought, still watching him.

Thinking he'd lose him when he went upstairs for the book signing, Scoville was jarred to see him standing right there, looking like a hulking mass of lard on a tray of petit fours.

When Scoville caught the guy's eye where he was standing at the bookcase, he didn't look away, but held Scoville's gaze, his dark irises barely visible beneath fleshy eyelids. Scoville jerked around to face front. Had the guy winked at him?

Maybe this character was some lowlife this Crowley had met in prison. Best to ignore him.

Deciding to forget about it, he opened a small handled shopping bag that had a gold sticker in the shape of a medallion on the front and took out a heavy lump in lilac-colored tissue paper. He unwrapped it, revealing a shiny chrome figure of a jungle cat in mid-leap.

"How beautiful," said the woman sitting beside him. She was of Asian descent, but either California-born or -raised given her speech. "Is that an antique hood ornament?"

"Yes, from a nineteen-thirties-era Jaguar. I found it at a little shop up the street." Scoville had suggested to Dena that they find such an ornament for her Jag. She'd of course had a negative, knee-jerk reaction, claiming that people used to be sliced up by such ornaments in car crashes, which was why, if they were installed at all, they were rinky-dink and had break-away wires. To hell with her and Ralph Nader. He thought the leaping cat was cool.

"Don't they have the best shops here? I love Pasadena."

Scoville noticed she wasn't wearing a wedding ring and appeared to be there by herself. She had several copies of *Razored Soul* in a bag by her feet. She was attractive. He indulged in a ten-second fantasy of him and her leaving the bookstore together, having a drink, and one thing leading to another leading to a tryst in a hotel room.

He had never cheated on Dena. There were call girls in Vegas, but he didn't consider that cheating. Things between him and Dena had been frosty for a long time. The separate-bedroom thing that had started as a work-week convenience had become a lifestyle. It was nice to have a woman look at him with something other than disdain or spreadsheets in her eyes.

"Are you going to put it on your car?" the woman asked.

"I was thinking of using it as a paperweight." He extended his hand. "I'm Mark Scoville."

"Hi, I'm Sally Kitamura." She pointed to Crowley's book on his lap. "Have you read it?"

"Not yet."

"Ohh. . . ." She sighed. "It's *so* powerful. I read it in one sitting. I didn't get up, cook dinner, do the laundry, nothing. I bought copies for my friends and family. It's scary and gritty, but inspirational too. Everyone should read it. I love the way he writes. His prose is spare but evocative. Hemingwayesque, I guess. Manly. Macho even, although I detest that word."

Her eyes widened as she was distracted by something behind Scoville. She gasped, then said, "There he is."

Scoville was quickly forgotten as Bowie Crowley made his way to the front of the room. After a gushing introduction by the store's promotions manager, Crowley took the podium. He was dressed in his trademark snug black T-shirt, scuffed motorcycle boots, faded Levi's button-front jeans, and a hand-painted leather belt with his name and red roses on it. Any fan knew the belt was made for him by his prison buddy, Spider, who was serving life without the possibility of parole for fatally shooting two people during a convenience store robbery.

"Thank you all for coming. I'm always blown away by the people who come out to see me, who've been touched by my book. It's awesome." Crowley tapped his closed fist against his heart. "Thank you. I'll read a little, then I'll take some questions."

"On anything?" a woman asked, accompanied by tittering from the crowd.

Crowley gave the questioner a guarded smile. "Sure. There are a few things I keep private, but most of my life is an open book, as they say."

He opened his book, nervously scratched at his face, and started reading from the beginning.

" 'Some people have it easy. Born lucky. By that, I don't mean just the good family, the nice house, the money. I mean they're born with a pure soul. They're just good people from the get-go. A person like that, you can take to the bank. No matter what things come down in their lives, they're going to do the right thing. Then there are people like me.' "

Scoville left without having his book signed, slipping away without saying goodbye to the cute girl, Sally. When he walked through the store on his way out, he kept his eyes open for the oily lug and was relieved when he didn't see him. He wrote the incident off to general weirdness in the universe.

He sat in his Porsche in the bookstore parking lot, having selected a dark spot that gave him a view of the back entrance and a Harley-Davidson motorcycle parked near it. He knew that Crowley rode a Harley. Scoville had thought about it a lot and decided the only thing he could do to get out of the mess he'd gotten himself into was to warn Crowley that some freak wanted him dead.

Scoville had turned off his cell phone and sat there in silence, chewing and spitting out his fingernails while he watched people get into their cars and leave.

He was startled when first one black-and-white Pasadena police cruiser and then a second sped into the parking lot. Four uniformed officers got out and jogged into the store. Scoville could hear chatter on the police band through the open windows of the patrol cars. More PPD prowlers arrived and more officers went inside the store.

The arrival of the cops caused the people leaving the parking lot to pick up their pace. It was nearly empty, and the store had passed its closing time.

A black sedan showed up, a police vehicle with chrome spotlights attached to both sides of the windshield. A good-looking Latino in a suit and tie got out and headed into the store. A uniformed officer called him Lieutenant Beltran.

Scoville thought the lieutenant looked vaguely familiar.

Finally, the police began returning to their cars and taking off. Two officers came out of the store leading a heavyset man whom Scoville had not seen before. His hands were cuffed behind his back.

Crowley brought up the rear, engaged in conversation

with the lieutenant, who was carrying a book. Scoville, sitting in the topless Porsche, could hear some of their conversation. They were talking about writing.

An officer tried to get the handcuffed man to go voluntarily into the back of a patrol car but he resisted when he saw Crowley coming.

"Crowley murdered my son. I've got a right to tell my side of the story."

Two officers were grappling to put him in the car when Crowley interrupted.

"Officers, if I might have a word with Donnie."

The officers looked at Lieutenant Beltran, who said, "Go ahead, Bowie. Just keep your distance."

"He's cool," Crowley said. "Aren't ya, Donnie? You're cool."

"Yeah, I'm cool. I'm cool." Baker stopped struggling, but the two officers still restrained him.

Crowley came closer. "Whatcha' doin', Donnie? What's happening here?"

"You're gonna have a word with me one day, Bowie."

"You don't want that, Donnie. Lookit chu. Now you're going to jail. Think Dallas would have wanted that for his old man?"

Baker bit his lip and looked away.

Crowley took a step closer to lay a hand on Baker's shoulder.

Baker kicked him in the shin.

"Get him outta here!" Beltran made a swooping motion with his hand.

"That's it, buddy, you're going to jail." The cops pressed Baker's head down while they shoved him into the back of the patrol car.

Crowley grimaced and limped. "You asshole. You always were a dipshit." He clenched and opened his fists.

"Look me in the eye and tell me that, Bowie."

Crowley took a step toward the patrol car as if he was about to take up Baker's dare, but an officer slammed the door shut.

Baker continued raging through the car window.

"You okay, Bowie?" Beltran asked. "You need medical attention?"

"Hell no. I'm fine." Crowley ran both hands through his hair and looked at the patrol car, which was taking off. A dimple formed in his cheek above his jaw as he clenched his teeth.

Baker had turned to stare at him through the back window.

Beltran hovered. "You want to press charges? Come down to the station and we'll take a picture of your leg."

"It's nothing." Crowley breathed heavily through his nose, watching the patrol car as it turned onto Colorado Boulevard and disappeared. Seeming to remember himself, he turned toward Beltran. "Thanks, Lieutenant. I'm good." He managed a tense smile. "Send me your screenplay. I'd like to read it."

Beltran flashed his broad smile. "Really? That's great. Thanks, Bowie."

"No problem." Crowley got on his Harley and took off.

The motorcycle's engine startled Scoville. All of his plans seemed to go to shit. After all, why should he care what happened to this pretty-boy murdering fuck? But then again, maybe it was the right thing to do. Hard to tell anymore.

Scoville thought he was doing a decent job of following Crowley without being detected, keeping a few cars between him and the Harley. He thought he'd lost him a couple of times, but was able to find the bright single headlight and taillight again.

Crowley took a route from Pasadena that was familiar to Scoville, entering the twisting Arroyo Parkway at its mouth, following it downtown, and then changing to the 101, the Hollywood Freeway. He exited at Melrose and headed west through the shabby neighborhoods of East Hollywood. At Rossmore, the eastern boundary of Hancock Park, Crowley turned left.

For Scoville, the route was not just familiar, it was *too* familiar.

Crowley slowed while he made a call on his cell phone and Scoville wondered if he was asking for directions.

A vague nausea again riled Scoville's stomach. It wasn't visions of blood and gore that tormented him now but thoughts of betrayal. Dena had interviewed Crowley on her show that morning. Why had she been so concerned about when he was coming home? He couldn't remember the last time she'd even asked. He knew the kids were gone.

When Crowley turned down Pinewood Lane, Scoville felt an acidic burn at the back of his throat as reflux rose. When Crowley turned into Scoville's driveway, Scoville kept driving.

Scoville parked his car around the corner and sprinted back. He skirted through the neighbors' yard, reaching over their unlocked back gate to pull the release. He knew they were still at their cabin in Big Bear. Their aged black Labrador wagged his tail and licked Scoville's hand, thinking the neighbor was there to feed him, as the Scoville family watched over the dog when the owners were traveling.

At the rear of the neighbors' yard, Scoville scampered up an oak tree, placing his feet on nails that Dahlia had driven into the trunk for footholds. Dena had told him about Dahlia's covert entryway onto their property. Easing over the spikes on top of his fence, he dropped into soft dirt behind the pool house.

He cursed when he tripped a motion-activated light. He waited for Dena's face to appear at one of the back windows. It did not.

Creeping around the side of the house, he peered into the kitchen. It was dark and empty. The dining room was too, although in the thin light from the night lamps, he saw a black blob on the light area rug. Could it be a black T-shirt?

Taking advantage of the old Tudor's many windows, he spotted more cast-off articles of clothing. The sight of each one was like a tender stab wound from a needle. Finally, he came upon them, the nightlights in the house and the diamond-shaped panes of glass creating a broken, dreamlike haze to the nightmare that was occurring before his eyes.

Crowley had Dena bent over a couch. Her back was arched, and she crushed the cushions between her fists.

Scoville could hear their moans. He watched. In spite of himself, he watched. He saw things differently. Maybe the freak had been right. The world would be a better place without Bowie Crowley.

EIGHTEEN

"More calls to Bennie Lusk," Vining said. "Must have been a big sports weekend."

It was Tuesday morning.

Vining and Kissick sat at one end of the large table in the conference-room-turned-war-room while Ruiz and Caspers took up the other. Each wielded a highlighting pen as they pored over pages of telephone records. Vining and Kissick were investigating Mark Scoville, and Ruiz and Caspers were on the trail of Lauren Richards's stalker, Dillon Somerset.

Vining and Kissick had learned that Lusk was a bookie who worked out of a hair salon in Burbank. Scoville's incoming and outgoing cell phone calls over the past twelve months showed an escalating number of calls to Lusk, which indicated a worsening gambling problem.

"Wish we could get Scoville's credit card data," Vining said. "I bet he gambles online."

"I'll take that bet and raise you." Kissick grinned. "Gambling is squeezing out the rest of his life. His business calls have cycled down, while his gambling-related calls have ramped up. Another call to the Wynn in Vegas. We can contact their security. If Scoville's a player, they would know what kind of dough he throws down."

"We know what makes him throw up," Vining said. "You heard about our two cadets seeing Scoville lose his cookies in the street in front of Mercer's house."

She felt energized, pumped up by the hunt. They were inching closer, peeling away the layers. Soon, she hoped, there would be that rare but glorious moment when they broke through and the truth spilled out like molten lava.

The other hunt, however, lurked in the background. She thought of Nitro sitting on a bed in a ward at the Big G, and counted down the hours until his release. She occasionally slipped from her slacks pocket the cropped photo she'd made of his eyes. Each time, it gave her a little shiver. She wanted Nitro at the Big G and not in jail for a reason. She had to act quickly.

The ticking clock on Nitro's incarceration had motivated her to call Lieutenant Owen Donahue with the Tucson P.D. She told him she'd like to come out and look through the Johnna Alwin homicide case files, as they might shed light on an unsolved attempted murder in Pasadena. He said anytime. That was Vining's problem: time.

She couldn't go to Tucson now, yet she had to. Was that T. B. Mann's plan? Pull her in too many directions, make her lose focus and let another murderer go? Let *another* murderer go?

"Somerset seriously needs to get a life." Caspers leaned over his documents with one arm circled around them on the table, as if protecting his plate from voracious brothers at dinnertime. "He called Richards like twenty times a day. One-minute calls. Calling and hanging up. Here's one that lasted three minutes. He probably connected with her and she told him to kiss off. She was cute, but man, no chick's worth that. Wake up, brother!"

"I'm having a bad feeling that Somerset is gone for good." Ruiz always frowned when he was doing detailed work, his dense eyebrows nearly forming a solid line. "His parents say he goes backpacking in these wilderness areas, and he's sometimes gone for weeks. He's into that survivalist, living-off-the-land crap."

He shook his head, his yellow marker motionless in his hand, not seeing the task in front of him but seeing his chance to snap the cuffs on a major bad guy fading away, and with it his big chance to prove his mettle as a homicide investigator. He was still having a hard time swallowing the fact that Vining had displaced him. It was a crock what Sergeant Early had told him about being rotated out as part of routine cross-training. He knew it. Worse, everyone knew it.

Vining tapped a highlighter pen against a page. "Dena Hale was spreading sunshine when talking about how everything was hearts and flowers between her and Scoville. What wife wants to put up with this level of gambling? These are not friendly wagers on a couple of favorite teams. This is a lifestyle."

"But Nan, he wins as much as he loses." Kissick joked, spouting the gambling addict's stock rationalization. "I spoke this morning with the owner of Drive By Media, the firm that wanted to merge with Marquis. He said Mercer thought Scoville was cooking the books. The real reason Scoville didn't want the merger to go through is because it would be revealed that he'd sucked the firm dry. Mercer felt Scoville had talked him into investing in Marquis not to expand but because he needed money to keep the doors open."

"Dena Hale . . ." Caspers let the name hang in the air.

After a beat, Vining said, "She's hot," timing it precisely to chime in with Caspers's identical pronouncement. She cackled maliciously.

Caspers was defensive. "She is. She's way hot." His cell phone rang, giving him an out. "Whassup, peckerhead? I'm gonna be there. You gonna be there? Ten o'clock. Later."

Ruiz gave his partner a baleful look. "You're going someplace at ten o'clock tonight? Better not be draggin' your ass in here tomorrow."

"It's my buddy's girlfriend's birthday," Caspers said. "Don't sweat it, T. I'm young."

"Youth is wasted on the young," Ruiz countered.

"Old people love to say that," Casper complained. "It's a crock."

Vining drew the highlighter across the page. "Tuesday,

August first, eleven-ten a.m., incoming call, sixteen minutes long from an eight-one-eight area code. I haven't come across this number before, have you, Jim?"

Kissick looked at the sheet she slid in front of him. He shook his head. "Eight-one-eight. That's most of the San Fernando Valley, with a gazillion people."

Vining picked her cell phone up from the table. "Let's see who answers." She placed the call and just as quickly ended it. "Number's out of service."

"Sixteen minutes," Kissick said. "Scoville's calls to his bookie barely last ten. Calls to his wife are done in less than five. He spends more time talking to his golf buddies than his wife."

He looked at Caspers. "Alex, you know who would be good to ask about your tattoo? Cameron Lam in SES. He's fluent in a couple of Chinese dialects. You know him?"

"Cam Lam. Sure I know him. Great guy," Caspers said. "Why would I want to ask him about my tattoo?"

"To make sure it says what you think it says."

"I don't *think* it says anything. It says 'crouching tiger.' "

Kissick rose from the table. "Just looking out for you, *brother*."

"Thanks, man, but I've got it under control."

"I'll find out who that eight-one-eight number belongs to."

"Wait a sec." Vining wrote a phone number on a scrap of paper and handed it to Kissick. "Another incoming call from a number we haven't seen before. Call was made yesterday at one-thirty-six in the afternoon. Eight minutes long. Area code nine-three-seven. Where's nine-three-seven?"

"I'll check it out." Kissick left the room.

She punched in the number on her department-issued cell phone.

After it rang several times, a man answered with a gruff "Hello."

"This is Detective Vining of the Pasadena Police Department. Who's this?"

"With whom would you like to speak?"

"The owner of this cell phone. Who are you?"

"I guess I'm the owner now, so you've reached the party to whom you wish to be speaking."

He was talking loud enough for Caspers and Ruiz to hear. They cracked up.

Vining's patience was thin. "And you are?"

"King Richard," he responded with gusto and a vaguely British accent.

Vining played along. "And where's your kingdom, King Richard?"

"The Strip, my lady."

Something about his speech put Vining in mind of an actor from the old movies she watched at night. Richard Harris or maybe Peter O'Toole. "You mean the Sunset Strip?"

"The same."

"This phone doesn't belong to you, does it?"

"They say that possession is nine-tenths of the law."

"King Richard, did you steal it?"

"My lady, I've held many an occupation in my day, but I've never stooped to thievery."

"How did you come to be in possession of this phone?"

"What if you answer a question for me first?"

Vining didn't like the idea of that. "Ask your question."

"What do you look like?"

That sent the men in the room over the edge.

"King Richard, I really need your help here." She resorted to the "take pity on the poor police lady" and "you seem like the kind of man who can get me out of a fix" strategies. She suspected he knew he was being played, but he gave her the information she needed.

King Richard lived on the streets in the Sunset Strip area. He had been foraging through a public trash can, still brimming since the holiday had postponed the garbage collection, when he had heard a phone ringing.

"And here we are, Detective Vining. It's our destiny."

While keeping King Richard on the phone, Vining wrote a note to Kissick, who contacted the West Hollywood sheriff's station.

After a couple of minutes, Vining heard sheriff's deputies arrive and confiscate the phone without incident. King Richard was a well-known local character. The phone's sign-on greeting indicated that it belonged to someone named Abby. Helpfully, she had a number in her contacts list labeled *Work*. Vining caught her there.

"I thought I'd left my cell phone in the airport bathroom," Abby said. "I reported it to their lost and found."

"A homeless man found it in a garbage can on the Sunset Strip."

"Sunset Strip?" Abby exclaimed. "That man stole it. That he-she or whatever he was. Here he was warning me that someone might steal from my bag and *he* stole my cell phone."

Abby relayed the story of her and her girlfriend's Sunset Strip encounter with the curious man who called himself Jill.

The tiny hairs on the back of Vining's neck prickled. This could be the oddball clue they needed.

"How old do you think he was?"

"Hard to tell. He had on heavy makeup. Forty?"

"Height and weight?"

"Wasn't real tall and he had on heels. Sandals with heels. And a French pedicure . . . Short, dark brown wig." Abby's voice trailed off as she recalled the scene. "He might have been five foot eight. Not fat, not thin."

Vining took notes. "Eye color?"

"Brown, I think. That reminds me. He had binoculars. He said he was looking at a hawk's nest on top of a building."

"Any scars, tattoos, distinguishing characteristics?"

"He had tattoos on his arms and shoulders. I don't remember what they were. But I remember he was ugly."

"How so?"

"Big hooked nose. Old acne scars on his face and neck. And with the makeup on top of it . . ."

Vining told Abby they'd return her phone after they'd retrieved any fingerprints from it. She told Kissick, "Our cross-dresser stole Abby's phone, made the call from the Sunset Strip, and dumped it. Scoville's office is on the Strip."

"I tracked down the owner of the eight-one-eight number," Kissick said. "Mr. Huan Yu Kang of Panorama City. He thought he lost his phone July twenty-ninth at the Municipal Court in Van Nuys. He was there suing his brother-in-law, who wouldn't pay fifteen hundred bucks he owed on a truck Kang had sold him."

"Small-claims court?" Vining said. "Wonder what other cases they had on the docket on July twenty-ninth. Doesn't tell us where the sixteen-minute call to Scoville on August first originated. We'll need a warrant to get the cell site data from the phone company to find out which phone tower the call pinged from. How good is your contact at AT&T?"

"We'll see. Want to take a ride out to the Van Nuys courthouse?" Kissick looked at his watch. "We can stop by the hair salon in Burbank where Scoville's bookie has his shop. And we can get a Cupid's hot dog when we're in the Valley."

Vining sadly shook her head as she gathered her work materials.

"Come on, Vining. What doesn't kill you makes you stronger."

"Tell that to my G.I. tract at three in the morning." She led the way out the door.

He followed her to her cubicle. "Take a Zantac. I have some in my desk."

"Zantac's your solution for everything."

Leaning in, he said, "Actually, sex is my solution for everything."

She looked over her shoulder at him. "Is that a one-size-fits-all solution?"

"If the shoe fits . . ."

She headed out. "Some shoes *are* more comfortable than others."

He thought about that. He didn't know what it meant, but it sounded good. He followed her.

As they took off, they drove past the front of the station, where Lieutenant Beltran was having another press conference on the front steps.

"Beltran in the spotlight," Vining said. "Our homicides again already?"

"No. You heard of that ex-con-turned-novelist Bowie Crowley?"

"Not another guy riding his criminal past to fame and fortune."

"Something like that, except I have to admit that this Crowley has literary talent. I'm reading his book. It's good. Last night, our guys arrested the father of the guy Crowley killed. He's been stalking Crowley and threatened him at a book signing at Vroman's. I think he's already out on bail, so I don't know what Beltran has to talk about."

"Probably likes his name being mentioned in the same breath as Bowie Crowley's."

NINETEEN

Scoville's bookie, Bennie Lusk, was not at the hair salon when Vining and Kissick stopped by. They suspected that he never was when cops came calling, slipping out a back door. The salon owner was a nice guy. He and Lusk had attended high school together thirty years ago. Wouldn't admit that Lusk was a bookie. Said he sold art reproductions out of the back of the shop. The owner claimed not to recognize a photo of Scoville.

At the Municipal Courthouse in Van Nuys, the detectives photocopied records of the small-claims-court cases heard on July 29. Along with Huan Yu Kang's case against his brother-in-law, another case heard that day was Alonso Mendoza versus Mark Scoville.

The detectives called Mendoza and learned that he had sued Scoville for the remaining two thousand dollars due on tile work he did in Scoville's home. According to Mendoza, Scoville claimed the tiles were laid unevenly and there were color variations in the materials.

Mendoza brought photos of the finished job to court.

He won his case. A few weeks later, he received a check for the balance due from Dena Hale.

The small-claims-court records proved that Scoville was at the same place the same day that Huan Yu Kang's cell phone was stolen. Three days later, August 1, someone used Kang's stolen cell phone to call Scoville and conduct a sixteen-minute conversation.

While Vining and Kissick were out, Caspers called to say he'd gotten ahold of his buddy with the Las Vegas P.D. The buddy had a buddy in security at the Wynn hotel who was familiar with Scoville. Said he was a high roller, throwing down five figures at a pop.

By early afternoon, Kissick was finally able to sit down with two Cupid's hot dogs. Vining joined him at an outdoor table in front of the hot-dog stand with a tuna salad sandwich from a nearby deli.

He bit into his hot dog, shedding sauerkraut and relish from the overburdened bun onto the wrapper. He wiped his mouth with a napkin.

"You missed some mustard."

He passed the napkin over his face again.

She rubbed the errant yellow blob off with her thumb.

He watched her as she pulled her hand away. "Thank you."

She picked up her sandwich. "You're welcome."

Her cell phone rang. It was Doug Sproul at the PPD, calling with the results of the criminal background checks he'd run on the thirty-two people who'd had cases in the Van Nuys small-claims court on July 29, the day Scoville was there.

"I turned up five with criminal histories, two females and three males. We've got DUIs, domestic violence, vandalism, drug possession, and one nice guy was busted for armed robbery and aggravated assault. I'll do a more thorough rundown on the males. AT&T got back with the cell site data on the August first call made to Scoville on Kang's phone. It originated from the vicinity of Niland, California."

"Originated from Niland?" Vining said for Kissick's benefit. "Where's that?"

"Turns out it's some burg on the eastern shore of the Salton Sea. Got a population of about eleven hundred people, mostly Hispanic. About fifteen percent are unemployed."

"The Salton Sea?" Vining repeated. "Isn't that out past Palm Springs?"

Kissick said, "It's a good hour and a half southeast of Palm Springs, out in the desert. Very strange place."

Holding the phone squeezed between her jaw and shoulder, Vining looked through photocopies of the July 29 small-claims-court cases. "Niland, Niland . . . aha. Defendant Connie Jenkins of Jenkins's Stop 'N Go Market, Niland, California. Plaintiff: Top-Notch Vending."

She read the plaintiff's description of the complaint. " 'Defendant owes me the sum of eleven hundred dollars and eighty-eight cents for product stocked in a cigarette machine at her business.' Says that Jenkins lost the case. Doug, can you run a DMV on her?" She gave the detective Jenkins's address.

She ate her sandwich while Sproul pulled the records. Kissick had finished both hot dogs and was scooping up the dropped condiments with a plastic fork. He chased it with the last of a large Pepsi while he reviewed the court documents.

Sproul came back on the line. "Connie Jenkins is seventy-four years old. Five feet tall. Ninety pounds. Gray over brown. Has a Niland home address. In her DMV photo, she looks like a white-haired grandma. I'll run her through NCIC and call you back."

"She's seventy-four," Vining told Kissick. "Why would

a seventy-four-year-old woman who lives near the Salton Sea call Mark Scoville on a stolen cell phone?"

After a while, Sproul reported back. "No criminal history. Owns Jenkins's Stop 'N Go and a couple of other properties in Niland. Got a six-year-old Saturn vehicle registered to her. Looks like a businesswoman and a citizen."

"Thanks, Doug." Vining ended the call. She said to Kissick, "How long to drive to the Salton Sea? Three to four hours?"

"Probably, given the time of day."

"I bet Connie Jenkins didn't drive herself to the Van Nuys courthouse. My grandmother wouldn't drive that far alone."

Kissick balled up the hot dog wrappers, got up, and shoved them and the empty drink cup into the garbage. "We could call her, pretend we're from Top-Notch Vending or something, but we have to be careful not to raise her or anyone else's suspicions. These calls made to Scoville on stolen cell phones are the first solid leads we have that he's hiding something. I don't want to blow it."

"Let's show Kang her DMV photo. See if he remembers seeing Jenkins at the courthouse and if he recalls her being with anyone. A tiny old lady in the company of a transvestite would stand out."

"Then let's take a drive out to Niland. See who's around, run some license plates. How many transvestites could they have there?"

"Mark Scoville's office is just over the hill. Let's pay him a visit right now."

"We can drive to Niland after," Kissick said. "Traffic will be better then anyway. We need to change into more casual clothes too. Get another vehicle."

Vining put on her sunglasses. They were sitting outside and Kissick was already wearing his. She put hers on because she was about to tell him a lie. "Can't go to Niland today. I have a doctor's appointment later. I've already rescheduled it once."

"Oh."

She saw his concern. If he was any other coworker, he'd let it go. He asked the follow-up question, showing that he was not just any other coworker.

"Everything okay?"

"Yeah. It's routine."

"Maybe I'll take a drive to Niland anyway."

"Not by yourself."

He got up. "I'll touch base with the local law. That would be, what? Imperial County sheriffs?"

"Sounds about right." She got up too and headed toward the car. She hated lying to Kissick, who was not only her partner but her friend. She'd also lied to Sergeant Early about the bogus doctor's appointment. She'd booked a flight to Tucson. Lieutenant Donahue had agreed to wait for her that evening to go over the Johnna Alwin case. T. B. Mann had upped the ante. She would match him.

TWENTY

Vining and Kissick found parking on Sunset near Scoville's office. They first walked across the street and down the block to Chin Chin, the restaurant where Abby Gilmore, the tourist from Ohio, had had the conversation with "Jill," whom she believed stole her cell phone.

Lunch was winding down, and the patrons, in $300 denim jeans, $200 T-shirts, and everyone looking rumpled, were migrating from their sidewalk tables into high-end vehicles without missing a conversational beat on their cell phones.

Kissick nudged Vining as they passed beneath a billboard advertising Chanel handbags that had a Marquis plaque on the bottom.

The Strip's buildings were lower than one might expect, one and two stories. The older ones were rehabbed to look fresh, and the new ones had been built to look old, but fresh. Some of the designer boutiques didn't carry women's sizes larger than ten.

"Look what they did to Ben Frank's." Kissick pointed at Mel's, a new diner designed to look mid-century. "Ben Frank's was a classic," he lamented. "Only in L.A. would they replace a genuine fifties-style joint with a fake fifties-style joint."

At Chin Chin, they found a waiter who'd worked the patio on Labor Day. They asked him if he remembered a male patron who was dressed as a woman.

The waiter gave a dismissive shrug. "This is the Strip, man. Men dressed as women. Women dressed as men. Androids. Vulcans. Whatever floats your boat. There might have been a guy like that. Yeah, I think there was, but I couldn't say I'd remember him if I saw him again."

Vining and Kissick thanked him and moved past the outdoor tables to stand on the sidewalk.

"Abby said Jill was looking at hawks," Kissick commented, peering through his compact binoculars. "I wonder if Jill was spying on Scoville. There's a rooftop patio on top of his building."

Vining had a look through Kissick's binoculars and

tried to tune out two women who were sitting at a nearby table.

"He's good-looking in the face but he's fat. Is it mean to tell him?"

The Marquis building had smoked-glass windows. The baby blue paint needed updating.

"There he is," Vining said. "Scoville's on the roof, leaning against the wall. Holding a drink cup. Wonder what's in it."

Kissick said, "Mercer and Richards were murdered last Saturday by a cross-dresser. The following Monday, Jill the cross-dresser steals a cell phone to call Scoville. Maybe Jill was concluding business with him?"

Vining was rankled by the women diners' conversation.

"I know body types. He'd look good if he worked out."

"Let's go." Vining skirted around a man with dread-locks interwoven with long metallic ribbons that trailed down his back.

They passed a bookstore with a large display of *Razored Soul* in the window.

"There's your buddy. Hot stuff," Vining commented, looking at Crowley's beefcake publicity photo.

"Does he turn you on?"

She looked at him with raised eyebrows. "He's not my type."

"What is your type?"

"What is this heightened sex thing with you lately?"

"I don't know. Life's short."

Her comment ended the discussion. "I already knew that."

The receptionist in the first-floor lobby was young, attractive, and polished, and probably thought she was skilled at keeping the world away from the inner sanctum of Marquis Outdoor Advertising.

Vining and Kissick didn't pause as they sped past her, holding out their shields.

The defense the receptionist mounted consisted of her rising from her chair and exclaiming, "Hey!" at Vining's and Kissick's backs as they climbed the exposed stairway.

Whenever Vining was successful at such a tactic, she wondered why citizens weren't better versed in their civil rights. Cops didn't have unrestricted access to private property.

On the third floor, they encountered a man dispatched to intercept them. He was earnest and young, and had been given a thankless job for which he would undoubtedly get his ass chewed by Scoville when he botched it.

Shields still in hand, the detectives sailed past him as he sputtered that they were to wait downstairs.

"We'll just be a minute," Vining said reassuringly as they circled the suite, cruising the corner offices until they found Scoville in the largest one with the best view. They went inside, closing the door on the minion.

Scoville was yammering into the phone, "I don't care if he's in court. I need him *now*." He stood when Vining and Kissick entered, slamming down the phone at the same time.

Vining put on her sweetest smile. "Hi, Mark. Howyadoin'?"

"You two can't burst in here like this without a search warrant. This is private property. I need to see a warrant."

Kissick took up his usual position, leaning against a wall. Vining had already turned on a microrecorder in her pocket.

"Search warrant?" Vining appeared bewildered. "We

just want to ask you some questions, Mark, not dig through your desk. We're here to verify a few facts, that's all. Will you help us do that?"

Scoville was neat and clean. His knit shirt bore the logo of the Wilshire Country Club on the breast. The creases on his chinos were knife-edged. His eyes were clear, the whites too bright, suggesting an application of Visine. His bearing was not as crisp. He grappled for words, and his movements were labored, suggesting he was either drunk or suffering from a powerful hangover.

Vining thought she detected alcohol behind the menthol aroma of the strong mints he was chewing. A drink cup with a lid and a straw was on his desk, the surface sweating condensation, leaving a ring on the coaster beneath it.

"I'm not talking to you without my attorney present," Scoville protested. "How do I get you out of here? Do I have to call the sheriffs?"

Vining winced as if wounded. "Mark, I'm confused. When we chatted the other day, you offered to help in any way you could. You volunteered to take a polygraph and we set it up. Then, next thing we knew, you left a message canceling it. Wouldn't take our calls. Didn't want to see us. Now you want your attorney here. What's changed?"

Scoville stood behind his desk as if it was a barrier.

"What's changed is I was naïve about the police. How you guys operate. You're desperate to hang those murders on somebody, and you'll twist anything I say to do it. I have a family and a business to consider. Bringing in an attorney was my wife's idea. She's the one who opened my eyes to what you guys are capable of."

"Mark, like I said, we're here to verify facts. It's routine. You can save everyone a lot of time and trouble by talking to us now, or we can bother your friends, family, and employees trying to track this stuff down." Vining apologetically raised her hands. "I know it's tedious. It's tedious for us too. Since you have nothing to hide, getting the facts straight can only help you. Am I right?"

Scoville ran a hand over his thinning hair and looked at the phone, waiting for the attorney's call.

"We'll be out of here in ten minutes tops," Vining said.

"I'm not talking without my attorney, and he's in court."

"In court? It could be hours before he's free. We'll just have to wait in the lobby. If you won't let us do that, we'll wait on the street near the front door. The three of us know you've got nothing to hide, but your employees are going to wonder why a couple of detectives are hanging around."

"I'd like to hear *that* water cooler gossip," Kissick added.

Scoville hungrily eyed the drink cup.

"Mark, it's simpler if you just help us out." From her briefcase, Vining took out copies of the forms pertaining to Alonso Mendoza's small-claims suit against Scoville and handed them to him.

"What's this? That small-claims-court thing?" He reluctantly took the papers, dropping into the chair behind his large mahogany desk. "What does that have to do with anything?"

"Tell us what happened that day." She didn't wait for an invitation but sat in a chair facing him.

He looked through the papers twice. "I refused to pay that Mendoza guy because he did bad work and he wouldn't fix it. The idiot judge sided with him." Beads of perspiration formed high on his forehead and on his scalp among the sparse strands of dark curly hair.

"Why are you asking me about this?" He set the

forms on the desk in front of Vining. While pulling his hand back, he snagged the drink cup, took a long drag through the straw, and set it back down. His hand had begun to tremble.

"You seem troubled, Mark." Vining affected a look of concern.

"I'm not troubled. I'm confused about why you're bringing this up. We paid Mendoza what he wanted."

"Something happened that day at small-claims court."

Vining noticed Scoville's eyes change from uneasiness to fear.

"A man named Huan Yu Kang had a case the same day as yours. His cell phone was stolen at the courthouse."

Scoville shrugged. "So what?"

"Someone used Mr. Kang's stolen cell phone to call you on August first."

Scoville began breathing through his mouth. "Call me?"

"Call you, for a sixteen-minute conversation."

"Must have been a wrong number."

"For sixteen minutes?"

Scoville took a handkerchief from his back pocket and wiped his forehead. "Dahlia, my stepdaughter . . . She uses my phone when she blows through the minutes on hers. Must have been one of her friends calling her."

Kissick shifted his feet. "You ought to get yourself one of those family plans. You know, the shared minutes."

"Yeah. Right. I'll look into that." Scoville drew circles on his desk with his fingers.

"That's what I've got with my two sons."

Scoville acknowledged Kissick's comment with a lack-luster raise of his eyebrows.

Kissick pushed away from the wall and left the office, not offering an explanation.

Scoville frowned as he watched him leave.

Vining didn't miss a beat. "What's interesting, Mark,

is that yesterday, Labor Day, you received another call. This one was eight minutes long, also made from a stolen cell phone."

Scoville again shrugged and began toying with a Mont Blanc pen that had been his father's favorite.

"This phone was stolen from a tourist visiting from Ohio. Funny, but it was stolen from her right down the street at Chin Chin." Vining hooked her thumb in the direction of the restaurant.

"I know where it is," Scoville said with irritation.

"The tourist says the individual who she thinks stole her phone was looking through binoculars in the direction of this building. Is somebody stalking you, Mark? Is there something you want to tell us?"

Scoville began shaking his head without pausing, a tiny movement, back and forth, like a bobblehead. He huffed out a laugh. "I don't know why anybody would watch me. Dena's had people follow her before."

"What were you doing at Oliver Mercer's house yesterday, Mark? A couple of our cadets reported that you vomited in the street."

Still staring at the pen and shaking his head, Scoville added a jostle of his shoulders. "A person can't go to Pasadena without the local cops knowing?"

The door opened without a knock and Kissick returned. "I called your wife, Mark. She says your stepdaughter never uses your cell phone." He resumed his position leaning against the wall.

Scoville's face flushed. "How the hell would she know? She doesn't even know where that girl is half the time." He bolted from his chair. "You two need to leave. If you don't get out right now, I'm going to sue both of you, the Pasadena Police Department, and the city."

Vining slowly rose, holding her arms open. "We're going, Mark. No problem. Didn't mean to disturb you.

We're all on the same team. We were just hoping you could help us sort out these unusual circumstances. People calling you on stolen cell phones. Someone watching your building. Maybe watching you. You throwing up in front of Mercer's house. And Mark, we've found out that you have some gambling issues."

"Issues? Who told you that?"

"Lots of people."

"I like to gamble. So what? It's not illegal." Scoville snatched the cup and thirstily pulled through the straw.

Vining pointedly looked at the cup. "We're hearing about alcohol problems too."

He set the cup down. "I have a few drinks every now and then. Whoever you're talking to is out to get me. Who's telling you these stories?"

"It doesn't matter, Mark. What matters is that I can see you're experiencing a lot of distress right now. You seem to be in a lot of pain. Holding a secret inside can really tear you up. Help us help you, Mark. You had your issues with Mercer, but no one deserves what happened to him. Certainly Lauren didn't deserve what happened to her. Two little children without their mother . . ."

"I told you, I don't know anything. You said you were leaving."

"We are leaving, but you seem so nervous and upset. You're drinking right now. I can smell the booze on you. You're a mess. Your family has to be suffering too. We can help, Mark."

He held his hand in the direction of the door. "We're through here."

"Sure, Mark. Whatever you want." She picked up her briefcase and took a file folder from inside.

"One last thing . . . You asked me what happened to Oliver and Lauren."

She tossed crime scene photos on his desk faceup, one after the other, arraying them as if dealing cards.

Scoville leaned on his hands against the desk. He blinked, not taking it in, his mouth gaping.

"That's what happened to them, Mark," Vining said.

Scoville wrenched himself from the photos and turned his back to the detectives. "Just go."

"Mark, it's clearly tearing you up. You can't live with this."

"Go."

TWENTY-ONE

It was dinnertime and the Scoville/Hale home was quiet. One wouldn't think the sprawling mansion would be anything but quiet, yet Hale had learned the design was an effective conduit even for sotto voce conversations held in distant corners. Normally, the silence would have been ambrosia to her, but tonight she found it unsettling to be left alone with her thoughts.

She had polled the kids about what they wanted to eat. On a normal Tuesday night, she would have cooked dinner. She avoided too many meals out or brought in, but it was the last week before school started, it was hot out, and frankly, she just didn't feel like cooking. They had agreed on a local family-owned Mexican place. Hale had left a message on Mark's cell phone an hour ago and had yet to hear from him. What else was new?

Luddy was in the family room, busy with his Nintendo

Wii. Dahlia was in her room, probably on the telephone or the computer, or both. And watching TV, while listening to her iPod. At least she was home. Hale was surprised when Dahlia told her she was going to hang out at home. Luddy declined Hale's suggestion to invite his friend who lived down the street, saying he was tired—unusual for him. The eight-year-old normally went full-bore all day until he collapsed into bed at night.

The situation with Mark was taking its toll on their children, and it pained her to see it. She embraced the Serenity Prayer, but recognizing its essential truth did nothing to make her feel serene tonight.

Mark was Lord-only-knows where. She hadn't seen him last night, even though he had slept in his suite of rooms, or all day today. His comings and goings and his behavior when he deigned to be around had been erratic before the double murders and were worse now. She refused to believe that Mark had had anything to do with the murders. Still, being the dutiful wife and standing by her man was especially hard in a loveless marriage.

She couldn't get what had happened yesterday with Bowie, that long, wonderful day, out of her mind. She felt a stab of shame thinking about it, but that didn't keep her from mentally going there again and again. She savored it all, starting from when she'd first laid eyes on him at the TV studio. His back was to her, and she'd done a double take at his butt and thighs in his well-worn jeans, the fabric softened so that it hugged his body just so. She remembered holding on to that butt, flesh against flesh. She felt tingly just thinking about it and wanted him all over again. All over.

She had seen his photo before. So when he'd turned to face her, she'd expected the square jaw and deep-set eyes, the sensitive lips. The photographer had tried to convey angst behind the macho swagger that she had figured was artifice. But when he'd turned and smiled . . .

She'd remembered her manners. "Hi, I'm Dena Hale. Very nice to meet you, Mr. Crowley."

"Call me Bowie, please. I'm happy to meet you. I'm a big fan. You're popular in San Quentin. We got some of the L.A. stations there."

"I'm big in San Quentin?"

"That's not as bad as it sounds. Those guys know what's good on TV. They watch a lot of it."

When she was younger, she used to joke to her friends that she fell in love at first sight once a week if not more often. She had been a poster child for the lost cause of those looking for love in all the wrong places. It was tied up in a bad childhood, narcissistic, substance-abusing parents, and the rest of that sad-sack genesis of a zillion tear-soaked tissues and therapy sessions. After tough work on herself, she'd cleaned up her act and married Mark, a businessman, owner of a hot restaurant, a man of means. When one of her friends, after a few cocktails, proclaimed him a milquetoast and "not someone I'd ever imagine you with," she had written off the catty remark as jealousy. What one friend had said, others were thinking, for sure.

Her friends didn't know Mark like she did. She knew he didn't fit the model of the perfect mate she and her friends had fashioned for themselves—*GQ* meets *The Wall Street Journal*—but to her that just showed how shallow they were. Beneath Mark's mildly dumpy exterior was surprising depth and a capacity for fun. She had once loved him deeply. Only later would she realize how closely their fun was tied in to alcohol and how what they considered fun was mere recklessness. She was only now plumbing those dark corners of her psyche.

Spinning out her car and plowing it into a telephone

pole on the PCH in Malibu after a "normal" night of drinks and dinner with friends had been her wake-up call.

Mark agreed, one tear-soaked night, that they needed to clean up their act for the sake of their kids. They dug in, the two of them, a team, and made it happen.

Time passed. Mark's father died.

Through faith and sheer will she had remained centered while Mark had floundered. They began cycling in the orbits of different planets, held by gravity from a different source. Now the separation in their lives was no longer benign indifference. The gambling, boozing, and whoring—she'd known about all that. Now there were two murders. Now there was Bowie.

That moment at the studio when he'd turned and offered his hand, a thought had entered her mind like a soothing balm, yet had struck her with sufficient force to make her feel like she'd been hollowed out, scraped clean, renewed.

The thought was: *I'm home.*

She was at the desk in her suite of rooms, addressing envelopes for Dahlia's eighteenth birthday party. Using her calligraphy pen, she painstakingly wrote out each one with swoops and curlicues. It would be much easier to just print address labels off her computer, but she liked the little personal touches that made life special. Genteel. A nod to times past. She and Dahlia had picked out the invitations together—velum attached to card stock backing with ribbons—and had them printed at the stationery store. It had been a fun mother-daughter time. She wistfully imagined doing the same thing for Dahlia's wedding.

After admiring her work, she set an envelope in the finished pile and picked up a blank one. She looked up to see Luddy at her elbow.

"Hey, chief. What's up?"

"Just watching."

He peered over her shoulder as she completed an address and waved the envelope in the air to dry the ink.

"You want to try? There are more pens in the box."

She began another. Luddy silently remained by her side. He picked up a lock of her hair and drew it through his fingers. He'd always loved to touch her hair, and she liked the gentleness of his touch.

She leaned into him and gave him a kiss on the cheek. "Something on your mind, pal?"

"What's going on with Dad?"

That was her boy. Direct. Unsubtle. An admirable personality trait, but one that required tempering or it would get him in trouble as he grew older.

She stopped working to look at him. Her old soul. Her deep thinker. Why did she imagine that she could shelter him from Mark's behavior? Wishful thinking.

He wasn't looking at her, but at the strands of hair he held. He released them and grabbed another lock at her scalp.

"Dad's been drunk a lot again."

The "again" cut her. She swiveled her chair and took his hands in hers. The dismay in his eyes nearly undid her. She burned with anger at Mark for having caused this. She could handle just about anything, but she couldn't tolerate someone hurting her children. She'd dreaded this moment with Luddy. He took family disturbances harder than Dahlia, who had always been more inward-directed than her brother, more concerned with herself and her issues. As long as her life wasn't affected, she cared little. Dena had worked to balance this trait with mixed success, fully aware of where that could lead the teenager.

While a happy boy, Luddy had always been the more

sensitive and intuitive of her children, aware of slight changes in his environment and in the people close to him.

She took a breath before beginning. "Luddy, things have been tough lately for Daddy. He was close to Mr. Mercer and he liked Mrs. Richards a lot. Their deaths were shocking, and it has affected Daddy. But he's going to be okay, sweetie. We're going to be okay." It would be years before he would realize the multitude of ways she'd painted a brighter picture to spare him. She hoped that he would at least understand and respect it.

He frowned, as he did when he was in a dark mood. His supple young skin was too elastic to form wrinkles, but made three ridges between his eyebrows. Dena visualized the creased brow of his adult face.

"Why does Daddy keep getting drunk? It makes him sick."

A voice sounded in her head.

Your father is weak.

Who was she to call Mark weak? Standing with Bowie on the terrace of the Malibu house, the coolly logical part of her mind had warned: Don't do it.

She had nerve, calling Mark weak, even if only in her mind.

With her thumb, she smoothed the ridges between Luddy's eyebrows as if she could force the worry from him. She pulled him into her arms and hugged him hard, breathing deeply of his neck. He was growing up quickly, but she thought she could still detect a whiff of that sweet baby scent, that fresh pure smell that was inevitably slipping away. She had the sad realization that recent events had hastened his march into adulthood.

She wanted her children's lives to be what her childhood hadn't been—happy and carefree. From her own experience she knew that sad, tough early years marred a person, like a strawberry birthmark. The stain faded over time, but never completely disappeared. One could always find it, if one looked hard enough.

As she gazed into her son's troubled eyes, she knew that the chickens had come home to roost.

"Sometimes adults do things that are hard for children to understand. Please always remember one thing, Luddy. Your daddy and I love you very much."

She tried a smile. It felt stiff and false. She kept it on anyway. Smiling was part of her profession. "Everything's going to be fine. Okay?"

His eyes grew hopeful. "Okay."

She released him. "Go get your sister and let's go eat."

"Great. I'm starving. Aren't we going to wait for Dad?"

"He has some things to take care of." One lie following another. It was all too easy.

Luddy again took her hand. "Mom, don't worry."

"I'll be down in a minute." She swatted him on the butt as he ran out.

She barely made it to the door, quietly closing it, before she broke down. She stumbled to the bathroom, sobbing, leaning against the sink. She wet a washcloth with cold water and pressed it against her face.

Snuffling, she looked in the mirror and splashed on more cold water to reduce the puffiness. She administered Visine and began fixing her hair and makeup, still feeling shaken.

She didn't know much right now, but she knew one thing. Her fling with Bowie Crowley was not helping anything. When something deep inside her began to wail at the thought of giving him up, she drowned it out with that cool voice of reason she'd been ignoring.

"It was a one-night stand during a time of emotional distress. It's over."

As for Mark, one day at a time.

TWENTY-TWO

*K*issick reached Indio, the ugly stepdaughter in the strip of fashionable desert towns that began with Palm Springs. Continuing south, he passed through the aptly named town of Thermal before reaching Highway 111, which would take him down the Salton Sea's eastern shore. The ribbon of highway slithered across the desert, moving up and down as if riding rolling ocean waves. He drove alongside a long train hauling containers from China and FedEx shipping trucks along the Southern Pacific tracks.

The sun was slipping behind the Santa Rosa Mountains to the west, tipping the peaks of the Orocopia and Chocolate Mountain ranges to the east with purple, and turning the Sea into a golden mirror. The land exulted in contrasts. Fields abundant with grapes, bell peppers, and cows grazing on alfalfa were across the highway from the flat expanse of natural desert with its sandstone, sagebrush, and manzanita. The flatlands between the mountains on the east had been appropriated by the military for live bombing areas.

Fields of overgrown palm and date trees, remnants of building foundations, and partially constructed concrete walls attested to abandoned moneymaking schemes. The area had lured dreamers for decades. Early in the last century, the Salton Sea was born because of a miscalculation in entrepreneurial vision on the part of men who sought to make the desert bloom with irrigation water from the Colorado River brought across the mountains via canals. Southern California was adept at expropriating others' water. An engineering mishap diverted the Colorado River into an ancient lakebed crusted with salt, creating the largest lake in California, thirty-five miles long, fifteen miles wide, and 195 feet below sea level.

The breach was finally repaired. The Imperial and Coachella Valleys became important agricultural regions. Visionaries then set their sights on the Sea as a vacation destination. But its glory days of speedboat regattas and celebrity sightings in the fifties and sixties were long gone, the shoreline resorts destroyed by hundred-year storms, the creeping salinity of the Sea— now 25 percent saltier than the ocean—and the slow determination of the desert. With no outlet, the water evaporated, leaving salt behind.

The Sea, against all odds, remained, fed by agricultural runoff. It still has its promoters, claiming the reports of its death are widely exaggerated. As the largest inland body of water on the Pacific flyway for migrating birds, it attracts one of the greatest concentrations of wildfowl in the country. Shortly before Kissick's visit, birders came from distant corners to see a rare Ross's Gull, an Arctic bird that flew several hundred miles farther south than normal, to feed in the muck.

Kissick knew the Sea was close when he detected its unique smell of sulfur and decay. It was especially pungent during the late summer, when algae overgrowth caused the tilapia, the only surviving fish species from those seeded decades ago, to die in even greater numbers.

The powerful odor was potent enough to waft to the

tony boutiques in Palm Desert, thirty-five miles north-west.

Kissick drove past the once-hopeful shoreline towns—Mecca, Corvina, Desert Shores, Bombay Beach—held together by paper clips and duct tape. Cobbled-together mobile homes and abandoned hotels lined broken streets near collapsing boat docks. Souls seeking respite from the rat race lived here, alongside those on the run and those who had washed up, like the beached tilapia gasping for air.

He entered Niland. The commercial district was right on the highway. There was a bar, the Ski Inn, a remnant from the area's salad days. There were dune buggies and vintage motorcycles in front—a gathering place for aficionados of the obscure. There was a small hardware store and a five-and-dime. A take-out stand advertised hamburgers, tacos, and pupusas.

The buildings were low to the ground, like any desert town, as if avoiding looking the sun in the eye. Most were built of utilitarian concrete blocks. Some were painted baby blue. Others sunflower yellow. Others pink. The cheap paint was the sole stylistic flourish.

Jenkins's Stop 'N Go Market and gas station stood out. It was on a big corner lot. Kissick pulled onto a side street off the highway across from Jenkins's to have a look. A neon sign on a pole brilliantly announced the store name in yellow and green. A series of red arrows flashing in a moving arc directed motorists inside. A wooden sign on the roof was encircled by chasing white lights.

There were three gas pumps. A sign on the road announced the price per gallon for regular, unleaded, and diesel, along with the price of a carton of Marlboro Lights, a six-pack of Bud Lite, and a gallon of milk. Bait was for sale. The property was surrounded by a fence made of chrome car bumpers atop wooden posts. The red stone mini-mart was built in a hacienda style, with arches lining a covered porch.

Behind the gas station was a house in the same style as the mini-mart, surrounded by a chain-link fence. The front yard boasted a well-established cactus garden with some otherworldly looking specimens as tall as the tile roof. Succulents were tucked between decorative boulders. Parked in the driveway in front of the detached garage were a tired Saturn sedan and a perfectly restored Triumph TR6 sports car painted British racing green. Kissick guessed it was from the seventies. The lights from the house and porch picked up a metallic flake in its undercoat.

Kissick didn't see anyone around. He took off, crossing the highway and heading down Main Street. On the corner of the building across from Jenkins's was a hand-painted sign that said "Salvation Mountain," with an arrow pointing toward the Chocolate Mountains.

The domiciles in the town were nearly all mobile homes on lots demarcated by chain-link fences. Two and three were slammed together, sometimes with a brick chimney rising from one end among the aluminum siding, like a granite headstone in a cemetery.

Yards were landscaped with cacti, succulents, and colored gravel or left natural with hard-packed sandy dirt and dry scrub brush. Grass and flowers, while rampant in the gated golf-course desert communities to the northwest, were rare luxuries here and were as carefully tended as hothouse orchids. Statuary abounded: wishing wells, cement burros, deer. Found objects—auto parts, farm tools, old mining implements—were transformed into decorative items. Some decorations, such as the plastic Holstein on the roof of one house, had no discernable genesis, like many of the people who ended up in this desert hamlet.

Kissick found the sheriff's substation. It was a square, flat-roofed prefab building on a dry grass lot where a tall flagpole flew the U.S. and California flags. Shades were pulled down inside over the windows. A window air conditioner hummed. A wooden placard on posts announced that this was the Imperial County Sheriff's Department in white with green letters, matching the colors of the SUV in the driveway and the patrol car at the curb. In the back was a satellite dish.

Beside the sheriff's substation was an old one-room jail, circa 1920, with thick walls and a pitched roof. Railroad ties braced the shingled awning over the porch. Old wagon wheels adorned the walls. The small windows in the front door and around the sides were fitted with thick iron bars. On the slab floor inside, a sleeping bag was wadded in one corner.

Across the street, people sat in resin chairs on the porch of a mobile home, talking and laughing. They were young Latino adults, friends and family, having drinks and kicking back after the workday was over. All talking stopped when Kissick got out of his car and walked up the front path to the sheriff's substation.

Just then a middle-aged man drove up in a mammoth Chevy Suburban. He wore a well-creased Angels cap over a brush cut. His short-sleeved Hawaiian shirt was snug around his belly over rumpled khakis.

Earlier in the day, Detective Mike Arnold had told Kissick he would be driving his wife's " 'burban." There was a trailer hitch on the back. A bumper sticker said: "My child's an honor student at Desert Middle School."

"Mike? Jim Kissick. Thanks for coming out on such short notice." Arnold had told him that the substation was not manned all the time. Any deputies there were based out of El Centro, thirty-five miles south.

"No problem. Welcome to Niland."

"Gee, thanks. Not much to do around here," Kissick observed.

"Nope. Just drink, smoke, talk, and fuck. This time of year, it's too hot even for much of that."

Arnold knocked on the door of the substation. A young deputy opened it. His nametag said R. Villalobos. The short sleeves on his dun-colored uniform barely hid a tattoo on his upper arm.

The interior was as spartan as Kissick had expected from the outside. A couple of desks, chairs, phones, computers, and maps.

"What we've got in Niland is a lot of drugs," Arnold said. "And everything that comes with it. There's high unemployment. Lots of transients. You've got Slab City. . . ."

"Slab City?"

"Oh, hell yeah. Slab City is a squatters' paradise. It's on the site of what used to be Camp Dunlap, a Navy base that was decommissioned after World War Two. Everything was razed, and all that's left are the guard station, bunkers, and concrete building foundation slabs. During the winter, as many as 3,000 people park their RVs there. A bunch of nutcases live there year-round. There's no water, power, or other services. But they've got a social club and even a church."

"What's Salvation Mountain? I saw a sign for it."

"That's on the way to Slab City. That's another piece of work. For decades, this old guy has been painting this mountain and pretty much everything else around it—trees, rocks, vehicles—with the Word. He's got biblical quotes, praise the Lord, Jesus is love, repent sinners. . . . He's gonna save the world."

"How do you paint a mountain?"

"With a lot of time and a lot of paint. About thirty thousand gallons of it, I understand. I learned this from my wife. She's given the guy paint. All this is on government land, by the way. The government came close to bulldozing it until the do-gooders got involved, claiming the mess was folk art."

Arnold sneered. "It's a toxic dump is what it is. Try and explain that to my wife. So you think somebody here knows something about a murder in Pasadena."

"We're following leads. Connie Jenkins's name came up. She owns the Jenkins's Stop 'N Go Market at the corner of Highway One-Eleven and Main. I want to see who's around. Run some license plates."

"I know that market out on the highway, but I don't know anything about it." Arnold turned to the deputy. "Villalobos, you know those people?"

"I know Connie Jenkins," Villalobos said. "She's a tough old bird. Winged a guy who tried to rob her a few years back with a shotgun she keeps behind the counter." The deputy laughed. "Her son's back in town, living there. Name of Jack Jenkins."

"Yeah?" Kissick said. "You know anything about him?"

"Got a criminal record as long as your arm. Did a dime in Quentin for robbery, aggravated assault, and mayhem. Sprung last year. Jack's a badass."

"Was he ever in for murder?"

"No. But he's the main suspect in his own wife's unsolved murder. Buddy of mine handled the case. Jack married Debbie about twelve years ago. Eighteen months later, she disappeared. Two years after that, her partially buried bones were found by a couple of guys riding dirt bikes out in the desert. They never had enough to arrest

Jack. He's one of those cool-as-a-cucumber guys. He's got those dead eyes."

Kissick knew those dead eyes well. "How old is he?"

"Late thirties."

"Anything else of interest?"

Villalobos began to chuckle. "I don't know if this is any help to you, but it's pretty interesting. Jack likes to wear makeup. I've never seen him in a dress, but I know some people who have."

The temperature dropped with the setting sun. The darkness brought out the stars in the clear desert sky, as well as the townspeople who'd been held hostage indoors by the heat. People sat in lawn chairs in front of their homes or with their feet dangling from pickup truck beds.

Mike Arnold pulled the Suburban up to the gas tanks at Jenkins's and he and Kissick got out. Arnold unscrewed the gas cap and started toward the mini-mart to prepay. The old pumps didn't have point-of-service devices installed.

Kissick saw the flickering of a TV through Venetian blinds over the mini-mart's windows. Through the open door, he heard the sound of Hollywood gunfire, which was more sonorous than the clipped pop-pop of real gunfire.

Arnold opened the screen door, sounding a bell attached at the top. The bell tinkled anew when the screen door, affixed by a tight spring, slammed shut.

Kissick walked toward the house behind the mini-mart. He passed salvaged rows of airplane and movie theater seats positioned to face the mountains. Some were near a brick firepit, allowing a person sitting there to rest his or her feet on the bricks. Scattered around were fanciful statues of people and animals made of scrap metal and found objects. The artwork was primitive yet showed a touch of whimsy. Some of the figures were dressed in clothing. Women's clothing.

When he got within a few feet of the chain-link fence, it was as if he'd tripped an invisible wire. Two large mongrel dogs appeared out of nowhere and began barking and snarling, flinging themselves against the fence, their big paws lopping over the top, the fence bowing with their girth. They were old and overweight, an observation that cheered Kissick. Fitter dogs that size could have easily cleared the fence.

Almost at the same time, a motion light on the roof of the house clicked on, flooding the yard. The cacti and boulders cast eerie shadows on the sandy dirt.

On a notepad, Kissick quickly jotted information about the Saturn sedan and Triumph TR6 that he saw earlier. Hearing the small bell on the mini-mart's screen door again ring, he turned, shoving the pad into his pocket.

"Slacker, Doobie, knock it off!"

Connie Jenkins approached. Kissick recognized her from her DMV photograph.

The dogs retreated to all fours and began whimpering and wagging their tails.

"Can I help you?"

Kissick had expected a rawboned, sun-hardened woman, and he was not disappointed. She was tiny, but her back was ramrod straight and her steps were sure.

She wore blue jeans and dusty Keds tennis shoes. Tucked into her jeans was a brown T-shirt imprinted with a drawing of a pistol and the slogan "We don't call 911." She wore a leather belt with a big turquoise-and-silver buckle where her waist used to be. She smelled of cigarettes. Her complexion was deeply tanned and weathered.

In contrast to her rugged attire, her nails were manicured and varnished red. Her hair was done in a puffy coif, the silver tone enhanced so it was bright as a newly minted quarter. Blue eye shadow matched her eyes.

Kissick recalled a comment Alex Caspers would sometimes make when he saw a woman past her prime: "She had her day." Meaning she'd been hot at some point. Kissick didn't believe that Jenkins had ever had her day.

"I'm sorry for upsetting your dogs. My buddy's getting gas, and I had to come over and check out this beautiful Triumph. I used to own one when I was in college, and I've wanted to buy another one ever since I sold it."

Kissick had never owned such a vehicle, but he had a buddy who had.

"They're starting up again." Jenkins pointed toward the mountains.

He turned to see a spectacular light show across the darkening desert sky from the Chocolate Mountains live bombing area. Explosions shook the ground and echoed through the peaks.

"That's enough to rattle your teeth," he said.

"Don't I know it? Sometimes I spend half the night putting stuff back on the shelves. Pretty though, isn't it?"

They both looked at the sky scarred by slashes of light turning blue and violet.

Kissick now understood why the airplane and movie theater seats were facing the mountains. He also guessed at the source of the abundant scrap metal for the sculptures. Someone had ventured onto the restricted area to gather it.

Kissick held out his hand. "I'm Jim Crockett." He cribbed the surname from one of the *Miami Vice* detectives, one of his all-time favorite TV shows.

"Connie Jenkins. Good to meetcha." Her handshake was firm.

"I'd like to make an offer on this car. Are you the owner?"

"Belongs to my son. You'll have to talk to him."

"Think he'd be interested in selling it?"

"I doubt it. He's had offers before."

"Is he around?"

"Not right now. I don't know where he is."

"Is there some way I can get in touch with him?"

"Gimme your number. Maybe he should call you."

"Sure." Kissick felt his pockets. "I don't have a business card." He didn't want her to see the spiral pad and pen he was carrying, fearing it would raise her suspicions.

"Let's go inside the store."

"What's your son's name?"

"Jack. Jack Jenkins. That's his given name."

"Does he go by a nickname?"

"Yeah. You don't want to get into that."

"I don't?"

"No."

The dogs began whining as she departed.

Passing the firepit, Kissick stopped when he saw a partially burned book atop a pile of charred wood. It was *Razored Soul*. He commented, "Someone's not a fan of literature."

She harrumphed. "Jack. Said it wasn't worth the paper it was printed on. Said he got it free anyway. I told him he could have sold it on eBay."

They walked to the store. Near the door was an old-fashioned pickle barrel. Kissick opened the screen door for Jenkins. She went inside and gave Arnold a hard look; he was holding open the door to a refrigerated case. He grabbed a Red Bull and took it to the counter.

Jenkins cursed as she restacked bottles of aspirin that the explosions had sent tumbling to the floor. "They've been doing that half the day. About to rattle my dentures out."

Kissick checked out the place. There were two rows of low shelves. Along the back wall were refrigerated cases. The hard liquor was stored on shelves behind the counter. An open door off the back led to what appeared to be a storeroom. Taped to the ancient cash register was a dollar bill, probably the first dollar the business had taken in. There were no other photos or mementos. A small TV behind the counter broadcasted a *Law & Order* episode. There was a desk chair with wheels. A glass ashtray was filled with cigarette butts. An open package of Kools and a matchbook was beside it.

Jenkins pushed buttons on the cash register. There was a "ding" when the drawer slid open. "That'll be thirty-two dollars and seventy-six cents for the gas and the soda."

While Arnold got cash from his wallet, Jenkins set a pad of paper and a pen on the counter. "Write your phone number down. I'll give it to my son."

Kissick wrote down the number for his personal cell phone. "You here all alone?"

"Why? You gonna rob me?"

"You're not afraid?"

Jenkins looked from Kissick to Arnold, her big grin revealing tobacco-stained teeth. "I'm not alone." From behind the counter, she took out a shotgun. "I've got Betsy to keep me company."

TWENTY-THREE

A cab dropped Vining in front of the Tucson police department just as the bells of St. Augustine Cathedral a block away chimed seven o'clock.

The police headquarters was a low-slung postmodern structure of bare cement, wooden beams, and glass and had stood in for a fictional city's police department in an eighties TV detective series.

Standing on the walkway outside, Vining announced her business to an officer behind a bulletproof window and slid her shield into a pull drawer. As she waited to be let inside, she watched a young officer wand a well-dressed, middle-aged woman for weapons.

The lobby was airy, with a flagstone-and-glass staircase in the middle. A sitting area had couches, chairs, and large vases of silk flowers. Despite the sunny atmosphere, the place had an institutional tension, like a hospital where the most skillful interior decorating is always foiled by anxiety.

Antique police equipment filled a display case. In another, Vining took in the collection of weapons confiscated from the Dillinger gang when they were captured in Tucson in the 1930s.

Her mind kept returning to the lies she'd told Kissick. She'd lied about the significance of Nitro's necklace and about why she had had to leave early. They weren't huge lies, but lies were lies. If she could link Johnna Alwin's murder to the assault on herself, she would reveal everything. Then they'd go to Sergeant Early and up the chain it would go. The brass might call in the FBI, the G-men with their college degrees and suits who just had to know more and know better than the local cops. A full-blown investigation would ensue and her role would shrink. The battle with T. B. Mann would become others' to fight even though she was the one who bore his scars.

The thought stuck in Vining's throat like a slender fish bone. She felt a hollowness in the pit of her stomach as if she was about to give away an heirloom that she knew the new owner would never hold as dear.

A tall man approached her as she gazed at the display cases.

"Detective Vining? Lieutenant Owen Donahue."

"Nice to meet you, Lieutenant. Thanks for seeing me."

"Call me Owen."

"Nan."

His eyes didn't leave hers but she felt him sizing her up. She did the same. She found him attractive. His closely shorn brown hair was liberally sprinkled with silver. He was fit and had a slight tan, suggesting that he participated in outdoor sports, but it may have been a side effect of desert life as it was for beach life. Tans happened. His attitude was polite but standoffish and rightfully so. He'd closed a grisly murder of one of the TPD's own. Vining's visit suggested he'd made a mistake.

Vining understood how it could have happened and didn't fault him. A likely perpetrator fell into his lap and Donahue went for him. Investigators bring a single-minded focus to a case. One has to act quickly and sometimes take a leap of faith before analyzing all the evidence. Time is the investigator's worst enemy. Haste can leave loose ends. Vining suspected her call out of the blue made Donahue recall such loose ends.

She walked with him to the elevators. On a nearby wall was a tribute to TPD officers killed in the line of duty, with photos above short descriptions of the circumstances. The first had occurred in 1892. Johnna Alwin's was the most recent.

Vining had seen this photo of Alwin on the TPD's Web site. It was her official portrait in uniform in front of the U.S. flag. She was not smiling, and her dark eyes were somber. Vining could not detect the essence of the woman from this uninspired representation on paper.

In the elevator, Donahue made no attempt at small talk and neither did she. They exited and walked down a narrow hallway decorated with large photos of Tucson's historic buildings.

Behind the counter in Evidence, a banker's box was waiting for him. He signed for it and carried it back to the elevator, which they took to the third floor.

At the end of a corridor, they reached a windowed door. A plaque beside it said CRIMES AGAINST PERSONS DIVISION. Donahue unlocked the door by flashing a Smart Card over the reader. They entered a large room divided into cubicles, the waist-high walls allowing full view across them, unlike the cubicles at the PPD. Most were empty. In the occupied ones, no one looked up as Vining followed Donahue.

A wall displayed a collection of patches from different police departments around the country. Detectives with cubicles on the perimeter had appropriated the extra wall space to post personal items and collages of snapshots. A banner pinned to one cubicle said "Remember. We work for God."

It was the homicide detective's maxim. They were the

last resort in this life to find the bad guys and mete out justice.

Donahue stopped at a table laden with two coffeepots, a coffee grinder, and an assortment of coffee, from gourmet beans to a can of Maxwell House.

He set down the box and raised an index finger and thumb toward a pot that was nearly empty. "Coffee?"

"I'm good. Thanks."

Donahue filled a Styrofoam cup and left the brew black. He returned the empty pot to the burner, flipping the switch to shut off the heat. He balanced his cup on the box, declining Vining's offer of assistance. They crossed the room to enter an area separated by tall partitions on three sides, the open side facing a wall of windows. Too many shabby rolling chairs were crowded around a conference table. A large map of Tucson was tacked to a fabric wall. On the table were two storage boxes with perforated holes for handles. Written on the short side of each in black marker was "Donahue." Beneath it was a "V" in a circle followed by "Johnna Alwin." There was a date and what Vining assumed was the case number. The "V" she knew stood for "victim."

He set the evidence box on the table beside the other two and raised his hand toward them, signaling Vining to have at it.

She opened the case file box labeled "1 of 2." On top were small manila envelopes that held audiotapes of interviews. File folders were beneath.

She found the folder that held the crime scene photos.

Donahue pulled over a rolling chair and sat at the opposite end of the table. He sipped coffee and gazed out the floor-to-ceiling window that gave a view of the cathedral down the street. His aloof attitude conveyed that he didn't consider her business worth his attention.

Vining reviewed the photos. The first one was of Alwin's bloody body, crumpled in a storeroom.

"Why do you think the murder attempt you're investigating is related to this homicide?" Donahue asked the question without looking at her.

Vining ignored him. "Was Alwin stabbed in the storeroom or was her body moved there?"

Donahue talked over his shoulder to her. "She was stabbed there. I figure her informant, Jesse Cuba, told her he had something he wanted her to see inside the storeroom. Stolen medical equipment or a cache of drugs."

Vining studied a close-up of Alwin. Beneath the open neck of her blouse, she spied a strand of pearls. The necklace was not in full view as depicted in Nitro's drawing. But his rendition of how her body was positioned and the clothes she was wearing was correct, down to her slingback shoes. Nitro had either seen the crime scene or the photos or an eyewitness had recounted the details to him—an eyewitness who had lovingly recollected the minutiae. In Nitro's drawing, the necklace had been emphasized. The necklace was important.

She made quick work of the rest of the photos, pausing at the corpse of Cuba lying on an unmade bed in a threadbare room, a length of rubber hose still tied around his heavily track-marked upper arm, the needle of a syringe dangling from his skin.

"Why did you conclude that Cuba's death was accidental?" she asked. "He was a longtime heroin user. He knew what he was doing."

"The dope we found on him was purer than the stuff that's cut for sale around here."

"Where did he get it?"

"Who knows? Who cares? He's dead."

Vining flipped through the remaining folders, replaced the lid on the box, and slid it aside. She started on the second box.

Donahue swiveled to face her, set his empty cup on the table, and casually leaned back, clasping his hands across his middle. "You didn't answer my question."

She didn't look up from the report she was reading. "What question was that?"

She'd heard his question. She suspected he knew this.

He repeated, "Why do you think the murder attempt you're investigating is related to this homicide?"

She set a couple of reports aside and closed the file. Pointedly meeting his eyes, she flipped her hair over her shoulder. She'd worn it down on purpose, even though it was twelve degrees hotter here than in L.A. She arched her neck and watched with satisfaction as his attitude evolved from cynical to commiserative when he took in the ugly scar.

"I was ambushed a year ago. The murder attempt I'm investigating is my own. The circumstances were similar to the Alwin homicide, but I saw the man who did it, and he was not Jesse Cuba."

She had planned that moment. Had devised it to throw him off-base, shake his conceit that he knew all about her and what she was up to. It worked. It worked great.

She'd saved the box of physical evidence for last. She'd asked to see many more items than she cared about to disguise the fact that there was just one thing she coveted. Donning latex gloves, she methodically removed items of Alwin's clothing from their protective envelopes and feigned interest in examining them. She took digital photos of the evidence.

Donahue had not left her alone with the materials, maintaining the proper chain of custody. Once she'd explained who she was and where she was coming from, his rancor toward her had faded. He'd turned off the catlike attention with which he'd observed everything while feigning apathy.

From the physical evidence box, Vining picked up a small manila envelope. The contents shifted seductively in just the right way. Her heart began to race even before she read the description on the evidence control form: "Pearl Necklace." The necklace that Johnna's husband had left behind when he recovered her personal belongings.

She upended the envelope onto her yellow pad. The necklace spilled out. She arranged it, moving the pendant to the center. Some of the pearls were flecked with blood. It was identical to her necklace except that the pendant had a large reddish stone surrounded by small glittering stones that she guessed were cubic zirconia, like hers.

"Is that a ruby?" Vining asked about the gem, knowing the answer.

"Garnet."

"Any significance?"

He shrugged.

"Was it her birthstone?"

"No."

Alwin had been murdered in January. In January the year before her murder, she had fatally shot a mob associate in an incident that had earned her fifteen minutes of fame. Garnet was the gem for January. Alwin's death stone. It was so obvious, Donahue hadn't seen it. Vining couldn't blame him. It had taken the pure instincts of her own daughter to connect the dots between the pearl pendant in her necklace and the date of Vining's spilled blood. She had shot the rock star in June. T. B. Mann had ambushed her in June. Pearl was the gem for June.

She took photos of the necklace and replaced the materials inside the evidence box.

When Donahue saw she had finished, he ended his phone call with a buddy about an upcoming fishing trip to Mexico.

"You're right," she told him. "The Alwin case is closed."

Waiting for her flight at the airport, Vining didn't flip through her magazine or make phone calls. She stared at a spot on the floor without seeing it. She realized she was smiling.

Once, she had tried to purge her life of the necklace by throwing it away. All she was really doing was trying to rid herself of what she had become. Returning the necklace to her home, to her life, was acceptance. T. B. Mann had changed her. Made her. She was his creation in more ways than she wanted to admit. He had colored her decision to lie to her boss and her partner, to come to Tucson, to do what she had done here, and what she was about to do. If someone had told her a year ago, even six months ago, that this is where she would be, she would have told that person he was nuts. T. B. Mann had sent her to the edge of infinity and she had crawled back, trailing dust from the dark side of the moon.

The T. B. Mann saga had become like a nightmare from which she'd awakened sweat-drenched and trembling. Trying to describe it, exposing it to the light of day in an attempt for others to understand, would only drain all its vivid colors. It would evaporate, the closer she drew, as if she was chasing a rainbow.

Other people would only muck it up. *She* was the one who had survived T. B. Mann. He had sent Nitro to provoke her. To show that he was in charge. Was T. B. Mann as obsessed with her as she was with him? If she belonged to him, he belonged to her in equal measure. Her and no other. He was hers.

She took out the slip of paper on which she'd written Richard Alwin's contact information when he'd called her three months ago. She caught him on his cell phone on his way home from work.

"Mr. Alwin, I've just gone through Johnna's case files with Lieutenant Donahue. I wanted to follow up on the similarities you spotted between your wife's murder and my attempted murder. Good news. They got the right guy. Jesse Cuba murdered Johnna. The fact that Johnna and I were given similar necklaces is just a coincidence. There are a lot of cop groupies out there."

She ended the call, confident she'd buried Richard Alwin's nascent serial-killer theory. Sometimes an investigator had to tell a small lie to get to a larger truth. While she was sitting at that table across from Donahue, holding Johnna Alwin's blouse, touching blood spilled by T. B. Mann, Vining knew she was prepared to do more than lie to get him. She knew she had it in her to pull off what she'd come to Tucson to do.

She put her hand in her pocket and drew out Alwin's pearl-and-garnet necklace, still flecked with dried blood. It was identical to hers except for the gem. The death stone.

By the time she'd gotten around to opening the envelope labeled "Pearl Necklace," Donahue was on his cell phone, mentally on his Mexican fishing trip. He'd been cowed by the story of the murder attempt on her. He'd played right into her hands.

With the evidence box shielding her, she'd gathered Alwin's necklace and shoved it into her jacket pocket, taking out a strand of cheap pearls she'd bought at Target before she'd left. She put that necklace inside the evidence envelope.

Donahue had done a cursory check of the contents before putting the lid on the box. She had bet that he wouldn't reopen the evidence envelopes and he hadn't.

She'd gone to Tucson intending to break the law to get Alwin's necklace. A photo was not enough. She had to possess it. It was more than just proof. She couldn't take the chance of it disappearing. T. B. Mann wouldn't. To get him, she had to think like him. She'd crossed a line, and there was no going back.

She crushed the necklace in her palm.

TWENTY-FOUR

*I*t took Scoville nearly two hours to reach the dusty town past San Bernardino. He was born and raised in Southern California but rarely ventured to what locals called the Inland Empire. For him, it was the place where smog went to die, trapped against the mountains. He pulled into the parking lot of Wrangler's Outpost, a sprawling rustic steakhouse that looked as if it had been putting out the feedbag and rye for buckaroos for decades, holding its own as urban sprawl encroached from all sides. A flashing neon sign portrayed a cowboy astride a bucking horse, twirling a lasso.

The interior was dim, lit by ersatz oil lamps on the walls and chandeliers made of wagon wheels hanging from the ceiling. A large sign announced the restaurant's no-necktie policy, and the walls and ceiling were covered with ties severed by scissor-wielding waitresses from men who had dared to enter sporting one. Waitresses wore off-the-shoulder gingham dresses with frilly petticoats beneath short skirts, and waiters wore gingham shirts and blue jeans. The place was loud and crass and the kind of theme restaurant Scoville had never considered fun, just phony. As a former restaurateur, he haughtily deplored the mountains of mediocre food they dispensed with the goal of making their non-discerning patrons feel they were receiving good value.

Scoville pushed through the bar, which seemed crowded with every guy in town who made his living with tools and the women who loved them. Televisions tuned to different sporting events were suspended from each end of the bar and every corner. He had money on some of the games, but he had bigger issues.

The floor crunched beneath his feet, and he realized it was covered with peanut shells that were making a mess of his Bruno Magli shoes. People were scooping roasted salted peanuts by the double handfuls from a large barrel. He found an empty stool and brushed peanut husks, damp from cocktail glasses, from the bar. A bratwurst-eating contest was being broadcast on one of the ESPN stations.

A bartender mopped the bar with a towel. He had a silver handlebar mustache and a full head of wavy silver hair of which he appeared proud, given the care paid to styling. He looked like the kind of guy who called women "doll."

"They call that a sport?" Scoville pointed at the TV.

The bartender barely looked at it. "Who knows anymore? What can I get ya, pardner?"

"Sierra Nevada if you have it."

Scoville wanted something stronger, but he had to keep his wits about him. He'd nearly blown it with those Pasadena detectives. The way they'd descended on him had been nothing less than an ambush. And that bitch Vining . . . the needling. The way she twisted words, trying to trap him, trying to mess him up. Dena had pulled that crap on him too. Vining and Dena must have learned their techniques from a canned course on interrogation. The tactics were so clunky, he could almost see the gears turning. The only reason Vining had nearly trapped him was because he'd been overwrought. He wouldn't let that happen again. He had to keep his head clear.

He'd reported the details as best as he could recall them to Leland Declues, his attorney, who was livid he hadn't immediately thrown the detectives out.

"Don't talk to the police about anything. They can't force you to talk to them, even if they wave warrants at you or arrest you. Especially if they arrest you."

Scoville knew that. He hated cops. He'd always hated cops. They had that smug attitude of every bully he'd ever come across, and he'd seen his share. He'd been a target of bullies since he was a kid. He could buy and sell each one of them twenty times over, but that didn't matter. Bullies had an innate sense for weakness, for that putty in his soul. He'd fired a couple of Marquis employees who had that smirking, condescending attitude. Fired them just because he could. They had been hired by his father, who liked that cockiness in people. Anyone who had worked for the old man had to be bold. Old Ludlow's abrasiveness could sear the skin off morefragile mortals.

His attorney didn't feel any harm had been done. The detectives were fishing, and Scoville had nothing to hide.

"Right," he'd replied. "I've got nothing to hide." Maybe if he said it often enough, he'd believe it.

He looked at his watch and rubbed his five o'clock shadow. Draining the last of his beer, he caught sight of himself in a mirror behind the bar. He looked gaunt, and had dark circles around his eyes. His life continued to unravel, the pace picking up, the ball of yarn growing smaller. The seed had been planted when he'd let his father lure him into the family business. He should have left well enough alone. Before that, he and Dena had had their problems but they'd been happy. Luddy was small and Dahlia was merely a handful, not a terror. And Dena . . . Dena . . .

He plastered his hands against his eyes, trying to block out the scene with her and Bowie Crowley.

It had been years since she'd responded that way to him. Had she ever? Unbridled passion hadn't just been evident on her face; it had sent tremors through her entire body. Her wonderful, perfect body . . . He couldn't remember the last time they'd had sex. His birthday last December: a mercy fuck.

And Crowley, with his movie-star looks and hairless, muscled torso, thrusting harder than Scoville physically could. His performance demonstrated he was better hung than Scoville.

Scoville used to take care of himself, going to the gym with Dena. He rarely went shirtless, embarrassed by the excessive body hair that covered his chest and back. He joked that he was the missing link. Dena used to tell him she found his hair sexy. He had never believed her. Now he knew what she found sexy. The truth had come out. It always does, like a body that eventually bobs to the surface.

If he'd had a gun, he would have shot them both dead right then. He swore he would have.

" 'Nother one?"

Scoville pulled his hands from his face and looked at the bartender. He thought he detected pity in his eyes. Rightfully so. He was a pitiful mother. A schlub. All show, no go. He could no more shoot Dena and Crowley than he could take the life of his own son.

The seed of his undoing hadn't been planted when he'd joined his father at Marquis, it was planted at his birth. Some guys, the Bowie Crowleys of the world, were born to raise hell. Others, like himself, were born to lap up what the tough guys dished out. Suck it up when the tough guys held their heads in the toilet bowl and flushed.

"Make it Grey Goose rocks."

The bartender swept away the empty beer bottle and glass and grabbed the vodka.

Out of the corner of his eye, Scoville saw a woman take the stool next to him. He couldn't be bothered to look, preferring the view of clear liquid and ice in the glass he cradled between both hands. She, however, had other plans.

"Buy me a drink?"

Thinking she couldn't possibly be talking to him, he ignored her.

She flirtatiously leaned into him, her perfume bold, and her voice husky. "I'm talking to you, cutie-pie."

Scoville slowly moved his eyes from his glass toward the woman, but didn't get past her hands. They were manicured but huge and masculine. On her ring finger she wore a USC class ring that looked jarringly like one Mercer used to wear.

His eyes trailed up wiry muscular arms and incongruous bouncy auburn hair to her face. The jolt made him splash his drink onto his hands.

"Hi, Mark. How's it hangin'?"

Scoville gaped at the well-made-up man with an expression of bewilderment and disgust. "Jack?"

"So how about that drink?" He tossed his hair over

one shoulder with a flick of his hand when the bartender came by. "I'll have a stinger, honey."

Scoville looked horrified. "You're Jack Jenkins, aren't you?"

"Just call me Jill and get that ugly, demeaning look off your face."

"Why are you dressed like that?"

"Why not?"

Scoville thought the answer was obvious.

"Do you find me attractive?" A carefully drawn perimeter and two shades of lipstick did little to enhance Jenkins's thin lips. His heavily made-up eyes, however, did draw attention away from his hooked nose.

Scoville hesitated a beat too long, giving his upper lip time to waver.

"For your information, two *very* attractive men made passes at me as I walked over here."

"You weren't dressed like this at—"

"Small-claims court that day? No. I had to drive my mother, and she refuses to be seen with Jill. She's a pain in the rear, but she's my dear old mom."

Scoville's eyes were drawn to Jenkins's cleavage. He winced, trying to make sense of it.

"They're prosthetics, Mark, but they're real to me, so don't get any ideas."

Dazed, Scoville turned away and raised his drink to his lips. Spilled booze dripped from the glass onto the bar.

"Thank you, sweetie." Jenkins winked at the bartender, who smoothed his silver mustache with his fingers, hiding his smirk. "Mark, let's get that booth over there."

Scoville settled the bar bill while Jenkins minced across the floor, gingerly navigating the discarded peanut shells on his stiletto heels. He slid onto the wooden bench, gathering the skirt of his dress.

A waitress who was well past the age when gingham and petticoats might have had a prayer of being attractive arrived as soon as they had sat down.

"I see you already have drinks. Would you like an appetizer? How about our hot artichoke dip with pita chips or an order of jalapeño poppers?"

Scoville wasn't hungry but figured he should eat something. He pulled over the laminated paper triangle on the table that listed the bar menu.

"You want anything, Ja . . . ah, Jill?"

"Hot wings . . ." the waitress continued to chant. "Fried mozzarella sticks, fried zucchini strips, our famous garlic fries, appetizer portion of our famous baby back ribs . . ."

"Get what you want and I'll just pick." Jenkins patted his flat midsection and said to the waitress, who chuckled gamely, "If us girls don't watch our figures, no one else will."

When Scoville frowned at the menu as if it was a calculus equation, Jenkins tugged it from between his fingers. "An order of hot wings and one of jalapeño poppers."

Scoville raised his eyes from where the menu had been, stopping at Jenkins's torso. He gaped at the tattoos covering his lean bare arms. His spare muscular frame in the strappy floral print sundress looked like a jackhammer dropped into a flowerbed.

Jenkins smiled at Scoville with a demonic and almost triumphant leer. His teeth were long and prominent. Dark eyes sparkled beneath plucked and painted eyebrows that looked like twin carets. A dusting of red paint and a pair of horns and he would have looked like a caricature of the devil.

"You look like you could use a good night's sleep, Mark. I hope I'm not being too bold."

Scoville felt dazed and disoriented. He felt as if he no longer even knew who he was. He had wanted to set Jenkins straight, but now he saw that by agreeing to meet him, he was only digging himself into a deeper hole. He glanced around. The people in the bar were too preoccupied with their fun to eavesdrop. The din made it impossible anyway.

"How could you have done that to them?"

"Done what to who, Mark?"

"You think this is a joke? The police showed me the photos."

"They would pull that tired trick out of the bag. But you were shocked, right? And disgusted. You had to turn away. Couldn't even look. So it was perfect. Just how I'd planned it. I did a Charlie Manson on them just for you."

Scoville sputtered, "For *me?* Why on earth would you have done that *for me?*"

"So that the police would never suspect you. Read my lips, Mark. I'll speak slowly. No offense, but you don't look like the kind of guy who has the balls to pull off something like that. It blows any theory about it being a hired hit because no professional would take the time for such bullshit. I know. I've done a few hits in my day. Not everything that's come my way, mind you. I'm selective. Wish I could get my hands on pictures of my work that night. It was downright artistic."

The waitress brought platters laden with saucy, greasy food. She set them on the table, a thick slab of wood. Shiny coins were embedded in the heavy varnish.

Jenkins plucked a jalapeño popper from the pile and bit it in half, retracting his lips to avoid smearing his lipstick. "Good, but hot. Temperature-hot. Careful."

Scoville shoved the platters toward Jenkins, who shoved them back.

"You'd better eat, pal. You need to keep up your strength. You've got work to do." He tossed the remaining half popper into his mouth. "You getting cold feet, frat boy? A deal's a deal, my friend."

"There was no deal. I was drunk. I was even drinking from a flask outside the courthouse while I was on the phone with my partner. You must have seen that."

"You were lit, all right, but you weren't too drunk to stand up in court and plead your case." Jenkins gave him a sardonic grin. "And lose."

"That's my point." Scoville flung his hands toward Jenkins. "I should have won. I barely remember standing in front of the judge, much less what I said."

"We shook hands, Mark. You gave me your business card."

"If you say so. But so what? I give it out all the time. I'm a businessman."

"You wrote your cell phone number on it."

"I'm always giving out my cell phone number."

"Why do you think I called you a couple of days later?"

Scoville rubbed his chin as he thought. "You called me?"

"I talked to you about putting up a billboard on some property near the Van Nuys courthouse. I asked questions about your business situation and specifically your business partner. What his background was. Where he lived."

"That was *you?*"

"Who the hell else did you think it was, Mark?"

"Someone who wanted to install a billboard on their property."

"Near the Van Nuys courthouse? That was a clue, Mark."

"How about telling me who you were and where we met? That would have been a clue."

"I didn't know who might be listening."

"I remember that phone call, but I swear I didn't know it was you."

Jenkins pursed his lips and arched an eyebrow at Scoville. "Mark, you knew it was me and why I was calling. Why else would a potential customer ask all those questions about your business partner and where he lives? And why would you answer?"

"I don't know. I thought you were trying to evaluate Marquis versus our competitors."

"Your argument is specious, Mark."

The erudite word coming out of Jenkins's mouth gave Scoville pause. He recovered and continued his rant. "That proves my point. That day at small-claims court, on top of being drunk, I was angry. I was under stress. I wasn't thinking clearly. Hell, I even forgot to pick up my son from school. How was I going to remember a stupid conversation with a stranger? I didn't even remember talking to you until the police started asking me questions. Then it flew into my head, this crazy conversation I had with some guy. You tell me it was you but, I'm not positive it *was* you."

"It was me. I had on a little foundation and mascara and simple clothes. My mother . . . Anyway, the point is, we shook hands, Mark. Where I come from, that's as good as a contract."

"All I remember was sitting there all morning waiting for the judge to call my case. Oliver kept text messaging me. By the time they cut us loose for lunch and I was able to call him back, I was plenty hot. I went outside, around the corner, found a bench, and Oliver and I got into it on the phone. I remember some guy—you, I guess—sitting there. You might have been smoking."

"I was smoking."

"Okay, so it was you."

"Thank you," Jenkins said with a bow.

"I vaguely remember ranting about Oliver."

"You offered me a drink. I would have taken it if I hadn't been driving my mother."

"I needed to vent, and you were a convenient ear. I was crazy mad. I guess I might have said my life would be easier if Oliver wasn't around."

"You were stronger than that. You said you wanted him dead. You wondered how someone went about hiring someone to do a job like that."

"I did not. I would never say that, drunk or sober."

"You do remember saying you wanted your partner dead."

Scoville raised a shoulder. "Maybe. So what? I used to say that half the time I got off the phone with Oliver at the end. Come on, Jack. Everyone's had some person some time that they wanted to see dead."

Jenkins darted a polished fingernail at him. "True words."

"When the lunch break was over, we went back into the courtroom. They called my case. I lost and I went home. That's all I remember about that day."

"I don't believe you, Mark. You're trying to get out of our deal."

"That's all I remember." Scoville nearly shouted.

"Shhh . . ."

Scoville lowered his voice. "Then a few weeks later, the police show up and tell me Oliver and Lauren were murdered. I can tell they think I have something to do with it. Then something clicks and I had a vague recollection of me raging about Oliver to a stranger. A chill just goes right down my spine. I can't remember what we talked about, but I get this sick feeling in the pit of my stomach. I think, Jesus, this can't have anything to do with that, could it? Then I get this call from you telling me I have to fulfill my part of the deal."

"That's right."

"Doesn't the fact that you had to explain everything we *allegedly* discussed prove to you that we didn't even have that conversation? You know what? You're lying. I never agreed to do anything for you. Even falling-down drunk, I would never agree to something like that."

Jenkins glanced around as Scoville's tone again spiraled out of control. "Mark, you've gotta calm down."

"Stop telling me what to do."

"Mark . . . you're attracting attention. Come on, boy. Easy does it." He nudged the platter of hot wings toward him. "Eat something. You're a mess. Look at you. Can't have the wheels coming off this thing."

Scoville sucked the flesh from a chicken wing. "What thing? We have no *thing*."

Jenkins caught the waitress' eye and drew a circle with his finger over the table, ordering another round of drinks.

"Mark, I don't know if you believe in fate, but that day at small-claims court was a cosmic coincidence. Manna from Heaven." Jenkins raised his drink toward Scoville.

Scoville writhed against the wooden bench. "I was venting to a stranger. How did I know I was talking to a, a . . ."

"To a what, Mark?"

Scoville shot a sideways glance at Jenkins. After the initial shock of seeing him in the bar, he hadn't been able to look him directly in the face. Every time he tried, the sheen of purple eye shadow or the carefully painted lips repelled him. "Who takes an angry comment made by someone who's had a couple of drinks . . . Okay, made by a *drunk* and runs with it? What kind of a lunatic are you?"

"There's no need to be harsh. Especially when you opened the door to the whole thing."

Scoville moaned, "*There is no thing.*"

"Answer me this. Is your life easier now that Oliver Mercer is out of the way?"

Scoville dug the heels of his hands into his eyes and raked his fingers slick with chicken grease through his hair.

Jenkins repeated his question. "Is your life easier now that Oliver Mercer is out of the way?"

The waitress brought the fresh drinks.

"Thanks, honey." Jenkins took a sip before continuing. "I'll answer for you. Yes, it is. Even if you won't stand up like a man and agree that there was a bargain, even you, Mark Scoville, has to admit that you owe me a huge debt for returning your life to you."

Scoville stared into the vodka. If only he could float away on that cold ice.

"Now, Mark, it's time for you to step up to the plate. I've brought you peace. Now I want peace. I will have no peace until Bowie Crowley is dead."

Jenkins's eyebrows danced on his forehead as he warmed to his subject. "The justice system determined that Bowie paid his debt to society and cut him loose. Now he's going around like the risen Christ, if Christ had been made over by a team of celebrity stylists. Everyone's listening to Bowie Crowley. Everyone wants to be seen with Bowie Crowley. Everyone wants to fuck Bowie Crowley. Hell, he's an *artiste.* They love it because he's a scary man. A criminal. An ex-con. A card-carrying killer. He's out there preaching, 'Parents, don't let your children grow up to be me.' Whoooooo . . ."

Jack waggled his fingers in Scoville's face, as if he should be scared.

"A killer . . ." Jenkins hawked up the word. "Fucking two-bit throwaway stint for voluntary manslaughter. Give me a break. Killer my ass. I'll show him killer. We'll see who the tough guy is."

Scoville imploringly raised his hands. "That's my point. I'm not a killer. I don't have it in me."

"Course you do, Mark. Everyone does. They just don't know it. Haven't gotten in touch with that part of themselves."

"Jack, you've murdered at least two people. You said you've done hits. Why don't you kill Bowie Crowley?"

"Because I want you to."

"*Why?*"

"Because."

"That's crazy."

"Mark, stop using those words, please. Crazy. Insane. Lunatic. I mean, I'm the one who's sitting here calm and cool and you're the one who's nearly busting a gasket."

Jenkins picked up a hot wing, picked off the meat with his fingers, and put it in his mouth. "Look, Mark. Bowie and I have a history, just like you and Mercer had a history. It's cleaner this way."

"What did Crowley do to you?" Scoville asked.

"That's between him and me. Make sure you tell him before you off him. 'This is for Jack.' Make sure you say that."

"I'm not doing it."

"You're boring me, Mark."

"Look, I'll come clean with you about something. This will surprise you. I would like to see Bowie Crowley blown off the face of the earth too, and I'll tell you why." Scoville took a breath and prepared to utter those terrible words. Telling someone would legitimize it. Make it real. He had no choice. He looked straight at Jenkins, having avoided it until now. He saw a heavily made-up ugly man. The fact that he'd gotten used to it was proof to him that he was on the road to hell.

Jenkins hijacked the moment. He began guffawing, sending those eyebrows higher on his forehead, setting his face between quotation marks. "Fucking-A. You caught 'em together, didn't cha? Didn't cha? I can tell you did by the look on your face. Crowley always was a swordsman. Hasn't lost his touch with the ladies."

After his laughter subsided, Jenkins asked, "What's your point?"

"What's my point?" Scoville was incredulous. "That *is* the point." He leaned toward Jenkins and lowered his voice. "Your plan, the way you described it to me later—because, my hand to God, we never discussed it that day in front of the courthouse—was to commit each other's murder and we'd never get caught because neither of us had a connection to the guy we killed or an obvious motive. Now I have a connection to Crowley and a motive. I'm the wronged husband. The cops would be on me like nobody's business."

"Not my problem. You owe me. You ain't got no way out. Kill Bowie Crowley or I will frame you for Mercer's and that girl's murder."

"Frame me?"

"Frame you." Jenkins held the back of his hand up to Scoville. "I've not only got Oliver's ring, I've got the hand it was on."

Scoville paled.

"Mark, can you say, 'death penalty'?" Jenkins tittered at Scoville's defeated expression. "Mark, Mark, Mark . . ."

He picked up his purse and alarmed Scoville by getting up and sliding onto the bench beside him. He opened his handbag and took something out that was wrapped in a silk scarf printed with colorful drawings of hot-air balloons. He pulled Scoville's hand beneath the table and shoved the bundle into it.

"That's an untraceable nine millimeter semiautomatic with a silencer. Got eight bullets in the clip and one in the chamber. You'll only need one clip because if you don't stop Bowie with that, he'll tear your head off and spit down your neck before you can reload. You sit there all self-righteous, thinking you're better than me. It's not clothing that makes a man a man. It's action. Stop whining and get it done, Mark."

Scoville made a wheezing noise when Jenkins grabbed his crotch.

"See, I knew you had cojones. Now use 'em."

On his way out, Jenkins muttered to himself, "I love messing with that wuss."

TWENTY-FIVE

Vining badged her way through the emergency room at the Big G, slowing only slightly as she passed the armed security guards with metal-detecting wands who screened all hospital visitors. Security had been beefed up after an incident in 1993 when a patient, disgruntled over having to wait too long for pain medication, opened fire in the emergency room, wounding three doctors and taking staff members hostage.

County-USC Medical Center on North State Street in East Los Angeles, with more square feet than the Pentagon, is one of the largest academic medical centers in the country and has one of the busiest emergency rooms. It is most famous for its art deco towers, which appear in the opening scenes of the soap opera *General Hospital*.

On the aged linoleum floor, seven lines, each a different color, lead to various sections of the mammoth facility. Vining didn't need to follow the orange line, as she knew the way. "Psychiatric Emergency Services" was painted on the wall of an alcove. Inside, closed double doors were painted a homely shade of aqua that someone twenty years ago had probably deemed a calming hue.

She hadn't called ahead and wasn't accompanied by a detainee for the facility, but the no-nonsense female security guard at a wooden podium didn't press her about her business. With her shield in her hand, Vining smiled and jived with the guard, behavior that didn't come naturally but that she thought she faked pretty well. She channeled Kaitlyn for inspiration.

Vining illegibly scribbled her name on the sign-in sheet on the clipboard. From a drawer, the guard produced a small key with a numbered fob for a gun locker. While police officers could keep their weapons in the hospital proper, guns were not allowed in the psych ward. The guard smacked a button and the two doors swung open. Inside was a waiting room. A psych tech sat in a small office behind a shatterproof, polycarbonate-reinforced glass window. A door with a similar window was at one end of the small room. Bolted to the wall was a set of numbered gun lockers that looked like large post office boxes.

Sitting on plastic and steel chairs were two uniformed officers, both young males, who sat a small distance from their handcuffed charge, likely because of her odor. She was a middle-aged African American woman whose filthy clothing, matted hair, and stench indicated that she lived on the streets. She incessantly muttered, "I know people in Trenton. Trenton. Don't mess with me, cuz I know people in Trenton."

It was after 11:00 p.m., known as "quiet time" in the psych ward. The doctors had gone home and a skeleton crew of psych techs and nurses was on duty. The staff made sure the patients were sufficiently medicated to sleep through the night.

Vining knew that Nitro was still incarcerated at the Big G. Despite patient confidentiality laws, she had been able to glean that much information through a phone call. She also knew about quiet time and protocol at the Big G psych ward. She was counting on being able to take advantage of an overburdened and overwhelmed system. Men's Central Jail was overburdened too, but she knew her odds were better at the Big G to accomplish what she had in mind. So far, so good.

A psych tech came to the window. He was a burly, dark-haired young man with a carefully sculpted short beard. A nametag on his uniform said: L. Chapel.

"You have a patient here called Nitro," Vining told him. "Young guy, white, tall, slight build. Won't speak." When the tech indicated he knew who she was talking about, she went on. "This guy has a necklace among his personal possessions. I want to have a look at it. We had a report of a piece of stolen jewelry that matches its description."

Without questioning her, Chapel left to fetch the necklace. Vining opened the gun locker that matched the key. In it she deposited her sidearm, the Glock .40. She did not remove her backup weapon, the Walther PPK in her ankle holster.

She remained standing. The two officers talked and laughed in low voices, leaning forward in their chairs, regaling each other with stories of conquests, Vining suspected, either on the street or in the bedroom. Meanwhile, the delusional woman blathered about Trenton.

Shortly, the psych tech returned. "Is this what you want?" He held up a plastic bag containing Nitro's necklace.

Vining took it from him and examined it, turning the bag over. She nodded. "Looks like our stolen necklace. I'm seizing it as evidence. I'll give you a receipt."

"Can you do that?"

"I already am." She put the bag with the necklace in her pocket and took out a memo pad. She pulled off the pen that was clipped to it and scribbled a receipt. As she tore it from the pad, she asked the tech, "Is Nitro talking?"

"Not yet."

"Can I see him for a few minutes?"

"I can't let anyone back there."

Vining shrugged. "It's quiet time."

"What do you want to see him for?"

"I've only seen a picture of him. I want to see him in person, see if he matches the description of a cat burglar working our area."

"I'm not supposed to let anyone back there without authorization."

Vining put away her notepad. When she pulled her hand out, she had a hundred-dollar bill hidden in her palm. "That's cool. I understand." She raised her hand to shake the tech's. "If you can work something out. . . ."

Taking the cash, the tech turned his palm to look at it. He glanced at the two cops, who were still deep in their own world. Their charge was immersed in *her* own world. "I can work something out. Did you lock up your weapon?"

Vining turned to show that the holster attached to her belt was empty.

He said quietly into her ear, "You've got five minutes and you'd better just be looking. Don't mess me up." He went behind the counter.

At the sound of the buzzer, Vining pushed through the door. She entered a large ward with hospital beds lining both sides of the walls. At the far end were chairs facing a TV suspended from the ceiling. A pay phone was on the wall. Most of the beds were occupied. A few patients were handcuffed to their bed. Some were strapped down. Patients wore their own clothing, which ran the gamut from clean pajamas, robes, and slippers to the grime-caked vestments of those who called the streets home.

It was quiet and the light was dim.

Vining walked down the aisle between the beds, peering at the faces. Her heart raced. With her left hand inside her pocket, she opened the plastic bag and touched the necklace, running her fingers up and down it as if it was a rosary.

A big Latino who was strapped to his bed hissed as she passed, "Chica . . . Come here, chica. I've got something for you. Chica, come see."

She saw a shock of white hair. Nitro. Beside his bed, she looked down at him, watching him sleeping. He looked even younger, and his unlined, trouble-free face filled her with rage.

Nitro opened his eyes with a start.

"Shhh . . ." Vining pressed her finger against her lips. "It's only me. Nan Vining. You remember me."

He wasn't glad to see her.

"Sure you do. You remember me."

She leaned as close as she dared, wanting to stand as close to him as T. B. Mann had stood to her during those final moments while he waited to watch her die. She felt a vibration from Nitro that was familiar, so much like T. B. Mann. It terrified and mesmerized her.

"Who put you up to this?" She knew he felt her breath on his face. That was what she wanted, just like she had felt T. B. Mann's breath on hers. Let her breath get under his skin and filter into his nightmares, just like T. B. Mann's had for her.

She was close, unwisely close. The hands can kill you, she'd learned in her Academy training. Keep your eyes on the hands. Distance is your biggest ally. She was disregarding those rules. He could grab her, bite her, jab his thumbs into her eyes, blind her.

He was not T. B. Mann but he was his messenger.

"You know who he is, don't you? You know who killed those women and who attacked me."

He squirmed until he was sitting up, crumpling the sheets in his fist.

"Am I bothering you? Why don't you yell for help?"

She imagined how she looked to him, looming malevolently. She delighted in the fear she detected in his eyes. T. B. Mann had watched her suffering the same way. Is that what they had come to now? Did they only fully exist when held by the other's gaze?

Nitro was panting. They both were. He scooted away from her until he'd backed against the head of the bed. He drew his knees to his chest and tried to hide behind them.

She followed the tortured movements of his head as he struggled to avoid her, remaining inches from his face.

"Did he send you? Tell me. I know this is a game, this not talking. *Tell me.* He put you up to this, didn't he? You're a victim of his just like I am. He's controlling you. You must be afraid of him to follow his orders even when he's not around. There is a way out. Tell me the truth, and I'll make sure you're protected."

When all he did was blink, her anger overwhelmed her concerns about safety. She knew she was treading in dangerous waters and should back away, but a different angel had grabbed her by the throat.

She spoke through clenched teeth. "I told you to tell me. Who are you?"

From her pocket, she took out the necklace and dangled it in front of him.

His eyes widened.

"This is mine now. I've seized it as evidence. You have a problem with that? I'll call over one of the staff and you can tell them about it. You can file a complaint."

Nitro blinked rapidly as if trying to awaken from this nightmare.

"No? No report? No official complaint. Let me tell you something. I know about the necklaces. I know *all* about them. This is a sapphire. The stone for September. Is that when the owner of this necklace was killed? Or is that when someone else is going to be killed?"

She took a quick glance around. The ward was quiet. She shook the necklace at Nitro, rattling the pearls like bones.

"You're a fake and I'm going to prove it. Are you here to hurt me? You want to hurt me? Come on, asshole. I'm right here."

They were both startled when the buzzer sounded and the door opened. With the tech that Vining had bribed leading the way, the two officers escorted the woman with Trenton connections. The tech gave Vining a stern look.

Vining shoved the necklace into her pocket and looked at Nitro a final time.

He understood her. There was no uncertainty.

"Everything okay?" the tech asked, annoyed.

"Yeah. He's still not talking."

It was late when Vining arrived home.

In the TV room, she found Emily curled up in the La-Z-Boy reading a book.

"Hi, sweet pea."

"Hi, Mom. You making progress on the case?"

Vining paused from her nightly routine of stashing her Glock in the empty box of Count Chocula to orient herself. Emily was talking about the Mercer/Richards homicides.

"Yes, we are. We've got a couple of good leads."

"That's great, Mom. You must be happy."

Vining thought about that. "I am."

Em knew nothing about the Tucson trip, Nitro, or the drawings. Vining had made the mistake of opening up to Emily about the T. B. Mann necklace and the link to Johnna Alwin. She knew she had been weak to do so. These were the times when she most missed having a significant other in her life. It wasn't fair to heap that burden on her daughter. Out of necessity, because she had no one else, Vining had reached out to Emily. And Emily, because she was closer to her mother than anyone else, had stood up.

But Vining was stronger now. She had put Em on a need-to-know basis.

Vining wouldn't say she was cured. She didn't believe in closure. Hated the feel-good concept. Hated the extra burden it put on victims and families to "get over it" and "move on." Some things in life were so horrible, there was no getting over them. There was only getting used to them. Living with them, like strange bedfellows one would toss out in a second if given the chance. They never got that chance. The twisted turn of events was handed to them. Here, live with it.

Vining spent her days living with it and not liking it. T. B. Mann was with her always, as integral a part of her life as a heart murmur. She knew he wasn't about to let her forget him, even for a moment. Still, she had to continue the fight. She couldn't undo what he'd done, but she could make him a memory rather than a day-to-day reality. He took his nourishment from her well-being. He was a leech on her soul. She had to burn him off. He had to die.

He had sent Nitro to goad her. It was a mistake. Potentially fatal. She would turn his device back on him. Before she'd left the Big G, she'd waited for L. Chapel, the psych tech, to return to the front. She'd pulled him aside and said there was another hundred in it for him if he let her know before Nitro was going to be released. She wrote down her cell number on a plain piece of paper. She'd be waiting for Nitro, and she'd follow him straight to T. B. Mann.

Emily looked up from her book. "I made goat cheese and fig quesadillas. It sounds awful, but it's good. The chef on the Food Network made it on the grill, but I cooked it on the griddle."

Vining snagged a quesadilla triangle from beneath the plastic wrap covering the plate in the refrigerator. "This is great, Em. Thanks."

"There's a bag of arugula in there too. Drizzle on vinaigrette from the bottle in the fridge. The chef on the show made it from scratch, but whatever."

"Bottled dressing . . . I don't know, Em." Vining walked behind Emily's chair, slid her arms around her, and kissed her on the cheek. "Whatcha reading?"

Emily turned the book to show the cover. "*Razored Soul*. It's fantastic. I can't put it down."

"That thing. Please don't tell me you bought that with your hard-earned babysitting money."

"Aubrey's mother lent it to me. She read it in one night and loved it. It's really good."

"That jerk murdered a twenty-two-year-old man in cold blood. Now he's a celebrity."

"You haven't even read the book. He did his time. He's reformed."

"Reformed."

"Mom, don't you believe in redemption? You've gotten cynical."

Vining let the dig slide. "He's good-looking."

"He's a total fox."

Closing her bedroom door, Vining thought about her daughter's question. Did she believe in redemption? Could she paint her dogged pursuit of the Nitro mystery and T. B. Mann in that rosy hue? Or was her true motive baser? Vengeance. Pure and simple.

From her purse, she took Johnna Alwin's blood-speckled necklace and carefully arranged it on the bed. Pearls and garnet. She followed with the necklace she'd confiscated from Nitro. Pearls and sapphire. Then she retrieved her own. Pearls and pearl.

All the same. All connected.

Who were the other women in Nitro's drawings?

The phone rang. Vining frowned when she glanced at the clock. It was close to midnight. She let Em answer it, as it was probably one of her friends. Teenagers occupied a different universe when it came to the appropriate time for phone calls.

Emily knocked on her door.

Vining quickly tossed a pillow over the necklaces. She felt ridiculous, like she was hiding contraband.

"It's Jim," her daughter said through the door.

Vining picked up the extension in her room. "Hey."

"Sorry to call so late."

They both heard a click as Emily hung up the other phone.

"It's all right. I'm up. What's going on?"

"I had an interesting trip down to Niland." He quickly filled her in. "The real reason I called is we found Dillon Somerset. He wasn't backpacking in the Sierras. He was living in Oliver Mercer's house."

"What a nut case."

"It gets better. He confessed to the Mercer and Richards murders."

TWENTY-SIX

The PPD Cadets who had been watching Oliver Mercer's house had noticed a dim light coming from inside. The patrol officers who burst in found lit candles surrounding the bloody area where Mercer's and Richards's bodies had been found. Somerset's sleeping bag was nearby. He had been keeping vigil.

He had gained entry to the house through an unlocked sliding glass door off the living room terrace, throwing a rope over the railing and climbing up. The cadets were positioned at the front of the house to keep sightseers and family and friends away until it was released by the PPD. The home's backyard was a terraced hillside that ran into the backyard of the house facing the street below it. It would have been easy for Somerset to hop the fence into Mercer's yard.

Vining and Kissick would have dismissed his confession as the ravings of a crackpot, but Somerset had revealed details about the crime that had not been released to the public. When the PPD officers arrested Somerset at Mercer's house, he was raving about having murdered Mercer and Richards. The officers reported that Somerset seemed delusional.

Even though the confession stemmed more from a twist of fate than from a searing interview by Ruiz, he was acting as if he'd broken the case. Kissick and Vining could not dispute the importance of a confession from a key suspect, but they were far from convinced that they should take their eyes off of Mark Scoville and Jack Jenkins, even for a second.

Lieutenant Beltran, who was all about closing cases, was already beating the drum.

Somerset refused to have an attorney present while he was being interviewed by the detectives. This did nothing to stop his father from hiring one. Before long, notorious criminal defense attorney Carmen Vidal showed up at the station. The detectives were surprised to learn that Vidal was much more petite than she appeared on television. The only part that seemed bigger was her black hair. Her abrasive demeanor, however, came through as effectively in person as it did over the tube as she argued with Sergeant Early.

Early kept her cool. "Ms. Vidal, Dillon Somerset has waived his right to an attorney. I can not allow you to speak with him until he asks for one."

"I'm not convinced that you've adequately explained Dillon's rights and the ramifications of waiving them to him."

"Ms. Vidal, our detectives are seasoned investigators. They've made Dillon aware of his rights and he said that he understands."

"Sergeant, you need to understand something. Dillon is a highly intelligent—a genius, actually—and sensitive young man. The only possible reason he would have confessed to these murders is because he was intimidated by your cops. One of your cops who apprehended Dillon has had several complaints filed against him for excessive use of force. The threats and intimidation started in the Mercer house and are continuing right now in your interview room. We'll be forced to make an example of the Pasadena Police Department to demonstrate that you cannot impinge on citizens' civil rights. Dillon has no criminal record. You can waste taxpayer money pursuing this charade, or you can let this clearly distraught young man go home and grieve for his murdered girlfriend in peace."

Early quipped, "Stalking her makes her his girlfriend?"

Vidal didn't respond.

"Ms. Vidal," Early began, remaining patient. "Six officers and one of our most seasoned field sergeants were on-scene when Dillon was arrested inside Mercer's home. We have statements from each of them, all reporting that Dillon did not resist and he repeatedly stated, without provocation, 'I killed them. I killed them both.' Further, the entire interview is being videotaped so there can be no question about what went on. You already know all of this, Ms. Vidal. You're wasting my time, and I don't enjoy people wasting my time. If Dillon requests an attorney, we'll let you know. For now, I'll have someone escort you downstairs. If you choose to wait, you can do so in the lobby."

"How long am I supposed to sit there?"

"As long as Dillon's parents are prepared to pay your hourly fee."

* * *

While Sergeant Early happily watched Carmen Vidal leave the area, Kissick came up to her.

"Isn't she that attorney who's on television all the time?" he asked.

"Yep. The highly paid advocate for the notorious. Has Dillon asked for an attorney yet?"

"Nope. He says attorneys are idiots. We're idiots. Everyone's an idiot, except Dillon."

"How's it going?"

Kissick looked dubious. "Well, we took his statement."

"You don't think much of it."

"He got some things right about the crime, but he spent a couple of days in that house. He's a smart, analytical guy."

"A genius," Early offered sarcastically.

"Makes sense that he would have figured a few things out, but he got key things wrong. He said he stabbed Lauren to death when her neck was broken. That's a big detail to muck up. Without any evidence, the best we can do is arrest him on a couple of rinky-dink charges."

"Maybe Nan and the others will find what we need in his apartment," Early said. "I just can't figure it out. Dillon seems lucid. He's intelligent. If he didn't do it, why confess?"

"Sarge, I'm gonna get to the bottom of it if it takes all night."

The PPD detectives searched for evidence at Somerset's apartment and his parents' house.

The main house was a burnt sienna–colored Mediterranean in San Marino, a city of 13,000 wealthy and merely affluent residents that bordered Pasadena to the south. The apartment above the four-car garage where Somerset lived was a studio with a small kitchen.

Caspers and Vining were tagging and bagging in the apartment. Other teams were going through the main house.

"This is a sweet crib," Caspers said. "I wonder how much Somerset's parents would rent it to me for, seeing as it's going to be empty when their son ends up on death row."

"I'm sure they'd appreciate having a new tenant already lined up. Though I doubt they need the money, judging from this spread." Vining was shaking out books she was taking from the shelves that lined the available wall space. "This guy lives like a monk."

"What does he read?"

Vining looked at the cover of the book she held. "Everything. Mostly science fiction and history. He's got some of the classics that my daughter's been reading in her classes."

Caspers was searching the large closet in the main room.

The only item of interest they'd found was a collage of photos of Lauren Richards covering the bathroom wall. Most of the photos appeared to have been taken without her knowledge. Richards's head had been sliced out of many of them. The detectives hadn't found the heads. It was curious that Somerset had defaced only some of the pictures.

So far, they hadn't found women's clothing, wigs, or makeup in Somerset's apartment. However, they were intrigued by the size of Somerset's mother and her fake hair.

"All this guy wears is khaki pants, white dress shirts, jeans, and T-shirts. Check this out." Caspers held up a hanger with a T-shirt emblazoned with "Grateful Dead" and the band's logo of a skeleton in a top hat. "Maybe he's not such a nerd after all."

"The kids in Emily's school are wearing those vintage rock band T-shirts." Vining saw that Caspers coveted the shirt. "They wearing them in the clubs, too?"

"They look good under a leather jacket."

"My mom used to be a deadhead."

"No way."

"Yep. Back in the day. She was a wild girl. All of her old clothes are still at my grandmother's house in Alhambra. I'll go through them and see if I can find any rock band T-shirts for you."

"Cool." Caspers searched the pockets of a pair of Somerset's pants. "So did your mom go to all the Grateful Dead concerts?"

"She went to a lot of them. She wanted to be a hippie, but she was a little young when that whole Haight-Ashbury thing was going on."

"She must have smoked a little weed in her day."

"Yes, she did."

"What's she doing now?"

"Dating a sales manager for a company that makes foam packaging and taking golf lessons so she can be part of his country club crowd. Hoping he'll be husband number five."

"She's been married four times?"

"Yep. My sister and I have different fathers. Neither of us knows our dads."

"Really? Here I thought you had this normal, boring family."

"Good."

"I'm the one with the normal, boring family," Caspers said. "You've never met your dad?"

"Never."

"Do you know anything about him?"

"Not much." Vining opened the futon that Somerset used as both a couch and bed. She pulled it away from the wall and exclaimed, "Aha!" as she held up a string of condoms. "Found his stash." She looked at the expiration dates on them. "These are pretty old. Shows he was hopeful."

"Three condoms is a stash?"

"What's that? A Friday night for you?"

"I'm just saying . . ."

"I shoulda stopped while I was ahead." Vining dropped to her knees and searched the futon mattress.

She didn't know why she'd told Caspers so much about her family. She wasn't trying to hide anything. She just didn't enjoy talking about it. She had researched her father. He'd received an honorable discharge from the Army in the late seventies. In the eighties, he'd done time in prison for selling drugs. After he'd gotten out of prison and completed parole, the trail went cold. She'd seen photos of him. While she had her mother's facial features, she had her father's dark coloring, height, and slender build. She wondered if he'd seen her on the news and had any clue that she was his daughter. She wondered if he was dead.

Beside the bed was a pair of Nike athletic shoes. She turned them over and studied the soles. She got to her feet with one and walked closer to a window for more light.

"Look at this." A dark brown substance covered part of the tread on the sole. "This look like dried blood to you?"

"Could be." Caspers took the shoe from her. He probed the sole with his gloved finger. "I think it's blood. If it's from the crime scene, it shows that Somerset was there even before he started camping out at Mercer's house."

Vining, instead of elation, felt empty. Somerset as the murderer felt cold to her while Scoville and the mysterious Jack Jenkins glowed.

Vining and Caspers were on their way out when Vining said, "The refrigerator and freezer."

"What about them?"

"Did you check them?"

"No."

"We need to check them out."

Caspers rubbed his hands together. "Maybe Dillon's got drugs in there."

"That too, but there's something more important we're looking for." Vining waved her hand. "Something very important. Something missing from the crime scene." She waggled her fingers in front of him. "This is a hint, Alex."

"The hand!" Caspers raised his index finger.

"The hand," Vining confirmed. "Possibly still wearing Mercer's USC class ring." She went into the kitchen and opened the freezer door.

TWENTY-SEVEN

Mark Scoville sat at his desk in the Marquis offices. His eyes had grown accustomed to the dark. He didn't want the lights on. He felt as if he was living in darkness anyway.

He held a photograph in a silver frame, seeing it dimly

by the light from the street and the moon. It was of his older brother, Ludlow Jr., at age three playing on the rug beneath that same desk while the old man did paperwork on top of it. The shot looked spontaneous, but Scoville's mother later told him that it had been staged by his father to imitate a famous photograph Ludlow Sr. had admired of President Kennedy at work in the Oval Office while John-John played on the floor.

Scoville picked up another framed photo of his father as a much older man. A toddler again played beneath the desk—Scoville's own son, Ludlow, the old man's pride and joy in his sunset years. His hope for the future. There was no such photo of Scoville and his father taking the roles of the slain president and his now-dead son. The only two photos of Scoville the old man had in his office were a family group shot when his brother was alive and a more current one of the three generations of Scoville men—grandfather, father, son—taken shortly after the old man's diagnosis.

Scoville had never known a time when he hadn't lived in someone's shadow. He'd thought his father's death would finally liberate him. But like brainwashed prisoners of war for whom the gates are finally flung open, he chose to stay inside his cell. He knew no other way.

He took his bottle from his desk drawer and poured the last of the Grey Goose vodka into his coffee mug over ice culled from the employee lunchroom. The mug, a joke gift from his secretary, was imprinted with the message "You don't have to be crazy to work here, but it helps."

He swirled the vodka until it was chilled and took a sip. From his desk he could see one of the firm's most prominent and profitable billboard faces, with an ad for a blockbuster swashbuckling pirate movie. The cleavage of the female costar, pushed up and out in a leather bustier, was at Scoville's eye level. Normally, he would have found such a coincidence amusing and entertaining. Tonight, it only made him think of Dena. Lately, the only way he could think of Dena, in spite of his efforts to shove the image from his mind, was of her bent over the back of the couch with Crowley ramming her.

He opened a bottom drawer of the desk and felt for Jenkins's gun. He was going to lock the drawer and leave it alone. Let it be. But it called to him. Just like that bottle of Grey Goose called to him. He heard the siren call of his dark angel, and he heeded. Could Jenkins have been right? Does everyone have a killer within?

Scoville set the gun on the desk and peeled back the scarf. It had been years since he'd fired a gun, but he knew how to shoot. His father had liked guns, owned some, and made sure his sons knew their way around firearms. Dena had of course gotten rid of his father's collection when Luddy was born.

Using the scarf, he picked the gun up by the barrel. Something had been filed off from an area on the grip. Jenkins had said the gun was untraceable. Scoville didn't know enough about things like that to know if it was even possible. SIG SAUER was etched on the barrel.

Scoville smiled. It sounded macho. The silencer made the gun seem criminal. He'd never fired a gun with a silencer, and wondered how it sounded.

Taking down his father's old unabridged dictionary, he stood it on a shelf against a row of books. He stepped back. Aiming the gun with both hands, he shoved his finger onto the trigger with the scarf around it, held his breath, and fired. The gun made a sharp clack, like a nail gun. The noise both surprised and thrilled him.

The bullet had made a precise hole in the dictionary. He took it down and saw that the bullet had lodged in the middle of the S's, between "sordid" and "sorehead."

He again stepped back and took aim, this time with one hand, feeling more comfortable with the gun. He squeezed off two rounds in quick succession, enjoying the adrenaline rush. He took down the dictionary to throw away later.

Sitting at his desk, he tapped his finger on his keyboard to wake up his computer and did a search on Sig Sauer. He found a photo of his weapon and learned it was widely used in the military, prized for its reliability and durability. He again picked up the gun and admired it anew.

Still holding the gun with the scarf, he walked to the window and aimed the gun at the heart of the starlet on the billboard, which for him was at the contact point of her two mounded breasts. He stood spread-legged, gripped the gun in both hands, and uttered a sharp, "Clack!" as if he'd fired it, jerking his hands up with pretend recoil. He imagined a perfect spot of red between those breasts, lasting just a moment before a trickle of blood appeared, followed by a torrent. The starlet's face became Dena's. She blinked and said, "I'm sorry, Mark. I love you," as the life faded from her eyes.

He paid her no heed, but turned his attention to her handsome male costar, the dashing pirate. The actor morphed into Bowie Crowley. It was an easy leap, as the actor also had long tousled hair and too-sensitive-for-this-world eyes. Scoville finished him off with a bullet right between those eyes.

"Clack!"

Recoil.

They were both bloody and dead. Scoville's feeling of triumph was fleeting, and was soon overwhelmed by despair.

He was not a killer. Despite what Jenkins had said, he couldn't be turned into a killer any more than he could be turned into an Olympic athlete. You either have that in you or you don't.

He should call the cops right now. He wasn't in any trouble with the police yet. He hadn't lied to them. Well, just a little. He should call those detectives. They'd probably make him wear a wire, meet with Jenkins, and try to get him to talk about how he'd murdered Oliver and Lauren. He could do that. That shouldn't be too hard.

On the other hand . . . His fury against Crowley and Dena was like a slow burn within him. He knew Dena had been thinking of leaving him. He'd felt it in his bones. Seen it in the slight, disdainful curve at the edge of her mouth when she spoke to him. He'd known that it was the beginning of the end when she got sober and stayed sober and he didn't. He'd tried it for a while. Sure, he felt healthier, and it was nice not being hungover. Ultimately, though, he'd concluded that reality was highly overrated. Reality couldn't hold a candle to getting a good toot on. He wasn't even talking about getting drunk. He just wanted those blurred edges. That's all. He knew his drinking lately had been over the top, but it hadn't always been that way. For years, all he sought was that nice, fuzzy haze. Ahh . . . That's better. It made the whole thing tolerable. But Dena had bought into the entire A.A. religion. All or nothing.

Maybe she would leave him, in spite of a divorce damaging her image. She'd take her substantial income with her. She'd been living paycheck to paycheck when they'd first met, but she was pulling down good money now, even though she didn't think so. He'd resisted putting her name on the deed to the house, but was forced to when they'd refinanced to get a lower interest rate. They'd needed her income to do the deal. Her name was on nearly everything now. Maybe she'd planned it all along. She'd leave and force him to sell out. She'd slowly and steadily built an investment portfolio of her own. He'd get part of it as community property under California law. Still, he'd be screwed. Her career was heading up. One of the big networks had been talking to her about joining its morning show. His career . . .

Well, he knew where his career was headed.

He peered into the coffee mug and the dwindling vodka. He took a miserly sip.

But if Dena died, he'd keep the house and the business and most of her assets. He was trustee over the portion she'd set aside for the two kids until they were twenty-five. He considered that his money too, for the time being. Plus she had a handsome life insurance policy. He and his son, Luddy, would make a fine life for themselves. He'd marry again, to someone who was actually nice to him. Someone less flashy than Dena. Less self-absorbed. Less beautiful, even. He'd settle for merely attractive. That was an acceptable trade-off for loyalty. As for Dena's daughter, Dahlia, he couldn't care less. She would be eighteen soon anyway. He'd kick her out that same day, if she hadn't already left on her own like she was always threatening to do.

Maybe murder wasn't as tough as he was making it out to be.

Scoville played out the thread. He could murder Crowley and Dena, and then, in a twist, plant the gun on Jenkins. He knew Jenkins lived with his mother out by the Salton Sea. Jenkins said she owned a gas station and mini-mart out there. That couldn't be hard to find. Jenkins wanted Crowley dead for some reason. Others must know about that. There must be a connection between Jenkins and Crowley that made Jenkins leery of killing Crowley himself.

On second thought, instead of planting the gun on Jenkins, it would be cleaner if he just killed him too. He could make it look like a suicide. He'd turn Jenkins's crazy murder plan back onto him. It would serve the freak right. Jenkins would get just what he deserved.

Scoville toyed with the scarf-cloaked gun and took another sip of vodka, feeling his blood pressure rise with indignation at the thought of Jenkins trying to turn him into his patsy. Guys like that were always getting the upper hand on him. Tried to walk right over him. His own father was like that. The old man had even had the nerve to call him a pussy. Because he wasn't a manly man, he'd taken crap from bolder men his whole life.

Now he had to deal with Jack Jenkins. Or Jill . . . Whatever. There seemed to be no end of schoolyard dramas and the long reach of bullies in his life.

He finished the vodka in the coffee cup, chewing on the ice. Taking the empty bottle from his desk, he put it in his briefcase. He picked up the gun and set it inside too. He pushed his chair back and stood, too fast. He staggered and steadied himself against the desk. Regaining his balance, he took his briefcase and left.

At first Scoville thought he'd go home, but once on the road in his Porsche, home didn't sound appealing. No place did. He felt rootless. Adrift. It was a feeling he'd never experienced before. There had never been a time when he hadn't known where "home" was. For him, it had always been the big Tudor mansion in Hancock Park. Even during the years he'd run from it, it had always been home.

Dena had ruined it for him. Dena, Crowley, Jenkins, and even Mercer. Mercer had started it. His ambitions had planted the evil little seed that had led to where Scoville was right now. It was as if all of them were in a line, like the tail of the Big Dipper. At a stoplight, he looked up and saw the constellation, his head tilted back. Not many stars shone through the city's smog and lights, but those of the Big Dipper made it. That single star off to the side was Lauren Richards. She was part of it. All of them together. Bad stars casting him under a bad sign.

Agitated honking from the cars behind roused him. Apparently, the light had turned green some time ago. Scoville gunned the Porsche's engine, the tires squealing, as he held his right arm aloft in the topless car, middle finger erect.

As he drove down the Strip, he passed billboard after billboard, most of them belonging to Marquis, all with photos of gorgeous thin models in Dolce & Gabbana, Armani, Chanel, or Prada. Or showing off their watches: Tag Heuer, Rolex, Baume & Mercier. The only relief was a billboard advertising a new animated film about farm animals. Even that had a vampish character—a slinky little filly. Scoville made his hand into a gun and shot all the pretty models in each of the billboards he passed, the women between the breasts, the men between the eyes. His signature kill.

Clack!

Turning onto a side street, he blew past the parking lot of a liquor store. The tires complained when he made a sharp right into the alley behind it, scraping the front fender against the thorny branches of a bougainvillea vine that had engulfed a fence. He stopped the car. A spray of blossoms on a potentially eye-obliterating woody stalk brushed his face and littered the car with magenta confetti.

Forgetting about his briefcase on the passenger seat but remembering to snatch the keys from the ignition, Scoville left his car and stumbled from the alley to the sidewalk and then to the liquor store.

Returning with a fifth of Grey Goose and a sack of ice,

he was startled to see someone sitting on the hood of the Porsche.

"Hey! What the fuck?"

The man slid off his big haunch and stood. "That's what I was gonna ask you, pal."

Scoville squinted through his vodka haze. He'd seen this man before. He thought back and remembered where he'd seen his fat, fleshy face, at Crowley's book signing in Pasadena. Scoville clutched his purchases tightly to his chest. The plastic bag filled with ice felt like the cold embrace of a corpse.

The man lumbered toward him. "Bennie Lusk sent me. You owe him for that thing last week and the vig on top of it."

Even though Scoville was drunk, he knew he was lighter on his feet than the overweight thug. He'd had it with people telling him what to do. "Fuck you."

He darted past, lobbed his purchases into the Porsche, and got the driver's door open.

"Fuck me? No, I'm gonna fuck *you* up."

The guy came at Scoville, slugging him in the kidney and sending him sprawling onto the seat, crashing into the bottle and bag of ice, and slamming his head against the gearshift.

The thug was on top of Scoville, hitting him in the face.

Scoville was crushed beneath him, pinned by the steering wheel and the gearshift. He grabbed a handful of the thug's oily hair and pulled hard enough to make the guy jerk back. It was enough for Scoville to slip out from under the steering wheel. The thug was on him again. Scoville could see that the guy was loving it. He felt himself losing consciousness. He blindly groped with his right hand, touching his briefcase and the bag of melting ice, but he couldn't grab them. He then touched something hard and solid that fit perfectly in his hand. He instinctively closed his fingers around it. As the thug drew back his hand for another punch, Scoville swung the vintage hood ornament, hitting him in the side of the head.

The thug reared back, blinking.

Still on his back, Scoville thrust both feet against the guy's belly.

The thug staggered backward, stumbled on the uneven asphalt, and fell to the ground.

Scoville could have gotten away, started his car and left, but something held him there. He got up and walked over.

Dazed, the thug couldn't get to his feet. He kept rolling back onto his butt. He reminded Scoville of a turtle stranded on its back. Standing a few feet away, Scoville saw dark shiny blood running down the thug's face. His own face felt wet and numb. He forgot about that as he watched the thug. Scoville laughed.

The thug slurred, "I'm gonna fuck you up."

Scoville darted forward and kicked him onto his back. He straddled him, swinging the heavy hunk of metal, and laughing.

"Look at you now, asshole. Look at you now."

He kept hitting and hitting and laughing until the man's head was mush, the blows no longer creating a sharp retort, but making their mark like a fist against oatmeal. The man's head now bloody pulp, Scoville roared as each blow struck home.

"Look at you now!"

TWENTY-EIGHT

Dillon Somerset's lanky form was hunched, his brow furrowed, his lips pursed beneath his toothbrush mustache. He leaned against the table with fingers interlaced, perfectly still but for his thumbs, which he ceaselessly tapped together. The fluorescent lights in the interview room reflected off his shaved head and black-framed glasses.

Kissick leaned against the wall, arms crossed. He sometimes used his height as an intimidation factor, but he had another reason for assuming that pose now: he'd spent most of the day sitting. His shirtsleeves on his periwinkle-blue shirt were rolled up but his tie was still snug around his neck.

Ruiz sat opposite Somerset. His tie was loose. His white shortsleeve shirt bloused over the top of his pants along with his waistline. His shirt hadn't held up to the long day as well as Kissick's. Ruiz's wife laundered and ironed his shirts herself and had bought Costco's Kirkland brand for him for years. Bachelor Kissick sent his shirts out and didn't scrimp on quality, shopping at Nordstrom—a habit he'd retained from his ex-wife.

Ruiz set glasses on his nose and began reading Somerset's statement aloud. "Dillon, this is what you told us. 'That Saturday night, I followed Lauren to Oliver Mercer's house. I watched the gate open and after she drove in, I parked down the street and hopped the fence onto

Mercer's property. I brought a knife with me. I rang the doorbell and when Mercer answered it, I stabbed him. He ran into the living room and I kept stabbing him. Lauren was screaming and I grabbed her and stabbed her too. When they were dead, I used their blood to write on the wall. Then I took a chain saw and cut Mercer into little pieces and put all his body parts into a big pile.' "

Taking off his glasses, Ruiz held them by an arm and tapped them against the report. "Dillon, this is bullshit. You need to tell us what really happened that night."

Somerset's voice was flat. "It's not bullshit. That's what happened. How many times are you going to ask me that?"

"As many times as it takes for you to tell us the truth." Ruiz pushed back from the table.

Somerset continued tapping his thumbs together.

Kissick began. "Dillon, why did you confess to two murders you didn't do?"

"I *did* murder them." Somerset sat straight. His head looked big atop his skinny neck. He stared at Kissick, his eyes intense. "I'm responsible. It was me. I wanted to be close to her. To Lauren. She and I belong together, forever. He was no good for her, that Oliver Mercer. I tried to tell her." The veins on his neck bulged as his voice became strident. "I warned her about him. Now that's all I hear. All everyone talks about. Lauren and Oliver, Lauren and Oliver, Lauren and that . . ." Somerset pursed his lips, struggling for an apt description of Mercer. He spat it out. "That *idiot*." His face was flushed and he was panting. He stroked his square mustache then continued tapping his thumbs.

Kissick looked at Somerset anew, intrigued by his lapse of control.

Ruiz tried to remain calm but didn't make it. He jabbed his finger toward the suspect. "Dillon, I sense you're holding back. I sense you're hiding something. Today is the day to tell the truth. The truth never hurt anyone."

Somerset mumbled, "I have told the truth."

"Dillon. Dillon, look at me." Kissick held up two fingers and pointed at his own eyes.

Somerset stopped his thumb-tapping and became eerily still.

Kissick raised his voice. "You're wasting our time with this bullshit. *Look at me.*"

Somerset defiantly swung his head to face him. He sniffed.

"Dillon, we know you're not telling the truth."

Somerset swallowed, and then darted out his hand to snatch a plastic bottle of water from the table. He unscrewed the sealed cap and guzzled most of it down. Finishing, he brushed his fingers against his lips and set the bottle back on the table but still held the cap.

Kissick loomed over him. "Okay, Dillon, this is what's going to happen. You'll go to trial and you'll be convicted. Your attorney will make a lot of money, but you'll go to prison. They'll put you on a train and take you to San Quentin and put you on death row. When you're laying on that table waiting for the needle, Detective Ruiz and I won't be there. Your parents will be there, outside the window, but you'll be on that table alone. Is that what you want?"

Somerset tightly squeezed the bottle cap between his fingers, bending the hard plastic.

"We're trying to help you out, Dillon," Ruiz said. "Tell us why you confessed."

"Are you dense?" Somerset said. "I confessed because I did it."

"I need to take a break." Kissick left the room.

Ruiz followed.

* * *

In the adjoining room, crowded around the two-way glass, were Sergeant Early, Lieutenant Beltran, and Vining.

"What do you think, guys?" Beltran asked Ruiz and Kissick.

Ruiz took a handkerchief from his back pocket and used it to blot his nearly bald head. "After a couple of hours of working on him, he won't retract his confession. That tells me all I need to know. That tells me he's our guy."

"I can't get past his problem with the facts," Kissick said.

"He talked about using a chain saw to dismember Mercer," Ruiz protested. "That's factual."

"He could have figured that out," Kissick argued. "He saw the little bits of flesh all over the room and the blood splatter pattern. What about Mercer's body parts? He said he stacked them. They weren't arbitrarily stacked. They were carefully arranged. What about Mercer's face being painted with blood? And how about the bloody footprint made by a size eleven high heel?"

Ruiz folded the handkerchief and shoved it back inside his pocket. "But he said he only dismembered Mercer and not Richards, which *is* accurate."

"I attribute that to him not being able to imagine her body being desecrated," Kissick said. "His description of what happened to Richards is wrong. That's what tells me he's lying."

"He was in some sort of a psychotic state when he did it," Ruiz said. "In his mind, that's how it happened."

"I agree," Beltran said.

"He's a nut," Kissick said. "But he's not our nut."

"Jim, how do you explain finding a key piece of evidence in his closet?" Beltran asked. "If the blood on that athletic shoe matches one of the victim's, that proves this isn't a false confession."

Early added, "It shows he was in the murder house before he set up his shrine there."

"How long are we going to keep working him?" Ruiz asked. "Let's charge him with the murders."

"I was just talking to Carmen Vidal," Beltran said. "She's madder than hell, having to sit in the lobby." He laughed. "I don't know what she has to complain about. It looks like she's opened up an office. Got her papers spread out, her Blackberry and everything."

"I don't know what she has to complain about either," Early said. "She's probably being paid six hundred dollars an hour to sit there."

Kissick let his eyes light upon Vining's.

She guessed what he was thinking. They could both see Lieutenant Beltran planning the press conference over which he'd preside like a conquering hero. One of the commanders was retiring and everyone knew that Beltran considered himself the heir apparent.

Vining turned and left without explanation.

"Somerset is hiding something, but he's not our killer. I'm not ready to charge him with the murders yet." Kissick stepped away from the group, as if anticipating the onslaught that was about to be directed at him. He wished Vining would return to help back him up and wondered why she'd abandoned him.

Beltran was first, keeping his voice low. "All due respect, Corporal, but why would he confess to two murders he didn't commit and not retract the confession after hours of being grilled?"

"Lieutenant, I don't know."

Vining returned carrying a large, manila evidence envelope. "I had a thought. Mind if I take a turn with Somerset?"

Ruiz didn't immediately respond, not wanting to cede any potential advantage to Vining. When Kissick said, "Be our guest," and Beltran said, "Give it a shot, Corporal," Ruiz climbed on board. "Go ahead."

Vining carried the envelope into the interview room.

TWENTY-NINE

"*I'm detective* Nan Vining."

She garnered the brightest spark of interest from Somerset that he'd shown since the interrogation had begun.

Taking latex gloves from her pocket, she put them on, then opened the envelope's brass clasps. She tipped the contents onto the table. Out tumbled a small wicker box and several small manila envelopes. She moved the wicker box to the middle of the table.

Somerset glared at the box and the small envelopes. His face and shaved head grew pink.

Vining took the lid off the box. "We found this among your possessions at Oliver Mercer's house. All these items were in it."

Somerset said through gritted teeth, "Don't touch that. That's mine."

"I know it's yours," Vining said.

Vining opened one of the envelopes and took out a white terrycloth headband. "What's this, Dillon?"

"That's Lauren's. It's mine."

"Where did you get it?"

Somerset's face grew more flushed and he didn't answer.

Vining answered for him. "Lauren's mother said that Lauren used to wear headbands like this at the gym. She probably dropped it on the way to her car."

"Give it to me." Somerset held out his hand.

"Sorry." Vining set it inside the wicker box. She opened and upended another envelope, spilling the contents into her palm. She held up the stub of a movie ticket and read the information on it. "One ticket to an animated kids' movie. Sunday matinee. You went by yourself to this, didn't you, Dillon? You followed Lauren when she took her kids, didn't you?"

"I don't like you touching my things." Somerset rubbed his hands over the top of his head.

Kissick silently slipped inside the room and stood near Somerset.

"Bet Lauren was real happy having you in the theater with her kids." Vining put the ticket stub inside the box.

Still holding his head, his elbows on the table, Somerset said, "I watched over her. That's mine. Don't touch it."

"Now, I'd really like to know what's behind this." Vining emptied a small envelope onto the large one. Tiny oval scraps of paper tumbled out. She began turning them over. They were the missing heads cut from the photos of Lauren they'd found in Somerset's apartment.

Somerset bolted from his chair and began to lunge for the severed heads. "Those are mine!"

Kissick grabbed his shoulders and pushed him back down.

"She can't touch those," Somerset complained, pointing at Vining.

Kissick left his one hand on Somerset's shoulder, reminding him that he was still there.

Vining left the severed heads where they were—tiny smiling Laurens, over and over. On top of them she poured out the contents of more envelopes. One held a brightly colored grosgrain ribbon. Another held a dried rosebud. Another held a ticket from a parking valet.

"What about this, Dillon?" she asked. "And this? And this?"

Somerset kept repeating, "It's mine. It's Lauren's. It's mine."

Vining dumped out the last envelope. It held an acrylic fingernail, painted with coral-colored polish. She picked it up in her gloved hand. It had been torn off. A patch of the wearer's real fingernail adhered to the glue.

"It's mine, it's Lauren's, it's—"

Vining held it toward Somerset. "This is not Lauren's."

"Yes, it is. It's Lauren's. It's mine."

Vining still held up the fingernail. "Where did you get this, Dillon?"

Somerset slid his hands toward his treasures.

Kissick again seized his shoulder. "Don't move."

Somerset looked at Vining. Tears were in his eyes. "They're mine. They're Lauren's. They're all I have left."

"Tell me where you got this fingernail, Dillon, and you can have them." She did not intend to return the items to him.

He blinked away tears. "In the house. I took it off Lauren's body. I took it from her hand."

"No you didn't, Dillon. You didn't take it from her hand. Lauren's fingernails were short and had clear polish. Why are you pretending that you killed her?"

"Because I loved her. If anyone was going to kill her, it should have been me."

"But it wasn't you."

He hung his head. "I wanted to protect her and make

life beautiful for her. If she had to be murdered, I should have done it, to protect her."

Vining began picking up Somerset's mementos and returning them to the small envelopes.

He didn't protest. His terrible secret now out, he seemed broken. He wiped his nose on his sleeve and rubbed his hand over his eyes. "Can I go now?"

Kissick had moved away from him. "No, you can't go. You broke into Oliver Mercer's house. You lied to us. That's not trivial."

"I guess maybe I need an attorney."

Vining looked at him. "Are you asking for an attorney?"

"Yes. And I need something to eat. I have low blood sugar issues."

After a break during which Somerset had an organic fruit and nut bar, he had calmed down sufficiently to tell his story.

After a long negotiation, Vidal, Kissick, Ruiz, and a prosecutor from the D.A.'s Pasadena office reached an agreement. In exchange for Somerset's complete and truthful account about how blood ended up on his Nike shoe and how he had come by the acrylic fingernail, the D.A. would not charge Dillon with burglary, usually filed as a felony, or the less-serious charges of making false statements to the police and vandalism. Somerset then detailed each occasion he'd entered Mercer's house. There had been several.

The day the murders were discovered, the PPD had brought Somerset in for questioning, starting his downward spiral. In the wee hours of the next morning, he gave in to his impulse to again visit Mercer's house—the scene of both Richards's betrayal of him and her murder. The sprinklers had been on in Mercer's yard. Somerset's damp tennis shoes on the bloody floor transferred blood to the sole of his Nike.

When he saw the crime scene, Somerset unraveled. He went home, gathered his camping gear, changed into hiking boots, leaving the bloody Nike beside the bed, and returned to Mercer's with no plans for the future other than never leaving Richards's side again.

Somerset had found the acrylic fingernail among sprays of white freesias in a vase on a sideboard in Mercer's living room. When Somerset had pulled out the flowers to incorporate them into his shrine around the blood-soaked living room floor, the torn acrylic fingernail had fallen out. Somerset believed the nail was Richards's, although he didn't recall her using something so artificial to enhance her appearance. He saw it as the corrupting influence of Oliver Mercer.

Vidal and the D.A. finally agreed to charge Somerset only with trespassing, a misdemeanor. At arraignment, the D.A. would recommend that Somerset pay a nominal fine and be released.

As Vidal led her client from the interview room, Kissick remarked to Vining, "You said Bowie Crowley wasn't your type. How about this guy? He's single now."

Vining looked deeply into his eyes. She opened her mouth as if to speak, but then turned away, saying nothing.

THIRTY

With *Somerset* no longer a suspect, the PPD turned its full attention to Jack Jenkins. Caspers, Ruiz, Jones, and Sproul set about following the paper trail and tracking down people who knew Jenkins. Vining and Kissick would return to the Salton Sea to surveil Jenkins's Stop 'N Go Market, hoping Jack would show up. Ideally, they would pick up a discarded cigarette butt, coffee cup, or something else that might carry his DNA, preferably obtained legally. The torn acrylic fingernail with the patch of DNA-laden real nail attached was already on its way for DNA testing. With any luck, they would also find skin cells or blood from Mercer or Richards.

Kissick had finished arrangements to borrow a car from Narcotics/Vice to take to the Salton Sea when Caspers approached his cubicle.

"I have a piece of business with you, Corporal Kissick," Caspers began.

"Shoot."

"Squatting dog . . ." Caspers turned around and lifted his dress shirt and T-shirt, displaying the tattooed Chinese calligraphy on his back.

"Squatting dog?" Kissick repeated, seemingly perplexed.

"Don't bullshit me, man." Caspers tucked in his shirt. Vining walked up and joined the exchange.

Kissick stifled a smile. "I don't know what you're talking about."

"Look how he laughs," said Caspers. "You *so* know what I'm talking about."

Vining chuckled too. "What's going on?"

Caspers continued riding Kissick. "I've asked two reliable sources about my tattoo. Both confirm that it says Crouching Tiger, *not* Squatting Dog." He pointed accusingly at Kissick. "You got Cameron Lam to—"

"Is that what Lam told you your tattoo says?" Kissick asked. "Squatting Dog?"

Vining cracked up.

Caspers continued pointing at Kissick. "I'm gonna get you, but good."

After shaking his finger one more time, Caspers left.

As soon as he did, Kissick wrestled harder with his laughter.

Still chuckling, Vining leaned in closer. "You had Cam Lam tell him his tattoo says Squatting Dog?"

Kissick succumbed, laughing as quietly as he could manage. Tears sprang into his eyes.

Vining raised her palm and Kissick high-fived her. Her cell phone began ringing. She took it from her pocket and looked at the display. She didn't recognize the number, but her interest was piqued by the area code: 213. Downtown L.A.

"This is Nan Vining."

"This is Leo Chapel. The psych tech down at County Hospital."

He didn't need to explain who he was.

"Yes?" she asked.

"Your guy was released."

"*What?*" Vining felt the air sucked out of her.

"About two this afternoon."

Vining looked at her watch. It was after 9:00 at night.

Mindful of Kissick nearby, she walked away from the cubicles. "You said you'd call me."

"I just started my shift. I didn't think they'd cut him loose so soon."

"Why did they?"

"He started talking. From what I've been told, when the psychiatrist on duty was making his rounds, he stopped by Nitro's bed and asked how he was doing. Nitro said, 'I'm fine.' The doctor pulled over a chair and they had a chat."

"Did Nitro say why he wouldn't talk before?"

"I read the doctor's notes in Nitro's chart. He wrote that the patient reported suffering from personal problems, was upset, and just didn't care about anything, so he stopped talking. He was sorry for the trouble he caused and wants to go home."

"What name did he sign on the release papers?"

"Nitro."

Vining closed her eyes. "Do you know if anybody picked him up?"

"My buddy who was here said he made a call from the phone in the ward, but didn't think anyone came inside to get him. He walked out and that was that."

"Thanks for calling," Vining said flatly.

"Not so fast. What about the hundred you'd said you'd give me?"

"You were supposed to call me when he was going to be released, not seven hours later."

"I told you he was gone by the time my shift started. I got all this information for you. That ought to be worth something."

"Yeah, right."

"Look, bitch. There's something here you'll want. We found it after Nitro left. Turned up at the reception desk."

"What is it?"

"An envelope that looks like it has a card in it, like an invitation. Handwriting on it says: 'Please deliver to Officer Vining, Pasadena Police Department.' "

Officer Vining. That's what T. B. Mann called her.

"If you want it, it'll be two hundred bucks."

"Excuse me?"

"I was going to give it to you when you came to pay me the hundred, but since you've been such a bitch . . . Take it or leave it."

"I'll be right down."

"I'll meet you in the parking lot in front of the E.R."

Kissick caught up with Vining while she was grabbing her purse from her locked desk drawer.

"I'm good to drive out to the Salton Sea whenever," he said. "If we went now, we'd beat the traffic. Get a couple of rooms nearby for the night. Something wrong?"

She slipped the strap of her purse over her shoulder. "Nitro was released at two o'clock this afternoon."

"They cut him loose? Why?"

She told him what the psych tech had said.

"So Nitro *was* faking," Kissick said. "What was that all about?"

"Who knows?"

"Why did this psych tech bother to call you?"

"Because someone left a letter for me down at the Big G."

"Who?"

"I don't know, Jim. I have to go down and find out."

"You going now?"

"Yes." She started walking toward the door.

He grabbed his jacket and followed. "Not alone."

"Jim, it's not a problem. I'll just pick up the letter and leave." She saw where this was heading. She didn't want him to go with her and stumble upon the true extent of her dealings with Chapel. Specifically, how she had confiscated Nitro's pearl necklace.

She continued walking.

He put his hand on her shoulder.

She turned, glaring first at his hand on her, then at him.

"Nan, I can't let you go down there and meet this guy in a dark alley. You're the one who's all about officer safety. You told me not to go around Niland by myself and you were right."

She didn't say anything at first. She knew there was no getting around him going with her, plus he was right. She had no business going there alone. She had no business taking Nitro's necklace and threatening him either, but there she was. Trapped.

"I'll drive," she said.

"That's all right. I'll drive."

Kissick parked the Crown Vic near the Big G's emergency room doors.

"There he is." Vining said. She started to get out of the car and he began to open his door.

"I don't think we should both go," she said. "One of us should stay and observe."

"Why?"

"Two of us showing up might spook him."

"Nan, you're here to pick up something that belongs to you. We're not doing a drug deal."

"Okay. Fine. Let me tell you this. That cash I got out of the ATM. It's not for me. It's for him. The psych tech."

"What? He's extorting you? How much does he want?"

"Two hundred."

"Bullshit." He looked at her as if he couldn't comprehend her. He got out and slammed the door.

She knew better than to press the issue. She was glad not to pay Chapel the money. The only reason she had gone along with the extortion was her feeling that it might buy her some confidentiality about their dealings. She knew there was no guarantee of that anyway. She'd rather keep the money. The withdrawl had nearly cleaned out her checking account until payday.

They approached the psych tech.

"Who's he?" Chapel threw down his cigarette butt and ground it out near a sign on a post that said "No Smoking. No Fumar."

"Doesn't matter," Vining said. "Where's my letter?"

He took the envelope from the shirt pocket of his uniform.

Vining immediately recognized the handwriting. The scrawl in black fountain pen ink was the same as on the note that had accompanied her pearl necklace. She felt more triumphant than afraid. He was coming out of the shadows. She was his unfinished project. He couldn't resist completing it.

Try it. Go ahead.

She took the envelope from Chapel, holding it by the corner. She would have it analyzed for fingerprints. Finding T. B. Mann's on it would confirm it came from him, but they wouldn't help her find him. He'd left prints at the El Alisal house, and they hadn't turned up in any of the criminal databases.

She slipped the envelope into her slacks pocket. "Okay, thanks." She and Kissick turned to leave.

"Wait," Chapel said. "Not so fast. Where's my money?"

Vining turned back. "No money."

Chapel aggressively stepped forward. "We had a deal."

He was bigger than Vining, but she knew how to hit him where it hurt and hit him fast, bringing him to his knees. She sensed Kissick tensing beside her, coiling to strike.

Vining met Chapel's eyes and shook her head.

"That's a bunch of crap," he said. "I didn't have to call you. You wouldn't have known anything if I hadn't called you."

Kissick's voice was low and even, but he more than made his point. "You were attempting to extort a police officer. You're lucky we don't arrest you."

"Fucking cops." Chapel raised a corner of his upper lip, showing nicotine-stained teeth. "Come down here and take whatever the hell you want. A patient's personal property, whatever. I took a ration of shit because I gave you Nitro's necklace. I had to explain to my boss, 'Well, you know, she said it looked like one that was stolen in Pasadena.' "

Vining felt a red flush prickle her chest. It would soon move up her neck and engulf her face.

Kissick betrayed no emotion. Vining, however, detected a shift, as if his aura had changed hue.

Chapel looked down, scuffed his shoe on the ground, and tried again. "C'mon. You've got twenty bucks in this for me, don't you?"

Kissick said, "Get lost."

He turned to leave and Vining did as well, glad to be out of one awkward situation, but knowing she was about to step into another.

"Fucking shit-ass cops," Chapel said to their backs.

"Yeah, yeah." Kissick opened the driver's door and got in.

In the passenger seat, Vining turned her head and fumbled with the seat belt. After she latched it, there was no place else she could look except at him.

"What went on there?" he asked.

She shrugged. "Whatever went on. You saw."

"You know what I'm talking about. You confiscated Nitro's necklace?"

"Yes."

"Why?"

"Because."

Their eyes didn't leave each other's. She knew he wouldn't believe her story about the necklace matching a report of one that had been stolen, so she didn't float it.

"You're not telling me everything."

"Right," she agreed.

He scratched his neck and turned away.

She knew he wouldn't press further now, but would later. When he reached to turn the key in the ignition, she said, "Let me borrow your Swiss Army knife."

He took out his keys, pulled down the small blade from the red knife's set of utensils, and gave it to her.

She sliced open the envelope. Inside was a card with a note written in that familiar spidery scrawl. It said "Officer Vining, your daughter looks just like you."

She again met Kissick's eyes and said, "Emily."

THIRTY-ONE

Kissick *sped* to Mt. Washington Code Three—lights and siren.

Vining called Emily while they were en route. It was

late, but the girl was still up, as was her habit during summer vacation.

Vining tried to remain calm, but nearly lost it when Em answered the phone.

"I'm reading. What's wrong, Mom? Are you okay?"

Hearing the anxiety spike in her daughter's voice made Vining wonder if maybe Kaitlyn, Emily's stepmother, was right after all about Vining's profession being a destructive influence on her daughter. Vining felt that she herself could endure anything except seeing her daughter suffer, especially when she was the cause.

"I'm okay, sweet pea. I need you to pack some things. You're going to stay with your dad for a few days."

Emily, every bit her mother's daughter, watchful and perspicacious, and, sadly, too aware of life's dark corners, said simply, "It's him."

Vining imagined her daughter rising from the easy chair where she'd likely been reading. Neither of them was good at taking bad news sitting down.

"Yes." Vining had already decided there was no point in glossing over the situation to Emily. Both of them preferred concrete facts, even if they were tough, over soft theories about what might be. Vining had tried to shield her daughter from the truth before, but it had never worked. Truth, like evil, follows its own course, like a river.

"Em, he left me a message. A note."

"Where? Did you see him?"

"I didn't see him. He left it someplace where he knew I would go. Not at the house or at work."

"What did the note say?"

In her mind, Vining saw the handwriting.

Officer Vining, your daughter looks just like you.

"It's like a taunt. He's jumped onto the chaos surrounding the double homicide and is manipulating it."

"He's messing with your mind. Scaring us."

"I believe so."

"He's like a terrorist."

After picking Emily up and making sure the house was secure, Kissick drove the thirty miles to Calabasas. At that late hour, traffic was light, but there were still plenty of cars on the road.

Vining was quiet with her thoughts, and Emily was sullen. After initially being cooperative about going to stay with her dad, the girl's adolescent defiance had found its teeth.

Kissick tried to keep the conversation light, talking about a movie he'd gone to see with his sons. Vining politely participated while Emily sulked. Conversation trailed into silence after the discussion had run its course.

While Vining appreciated his efforts, she and Emily were elsewhere. If T. B. Mann wanted to get their attention, he'd succeeded.

Emily grabbed on to Vining's seat and leaned forward. "But Mom, if T. B. Mann is just trying to scare us, why are we letting him? Why are we leaving the house?"

"Jim and I have to go out of town, possibly overnight, to follow a lead, and I don't want you to be alone."

"We can't keep running. When can I go home? Aubrey and I and a bunch of us were going to go to the movies tomorrow. I already told you. Remember?"

Vining didn't remember. "You might have to miss it if I'm not back by then."

"*Mom,* I told you. I had plans."

"Your plans have changed. I don't want you in that house alone when I'm three hours away."

"Granny can stay with me."

Emily flung herself against the backseat with a huff, her arms tightly folded across her chest. "I hate running.

I thought we weren't going to run. That we weren't going to let him control our lives or mess things up more than he already has."

"Em." Vining's tone conveyed the message that the conversation was over.

Kissick kept his eyes on the road and drove.

He knew too well the devastating effects of crime on its victims, including the victims' loved ones, especially a crime as heinous as the one inflicted upon Vining. Listening to Vining and Emily, hearing their tension and anger, brought it home to him in a personal way. He was still the lead investigator in Vining's murder attempt case. The unsolved cases haunted the most, but this one did especially. He'd never had such a close relationship with a victim before, and didn't like what it was doing to his objectivity. He'd experienced victims holding back the truth to protect their assailants if they were afraid of the assailant or if he or she was a loved one. Neither of these reasons explained why Vining wouldn't tell him what the deal was with Nitro's pearl necklace. He'd given her the chance to tell him what was going on and she'd chosen not to. Only one explanation made sense— Vining was cowboying, going it alone. The Lone Ranger, again. Her bad habit was affecting his ability to do his job, both his official job and his personal commitment to protect his loved ones, which included Vining and Emily.

As he drove, his anger with Vining grew. He would pick the time and place, but he would get to the bottom of what she was up to. He fell into his own heavy silence.

After exiting the 101, they drove down clean streets lined with older storefront businesses interspersed with newer Southwestern-inspired mini-malls. Kissick took a road that led back into golden rolling hills and arrived at the entrance to a gated neighborhood tucked there. He stopped at a kiosk, waking up a gray-haired guard inside. He flashed his shield.

Vining leaned across and explained that they were dropping off her daughter.

When they had driven through the gates, Vining goaded Kissick. "Just couldn't resist badging him."

"It's who I am, Nan," he responded dryly. He followed Vining's directions through the exclusive housing development, wending up to the crest of a hill, where the largest homes with the best views were located.

"It's the big white one there," Vining said. "I haven't seen it since they finished the addition."

Kissick whistled. "They added on to this thing?"

"Yep. The media room and family room weren't big enough," Vining explained. "And they wanted a full gym. They added two thousand square feet, so it's now about ten thousand."

"Where's the moat?" Kissick joked.

"Now the house looks even more like Tara," Emily added with a touch of sarcasm. "*Gone with the Wind* is Kaitlyn's favorite movie."

"Where shall I go? What shall I do?" Kissick pondered in a falsetto Scarlett O'Hara voice, working to lighten the mood.

"How about pulling into the driveway and stopping the car?" Vining said.

Kissick followed her orders but chided, "Come on, Vining. That's not the right answer. Ladies, work with me here."

Emily and Vining recited at the same time, "Frankly, my dear, we don't give a damn!"

"A little too much enthusiasm, but okay."

Then Kissick was distracted by a lithesome woman standing on the front porch. She wore a low-cut cotton shift that showed off her reed-thin figure and substantial assets.

A large yellow Labrador obediently stood beside her, trembling with excitement.

"The dreaded Kaitlyn, I presume," Kissick said.

Vining felt a twinge of guilt over all the Kaitlyn-bashing she'd done, though some of it was well-deserved. Kaitlyn had lured a married man from his home and young daughter. Granted, Wes wasn't an unwilling patsy. Still, Vining could only imagine Kaitlyn's romantic pillow talk early on: "It's not fair for you to be so unhappy, Wes. . . ."

But now, Kaitlyn had walked in Vining's shoes. "She's just making her way, like the rest of us."

Kissick paused in opening his door, one eyebrow arched. "Did you get religion or something, Nan?"

She got out and shot back as she headed toward the house, "Things change, James. Things change."

Emily bolted from the car and called, "Woofster!" Her malaise dissipated at the sight of the Lab.

She dropped to her knees on the grass and the dog bounded toward her, knocking her over. They wrestled on the lawn, the dog prancing and barking. He licked Emily's face while she laughed and tried to restrain his big head.

Vining smiled.

She and Kaitlyn exchanged a sincere hug. "Sorry to get you up and to impose on you like this."

"I wasn't asleep. I'm glad to help."

"I really appreciate it. Meet my partner and friend, Jim Kissick."

"Oh, yes . . . Hello."

Vining guessed that Kaitlyn had heard the rumors about romance between them.

He extended his hand. "Nice to meet you."

Vining saw that he politely and probably with effort

kept his eyes on her face. The woman didn't seem to own clothing that didn't reveal cleavage. Vining was grateful Caspers wasn't with them.

"Very nice to meet you too. Nan, is it bad? What happened?"

Vining tried to put her at ease. "It's just confusing. Saber rattling. I have to go out of town overnight for work, and I don't want Emily to be by herself. Again, I'm sorry to drop this on you at the last minute, Kaitlyn."

She took Vining's hand. "It's all right, Nan. We're family."

Vining sensed the wistfulness behind Kaitlyn's words. She gave her hand a squeeze before letting it go. "Is Wes here?"

"No." Kaitlyn's clipped response precluded any follow-up.

Vining patted her shoulder and moved on. She raised her arms toward the house as if before one of the world's seven wonders. "Look at the house. It's spectacular. Wow." She heaped praised on the house that she loathed, which represented a side of Wes that she despised.

"Thank you. Come inside and have a look."

"Love to."

They left Emily playing with the dog on the lawn.

The new rooms were big, airy, and expensively decorated, with the latest in contemporary furniture styles.

As Kaitlyn showed them around, Vining detected that she no longer had the enthusiasm she'd once had about her showcase home. Her suspicions were confirmed when Kaitlyn said with a shrug, "Wes wanted the addition more than I did. I almost think he did it to keep me busy."

*   *   *

Back outside, they said their good-byes.

Vining was pensive as Kissick drove out of the development, stopping to wait for the gate to open.

"That's a big, expensive place," he commented. "It's beautiful, but frankly it reminds me of a hotel, and it's about as warm. I'll take my little shack any day."

"I love your little shack."

"Do you? You missed my barbecue earlier this summer."

"We had other plans."

"You haven't even seen the landscaping I put in."

During the few months of their brief romance, Vining had spent days off with Kissick looking for authentic fixtures and hardware to restore his Craftsman bungalow at swap meets and salvage yards. She'd since made excuses not to attend the couple of events he'd had. The house was too uniquely him for her to feel comfortable there after they'd split.

Vining changed the subject. "Kaitlyn's learned that a house doesn't make a home."

"There's trouble in paradise?"

"My grandmother has a saying. 'When a man marries his mistress, he creates a job opening.' "

"Got it. They've got a couple of little kids, don't they?"

"Two boys. Kyle's five and Kelsey's three."

"That's a shame. Think they'll get divorced?"

"Knowing Wes, he's not going to want to pay more child support. Kaitlyn will get spousal support too. She doesn't work."

"Wasn't she a hairstylist?"

"At Supercuts. She used to cut Wes's hair."

"Boy, I need to change where I get my hair cut. My barber is seventy years old, had quadruple bypass surgery, and still smokes two packs a day."

She gave him a pained smile.

"Off to the Salton Sea?"

"It would be the middle of the night by the time we got there. Maybe it's better to arrive first thing in the morning when Connie Jenkins opens up her business." She yawned.

"You want to go to bed first?"

She gave him a baleful look.

"I didn't mean that."

"I hope not. I thought you'd at least buy me dinner first."

"Okay. I'd buy you dinner."

"I bet you would," she retorted.

THIRTY-TWO

"Mark won't answer his cell phone or return my calls. His secretary said he slept in his office last night. She said he left to shower and shave, but he must have done it at the club because he didn't come home. He keeps clothes in his gym locker. His secretary said he was upset after those detectives came by. Everyone in the office is wondering what's going on."

"Is it unusual for him not to take your calls?" Crowley's calmness soothed Hale. She wished he was there with her instead of just on the phone. It was an illicit thought, but she indulged in it.

"Yes. Even when he goes on benders in Vegas, he calls to check in."

"It's too soon to report him missing. His secretary saw him this morning. You said he's erratic sometimes."

"I just have a bad feeling." Hale paced the floor of her bedroom. "I'm afraid he suspects something . . . You know, between us."

"How could he? It barely happened."

"Hard to believe it was only Monday."

"I can't believe it either, Dena. This is going to sound corny, but I feel like I've known you my whole life."

Hale let out a sob. She had vowed to end it with Crowley, but he was the only one she felt she could turn to now.

"Babe, I didn't mean to make you cry. That's not the response I expected."

"I'm sorry, Bowie. I'm just so confused right now. We got hot and heavy pretty fast."

"Yeah, did we . . ."

His comment made her feel embarrassed about the way she'd impulsively jumped in the sack with him. She was so stupid. She blurted, "I think we should just be friends," which made her cry harder. "That sounds stupid, doesn't it?"

"It's not stupid. You're right. We shouldn't be having sex."

"It's wrong and I feel so guilty. I don't know what I was thinking."

"I know, Dena. Look, I'm your friend. I really am. You can count on me. You can talk to me. Anything. Whatever you need, I'm there. Promise."

In the ensuing silence, he heard her sniffling.

"You gonna be okay, Dena? You want me to come over?"

"I'd love it, but it's a bad idea."

"Why don't you try to get some sleep? Things always look worse when you're tired."

"I'll make some chamomile tea and curl up in bed with *House and Garden*."

"Still, I can't help but wish you were curling up with me."

"Bowie . . ."

"All right. I'll stop."

She didn't want him to stop, but it was the right thing to do.

"Dena, I'm right here at home. Call me if you need me."

Having put on her favorite cotton nightgown, the one with hand shirring, Hale brewed chamomile tea in the mug that Dahlia had brought back from a trip to Italy she had taken with her high school girls' chorus. Hale splurged and nibbled on a piece of buttery shortbread from a basket of treats a corporate sponsor had sent to her TV show. Before she realized it, she'd consumed an entire wedge and was halfway through a second. She tucked the remaining half back beneath the cellophane wrapper and took her mug of tea upstairs, where her magazine waited.

Before heading to bed, she went into Luddy's room. He was sound asleep. As she straightened his bed coverings, her sadness and confusion overwhelmed her. Her eyes grew teary, but she didn't give in. No more. She had to keep her head on straight. She gave her son a kiss while he slept.

She then knocked on Dahlia's door and found her sitting cross-legged on the bed with her laptop on her thighs and her iPod headphones in her ears.

Her daughter greeted her with a put-out look and a question whose delivery sounded more academic than caring. "Have you been crying, Mom?"

"I was watching a sad movie. You know me."

Dahlia resumed tapping the keyboard. "Oh, okay."

"I'm going to bed. I'm kind of tired."

"Okay . . . G'night."

"Don't stay up too late."

"G'night."

In her suite of rooms, Hale called her husband again on his cell phone, not leaving a message this time. She'd already left two. Before she climbed into bed, she said a prayer for his safety and requested divine intervention in her life to help show her the way. She turned out the lights. Through the open windows, a gentle, cooling breeze blew across her skin and the sheet that covered her.

The herbal tea made her drowsy, but even as exhausted as she was, her mind raced. She tried deep breathing and relaxation techniques. When that didn't help, she focused on the hypnotic sawing of the crickets. What finally helped was a forbidden image of herself in Bowie's arms. They were on a sailboat on a calm turquoise sea, far away, and the waves rocked the boat, back and forth. . . .

Sometime later, she woke to sounds of splashing in the pool. She groggily squinted at the clock and saw that it was 2:13 a.m. She rose from her bed and went to the window. The motion lights at the rear of the property had been tripped. Someone was in the pool. She couldn't see clearly, as the lights only illuminated the part of the pool closest to the gate, but she could tell it was Mark by the noise he was making. He was a graceless swimmer, uncomfortable with the fluidity of water. He didn't like the pool much. She was surprised to find him there, of all places.

She grabbed a light robe, slid her feet into flip-flops, and went outside through the French doors in the library.

When he saw her coming toward him across the garden, he dogpaddled beyond the range of the light and began treading water. He was nude. "There she is, Miss America," he sang, off-key and out of breath. "Dena. My wife. My reason for living."

"Mark, what are you doing?"

"Swimming!" he exclaimed, as if it couldn't be more obvious.

"I can see that. Why?"

He moved to where his feet touched the bottom, yet he remained in shadows.

She noticed his clothes piled on one of the chairs that was pulled away from a table in the corner of the pool deck.

"Why am I swimming, you ask, my wifely? Because I feel like it. You say I never do anything creative. That I'm not *spontaneous*." He intentionally draped the word with sibilant hissing that he hoped Dena found intimidating.

Scoville was in a great mood. He didn't feel bad about bashing in the thug's head. That guy was vermin. It had been a case of survival of the fittest. It was the law of the jungle and the Wild West. He had prevailed. He was *the man*. He had never been "the man." He had to admit, it felt great. Maybe even better than sex. He had always been intrigued by murder's practical aspects, but he was surprised to find it so empowering. He understood its enduring appeal.

"I'll get you a robe." She headed toward his pile of clothes.

"Whoa. What are you doing?"

"I'm going to pick up your clothes."

"Don't worry about them."

"I'll put them away for you."

"Dena, leave the clothes alone." His tone was more insistent yet flat, as if issuing a command to a dog.

She stopped a few feet from the patio table and chairs, wincing, not certain she'd heard him correctly. "Mark, what's going on?"

"I was about to ask you the same thing, my lovely. My lovely wifely."

She was startled when the motion lights shut off. When her eyes adjusted to the darkness, she noticed how bright the moon was. Still, with the dark bushes behind him, she couldn't see him at all. "I was asleep. I heard you splashing out here."

"That wasn't what I meant."

"I'm not getting this conversation."

"Oh, I bet you are."

The tone of his voice confused her. He was clearly putting on an act, but there was something else there. Something different and unnerving. "You must be cold."

"Dena, why are you so concerned about my comfort all of a sudden?"

"I'm always concerned about you. Of course I am."

"Save your concern for Bowie Crowley."

Her lips parted. The moment of surprise was fleeting, and she wondered if he detected it. "What do you mean?"

"You know what I mean. Stop treating me like I'm stupid. I know about you and the *author*."

He correctly interpreted her silence. "I *saw* you, Dena. I saw you with him through the living room windows."

She closed her eyes.

"Don't think about leaving me."

Her distress turned to outrage. "Are you threatening me?"

"You know what they say. Shit happens."

She planted her hands on her hips and gaped at his silhouette, the only view the moon allowed.

"You seem bewildered, Dena. What's the problem, my

sweet? I bet I know what it is. You don't think I have it in me. You don't think I have the balls to do something . . . dangerous."

She stared at his dark shadow and the water flecked with moonlight.

"You think I'm too big a wuss to pose a real threat, don't you?"

He continued speaking in that low, insidious tone, slapping the surface of the water as he made his points.

"Dena, you think you're the great interviewer. You know how to *read* people, how to *work* them, how to get them to spill their guts on TV for entertainment." He moved closer, walking in the water. "But your critics are right. You *are* all fluff and no substance. You can't see past the surface of people. Take me, for example. You have no idea who I am and what I might be capable of. After all these years, my subtleties elude you. You thought there *were* no subtleties, didn't you? In fact, you have no idea who you're married to."

Maybe she wasn't Barbara Walters, but she knew enough not to discount a threat. She unhinged her arms, letting them drop to her sides. The better to flee. Keeping her eyes on him, she took a step backward.

The motion lights clicked on. She saw his battered face. Her hand flew to her mouth. "What happened to . . . ?"

Something else caught her attention out of the corner of her eye. Walking quickly to his clothing on the patio chair, she picked up his shirt. Her mouth twisted with revulsion when she saw the blood-soaked garments.

"There's blood on your clothes."

He started furiously splashing through the water as he moved toward the pool steps.

Still clutching the shirt, she ran, not looking back. Her flip-flops somehow stayed on her feet as she sprinted across the gravel path through the garden. He was behind her. She heard him cursing, the pea-size gravel cutting his bare feet.

Reaching the house, she dashed into the library through the glass door, locking it behind her. She snatched up a cordless phone and punched 911 as she headed for the stairs. Her footsteps alternately slapped against hardwood and were muffled against the Oriental rugs as she ran.

Scoville was outside the library doors, pounding on the wooden frame, shaking the doorknob. "Dena! Let me in if you know what's good for you."

She prayed he wouldn't break the glass, counting on him not wanting to destroy the panes of handblown glass imprinted with the family crest that his father had imported from Italy. Running up the curved staircase, taking the steps two at a time, still clutching the bloody shirt, she panted into the phone, "Hello? I need . . . the police . . . right away. My husband. I'm afraid he's . . . going to hurt me. My children."

Dahlia's door opened and she appeared on the landing.

Hale grabbed Dahlia's arm and flung her in the direction of Hale's suite of rooms. When the girl staggered a few steps and seemed confused, Hale forcefully pointed and ordered, "Go."

She then ran to Luddy's room, saying into the phone, "He's outside. I've locked him outside."

She jumped and Dahlia screamed at the sound of broken glass, followed by a thud of something hitting the dining room table, crashing into the crystal chandelier.

Banging open the door to Luddy's room, Hale saw her son, the deep sleeper, rubbing his eyes and yawning.

"He's broken in. I'm getting my children." Hale jerked Luddy harder than she had intended to. She was losing her composure. She told the dispatcher, "Get the police here now!"

Downstairs, she heard Scoville cursing and hoped he'd cut his feet on the broken glass.

"Run to Mommy's bedroom, Luddy. Fast. Don't stop. Wait there for me."

The boy was faster than she was, running like mad to where his sister held her arms open in the doorway to Hale's suite.

As Hale crossed the top of the broad staircase right behind her son, the toe of her rubber flip-flop caught on the edge of the runner. She yelped and windmilled her arms, trying to regain her balance. The phone, still connected to 911, was in one hand, Scoville's bloody shirt in the other.

He was running up the staircase, raging incoherently.

Hale regained her footing and ran, but not quickly enough. He lunged at her, grabbing one ankle, landing across the steps, and bashing into the banister, pulling her foot out from under her. He broke through several of the old balusters and slipped halfway over the edge of the staircase. He held on to her to keep from falling.

She began slipping backward with him, and with both hands she grabbed the leg of an armoire on the landing. The heavy piece of furniture slid on the floor under the pressure of their combined weight, stopping when it hit the runner.

Scoville swung one leg back onto the stairs and pulled himself up, his fist twisting Hale's thin nightgown, which was now pulled taut around her neck. She choked and struggled to breathe. The armoire teetered against the edge of the runner, threatening to tumble onto them.

Dahlia ran from where she'd been crouching in the doorway, shielding Luddy. She picked up the phone that Hale had dropped and, with a roundhouse swing, bashed it against the side of Scoville's head. It stunned him long enough for Hale to break free.

Dahlia helped her up and they ran to the open door of the suite. Hale shoved Dahlia inside and leaped to clear the distance herself, one hand flinging the door closed, when she was brought up short.

Scoville had grabbed hold of her ponytail. Hale's head snapped back.

Dahlia snatched her mother's arm.

Hale held on to the heavy old door, smashing it against herself. Scoville still held fast to her hair. Her lower body was inside while her head and shoulders belonged to him. Dahlia wailed and cried, but she held on to Hale's arm as hard as she could. Scoville got his hands around Hale's throat.

She couldn't breathe.

Dahlia braced her foot against the doorjamb, pulling on Hale's arm with both hands. She screamed, "Let her go, let her go!"

Hale saw spots before her eyes. Still she clung to the door, the weight of her body painfully squeezing it against her.

All of a sudden, Scoville cried out and released Hale. Dahlia pulled her inside, the momentum causing them to collide and crash to the floor.

Luddy slammed the door closed and turned the bolt lock, a remnant from when Mark's mother used to barricade herself from her husband's rages. Luddy leaned against the secured door.

Bewildered, his mother and sister looked up at him from the floor. Breathing hoarsely, Hale gingerly rubbed her neck.

Luddy opened his hand and dropped a sterling silver letter opener Hale kept on her desk. It had been a gift from Scoville when she'd landed the cohost spot on *Hello L.A.* He'd had it engraved "To Dena, the costar of my heart."

Outside, they heard Scoville's Porsche.

Dahlia bolted to her feet and ran to the side window in time to see the sports car's taillights veer crazily as it sped around the corner and out of sight.

THIRTY-THREE

S coville wondered why the police were taking so long to respond to Dena's 911 call. He was prepared to go out in a gunfight. A hail of bullets. At least he'd leave this world standing on his feet. Nude, but on his feet.

He drove fast, yet not too fast, on the surface streets, avoiding major thoroughfares when he could and keeping off the freeway, where he'd be easy to spot. He'd lived most of his life in this part of the city and knew it like the back of his hand.

While he was driving, he dug inside his gym bag in the storage area behind the seats and pulled out shorts, a T-shirt, and tennis shoes. He twisted the rearview mirror to get a look at his face and almost didn't recognize himself. The sight was both horrifying yet strangely fun, as if he was wearing a Halloween mask.

At a stoplight, he pulled on the shorts and T. He ran his hand down the blood on his thigh from where Luddy had stabbed him. At another stop, he opened his briefcase, took out the gun Jenkins had given him, and set it beneath his seat. On the floor of the passenger side was the leaping cat hood ornament, sticky with blood and brain matter from his bookie's hapless henchman.

Scoville recalled something his mother used to tell him, claiming it was a Native American proverb: "Don't judge a man until you've walked a mile in his moccasins." The sort of Hallmark-card philosophy his mother tried to pass off as wisdom. His father, of course, had laughed at her. But now, Scoville saw the truth in the adage, and he enhanced it with personal experience: Don't judge a murderer until you've wielded your own bloodied blunt instrument.

Scoville was now a member of a different club. He was no longer one of the men who lived in the shadow of demanding fathers and passive mothers. He no longer shuffled along in the great line of also-rans, wielding good but not stellar report cards, bringing home trophies for "Most Improved" and "Best Sportsmanship" while he watched others collect honors for first, second, or third place. He'd have been happy with third place. Now, he possessed a more potent trophy—a heavy hood ornament covered with a man's blood and brains. A dead man. And Mark Scoville was the man—the *man*— who had made him that way.

Now he was off with a loaded gun to make his next kill. Bowie Crowley. He didn't have to take crap from the Bowie Crowleys of the world any longer. Or even from the Dena Hales. Both of them were social-climbing hicks who overestimated their value in the world. Or even from bullies like Jack Jenkins. He'd kill Crowley all right. He'd kill him and then kill Jenkins and frame him. He had wanted to kill Dena too, but whatever. Best in the long run not to leave his son motherless. Still, it had been good fun seeing her face when he'd messed with her by the pool. He chuckled, just thinking about it.

He knew where Crowley lived. After the night he'd happened upon him and Dena going at it in his own living room, he'd followed him to his Hollywood Hills home. He'd lurked in the shadows and watched him through the windows of his house. He didn't even have window coverings, a detail that ticked Scoville off. Here was a guy who thought he could get away with anything: murder, writing a book about the murder, screwing someone's wife, and walking around in the altogether for anyone to see.

Crowley had come to the window at one point when Scoville had tripped over a bowl of water left out for a cat. Big, manly, macho Bowie Crowley owned a scrawny, battle-scarred black cat that must have come from the same pit from which Crowley had crawled. If Scoville had been the man he was now, the *killer* he was now, he would have lured Crowley outside and whaled at his head with a brick.

But that night, he'd lost his nerve.

That was *before*. Now he'd found a gun and his co-jones. In a way, he was grateful to Jenkins for showing him the light. He would thank him before he blew his head off.

Scoville navigated the meandering road off Laurel Canyon Boulevard. The neighborhood had always been artsy and hippieish. Figures that Crowley would live in a pseudowoodsy house in Laurel Canyon with a hot tub on the back deck overlooking a eucalyptus grove. A freaking Writer's Retreat. Scoville had seen a photo of Crowley in his home office there. Where The Writer Works. The Writer. . . .

Scoville sneered as he slugged down a bracer from the bottle of Grey Goose, which luckily hadn't broken during his fight with the thug.

He cut his headlights and drove slowly as he approached Crowley's house. He passed it, looking for suspicious cars or the police. Dena had probably called Crowley to warn him, but when Scoville didn't see anyone around, he wondered. Maybe she was too busy with all the cops she'd rained down upon Hancock Park.

He parked down the street from Crowley's house. Opening the car door, he put on his tennis shoes. Standing, he slipped the gun under the waistband of his gym shorts, then snatched it before it hit the ground when it slid from beneath the elastic and headed down his leg. He had sought the gangster, gangbanger panache of the gun beneath the waistband, but he was having a wardrobe malfunction. Instead, he put the gun in his shorts pocket and pulled his T-shirt over it.

Walking around the car, he reached inside, opened the glove compartment, and took out a small flashlight. Dena had put it there, along with a disposable camera. In case he was ever in a car accident, it was important to have a camera to take photos, she'd said. The safety precautions seemed ludicrous now.

He took another pull from the bottle of vodka, wrapped it inside the paper bag, and set it on the floor.

He walked up the street to the house, then sprinted and ducked behind a large willow tree in the middle of the lawn. Crowley's motorcycle was in the driveway. Scoville guessed he was home.

The house was small, made of stained redwood and river rock in a boxy, utilitarian style. It looked as if it had been built by the tender hands of hippies in the sixties, with that homespun natural look that Scoville had always found pretentious in its attempt to look unpretentious. Give him the genuine pretension of an overblown mansion any day. Looking at Crowley's cottage, Scoville could almost smell the decades-old pot smoke that had permeated the wood and the spilled sangria that had leached into the floor.

The house was completely dark. Scoville saw that as another example of Crowley's unbridled arrogance.

Look at me. I'm the big Bowie Crowley. I don't care who looks through my windows. I don't even keep a light on at night. I'm not afraid of anything.

The motherfucker.

Scoville darted to the side of the house, avoiding the front picture windows. He stretched to peer into a side window. The full moon cast enough light for him to see that the sparsely furnished living room right off the front door was empty.

Creeping farther, he stepped over the cat's water bowl and empty food bowl on the cement back porch. From there, he could see into the kitchen. He slid a hand beneath his T-shirt and yanked up his shorts that had slid well beneath his healthy belly from the weight of the gun. He couldn't see much of the kitchen, but it seemed empty.

He tried the back door. The doorknob turned. It was unlocked.

Of course it's unlocked. I'm Bowie Crowley. I can fuck a guy's wife in his own house in front of his living room windows.

Scoville felt a jolt of excitement as he slowly pushed the door open.

It's a new day, Bowie. Time to wake up and smell the gun smoke.

He set a foot on the linoleum floor. The thin light that filtered in through the backdoor showed that the kitchen was undergoing renovations. The cabinets had been yanked out. Sawhorses and power tools strewn about suggested that Crowley was doing the work himself.

It was yet another thing that frosted Scoville.

Inside the kitchen, he risked turning on the flashlight. It was cheap, the hardware-store brand, and didn't cast a bright beam. He didn't know whether it was better to leave the door open or closed. He opted for closed.

A door to the right led to a dining room. An opening off it led to what looked like a living room. Scoville navigated around the construction project and went into the tiny dining room. The table was covered with a tarp. On it were piled the dinette table and chairs that must have been in the kitchen.

He crept from there into the living room. A hallway extended off it. Crowley's bedroom had to be back there.

The house was silent. Dena must not have called him. Maybe she did call him and he'd left in a vehicle other than the Harley. He'd gone flying over there to be by Dena's side, the chivalrous prick. Of course he would.

Maybe he was asleep. Early to bed. Up to see the sunrise. The dawning of a new day in the glorious life of Bowie Crowley.

Scoville's hate for Crowley burned like unrequited love.

He turned off the flashlight, not wanting to signal his approach. He took the gun from his pocket and put the flashlight in, again tugging his shorts up around his waist. He moved down the hallway until he reached a doorway. Holding the gun between both hands, he spun inside, staying close to the wall, as he'd seen in a million TV cop shows. It was Crowley's office. Flashlight again out, he saw that the small room was crammed with a 1940's vintage desk, an Aeron chair, and a computer with a large monitor. A flat-screen television was on a wall. There was a printer/fax/scanner combo. While other parts of Crowley's life were spartan, his work area was not.

He looked at the answering machine. The display showed that he had no messages.

Scoville moved back into the hallway. A doorway across it led to a small family room off the kitchen. There were two more doors. The first one was likely a bathroom. The last had to be Crowley's bedroom.

Scoville took a second to think about his next steps and to try to calm his pounding heart. He wiped his sweaty palms against his T-shirt, shuffling the gun and flashlight. He was annoyed that his body was sabotaging him while his mind was gung ho. His hands were trembling. His machismo was melting.

Keep your wits about you, Skipper.

He smiled as he recalled his father's advice and the nickname the old man had called him. Would his father be proud of him? One never knew with Ludlow, but Scoville thought he might. Ludlow considered himself an outlaw, and took pride in it.

He took a deep breath, one of Dena's five million relaxation techniques, and mentally said, *Inhale.* He then exhaled at length. *Relax.* Two breaths in. Two breaths out. He did it several more times. He had to admit that he felt calmer.

Clicking on the flashlight, holding it in his left hand and the gun in his right, he forced his feet to move to the next doorway.

Bathroom, as he had thought. Empty.

One room left. The door was open. Of course. That was Crowley's M.O. Everything open for the world to see. C'mon in.

He hated him—more than he hated life itself.

What to do? What to do next?

He would march down there and announce himself. He wouldn't shoot until he saw the whites of Crowley's eyes.

Wait, wait, wait. . . . He had to think about this.

He shut off the flashlight.

What if Crowley slept with a gun or a knife under his pillow? That was what got him sent to prison, throwing a knife at a guy and hitting him in the heart.

Best thing would be to shoot first and sort it out later.

Maybe he had a woman with him. He'd have to kill the woman too. If he was going to succeed in framing Jenkins for Crowley's murder, he couldn't leave witnesses.

Crowley had a son. He'd TiVo'd Dena's interview with Bowie, and they'd talked about a son, a boy Luddy's age. What if the boy was there?

Scoville talked himself out of that idea. If the boy was here, he wouldn't be sleeping with his father. One of those couches had to be a pullout. Hell, Luddy slept like a log anywhere.

He was losing his nerve. Stop thinking and start shooting.

He took a deep breath, mentally counting *One*. Another breath. *Two*. One more. *Three*.

He turned on the flashlight and stomped toward the final door. His tennis shoes squeaked against the hardwood floor. He was all about action. Man of action.

He was at the door. The flashlight beam flit across the bed. Crowley was there. In bed. Beneath the covers.

Scoville started shooting. Shooting and shooting. Shooting wildly. The silencer muffled the timbre of the shots, but in Scoville's mind, the room exploded. The comforter danced from the impact of the bullets. No noise came from beneath the covers. Sometimes death was quiet. Like with the thug and the hood ornament. Sometimes death was as subtle as the quiet thwack of a skull cracking open against asphalt.

He kept firing. The empty gun made anemic clicks but he kept on, finally letting his hand drop to his side. A haze of feather fragments from the down comforter swirled in the moonlight that spilled through the naked window.

The overhead light went on.

Scoville let out a bleat of surprise and spun on his heel.

"Whatcha doin', Mark?" Crowley stood behind him, wearing only boxer shorts, a knife in his hand.

Scoville fired at the bare chest of his nemesis, using a gun that had no bullets, an apt metaphor for his life. The gun not achieving the desired result, he raised it in his hand and charged Crowley, intending to do to him what he had done to the thug.

In one smooth motion, Crowley set the knife on a dresser, seized Scoville's wrist, and twisted it behind his back, pinning it there.

Scoville yelped and the gun clattered to the floor. He cried out again when Crowley sharply tugged on his arm as if he was going to pull it out of the socket. He felt Crowley's body heat and his rock-hard chest through the back of his T-shirt. It repulsed him.

"Mark, quiet down. I don't want to have to hurt you."

Facing the bed, looking at the bullet-riddled comforter, Scoville saw the flaw in his logic. It was too warm a night for a heavy down comforter.

"You *are* hurting me. Let me go."

"Not until you promise to stop acting stupid."

"You screw my wife in my own home and I'm supposed to do nothing."

Crowley leaned to speak into Scoville's ear. "I'll admit that was uncool. If I was you, I'd be pissed too. I'd want to do to me exactly what you came here to do. But Mark, what kind of man terrorizes his wife and children? If you have a situation with me, deal with me."

"Dena called you."

"She called me."

"I guess the police are there."

"They are."

"Are they coming here?" Scoville asked almost hopefully.

Crowley released Scoville's arm and pushed him away. "I don't need to settle this with cops."

Scoville faced Crowley, rotating his shoulder and rubbing the socket. "Do you have anything to drink?"

"There's no alcohol in this house. From what I see, you don't need any booze."

"Don't fucking preach to me, okay? You A.A.-ers, you're like evangelicals. You have a gospel tract you want to give me?"

"I have water, orange juice, or punch. What would you like?"

"I've got vodka in my car."

"Water, orange juice, or punch."

"Whatever." Scoville was somber, his bluster spent like the last of his bullets.

Crowley grabbed a pair of Levi's from the back of a chair. Scoville looked away as he put them on, buttoned the fly, and buckled the belt that was already through the loops. He slipped his feet into worn huaraches and the knife into a leather sleeve on the belt. He waved his hand, indicating that he wanted Scoville to walk ahead of him.

In the kitchen, Crowley turned on the overhead light and surveyed the tools scattered around from his remodeling project. "Mark, clasp your hands behind your head."

"I'm not gonna—"

"Just do it."

Scoville complied.

In the bright kitchen, Crowley got a good look at Scoville. "You get in a fight?"

"Yeah." Scoville chuckled. "You should see the other guy."

Crowley appraised Scoville's injuries. "You might need a couple of stitches. I'll take you to the E.R."

"No."

"It's your face." Crowley opened the refrigerator. "I've got water and punch. I'm out of orange juice. Need to go to the market."

"I'll take punch."

Crowley took out two small flexible pouches with plastic straws attached. The back of the pouch was transparent, showing blue liquid inside.

Scoville made a face and dropped his hands.

"It's my son's Kool-Aid. Sugar-free. Hundred percent of your daily requirement of vitamin C. Keep your hands behind your head, Mark."

Scoville huffed and again laced his fingers behind his head.

"Let's go in the front room. Watch your step."

Scoville wove around the clutter, leading the way into the living room. "You doing this work yourself?"

"It's a hobby. I learned cabinetmaking in the joint. Helps keep my head clear."

On the way, Crowley grabbed a chair from the dinette set stacked on top of the dining room table. He plunked it in the middle of the living room and turned on a lamp.

"Sit down."

Crowley handed him a pouch of punch. He sat in a deep leather chair, unpeeled a straw from its wrapper, and stabbed it into the opening of his own pouch.

Scoville did the same, sucking up the blue Kool-Aid. Only a couple of hours ago, he'd left his office and gone to the liquor store, where he'd encountered the thug. Earlier, he had considered going to the police and telling them everything about Jenkins and the double homicide.

At that time, his worst crime had been lying. He'd since broken through that invisible veil in everyone's life, the membrane that separates before and after, the barrier that one might not even know is there until it's pierced, never to be restored.

In life, there are, of course, normal, recognized milestones. Graduations, marriage, children. Certain deaths are expected. Normal. Then there's the unpredictable rest. Falling in love. Landing a sought-after job. Making a friend. But the melodrama of before and after comes not from the best life has to offer, but the worst. Those dark nights of the soul in which one cries out for the boring, unsatisfying before. If one could have only known what the future held. How a simple twist of fate could set in motion a landslide of destruction.

I didn't realize how good I had it. Scoville drank the last of the blue Kool-Aid. He squeezed the empty container and hung his head, wiping tears and mucus from his swollen face.

"You want to talk about it?" Crowley looked like a Roman statue. His smooth upper body descended in a V shape to the waistband of his faded Levi's. His legs were relaxed and open. His long hair was sleep-tousled. His famous tattoo was on his right bicep. On his hip, the hilt of his bowie knife protruded from a well-worn case.

Scoville did want to talk about it. The horrible secrets he'd been harboring were eating him from the inside out, just like the Prestone patty Jenkins had fed Mercer's dog. There wasn't enough booze in the world to drown it. He could kill all his enemies in the world and it wouldn't help. Nothing could restore before. The best he could do was to deal with after like a man.

Finally, he met Crowley's eyes. Scoville would never have believed it was possible, but they had a lot in common. Both had murdered in a fit of rage. But Crowley had found redemption. He'd come far enough back to win the heart of a woman like Dena. Yeah, Scoville knew he'd lost her for good. He couldn't blame her.

He started talking. He told Crowley everything, beginning with the moment he set eyes on Jenkins outside the courthouse in Van Nuys, up through the bludgeoning of the thug, and how he'd come after Dena.

After he'd finished, he asked Crowley, "What's Jenkins's beef with you anyway?"

Bowie raised his hands and laced his fingers behind his neck, unintentionally creating the famous beefcake pose from his *Vanity Fair* photo shoot.

After a while, he said, "It's a long story." He dropped his hands onto the chair arms. "Actually, it's a short story."

Crowley had changed into boots, his trademark black T-shirt, and a leather jacket. His knife was still in its sleeve on his hip.

Mounting his bike, he picked up his helmet from the handlebars and put it on. He released the brake and rolled the Harley down the street until he passed his neighbors' houses before firing up the engine and heading out of the canyon toward the freeway.

THIRTY-FOUR

Kissick and Vining decided to get a few hours' sleep before driving out to the Salton Sea. Returning to the station, they borrowed a pickup truck from Vice that had been confiscated from drug dealers. It had tinted windows, four-wheel drive, big off-road tires, and a roll bar.

They went by Vining's house so she could pick up a change of clothes and make sure everything was okay. It was. The alarm was still set and, as near as she could see, no one had bothered her house. She could have spent the night there—Kissick would have picked her up later— but she had taken him up on his offer to bunk at his house. It was a few miles farther east and closer to their destination. That was the trivial reason they'd settled on. Neither one shared their true motives. Vining guessed he had hoped for more than sleep. As for her, sleeping beneath his roof and sharing coffee in the morning was all she wanted. She'd had enough of saying good-bye to him.

They picked up carne asada burritos from Taco Fiesta near Vining's house and ate in his dining room, drinking bottles of beer from his refrigerator. The old Craftsman-style house's original wood chandelier with its amber frosted glass shades gave off a warm light and made even the humblest of meals special. Sitting there in the easy silence made her acutely aware of how painfully empty her cluttered life was.

All of a sudden, emotion welled within her. She knew that when she was tired issues took on a magnitude they wouldn't normally. She ran her hands over her face and eyes, rubbing off the last traces of the makeup she'd put on that morning.

He slid his hand across the table and touched hers. He misinterpreted the source of her distress. "Hey, we don't need to figure anything out tonight about Nitro, T. B. Mann, or whatever you're not telling me about that necklace. Let's get some sleep and tomorrow maybe we'll catch us a bad guy."

She dared to meet his eyes. She opened her hand and he laced his fingers with hers.

This was how they'd started three months ago. They'd gone for drinks and his hand on hers had led to a soulful kiss. That had happened in a public place, and it had been easy to back away, to listen to all the practical reasons they were not a good idea. Now they were alone. It had been her call to come here. And it was her call now. She knew why she'd come. Another person she needed to stop lying to was herself. His hand on hers swept away the cobwebs. She'd thought barbed wire had encased her heart, but it was only cobwebs, scary but harmless.

She withdrew her hand. She could tell by his eyes that he thought she was backing away again. If she did it again, here where everything was perfect, it would be the last time; he wouldn't keep putting himself out there. She wouldn't respect him if he did.

She pushed herself up, her eyes not leaving his.

He slowly pulled his arm across the table and into his lap, but didn't move to stand. His lips parted slightly as she rounded the table. The old wooden floorboards creaked beneath her deliberate steps. He slid back his chair. She took her spot on his lap and reached to hold his face between her hands. They kissed. He tasted like spicy beef, beer, and some long-missed but never-forgotten delicacy.

After a while, she got to her feet, took his hand, and led him through the living room. They passed the fireplace and the rug in front where they'd last made love two years ago and he'd made the mistake of confessing his love for her. She led him down the hallway and into his bedroom. She had much to confess, but it could wait. He closed the bedroom door behind them.

It was dawn when they arrived at the Salton Sea. They had roared across the Southland and into the desert at high speed, encountering little traffic. They'd only been stopped once by the CHP outside Redlands. A flash of their shields had quickly resolved the situation.

While Kissick drove, Vining touched base with the Imperial County Sheriff's El Centro station to give them a heads-up that they were working in the vicinity. She also checked in with Sergeant Early. They didn't expect any fireworks, just a couple of uneventful hours seeing if Jack Jenkins was around, who he associated with, where he went, and possibly snatching something with his DNA on it.

They had dressed like tourists, wearing light trousers and loose shirts over their belts, which hid their guns. Vining had her backup Walther in its usual spot—her ankle holster. Kissick had suggested that she wear shorts and a thigh holster, but she didn't have a thigh holster and wouldn't have indulged his prurient fantasies even if she did.

He wore a Dodgers baseball cap, and she had brought the floppy sun hat she put on when working in the minuscule portion of her yard that was landscaped, if a patch of lawn and a few ancient rosebushes could be considered landscaping.

They didn't talk about what had happened the night before. For Vining, the silence was comfortable, as had been their lovemaking last night. New but familiar, like a favorite food one hadn't enjoyed in a long time, sampled again with trepidation that one's tastes had changed, which would ruin not only the present experience but taint the fond memories. But it had all been just as good as she'd remembered.

As for Kissick, he had held her in his arms and whispered, "I missed you. You have no idea how much."

In Mecca, the last big town before the Salton Sea, they found a diner open, busy with workers headed for the fields. They had breakfast and picked up sandwiches and coffee for later. A shop beside the diner carried old-time candy and sodas. Kissick carried on like a kid as he snatched up boxes of Good & Plenty, Red Hots, and Boston Baked Beans. From the cooler, he grabbed a six-pack of Dad's Root Beer in bottles. She grabbed a couple bottles of water.

She selected magazines for the long hours of surveillance, indulging in guilty pleasures: *People, Cosmopolitan,* and *Guns & Ammo.* Kissick had brought a book from home. At the counter, she tossed in a pack of gum and picked up wrapped flexible straws for the root beer.

She surveyed his stash at the checkout stand. "Thought you were on a diet."

"That's only valid in L.A. County."

She grabbed a roll of Rolaids. "Carne asada."

"It wasn't that spicy."

"It was to me."

He took out his wallet to pay, and she made a motion toward hers.

"Get the next one," he said.

"All right." She found herself already making a plan to invite him over for a steak dinner. She could see it unfolding in her mind. She didn't know if it would ever happen, or could happen, but it was another guilty pleasure of their pseudovacation, like her magazines.

They drove along the sea's eastern shore. The sunrise cast a pink haze on the surface of the water and across the tips of the Santa Rosas to the west. At evening, the effect would be reversed; the fading sun would tint the sky purple and gold, and the sea would shine with a reflection of the Orocopia and the Chocolate Mountains to the east.

The traffic on Highway 111 was light, mostly large flatbed trucks either empty or piled high with bales of hay. Latino farmworkers headed to the fields crowded into the open beds of pickup trucks, pinch-front straw cowboy hats pulled down low, jacket collars pulled up against the cool morning air, which would slowly turn brutal as the sun completed its ascent.

Kissick took the turnoff to the Visitor's Center. "I stopped by here the other day. Let's take a look. The birds will be feeding."

They traveled down a narrow paved road, passing a closed kiosk where the fees for day use and overnight camping were posted. They drove off the pavement to go around the chain pulled across the road. At the end of the road was a large parking lot with the Visitor's Center on one side. It wouldn't be open for hours. Only two RVs were parked there, lawn chairs set up in semicircles, awnings pulled out for shade. It was still summer, and hotter than Hades during the day. Only the most stalwart RV-ers would camp there.

Kissick parked close to the wide white beach, which had a few deteriorating wooden picnic tables.

When they opened the truck's doors, the potent odor

of decay that had been filtering into the vehicle hit them full on.

"Phew!" she exclaimed.

A couple of flies flew inside. They chased them for a while and then left them alone, figuring they'd get them later.

The lake was bathed in that early-morning soft pink desert light that teased out hidden creatures and colors. Later, its ruthlessness would be revealed, like the fanatical gaze of a jealous lover, its white haze devouring all life and shades of variation. But for now, the magic was working. Insects, fish, and fowl were feeding. Like the pink light, the birdsongs bounced off the water and ragged mountains.

Sagebrush and saltbush grew densely on the sandy dirt. The beach was loaded with small dead fish in various states of decay. Vining stepped onto the pure white shore that from a distance looked composed of rough sand. She was surprised when her feet sank and she had the sensation of walking on cornflakes. She reached down to scoop up a handful of what she discovered were barnacle shells, bleached white by the sun.

"Barnacles in the desert?" She showed the shells to Kissick.

"Lots of theories about how they got here. Most likely, they were attached to ocean craft towed here from San Diego during World War Two, when the Salton Sea was used as a naval base."

They walked toward the water, which was deep blue in the middle but lapped shallow brown waves onto the shore. The closer they got, the thicker the layer of dead fish grew. At first, they walked on skeletons, but near the water's edge, the fish hadn't yet fully decomposed.

She frowned at the carnage and decay beneath her feet. He nudged her and jerked his head toward the sky.

She looked up to see flocks of birds soaring and diving into the water, the surface covered with little pockmarks made by the tilapia feeding. There were seagulls and pelicans and hundreds of smaller birds.

She closed her eyes to take in the birds' cawing and singing. In this place that reeked of decay, teetering on the edge of death, life persisted in spite of everything.

She opened her eyes and saw him looking at her. She didn't overanalyze the situation. She simply walked into his arms.

They kissed, their passion rising on the music of birdcalls.

Taking her hand, he led her to a picnic table, backing her up until she was sitting on top of it.

"Oh no we don't," she weakly protested.

He was already unzipping her khaki pants. "No one's watching. No one knows us here."

She looked around. The beach sloped down, and they were out of sight of the RVs.

"No one knows us." She liked saying it. She let herself go.

He didn't need any encouragement.

For too brief a moment, they did not exist. They were part of the birds, fish, air, mountains, and water. She melted into him and was carried away. She had been carried away before, on the wings of death, and had returned changed. This journey would also change her. Only time would tell in what ways.

Afterward, he held her face in his hands and said, "Good morning."

"Good morning."

He climbed onto the tabletop and wrapped his arms around her. She looked at the water and its changing colors.

Holding her tightly, he rubbed his nose in her hair. Together, they watched a spectacle in the sky. A flock of white birds was flying so closely aligned, they looked like a sheet gliding on the air. They dipped, banked, and changed direction without losing form.

She snuggled against him. The years that had passed since they had been a couple collapsed. It seemed as if it had only been yesterday. That was the enduring power of love, she thought. She had denied it for years. Still it persisted, latent, waiting for the right trigger. Still, she couldn't quite release it.

"What are we doing, Nan?"

She raised a shoulder. "Living in the moment. This now that will never be again."

He craned his neck to look into her face. "That's profound. I had something more mundane in mind, like why don't we get back together? Warning: I'm only going to ask another two, three dozen times."

All she had to do was let him back into her life. That was the temptation and also the problem. She was no longer the woman she'd been then, and she was no longer alone. Now there were T. B. Mann and Nitro and their secrets. Their secrets had become her secrets, to have and to hold from this day forward, until . . .

She turned and raised her hands to caress his face, that good strong face that was pure and simple, like his heart. She was simple too. Simple wants, needs, motives, principles. But her purity had been lost, clouded by spilled blood. If she got too close, she would taint him too. She loved him too much to do that.

"What are we doing?" he asked again.

"Enjoying the now."

He pulled her close. Lost in each other, they didn't hear the Harley-Davidson roar past on the highway. They wouldn't have thought it important even if they had.

THIRTY-FIVE

*I*t *had* taken Crowley a couple of hours to make the drive to the Salton Sea, having adhered to the speed limit the entire drive. The CHP loved to mess with motorcyclists, especially if they were driving in the wee hours of the morning, and particularly if they had long hair. If he was going to be jacked up by cops, he wanted it to be for something he'd *done*, not something he *was*. He was contemplating doing something that would give them a reason.

Scoville had told him that Jack Jenkins was living at his mother's place. Crowley knew all about Jenkins's mother, the desert gas station, and the no-good wife who'd gotten herself murdered. During their long hours together when they'd shared a cell at San Quentin, Jenkins had lovingly recounted his bar fights, assaults, and burglaries the way other guys talk about athletic or sexual triumphs. The way Jenkins had spoken of his wife's murder had creeped Crowley out the most. Jenkins kept a photo of her. Tiffany. She was cute. Fresh-faced and unsophisticated, she'd grown up in a double-wide trailer with a gaggle of siblings and a mother on disability in Slab City, the squatters' settlement not far from the Salton Sea.

Tiffany had her high school diploma, Jenkins was quick to add. Crowley had known lots of girls like Tiffany in his day. In Jenkins's photo of her, Crowley saw the earnestness in her eyes that nearly cried, "Love me." No doubt Jenkins, with the family spread and business, was a good catch for someone like her.

Jenkins was too cagey to admit that he'd murdered Tiffany. He was nobody's fool. It sickened Crowley how Jenkins would talk about Tiffany's murder with near glee, recounting how her bones, found months later in a shallow desert grave, indicated multiple fractures, especially to her skull.

"He really did a number on the bitch," Jenkins would say with a faraway look in his eye.

"Who do you think did it?"

Jenkins shrugged. "She was a bitch. Bitches get murdered."

He talked about other women who had disappeared from Niland, his desert-rat town, and the surrounding area. It was a transient haven, so most people didn't know when people were gone—really gone. Prostitutes. Illegals. Crowley thought that if they dug up the desert around the Chocolate Mountains, they'd find a boneyard. Jenkins was careful to withhold details, so there wasn't enough for Crowley to take to the cops. But then maybe most of Jenkins's talk had been jailhouse swagger. Everyone wanted to be a badass. Few were.

Crowley was fascinated by Jenkins, by his personality, habits, and tales. The guys in the Q with histories of violence had usually had something to gain from it: prestige, revenge, money. If Jenkins's stories were even partially true, he was among the minority that mutilated and killed for the sheer pleasure of it. That made Jenkins a genuine scary guy.

Crowley had become friends with Jenkins, after a fashion. They sort of complemented each other. Crowley had the intimidating size and Jenkins those empty eyes that suggested that nothing was off the table. Sure, Crowley had been a bad guy in his day, but his antics were penny-ante compared to the things Jenkins hinted at. Crowley suspected Jenkins was at least half bullshit, but Scoville's recounting of Jenkins's slaughter of the Pasadena couple finally confirmed to Crowley that Jenkins was just as bad as he'd wanted to be.

When Crowley was in prison, out of necessity he'd aligned himself with the Aryan Brotherhood. Jenkins was a high-ranking member of the gang and had vouched for him. If you didn't run with a gang in prison, you were alone—not a good place to be.

Crowley had had his own reputation in the Q for being a badass, wielding the persona as protection, even after he'd undergone a transformation. Over time, all that mattered to him was his son, his faith, and his writing—and getting out in one piece. Still, he kept up the ruse.

He liked to read and even got Jenkins to read a book cover to cover for the first time. It was *I, The Jury* by Mickey Spillane. Jenkins pronounced it brilliant. Crowley fed Jenkins more fiction, mostly crime novels, and Jenkins sometimes finished them. He also took an interest in Crowley's vocabulary list where Crowley recorded and tried to learn words he came across that he didn't know. Like Crowley, Jenkins would include the vocabulary words in his speech, but in Jenkins's mouth, the words had the same effect on listeners' ears as biting into sandy, insufficiently washed spinach has on the teeth.

Inmates knew Crowley liked to write, but he didn't speak of it. If asked, he said he was writing letters home or his memoirs. He didn't want the guys to think he was writing about them. Of course he was inspired by them, but he took care to camouflage his fictional characters, making them as different from the source material as he could without stretching credulity. Small literary magazines began publishing his stories, paying him with copies of the publication. Thus, word by word, he began to build a life outside the joint. Given the obscure forum for his published works, it was unlikely that his worlds would collide. He wanted to keep them separate. His writing belonged to him and him alone.

Like any good writer, Crowley listened more than he talked, took in more than he gave. As their time together wore on, Jenkins opened up more and more.

Then there was the night Crowley had returned from his shift in the laundry and Jenkins had confronted him with a copy of the *Bloomsbury Quarterly*. He shoved it in his face, the pages rolled back to the title page of a story: "Call Me Diva," by Bowie Crowley. It was about an angst-ridden male cross-dresser who has a vitriolic relationship with his overbearing mother and who slaughters a woman in a frenzy.

"What the fuck is this?" Jenkins demanded. He didn't give Crowley a chance to respond.

"I open up to you," Jenkins went on. "I open up to you and this is the thanks I get?"

"That story isn't about you, Jack. It's set in Paris in nineteen thirty-eight. The protagonist is African American."

The magazine hid a shank, a sharpened piece of Plexiglas culled from a broken cafeteria tray. Crowley was able to prevent a lethal wound, but Jenkins managed to stab him in the shoulder. With the shank still embedded in his body, Crowley flung Jenkins across the room. Jenkins was smaller than Crowley, but built like a bulldog. He kept coming. The guards finally intervened after what Crowley thought was too long a time.

Jenkins wouldn't reveal to anyone what had provoked the attack, but guys in nearby cells heard, and word got out. Crowley learned that the magazine had been passed to Jenkins by a bespectacled former financial advisor who'd cleaned out the accounts of several elderly clients. He worked in the prison library, had literary aspirations of his own, and had finagled subscriptions to the *Bloomsbury Quarterly* and similar publications. When Crowley later confronted the financial advisor, the wimpy thief said he'd thought Jenkins would be proud of his cellmate. He wouldn't cop to professional jealousy.

After Jenkins's stint in the hole, Crowley and Jenkins were separated, and Crowley steered clear of him. He wasn't the only one.

There were few secrets in the Q, and fewer still within the prison gangs. News of Crowley's short story and how it was allegedly inspired by Jenkins spread among the Aryan Brotherhood. While the gang's leader admired the frenzy murder attributed to the supposedly fictionalized Jenkins, he couldn't go along with the cross-dressing. He ordered damage inflicted until tough-guy Jenkins came clean and told the truth about his double life. Jenkins was beat even longer for refusing to renounce it.

Once the secret was out, the Brotherhood had to take action or risk tarnishing their standing in the Q. Killing Jenkins was proposed. Crowley influenced their decision to simply spurn him. Now this was the thanks Crowley got.

Jenkins spent the last months of his sentence watching his own back. He was released a year before Crowley and that was the last Crowley had heard of him.

Crowley had wondered what had become of old Jack. Now he knew.

Jenkins's Stop 'N Go market was easy to find. It looked just like Jenkins had described it.

It was early morning, and the place was shuttered. Crowley drove onto the property and circled past the front door to see what time it opened. Eight a.m. He remembered Jenkins talking about the long hours his mother worked. He spoke often about Connie, a tiny yet tough woman who had saved the first penny she'd earned. His father, an affable, malleable man, had been dead for thirty years. Jenkins said his mother had a love/hate relationship with him, her only child. He had never succeeded in making his mother understand that Jill was not a part of him that he could shed like an outmoded fur coat.

Connie had learned of Jenkins's alter ego years ago. Even though his only occupation was being a criminal, she didn't mind him living with her. There was one condition—she lived with Jack, not Jill. She didn't want to see or hear of Jill. Jill had been a source of distress and disappointment to Jenkins's father and, Connie claimed, had led to his early death from a heart attack. She insisted that this was so even though, of his two parents, Jenkins felt that she was the more critical one. She was the one who had ridden his behind about Jill. His father hadn't liked Jill but hadn't been cruel to Jenkins about her. Yet Connie was his mother, the only blood relative he had. So he respected his mother's wishes. Jill led a separate life.

In their cell, Crowley had listened to Jenkins pour out his heart without judgment. He had listened, and had taken it all in.

Crowley left Niland and drove on into the desert. The rising sun cast long shadows from the mesquite and Joshua trees. After several miles, he reached the remnants of a concrete guard station that had stood at the entrance to the long-decommissioned naval base. The squatters on the government land had fancifully painted the guard station: "Slab City. Welcome." It was decorated with rough depictions of pine trees and birds, the birds looking like a swarm of arrowheads, all in white and green paint as if purchased at a closeout sale.

Just beyond the guard station was where the snowbird retirees parked their RVs. They clustered together and didn't venture farther in, where the oddball full-time residents lived. Permanent residents had laid claim to the coveted concrete slabs and especially the bunkers, which provided superior shelter from the sweltering heat. The domiciles, sun-bleached mobile homes and converted buses and trailers, were decorated with flowers and fanciful designs. Homesteads were established far apart. There was plenty of desert. No need to crowd. Scrub brush sprouted through the hard desert floor and cracks in the concrete slabs. Abandoned cars and cast-off car parts were ubiquitous. Tires made excellent flowerpots.

Crowley buzzed down Low Street, the main drag, aptly named as it crossed the flat land at the base of the mountains. He attracted the attention of residents who were just beginning to stir. A child on a plastic three-wheeler waved.

The vegetation was also low and sprawling, and added little color. What God had not bestowed upon the desert, a man had in the form of a mountain hand-painted in psychedelic colors.

Salvation Mountain rose from the flat barren landscape like a rainbow vision of Christian fervor filtered through an LSD lens. It was as tall as a three-story building and as long as a football field. The subtle desert aromas of dust and sage were overpowered by the commanding odor of paint.

"God Is Love" in red and pink cascaded down the face against a multicolored whimsical background. A giant red heart in the center displayed a sinner's plaint in white letters, asking for Jesus's intercession. Bright flowers, trees, birds, and hearts were in bas-relief across the hill, made of straw coated with adobe and latex paint. Painted waterfalls of white and blue stripes coursed to the bottom, where they flowed into an "ocean" in shades of blue in which a dingy was partially submerged in the painted earth.

On the crest stood a giant cross of white PVC pipe. Beams from the rising sun broke around it. A narrow road of adobe-coated straw steps painted bright yellow traced precipitously across the face to the top.

At the self-styled entrance to the area, Crowley passed a large rectangular sign that announced, "Salvation Mountain," decorated with the same primitive painting and bas-relief molding that adorned the foothill. The sign sat atop a base of tires slathered with adobe and painted to look like a tree trunk. Above, branches of real trees were arrayed as if growing out the top. A wooden sign bore the message: "God never fails."

Crowley circled the area on his Harley, not seeing anyone. The back of the hill was plain dirt and clay. He got off his bike, took off his leather jacket, and tossed it across the seat. He looked around, looked up at the hilltop and at the bright yellow steps that led there. He spontaneously began to climb them, the steps barely broad enough for his boots. The painted adobe had broken away in spots and tore further with his weight. Patches of paint were thick and tacky, sticking to the soles of his boots.

He was breathing heavily when he reached the top. The "God" from the "God Is Love" message protruded above the summit, the letters open in the middle, revealing blue sky.

Bracing himself against the cross at the crest, Crowley turned to face the rising sun.

Today he once more found himself at a crossroads, as if he was again poised to throw his knife into Dallas

Baker's heart. Everything could change again. This was the time before the time.

He still struggled with the fact that Baker's blood had been the source of his own rebirth. With the warmth of the morning sun upon him, he visited this dilemma anew.

There was good in the world and there was evil. Crowley wasn't an evil man. He'd done bad things, but he wasn't evil. Jenkins was evil. And just as good will out, so will evil.

If he terminated Jenkins's life, was that any different from how he had ended Baker's life? Did motive matter in the end? Were his motives regarding Jenkins clean? Must good fight evil with evil? Does a killing carried out under the auspices of a higher motive make it good?

Crowley didn't know. These were eternal questions. He was mortal, merely a man.

He dropped to his knees and prayed.

THIRTY-SIX

Vining and Kissick arrived at Jenkins's Stop 'N Go market at 6:50 a.m., more than an hour before opening. Kissick drove slowly past while Vining cased it through binoculars.

"Jenkins's mother has a shotgun," Kissick said. "She made no bones about showing off Betsy."

In a town where the majority of dwellings were mobile homes with chain-link fences to mark the kingdoms' scruffy boundaries, Connie Jenkins's house and business constructed of red stone looked as imposing as boulders in a field of tumbleweeds.

Vining took digital photos of the house and its detached garage, which were set off the main road behind the gas station and mini-mart. Using the telephoto lens, she zoomed in on the collection of wrought-metal sculptures and the rows of discarded airplane and movie theater seats near the firepit. She commented, "One man's trash is another man's treasure."

Kissick drove a hundred yards past the location before making a U-turn and coming back. He parked on a small street that intersected the highway just north of the Jenkins complex, where they had a view of the mini-mart's front door, the gas pumps, and the house.

Kissick cracked the truck windows a couple of inches. There was no shade, and it was already approaching eighty degrees.

Using the bottle opener on his Swiss Army knife, he popped open two bottles of root beer. He handed one to Vining, who stuck a straw in the neck.

"Why don't you drink it from the bottle?"

"Because I like straws."

He took a long drink, then another, and then indulged in a long, gassy burp.

She made a noise of disgust. "Already we're burping and farting in front of each other."

"I haven't farted." He looked askance at her. "That was *you?* I thought that was the stink off the Salton Sea."

She demurely sipped the root beer. "Carne asada. You know I can't eat that stuff, even though I love it."

He set the empty bottle inside the cardboard carrier and set it behind their seats. Turning back, he picked up the Rolaids and held the roll out to her. "Maybe you'd better take a few dozen more."

She glowered at him.

Smiling, he opened the boxes of candy one by one, tipping some of each into his mouth and crunching noisily.

She gave him a reproachful look.

"What?" he protested.

"You just ate breakfast."

"This comes from Mrs. Count Chocula." He shook the box of Boston Baked Beans at her. "Last chance."

"They're all yours."

He emptied the box of candy into his mouth and again noisily crunched as he rummaged in his duffel bag. He took out a copy of *Razored Soul*.

"Not you too," she complained. "I caught Emily with it."

"It's great. You should read it."

"No thanks." She took the book from him and looked over the author biography.

"You and Jenkins," said Kissick. "Did I tell you that when I was here with Detective Arnold, I saw a copy of this book half burned in the firepit? It's probably still there. Connie complained about it. Said if Jack didn't like the book, he could have sold it on eBay."

Vining tapped the book jacket back flap. "Says here that Crowley was in San Quentin. He would have been there the same time as Jenkins. Think they knew each other?"

"That's a big place."

"They're both Caucasian tough guys."

"Aryan Brotherhood? Guess it's possible. Maybe we should talk to Crowley and see if he has any intel on Jenkins."

"I bet you could get Lieutenant Beltran to go with you."

"I bet I could." He took his book back from her.

She grinned as she took out her cell phone. "I'm gonna check in with Sarge." She punched the speed-dial number for PPD dispatch and got through. After a few seconds, she was saying, "Hello . . . Can you hear me? Shoot . . ." She scowled at the phone's display.

"Call dropped?"

She called again, getting through only to growl with frustration. "Try your phone."

He did. The call connected briefly before dropping. He tried again, first rolling down the window. The reception was so bad, he finally said, "Forget it. We're okay. We'll call in later."

"I'll get out." The passenger side was not facing Jenkins's property and she was able to slip out without being seen.

He heard her talking to dispatch.

She returned shortly. "At least they know where we are." She raised her chin in the direction of a phone booth in a corner of the gas station. "We have that in a pinch. Assuming it works."

He opened his book and started reading.

She flipped through *People* magazine. After a few minutes, she looked at her watch. "How long do you want to stay?"

"One o'clock. It's supposed to be over a hundred here today. If anyone's around, they'll come out before then or wait until night. We could get a room and come back after dark. Maybe go up to La Quinta. Palm Desert. Have a nice dinner."

She gave him her dubious arched eyebrow.

"We'd get two rooms." He blithely returned to his book. "For our expense reports." He shot her a sideways glance.

"You're making a lot of assumptions here."

"Like my father used to say, live in hope, die in despair."

"I vote we leave at noon."

He screwed off the top of a plastic water bottle and took a swig. "Have it your way."

Vining looked at the storefront businesses along the highway, which were mostly shuttered for the summer. "Wonder why the Jenkinses don't close up."

"I bet Connie would stay open all summer if all she sold was a pack of cigarettes. Speak of the devil."

Vining and Kissick looked through binoculars at the diminutive but wiry old woman who left the house through the front door. Two dogs burst out with her. She walked through the cactus garden toward the front gate, the old dogs ambling alongside, tussling with each other.

She wore lightweight cotton pants and a tucked-in, short-sleeved, floral print T-shirt that showed off thin, deeply tanned arms. A broad white belt encircled her apple-shaped middle. Her silver hair was perfect.

She opened the gate, leaving the dogs inside. Her gait was definitive. She held her arms slightly bent and swung them in time with her legs, almost as if she was marching.

Inside the truck, Vining and Kissick didn't move. The tinted windows, especially with the reflection from the sun, did a good job of concealing them.

They watched as Connie kept walking in a straight line toward them.

"Is she coming over here?" Kissick wondered.

She stopped at the edge of the property near the highway to pick up a tied bundle of newspapers. She easily bent over and hauled up the stack, carrying it to the mini-mart, where she dropped it on a bench outside. Taking keys from her pocket, she unlocked the screen door and the front door.

The door of the house opened again.

"Jack Jenkins." Kissick bored in with his binoculars. "He looks older than his mug shot."

"And blonder."

Jenkins's black hair was bleached platinum. It was short at the back and sides but long on top, where it had been teased, styled, and sprayed. He was holding a lit cigarette.

"Couldn't resist a little lip gloss, mascara, and foundation," Vining observed.

He headed toward the mini-mart's front door. He wasn't a big man, but he had a powerful build. He wore a Western-style short-sleeved shirt. Silver metallic thread ran through the pink-and-white stripes, catching the sun. His white jeans were snug. A silver belt and white sandals accented his outfit.

"Buttons are on the left. That's a woman's blouse." Vining scrutinized his attire. "He hasn't had sex reassignment surgery. He still has his private parts."

"I didn't go there."

She frowned at Jenkins's white pants in a five-pocket jeans style. "I think I have those pants. Cotton with a little spandex."

"Spandex . . ." Kissick let the word dangle.

"Am I here with Alex 'All Sex, All the Time' Caspers? I thought you would have been satiated after last night . . . and early this morning."

"Oh, darlin'. It just whets my appetite for more."

"He's wearing women's clothing but nothing to make you turn your head. Guess he saves the high heels and pearls for when he goes into the big city."

"High heels and pearls . . ." Kissick seemed to savor an image that had nothing to do with what Vining had described.

"Now you're starting to get on my nerves."

"Remember that time when you wore high heels and pearls? That was *all* you wore. . . ."

"Is the sun shining on that thing or something?"

"It's just the closeness of you, dear."

She noisily exhaled and returned her attention to Jenkins.

He went inside the mini-mart and came out again soon after. He tossed the cigarette on the ground, mashed it out, then went to the gas pumps. He fiddled with each one, unlocking them. He turned to look down the road that led toward Slab City and the mountains.

In the distance was the rumble of a heavy motorcycle.

Jenkins finished his work and started back inside, turning when the motorcycle became visible in the distance and quickly approached. It was a large Harley. The rider was cloaked in black, his face hidden beneath a black helmet with a tinted visor. He didn't turn onto the highway but instead rode onto the Jenkins property, stopping a few feet from Jenkins.

Crowley dismounted, took off his helmet, and shook out his long hair.

"Hello, Jack."

"Well, look what the cat dragged in. Bowie Crowley." Jenkins smirked.

Crowley set his helmet on the seat and moved to stand a few feet from Jenkins. His sheathed knife was over his right thigh. "Didn't expect to see me again, Jack? At least not vertical."

"What brings you to our fair city, Bowie?"

"You oughta know, Jack."

They stood with their hands slightly away from their sides, like gunslingers facing off.

THIRTY-SEVEN

*K*issick checked that the truck's radio was off before turning the key in the ignition just far enough to activate the power so he could roll down the windows a little more. The two men by the gas pumps were too focused on their own drama to notice.

"The motorcycle guy has a big knife on his belt." Kissick grimaced as he studied the bike's license plate number through binoculars. "I can only make out a partial number." He jotted it down.

"I can't hear what they're saying. Can you?" Vining watched through her binoculars.

He shook his head as he picked up the camera to take photos. "Jenkins is not happy to see this guy. Judging from their body language, they have a history."

They watched as the two men shifted position, circling each other.

"Wait a minute . . ." Vining said as Crowley's face came into view.

"Yeah." Kissick grabbed his copy of *Razored Soul*, opened the cover to the author photo, and compared that image with the man talking to Jenkins. "That answers that question. They know each other."

Vining moved magazines and anything else blocking her exit from the truck.

Kissick did the same. He took out his cell phone and found the Sheriff's El Centro station in the list of recently dialed calls. He got through and kept his voice low.

"This is Detective Jim Kissick with the Pasadena Police Department. I'm in Niland with Detective Nan Vining doing surveillance of Jenkins's Stop 'N Go Market at the corner of Main Street and Highway One-Eleven. We've got two adult males having a heated discussion. One is Jack Jenkins, convicted felon, career criminal, and a suspect in a double homicide. He's the son of the store's owner. The other we've tentatively identified as Bowie Crowley, who did time in San Quentin for voluntary manslaughter. Crowley is wearing a knife that has about a six-inch blade. He's got on a leather jacket so I can't tell if he's in possession of other weapons. Jenkins does not appear to be armed." He gave them the partial license plate number off the motorcycle. "They're just talking, but I've got a funny feeling. You got anybody at your Niland substation who could roll over here just in case something pops so we won't blow our surveillance? Hello? Hello . . ."

Kissick angrily snapped the phone closed.

Vining looked at him.

"I think she said she'd send a car from El Centro, thirty-five miles away. Probably won't need them, but . . ."

"Right."

"So Scoville found the balls to come after you." Jenkins let out a sinister laugh. "Course, you helped by screwing his wife." He laughed louder.

As Jenkins stepped to the side, Crowley matched him, but didn't respond.

"Is Scoville dead?"

"Scoville's not your problem, Jack. I am."

"That's not news to me, Bowie. You've been my problem since Quentin. I should say, since you betrayed me in Quentin."

"You're still stuck on that, Jack? Get over it."

"Get over it?" Jenkins's sarcastically joking demeanor changed. His body grew rigid, as if his tendons were retracting, like a sling on a catapult. "How do you get over betrayal, Bowie? How do you get over someone who you thought was your friend making fun of you in public? All those hours. All that conversation. Opening up, telling you about my life. My secrets. Then I find out that you didn't give a rat's ass about me."

"I *was* your friend."

"Bullshit!" Jenkins began shouting. "You pretended you were cool with my lifestyle just so you could pick my brain about it. You know what the Brotherhood did to me. I took twenty-eight stitches, man. All because of you."

"I *am* cool with your lifestyle."

"You called me a freak."

"A *character* in my story called *the protagonist* a freak, not me. That's not my opinion."

Vining and Kissick could hear the two men now that they'd raised their voices.

"What do you want to do?" she asked.

"So far, they're just talking. I hate blowing our cover. We found Jenkins, and we're going to take him down. I don't want him going across the border and disappearing." He looked at his watch. "Even if the sheriffs sent a car, who knows when they'll get here. I'll try to get through again and tell them it's a code three."

"On the other hand, if Jenkins does something that causes us to arrest him, he'll be safely locked up while we continue our investigation."

"There's that."

Vining pulled her shield from her belt and clipped it onto her shirt pocket. Kissick displayed his as well.

Crowley and Jenkins paced in front of the gas pumps turning like spokes on a wheel, keeping the same distance between them.

"Jack, I'll admit my story was inspired by some of the things you told me, but it's fiction. The main character couldn't be more different from you."

"Yeah, as different as a cross-dressing criminal with a hard-assed mother can be." Jenkins snickered.

Jenkins and Crowley stared at each other, their pacing and positioning over.

"Jack, you not only tried to kill me yourself, you sent some guy to try to kill me. You'd leave my son without a father all because of a story I wrote."

Jenkins made a face as if he didn't get Crowley's point.

Crowley clenched and opened his fists, as if wrestling with his impulses. "Okay, look . . . my actions harmed you, even though I didn't do it intentionally. For that, Jack, I'm sorry. Will you accept my apology?" He wiped his hand against his jeans, then held out his palm. "I'm willing to forget the whole thing. Can we put it behind us?"

Jenkins stared at Crowley's hand and laughed. His laughter grew, riding a wave. He slapped his knee and doubled over, holding his ribs. He then bowed his back and laughed at the whitening sky.

Crowley let his hand drop and sucked in his cheeks.

"Put it behind us, he says." Howling with laughter, Jenkins staggered, heading toward the front door of the mini-mart. "Let bygones be bygones." He wiped tears from his eyes. "Sure, Bowie." When he was within striking distance of an old wooden pickle barrel, he lunged for it, tossing aside the lid and grabbing an AK-47 assault rifle. By the time he had the gun in his hands and had spun around, Crowley had snatched his knife and was holding it ready to throw.

"Police! Drop your weapons!" Kissick and Vining burst from the truck's passenger door and crouched behind the engine block, the most solid barrier the truck provided.

"Drop your weapons now or someone's going to get hurt," Vining commanded.

If the two men were surprised that the police were there, they didn't show it.

"Drop it, Jack," Crowley said. "I'll drop mine."

"You're a riot," Jenkins retorted.

Kissick yelled, "On the count of three, your weapons need to be on the ground and your hands behind your heads. One, two—"

The world exploded and Crowley was thrown backward off his feet before hitting the ground.

Jenkins ran for Crowley's motorcycle, haphazardly firing a stream of bullets toward the detectives.

Vining and Kissick maintained their cover and returned Jenkins's gunfire.

He revved the motorcycle's engine and headed toward the mountains, the AK-47 slung across his back by a strap.

Vining and Kissick got off a few rounds, but he didn't stop.

Crowley moaned and bled on the asphalt as Connie Jenkins, carrying the shotgun with which she'd shot him, ran inside the mini-mart and locked the door.

They looked at each other, at Crowley writhing, at Jenkins getting away, and at the mini-mart, where Connie was holed up.

Kissick tried to call 911 on his cell phone, looking as if he was about to throw the device as far as he could.

Vining darted back inside the truck and cranked the ignition. Kissick barely managed to get inside before she burned rubber as she turned around. She came to a screeching halt in front of the telephone booth. Using the truck as a shield, Kissick got out and called for assistance while Vining assumed a firing position behind the engine block, aiming at the mini-mart. She chewed her lip at the sight of Crowley bleeding and in pain but she couldn't do anything to help him without endangering herself.

As Kissick called for help, they were surprised to hear sirens in the distance. Two Imperial County Sheriffs' SUVs sped on scene, followed by paramedics.

Kissick and Vining held up their shields.

The deputies pulled their vehicles close to the truck, creating a barrier, and took position.

Kissick explained what had gone on to the field sergeant.

The paramedics remained in their van across the street, waiting for word that it was safe for them to move in and do their work.

Crowley became listless. He slowly dragged his arm across the asphalt and over his face to block the sun.

A bell tinkled when the mini-mart's screen door opened. A white cloth jerkily waved through the opening.

"Don't shoot," Connie said in a raspy voice. "Don't shoot me."

A chorus of commands went up. "Come out with your hands—"

"Put your hands—"

"Walk out—"

The shotgun hit the ground when Connie tossed it out. She moved quickly, as if she'd been shoved, crossing the porch and walking into the clearing by the gas pumps with her hands in the air. "I called the police. I didn't want him to hurt my boy."

Once she had cleared the building, deputies swarmed her, roughly forcing her facedown on the ground, twisting her arms behind her, and snapping on handcuffs.

The paramedics moved in but Vining and Kissick got to Crowley first.

"Are you Bowie Crowley?" Kissick asked.

He was struggling to breathe but lucid. Grimacing, he rasped, "Yes."

Vining crouched beside him. She saw that buckshot had peppered his torso. "What are you doing here? What's your business with Jack Jenkins?"

"Officers, could you please . . . ?" The EMTs were trying to do their work.

Crowley managed to croak, "Old business."

As the deputies walked Connie past in handcuffs, she kicked loose pebbles in Crowley's direction, hitting Vining as well.

"Hey! Cool it, Grandma," Vining snapped.

Connie muttered, "Asshole," as they hauled her off.

Vining persisted, leaning closer to Crowley. "Do you know who murdered Oliver Mercer and Lauren Richards?"

"Officer, please." An EMT forced himself between Crowley and Vining. "You can talk to him later."

Crowley's eyes fluttered closed as he passed out.

Vining straightened to see one of the sheriffs' vehicles peel out and head toward the mountains. She ran toward the truck as Kissick turned it around, the tires skidding.

THIRTY-EIGHT

*G*oing *at* high speed through the small town, they quickly reached a crossroads. Kissick rolled down his window to confer with the deputies. They would take off in opposite directions, the deputies going left and Kissick and Vining to the right.

Kissick gave them his cell phone number. "But the reception is flaky."

One of the deputies looked at his own cell phone. "Shows good reception here. We've got more units en route and we've requested a helicopter. We'll get your bad guy."

They parted.

Before long, Vining and Kissick seemed to leave the desert behind, passing expansive fields planted with bell peppers and alfalfa. Cows grazed. Sprinklers released great fans of water.

They drove with the windows down but did not hear the big motorcycle's engine.

Vining ran her hand over her sweaty face. "Jenkins is gone. He knows these roads. We'll never find him."

"I need some water."

Vining grabbed the liter bottle and opened it for him.

They passed a group of men at the side of the road unloading hay from a truck.

"Stop," Vining said. "Let's ask those guys if they saw anything."

Kissick threw the truck into reverse and backed up to where the men were working. Vining rolled down the window and called out to them. She did not identify herself.

They didn't know much English. Vining and Kissick had a rudimentary command of Spanish. Between them, they managed to communicate. Minutes ago, the men had seen a big motorcycle traveling at high speed. They'd swerved to avoid it when exiting a side road as the cyclist turned onto it.

Kissick again took off, making a sharp left onto the road the farmworkers had indicated, a gravel ribbon cutting across the fields, stretching for miles. They bounced along the uneven road at high speed. Bales of hay piled twelve feet high were stacked along the sides, periodically blocking their view.

Vining struggled to hold her binoculars steady. She peered at a large barn set back in a field where workers were moving equipment. The men were busy finishing the day's labor before the sun turned brutal.

"Something in the road up ahead," Kissick said, not decreasing his speed as they closed in on the obstruction.

In the distance, Vining zeroed in on a flatbed truck loaded with hay that was partially blocking the road. Men were gathered around. Dozens of bales of hay had spilled onto the ground.

Her view was obliterated when the road disappeared behind a low rise. When they surfaced, they saw men hoisting a fallen motorcycle. In the middle of the dungaree-clad Latino farmworkers, Jenkins stood out with his platinum hair, sparkly striped shirt, and white pants. He was bent over, his hand braced against the truck as he examined his leg.

Through the binoculars, Vining could see blood on his pants. "Jenkins took a tumble."

Kissick stepped on the accelerator. Vining nearly dropped the binoculars when he hit an incline and landed heavily. When she again got Jenkins in view, he was already astride the bike, scattering the farmworkers as he took off.

Kissick laid on the truck's horn as he bore down on the scene. Men dove out of the way as he steered the truck in a broad arc around the activity, cutting across rows of bell peppers. The ripe orbs crunched crisply beneath the tires, filling the air with a sharp, sweet aroma.

They got back onto the road in time to see Jenkins nearly topple the bike again as he made a hard left onto the frontage road that followed the Coachella Canal, which was flowing with Colorado River water.

Kissick and Vining made the turn, sending the truck rising onto the berm that bordered the canal, plowing through thick bunches of rushes and cattails.

The motorcycle kicked up gravel and dust as it stayed ahead of the truck, yet it was losing its substantial lead.

"He's slowing down," Kissick said with disbelief.

Vining pulled the shotgun from behind the seats as Kissick closed the distance between them and Jenkins. She racked in a shell and took aim. Jenkins surprised them by making an abrupt right onto a narrow bridge that crossed the canal. The bridge was nearly hidden by the tall marsh plants. The bike fishtailed, but Jenkins recovered and kept going.

Kissick sailed past the bridge, losing sight of Jenkins.

"Son of a bitch." Kissick slammed on the brakes and turned around. The truck's big tires chewed up alfalfa when he went off the road. They cleared the bridge but didn't see Jenkins.

After traveling a hundred yards on an improved road, they left the nourishing canal water behind for the commanding desert. Jenkins was ahead of them, steering the bike down a dry riverbed, heading toward the craggy Chocolate Mountains.

The rocky terrain caused the motorcycle more problems than the truck, and Kissick soon gained on Jenkins.

Vining wore a seat belt but held on to the top of the open passenger's window with one hand and steadied the other against the dashboard. The shotgun was on the floor.

Jenkins risked glancing back at them and fired a volley over his shoulder, a mistake because he then had to swerve violently to avoid a Joshua tree. His rear wheel slid and he slashed across the sandy dirt but didn't go down.

Bullets breezed past the truck.

Kissick got closer. Jenkins was in range. Vining again drew a bead on him with the shotgun, but her shot missed when Kissick veered to dodge a boulder. The blast reverberated through the mountains.

Jenkins climbed the side of the riverbed and headed toward a forest of boulders, where the motorcycle would have the advantage.

Gripping the steering wheel tightly between both hands, Kissick darted the truck back and forth, forced to circle narrow passages that the motorcycle slipped through. They again lost sight of Jenkins. The truck soared over a low hill and the suspension responded brutally on landing. The seat belts engaged and seized them so tightly they could barely breathe. The root beer bottles behind the seat shattered.

They hit another ridge and sailed over. The raised front end of the truck blocked their view of the ground and Kissick was powerless to steer. When the truck leveled again on the way down, Vining yelled at the sight of the fallen motorcycle directly in their path. Airborne,

Kissick could do nothing until they hit the ground. The truck bounced down, rattling their teeth and landing on top of the bike. The air bags deployed. The truck and bike skidded across the sand. Kissick turned in to the skid, the tires kicking up a cloud of sand and rocks, dragging the bike. They finally landed in a small ravine. The truck listed to the left side, its tires deflated, the motorcycle beneath it. The engine stalled.

Stunned, Vining and Kissick blinked at each other.

Kissick smashed the deflating air bag. "Are you all right?"

"I'm okay." Vining punched her air bag out of the way. "Did we hit Jenkins?"

A volley of gunfire answered her question. Bullets hit the truck through the sand and dirt which was still settling. A web of cracks crossed the windshield but it didn't break. The bullets came within inches of them as they dove for cover on the truck's floor. Kissick was impeded by the steering wheel.

There was silence.

Crouched beneath the dashboard, Vining rose to draw her Glock from her belt holster. "Got any ideas, Batman?"

He cautiously raised his head to look out the windshield. A bullet sailed through the glass and embedded itself in the passenger seat.

"I think he's hiding in those boulders," Kissick said. "Cover me while I take another look."

"Look up on three." She grasped the door handle. "One, two . . . three." She thrust the door open, remaining squeezed on the floor. The door would only open halfway, impeded by the rise of the ravine in which they'd landed.

While bullets hit the truck's passenger side, Kissick looked around, then ducked again.

"There's a low hill about fifty yards away. If I can get around it I can come up behind him. If you cover me I can reach it."

"That's far to run in the open."

"I'm fast."

"You're not faster than a speeding bullet."

"So I'm just Batman, not Superman. You have a better idea?"

"Just staying alive while that asshole is shooting at us. Where's the cavalry anyway?" She pulled out her cell phone and laughed joylessly. "No service."

He picked up the water bottle and took a drink. "I think I ate a pound of sand."

She looked at the remaining water. "Hope we don't have to worry about running out of water. It's hotter than hell already."

"This isn't going to go on all day. The sheriffs should have their copter up by now."

She checked her watch. "You'd think so. Hopefully in all the chaos of their crime scene back at Jenkins's store, they've noticed that we're missing."

He rubbed his back, where he was bent double. "I've got to stretch or I'm going to be a cripple."

She leaned to look out the open passenger door. "This ditch we're in gives cover on this side. Slide out."

Bullets hit the truck's left front quarter panel.

"We know you're out there, asshole," Vining shouted.

"I'm gonna kill you cops," Jenkins yelled in return.

"All work, no play," Vining retorted, reciting the bloody message on Oliver Mercer's wall. When Jenkins didn't respond, she tried again. "All work, no play, Jack. Sound familiar?"

"I don't know what you're talking about," Jenkins said in a snide singsong.

"Cagey ex-con." Kissick unhinged his legs and slid

past her on his back, dropping his feet onto the ground with a long, "Ahhh . . ."

"Wait. Make sure there aren't any snakes."

He retracted his legs. "Oh, shit. Snakes."

She giggled, knowing he hated snakes.

"She laughs. There's gotta be rattlesnakes all over the place."

"Stay there." She clambered from her own tight hiding space on the floor beneath him, stuck out her head, and looked beneath the truck. "There aren't any rocks here for snakes to hide under. I smell gasoline, though."

"Me too. That's not good. Probably crushed the motorcycle's tank."

She pulled herself the rest of the way out. On her knees in the packed sand, she aimed her gun in the opening between the door and the windshield. She saw movement and fired. "You think you're going to sneak away from me, you crazy bastard?"

Kissick reached inside his duffel bag and grabbed extra gun magazines. He handed one to her and shoved one into his pants pocket before sitting on the ridge beside her. "Wonder how many rounds Jenkins has in that banana clip."

"Could be a lot." She again fired toward the boulders, sending up rock shards where the bullets hit.

They both ducked Jenkins's return volley from the AK-47.

Kissick looked at his watch. "Sergeant Early has gotta be wondering why we haven't checked in."

"She'll raise hell and drive here herself if she has to."

"Ask Jenkins about him and Crowley."

She yelled, "Hey Jack, what's up between you and Crowley?"

"Fuck you."

"Did you know each other in Quentin?"

"None of your fucking business."

"Bowie wasn't hurt bad, Jack," she shouted. "He's probably already told the sheriffs everything."

"He lies."

Vining cocked her head. "Oh-kay."

Kissick frowned as he sniffed the air. "Gasoline smells stronger." He dropped to his hands and knees and looked beneath the truck, aided by the way it was tilted. "The truck's gas tank is busted. Gas is running out. That tank was nearly full."

"I hope Jenkins can't smell it. He was smoking a cigarette by the mini-mart. He might have a match or a lighter on him."

"I doubt he can smell it from over there," Kissick said. "I'm more worried about these vapors. We're firing guns. Could ignite."

They looked at each other.

She said, "We've gotta get out of here. No part of this scenario has a happy ending."

He saw the stress in her face. "Let me take over."

They traded places.

She sat on the ground and rubbed the back of her neck. "We need to chase Jenkins out into the open." She rested her head in one palm, supporting her elbow against her knee as she considered their options. "Wait a minute. . . ."

She rose and crept inside the truck, keeping away from the windshield. She reached behind the seats.

"Careful, Nan. There's broken glass back there."

Her lips spread in a grin as she retracted her hand. In it she held a full bottle of root beer. "One bottle didn't break. We can make a Molotov cocktail."

He glanced from the boulders to her. "A Molotov cocktail? Talk about blowing ourselves up."

She opened the root beer, took a drink, and handed it

to him to finish. "Weren't you on a champion high school baseball team?"

"We were state semifinalists. I played left field."

"I'll cover you. You run clear of the truck and throw the bottle at the rocks where Jenkins is hiding. It'll explode, he'll run out, and we'll nail him."

"There's so much about that scheme that's a bad idea."

"Sitting around in gasoline and firing guns while dodging bullets from a maniac with an assault rifle is a good idea?"

"Okay, how are we going to light it?"

"You were a Boy Scout. Can't you rub two sticks together or something?"

"It's not that easy and you know it. Plus, we don't want fire anywhere near this truck."

She opened the glove compartment and rummaged around, pulling out candy wrappers and fast-food restaurant napkins. She flung a wrapped condom at him.

He glared when it bounced off his arm.

"Aha." She held up a plastic lighter. "Vice and their vices."

"I don't know about this, Nan."

"If you have a better idea, speak up. The way I see it, if we don't flush him out, we have two choices. We can storm his position and one or both of us could get shot, or we can wait for something to happen. Two choices and both stink."

"Take over. Give me the bottle."

They changed positions.

She aimed at a spot and fired a couple of rounds, sending rock shooting into the air at the exact location where she was aiming. She was pleased with herself.

He dropped to the ground and crawled beneath the truck.

After awhile, he resurfaced, holding up the root beer bottle now full of gasoline. "So, Martha Stewart, what are we going to use for a wick? Tear off strips from our clothes?"

"That would work. I know . . . get my purse behind the seat."

He found it and held it out for her.

"I'm covering him. Open it."

"I don't want to look through your purse."

"Just open it. Get a tampon out of the plastic case."

"Tampon?"

"It'll make a perfect wick."

"Tampon," he repeated.

"They won't hurt you, tough guy."

He plunged his hand in. "There's nothing in here that's going to stick or cut me, is there?" It was a joke. That was the question cops asked whenever they searched someone's pockets or belongings.

He found the pink plastic container. He popped it open, took out a tampon, and picked at the slippery plastic wrapper.

She sighed. "Grab an edge and tear it open. Then take it out of the applicator."

He took the tampon from its wrapper and held it up. "How do you women *do* this?"

"Just take it out."

"When you think you've done everything. *Voilà*." He dangled the cotton cylinder by the attached string. "Here goes nothing." He sat on the floor of the truck and went about finishing the incendiary device.

She squeezed off several rounds. "Try it again, Jenkins. Make my day." She heard fabric tearing and looked to see Kissick hacking a length of fabric from the hem of his pants with his Swiss Army knife.

After a few minutes, he said, "Okay . . . here's how

this works. I put the cap back on the bottle. That way, gas won't spill when I throw it. I've soaked the wick in gasoline and I'm tying it around the bottleneck." He held it up. "Done."

She noticed that he refused to say "tampon." She didn't give him grief about it. "Looks great."

He raised himself to see through the cracked windshield. "It's gotta hit one of those rocks by Jenkins, and it's gotta break. It's gotta stay lit." He silently examined the scene. "That's pretty far to throw."

"Can you do it?"

"Don't know. I haven't tried to throw that far in a long time. I'll run away from the truck in that direction. You've gotta cover me, but good."

"I will." When she crooked her neck to look over her shoulder, she saw him working his jaw.

"This could be very messed up, Nan. The thing could blow up in my hands. He could shoot me. I could drop the lighter. All this gasoline . . ."

She hiked a shoulder. "You're right. Let's hold off. Somebody's bound to come looking for us soon. We could move to a position away from the truck." She looked around at the flat open terrain. The only other good cover was many yards away.

"A lot of hours of daylight left and we don't have much water."

"There's that . . ."

"Screw it," he said. "I didn't take this job to sit and wait. Worse case it falls short. Ready, Sundance?"

She flicked the end of her nose with her index finger.

"That was a different movie."

"I know." She grinned. "Go for it, Butch."

"On my three."

She again took aim.

"One . . . two . . . three."

As Kissick ran, Jenkins began firing. Vining returned fire, forcing him back. She watched as the lit Molotov cocktail flew in a fast straight line right at the boulders. It exploded on impact, igniting the surrounding dry brush.

Jenkins took off, limping as he ran, the fire helping shield him.

"Shit." Vining ran, looking back at Kissick, who was also on the move. When he saw her, he pointed indicating that he was heading around the other side.

Even with his injured leg, Jenkins reached the low hill and was again out of sight.

She, however, was in the open. The boulders Jenkins had hidden behind were inaccessible because of the spreading fire. She kept running, cursing herself. Molotov cocktail . . . Stupid Rambo cops with harebrained ideas. Jenkins had gotten away anyway. She reached the hill and decided to head for the top. With their luck, she figured she'd find more hills on the other side in which Jenkins could hide for good. She jogged as far as she could until it got too steep and she had to crawl. She didn't see Jenkins or Kissick.

Holding her gun in her right hand, she crept up the hill, mindful of where she was stepping and putting her other hand. Her tennis shoes slid on the loose rocks. Lizards scurried for cover. She snagged the tail of one and it went running away without it. If only people were so versatile, she thought.

"Nan, above!"

It was Kissick, somewhere off to her left.

She instinctively threw herself to the side as Jenkins, atop the ridge, fired at her. She started tumbling down the slope, losing her gun on the hillside, rolling over rocks, dry brush, and shrubs. Finally, she slid to a stop with her head pointed downhill. Twigs and thorns were stuck in her hair and clothes. Her palms and exposed skin were scratched. Dirt was in her eye. She was disoriented.

Blinking the grit from her eyes, she quickly looked around. A rocky outcrop was several yards away. It was the closest place for her to seek cover.

She saw Jenkins above her on the hillside, climbing to his knees with difficulty. His left arm dangled. He was using his rifle as a cane to help himself up. Kissick must have shot him. She didn't see Kissick.

Her legs still above her head, she started to pull them toward her as she reached for her backup Walther in her ankle holster. Before she could grab it, Jenkins had raised the AK-47 with his good arm.

Did she see movement across the crest of the hill? She didn't take the time to find out. She kicked off and again began toppling down, going head over heels. She heard a blast from Jenkins's gun and didn't know whether she'd been shot. The world was spinning as she rolled out of control. She finally stopped when she hit the rocky outcrop, knocking the air from her.

Something hit her, crushing her body against the rocks.

It was Jenkins. His hair, stiff with hair spray, was in her face. Mixed with the odor of dirt, blood, and gun smoke was sweet perfume.

Repulsed, she tried to get out from under him. For a split second, she didn't know if he was alive. Then he let out an inhuman gasp. She squirmed, struggling to free the leg that was entangled in the strap of his AK-47. She grappled with her ankle holster and managed to pull out her Walther.

Flinging out his good arm, he grabbed the Walther's muzzle. He broke her grip on the gun and took it from her. She heard gunfire from the hillside above. Jenkins returned fire with the Walther. The distraction was sufficient for her to break free.

She scampered to the opposite side of the outcrop. The stacked boulders created a shady cave. It was tall enough for her to stand in. She assessed her physical condition. She was battered and bruised, but nothing serious. She would ache like hell tomorrow, but for now she was okay.

She heard the gun battle continuing on the other side. From the sounds, she surmised that Kissick had moved down the hill, closer, as Jenkins's tumble would have put him out of range of Kissick's gun. Jenkins was again firing the assault rifle.

She picked up rocks, the only weapons she could find.

The truck was straight ahead at the bottom of the hill across a clearing. She could try to make a run for it and the shotgun inside. A fearsome image flashed in her mind of Jenkins shooting her in the back and her dying here in the desert.

Suddenly, everything went quiet.

She listened. The silence spoke volumes. She quickly moved away from the shade beneath the boulders. Creeping around the outcrop, she saw Kissick peek up from behind jagged rocks about ten yards away, where he'd taken cover. It wasn't a large enough barrier to protect him.

Jenkins was rising onto one knee, dragging himself from the crevice in which he'd been wedged. His white pants were blood-soaked. Blood stained his shirt. A thick lock of sticky blond hair flopped over one side of his head. Using the outcrop as support, he climbed to his feet.

Vining gaped at her Walther stuck beneath his belt.

Kissick could have easily shot Jenkins now. Vining wondered if he was out of ammunition. She looked at the hillside and saw him on his belly, crawling toward a ravine a few yards away that would provide more substantial cover from Jenkins's bullets.

Jenkins fired, kicking up dirt near Kissick. Too near.

"Got bullets?" Jenkins shouted, laughing as he released a burst from his rifle.

He was leaning heavily against the rocks, and Vining could tell he was weak.

She threw a rock at him, hitting him in the back of the head. As he turned, she ducked back behind the outcrop.

"Did you forget about me, asshole?" she taunted.

"I've got nothing but time, baby. And all the bullets."

When she saw Jenkins's shadow approach, she threw a rock as hard as she could into the shady spot at the base of the boulders and kept running.

By the time Jenkins had rounded the outcrop, she was tearing across the desert toward the truck. He took aim. His arm was wobbly, but he was focused on her and nothing else. If his mind had been clearer, he might have wondered what she was up to. He might have heard what she had heard coming from the shade beneath the rocks.

She threw herself onto the ground. He fired at the same time and missed.

Cursing, he again started lumbering toward her, but paused for a second as another presence made itself known.

Riled by the rock Vining had thrown, the nest of Western diamondbacks clattered their rattles fearsomely.

Living in the desert, Jenkins was familiar with that sound. He limped as fast as he could, dragging his wounded leg. He wasn't fast enough.

A coiled rattlesnake struck, burying its fangs in his

calf. He yelled and jerked away, giving another snake access to his buttocks.

Vining guardedly rose from the ground, at first keeping low, then lured to her feet by the gruesome scene. She gaped in horror, having to look away before again drawing back. As much as she despised Jenkins, two glances at his demise were more than enough. She dashed for the truck and the shotgun there.

As Jenkins flailed, he stepped fully into the nest. Snake after snake struck. Still holding the rifle, his finger was clamped on to the trigger as if by instinct. Bursts of bullets went into the air as he spun, trying to break free from the serpents' kisses. The snakes held fast as he twisted in agony. Their elliptical pupils beneath their scaly hoods were cold and empty, with no sign of triumph or fury. Only their jaws demonstrated their determination, holding tight as venom flowed through needle-sharp fangs. Their triangular heads pointed at him like arrows.

Jenkins lost his balance and fell backward into the nest. The snakes swarmed him. Their rattles sounded as if the gates of hell had opened. Jenkins screamed, his body writhing and twitching. He tore at his clothes as if by shedding them he could be free of the snakes. His arms and hands were heavy with vipers, but still he ripped open his shirt, revealing a pink eyelet brassiere. His carefully depilated torso was already growing discolored from snakebites. He tore at the bra, breaking the front clasp. Beneath, near his heart, was a flowery tattoo, the edges a lacy doily. It was inscribed "Diva."

Shotgun in hand, Vining returned to witness Jenkins's final moments, standing a safe distance away from both the rattlers and the brutality.

Kissick joined her, his clothes torn and dirty. He shook his head. "Lord have mercy."

They heard a helicopter and began waving their arms

when it came into view. The copter flew closer, swooping down. Kissick gave it a thumbs-up.

In the distance, vehicles approached across the desert.

"Finally," he said. He turned to leave but she didn't budge.

"Nan, what's wrong?"

"He's got my Walther. It's my favorite gun. It saved my life once." She reluctantly turned away.

He held out his palm. "Good job, Corporal."

"Back atcha."

They held each other's hands for longer than just a handshake. She felt like kissing him, but didn't make a move.

He did.

She tasted dirt, sweat, and a hint of Boston Baked Beans candy.

THIRTY-NINE

*O*n *his* way to his Salton Sea showdown with Jack Jenkins, Bowie Crowley had called Dena Hale to assure her that he and Mark Scoville were fine. He asked that she wait a couple of hours before having the police fetch Scoville so he could conclude his business with Jenkins without interruption. The police found Scoville tied to a dinette chair in Crowley's living room, just like Crowley had left him. Scoville started bleating for his attorney as soon as an officer pulled the rectangle of duct tape from his mouth.

The police confiscated the bloody hood ornament as evidence in the bludgeoning murder of Lloyd McBroom, an enforcer for a couple of local bookies and loan sharks. McBroom's corpse had been discovered by a homeless man Dumpster-diving for recyclables in the alley behind the liquor store. The thug had died in the shadow of a Marquis billboard that bore a sexy ad for a premium vodka brand.

Connie Jenkins was arrested for attempted murder. She was put on suicide watch, as she was bereft over the death of her only child.

Crowley had been hit with dozens of shotgun pellets. The wounds were not life-threatening, and he was expected to make a full recovery. Hale rushed to be by his side. There was a media circus outside the hospital in Rancho Mirage. Fortunately for Crowley, due to the preponderance of well-heeled retirees in the greater Palm Springs area, medical care and hospitals were excellent.

Since Scoville had clammed up, the police had to wait until Crowley was lucid before they could learn the details of Jenkins's and Scoville's crisscross murder plot.

Hale wasted no time in having her attorney begin divorce proceedings.

Vining and Kissick had stayed at the Salton Sea until late, processing the crime scene with the sheriffs. Vining recovered her Walther PPK from Jenkins's corpse.

It was daylight before Vining was back home, crawling into bed with only her Walther beneath her pillow as company. Emily was still at her dad's, and it would have been easy for Vining to have invited Kissick to stay. They had been together constantly over the past several days. Vining detected a flicker of loss in his eyes when he left. Their parting was bittersweet for her, but she needed a little distance from him. She needed time to think. A different unsolved murder was again at the forefront of her mind: hers.

The next day, there was a news conference at the Pasadena Police Department. Vining and Kissick stood with Sergeant Early and Lieutenant Beltran on the station steps. Beltran boasted about his detectives having broken this important case. He announced that thanks to the work of the PPD, law enforcement agencies were looking into the disappearance of numerous females in the Salton Sea area.

The DNA analysis of the acrylic fingernail found at the Mercer house had not yet come back. No one had any doubt that the DNA would match Jenkins's. Mercer's USC class ring had been recovered from Jenkins's finger. Mercer's severed right hand was found in the freezer in Connie Jenkins's house, wrapped in aluminum foil, sealed inside a Glad zipper bag, and stashed behind leftover Easter ham and freezer-burned ground meat.

After Crowley's condition had improved, Donnie Baker, the father of the man Crowley had murdered, came to see him in the hospital. Hale had orchestrated the event to be captured by a camera crew from her TV show. Crowley's eight-year-old son Luke, who shared his father's cinematic looks and love of writing, was also there.

In an Oprah moment, Baker told Crowley that he forgave him for killing his son. He realized he'd been a prisoner of his grief and anger. They embraced and both men wept. Then Baker, tears streaking his face, hugged Luke.

Crowley had agreed to the TV cameras because he believed the issue of forgiveness was important. The publicity kept *Razored Soul* on the *New York Times* bestseller list a few more weeks.

FORTY

Vining's life returned to manageable chaos, the best any single mom could hope for.

It was a quiet weeknight at the Vining home. Emily was in her room busy making photo collages on her computer, archiving the events of the summer of her fourteenth year. Vining was glad that the summer had been happy and eventful, and that Em had fond memories to keep close the rest of her life. It was in sharp contrast to the summer the year before. T. B. Mann had robbed them of that time and much more.

Vining was at her desk in her room. She wore her favorite short cotton pajamas. They were ragged, but she wasn't yet ready to part with them. After the heat of the desert, the Los Angeles early September evening felt cool. She had the windows open through the house to take advantage.

She'd arrayed the artifacts she'd collected from Nitro and T. B. Mann across her desk. There were three necklaces: hers, Johnna Alwin's, and Nitro's. There were two notes handwritten in fountain pen on panel cards: "Congratulations, Officer Vining" and the new one: "Officer Vining, your daughter looks just like you." There were the violent drawings Nitro had. One showed her. Another depicted Alwin. Who were the other two women?

She was roused from her thoughts by the sonorous ringing of the wind chimes hanging on the terrace.

She angrily marched down the hallway and into the living room. The sliding glass door was open, as she had left it. The lights were off, as was her habit when she left the drapes open at night. The air was still, yet the chimes continued to ring.

Ducking into the kitchen to grab the stepstool, she saw Emily heading out the door to the garage. She was carrying clothes hangers for the laundry that had finished drying hours ago.

"Frankie's talking," she said matter-of-factly.

"She's gonna have to find another way because I'm taking down those blasted chimes."

Vining went out the screen door onto the terrace, where the stool slipped from her hands and clattered to the ground.

There was a woman on the terrace. She was running her fingers over the wind chimes, waving her hand back and forth, making them ring. She looked like Frankie Lynde, but it couldn't be. The LAPD vice officer's body had been dumped beneath the Colorado Street Bridge in June, three months ago.

Lynde was in full dress uniform, as she'd always appeared in Vining's dreams. Brass polished, creases pressed, hair in a tight bun beneath her cap, eyes bright. Vining had only seen her in her waking life as a brutalized corpse, but in dreams, Lynde was perfection.

She smiled cryptically at Vining, as if she had the answers to everything if only Vining knew how to ask.

Vining heard a voice in her head. Not a ghostly whisper, but an authoritative decree.

He's closer than you think.

Vining was reaching to pick up the stool when she heard Emily shout.

"Mom, come here. Mom!"

In the garage, Vining found Emily backed up against the car, her face ashen.

"Em, what is it?"

"Look in the basket."

In the laundry basket on the washer, among the sheets and towels Vining had set out to wash, was something yellow. She picked it up. It was a polo-style shirt that had an embroidered logo of a lamb dangling from a ribbon. The shirt was caked with something dark brown. Dried blood. Her blood.

"What is it, Mom?"

Vining knew that shirt. It was the one T. B. Mann had worn when he'd attacked her.

She quickly pulled Emily away and searched the garage. He wasn't there. She didn't think he would be.

She carried the shirt into the kitchen. He'd attacked her in a kitchen. As she dropped the shirt inside a paper bag, she reflected that the circle was now complete.

Off the terrace, the chimes rang their last notes, musically echoing Frankie Lynde's message.

He's closer than you think, think . . . think . . .

Please read on for a preview of

THE DEEPEST CUT

by Dianne Emley
Coming soon in hardcover
from Ballantine Books

Montaña de Oro State Park
Central California Coast
Eight years ago

This was his chance to get it right. He was nervous but confident. This was good. No . . . Great. Perfect. A fresh start. A new day. His first time had been a bloody mess. Of course, it counted. It had been *everything*— which was part of the problem. He'd lost control. He wouldn't do that again. Because he'd learned that killing is never as easy as you hope, but it's so worth taking the time and trouble to do it with style. Practice makes perfect. Here he was and here she was. Take two.

Looking up at California State Park Ranger Marilu Feathers, he let a smile tickle his lips and said, "Where there's smoke, there's fire."

He pulled one corner of his mouth higher than the other, crafting what was intended to be a rakish grin. She'd know that he knew it was a corny old saying, and that would show his mastery of the situation. While he was at it, he arched an eyebrow, aiming to look clever, disarming, maybe even handsome. He was rewarded. She smiled. She was flirting with him.

In no mood, Feathers smirked. It was Christmas Eve and this clown was about to make her late to dinner at her parents' house with her brother and his family. Her young niece and nephew wouldn't care, but her sister-in-law would find it an opportunity to remind single, childless, thirtysomething Feathers about the importance of schedules for children.

She'd taken her horse instead of the Jeep to do one last patrol of the nearly deserted sand spit, ringing in the holiday and a well-earned break with a sunset gallop. And now this.

The stranger looked Feathers over with a measure of scrutiny and delight, as if examining a long-sought-after rare book found by chance at a yard sale. He had watched in awe from the moment she'd appeared with Gypsy, her big roan mare, from the pass-through between the dunes and had begun galloping across the sand. She scattered spindly legged sandpipers and inky black cormorants feeding in the surf while brown pelicans and Western gulls circled above, the gulls calling, *"Kuk, kuk, kuk."*

He had known she'd take Gypsy from the stable behind the dunes, would go down the Jeep path onto the spit, and would turn right, toward the Rock. He had known exactly where to position himself. She often rode at sunset, when the sand spit was quiet, but not always. He'd spent disappointing hours, primed, waiting, only to return home unfulfilled. While frustrating, waiting taught him discipline, which he knew he sorely needed. Now, at last, his *reward*. His heart had thrilled with each beat of the horse's hooves upon the sand.

He felt his emotions running away with him and, like Feathers reining in her horse, he seized command of himself. His reward was near. His memories of this moment would keep it alive and fresh forever. All he had to do was hold on. *Hold on.*

Feathers pulled up her horse beside the makeshift barrier and managed an insincere, "Good evening, sir," and then the admonishment. "You're in the snowy plover restricted habitat. You can't be here, let alone have a campfire."

He knew that. Who could miss the miles of yellow nylon rope on four-foot metal stakes marked with signs, some drawn by schoolchildren, "Share the beach!" "We love the snowy plover!" He thought the stupid bird deserved to go extinct, but he knew that if she could, Ranger Feathers would sit on their nests—mere shallows in the sand, lazy birds. He'd not only purposefully gone into the restricted habitat, he'd built a fire with driftwood. Brilliant. Did he know how to push her buttons, or what?

Standing near him now, she was a sight to behold, tall in the saddle, her dun-colored uniform fitting loosely on her big-boned, lean frame. He was beguiled by her uniform, her round, flat-brimmed Ranger Stetson hat, her gun, and her badge. Her plain face so easily adopted that no-nonsense bearing. He'd seen her laugh, but soon after, her face would reassume that stern countenance, that *command presence* coveted by cops. It came naturally to Feathers. She had been born for the job.

He'd told her, "Where there's smoke, there's fire." Rakish grin. Arched eyebrow.

He returned his attention to the marshmallow he was roasting on the end of an opened wire hanger. The next move was hers. He was so excited, he could hardly stand it. *Get a grip, buddy!*

Feathers thought, "What's he doing? Trying to flirt with me?" She guessed he was one of the college kids that abounded in Morro Bay and Los Osos, the relaxed beach cities adjacent to the sprawling state park. A state university was nearby and students frequented the park to hike in the jagged coastal mountains or to surf and raise hell on the long stretch of secluded sandy beach reached by foot or horseback via twisting, steep trails that traversed the dunes. Only rangers were allowed to drive there.

She had invested a lot of time over her years at the park reprimanding, citing, and sometimes arresting the drunken, the loaded, and the pugnacious of all ages. In addition to providing the public with information about hiking trails, campsites, local flora and fauna, and the locations of public restrooms, her job was to enforce the law in the park. Those who did not revere this sacred space would feel her iron hand. She was protective of these eight thousand acres. Her corner of paradise. Her mountain of gold.

The young adult visitors were usually in packs, or at least pairs. This jackass was alone, sitting on a cheap, webbed-nylon folding chair. He wore a heavy plaid wool jacket, buttoned to the top, blue jeans, and sand-caked athletic shoes. A wool watchman's cap was pulled low over his ears. She saw no belongings other than the chair, the open bag of marshmallows on the sand near his feet, and the wire hanger. The jacket, though, had deep pockets.

The park was nearly empty. Only a few campsites were occupied. The sand spit was deserted except for this guy. He was burning driftwood, an additional insult to the park. Her park.

"Sir, you're going to have to put out that fire and move out of the restricted area. Now."

"I know, Ranger Feathers." He pulled the golden, softly melting marshmallow from the flames and swung the wire toward Feathers. "Toasted marshmallow?"

The sudden motion startled the horse and she pranced backward. Gypsy was Feathers's personal horse and un-accustomed to aggressive movements.

"Watch it, pal." Feathers steadied Gypsy, the horse moving so that Morro Rock was behind them. The giant, crown-shaped, long-extinct volcano at the mouth of the bay was silhouetted by the fading winter sun.

She was wearing a brass name tag, but his vision had to be extraordinary if he could read it at that distance in the fading light. She leaned forward and gave the horse a couple of firm pats while eyeballing the stranger.

The watch cap covered his hair and part of his eye-brows. He was seated, but his legs and arms were long. She guessed that standing he would be at least six feet. His clothes were bulky, but his build looked average. His face was ordinary. Not handsome or ugly. No distin-guishing scars or marks. It was a blank canvas, bright-ened only by the way he looked at her: adoring and consuming. It put her in mind the way her brother played with her infant niece, slobbering kisses over the baby while taunting, "I'm gonna eat you up. *Eat you up.*"

"Didn't mean to scare Gypsy." Tossing off the horse's name was good. He was golden. He could almost see the wheels turning as she sized him up, wondering, "Do I know this guy?" It was all this nondescript, young Cau-casian male could do to keep from grinning. He knew how the world saw him. He had learned to use it to his advantage.

His adoring gaze made her wary. It aroused her in-stincts of danger. He hoped it also appealed to another part of her. She would be unaccustomed to such atten-tion from men. She was a raw-boned woman with a lantern jaw, a squat nose, and thin lips framing a gash of a mouth. Calling her handsome would be generous. She wasn't the type of woman who inspired sonnets. But *he* loved her. He could hardly wait to show her how much. He caught his breath, feeling overwhelmed.

Control, he told himself. *Control.*

Christmas always made him emotional.

She asked, "Do I know you?" She searched her mind, grabbing at a memory that stubbornly slipped back into the shadows. "Where have I seen you?"

He pulled the sticky marshmallow from the end of the hanger with his fingers and blew on it before tossing it into his mouth. He chewed with obvious pleasure, letting out a little moan. He stood and stabbed the wire into the sand where it wobbled back and forth.

He struggled to calm his breath. "Nowhere. Everywhere."

"What's your name?"

He retrieved the wire hanger and intentionally held it by his side in his left hand, the one farthest from her, in a nonthreatening manner. He ducked beneath the yellow rope and walked a few feet toward the surf. He wrote in the wet, smooth sand.

Feathers cocked her head and squinted at the scrawling. "What does that say?"

He shrugged, chucking the wire away. "Doesn't matter."

"Okay, pal . . ." Feathers reached behind her and pulled a small spade from a loop on the saddle bag. "You're gonna put out that fire and I'm gonna escort you out of the park. Being Christmas Eve, if you cooperate, I won't cite you. If you don't, I'll arrest you and you'll spend the night in jail. Got it?"

"Ranger Feathers, you know about death."

He was standing a few feet away from her and the horse, his hands by his sides. He didn't want to breathe through his mouth, but he couldn't help it. He'd never been more rock hard. He was afraid that the slightest movement would make him explode, which would be awkward.

Control.

"Tell me what you know about death, Ranger Feathers. I want to know. I want to know everything."

She shifted the spade to her left hand and pulled out her two-way.

The call would go to Ranger Dispatch. Budget cuts had made staffing thin. They would probably reach out to the San Luis Obispo Sheriff's Department. Backup would arrive, but not in time.

"Do you wear the pearl necklace?"

The question caught her off guard. She released the radio button.

"Yes, Marilu. *That* necklace. Do you like it?"

"So you're the one who gave it to me."

"That's right."

"Why?"

"You earned it. The heroism you showed the day you brought down Bud Lilly . . . You were judge, jury, and executioner, ridding the world of a worthless creep. That should be honored in a special way."

Finally, she raised Dispatch.

He detected relief in her eyes. A crack in the armor.

She announced her location into the two-way and asked for an assist with a nine-eighteen—a psycho/insane person.

Now.

In a flash, his hand was in and out of his pocket. He aimed the snub-nose .38 at a spot between her eyes as if it was something he did every day, even though it was the first time he'd aimed a gun at a human being, other than at his own reflection in the mirror.

She reacted quickly, but not quickly enough. He fired.

He couldn't believe he'd missed. He looked at his gun as if it had betrayed him.

At the sound of the gun blast, the horse had reared. With one hand, Feathers tried to rein in Gypsy while pulling out her gun with the other. Struggling with the frantic horse, Feathers got off a shot. The horse reeled.

His hand flew to his neck that stung like crazy. He drew back bloody fingers. He stared at the blood. She'd grazed him. He started to giggle. She'd only grazed him. But the blood . . . And the heat radiating from the long fissure across his skin. It thrilled and calmed him. His hand was steady. It was like magic. He aimed again.

Feathers did too, but this time, his aim was true.

Gypsy took off at full gallop. After fifty yards, mortally wounded Feathers fell from the horse into the surf, scattering the sandpipers and cormorants. The calls from the soaring birds grew more frantic.

Overwhelmed, he dropped to his knees. He tried to keep his eyes open, but the pleasure of release was so sublime, he had to close them as he cried out, his hands clutching the sand.

Still panting and fuzzy-headed with bliss, he pulled himself together to finish his mission. He picked up his beach chair and bag of marshmallows and walked to retrieve Feathers' Ranger Stetson from where it had fallen just within reach of the foamy fingers of the surf. The mare, Gypsy, hovering near her fallen master, galloped off at his approach.

He took a long, final look at his prize, Ranger Marilu Feathers, bleeding into the sand. The young man, whom years later Detective Nan Vining would give the nickname T. B. Mann, then turned and walked into the lengthening shadows. The next phase of his life had begun.

A wave washed away his handwriting in the sand.